For T... l

CW00481787

THE BUZZARDS OF
ZINN

THE BUZZARDS OF
ZINN

A story of war and peace

George Miller

THE MEDLAR PRESS
2010

Published by The Medlar Press Limited,
The Grange, Ellesmere, Shropshire SY12 9DE
www.medlarpress.com

ISBN 978-1-907110-08-5

Designed and typeset in $11^{1}/_{2}$ on 13 point Bembo Roman.
Produced in England by The Medlar Press Limited, Ellesmere, England.

Contents

I would like to thank Rosie and Jon Ward-Allen for their close attention to every aspect of the editing and production of this book; my wife Sue, Steve Phillips, Jean Saunders and John Sykes for corrections and comments; Adam Daly for permission to adapt an idea from his story 'The Sacrificial Spire'; and all of the above for their encouragement.

GM

CHAPTER ONE

A Road Not Travelled

ZINN WAS a closed city. No Western traveller ever set foot inside it, and neither did I. But I stared wide-eyed into the heart of its darkness.

My first sight of it was from a great distance. I was travelling with a guide in a mountainous region. We were trekking along a narrow path with a sheer drop on one side. A misty blue-green valley spread below us and beyond that another range of mountains, lit randomly by shafts of sunlight breaking through the clouds. As I paused a moment to take in the view, a city appeared and disappeared on a mountain peak so swiftly I thought I must have imagined it, and indeed, with its shining towers and spires it seemed to belong more to the world of fantasy than reality. I questioned my guide about it. He told me it was the city of Zinn, and he had never been there. Though talkative as a rule he was unable or unwilling to tell me more.

At the next village we came to I made more enquiries but could discover little further. Outsiders were not welcome, and there were buzzards of enormous size that soared above the city and, it was rumoured, could swoop down and carry off a fully grown man. I was advised to forget about the city of Zinn, and there were no guides prepared to take me. Nothing could have aroused my curiosity more, and as an intrepid British traveller I felt honour bound to go there. So I set out alone.

The people of the valleys had known peace for centuries. They were wise, gentle, innocent folk who cultivated small terraced fields and grazed their herds on the wide upland plains. They had come so to depend on one another for their livelihood they had forgotten how to hate and fight, and how to push and scheme for their own advantage. I had never known such hospitality. Everywhere I was welcomed and fêted and feasted; beautiful and modest young maidens shyly approached and eagerly listened to my stories of other worlds (though understanding little of what I said in a tongue which seemed uncouth beside their own). My hosts hinted that I might find one who especially pleased me, and after due courtship and ceremony make my home among them. Only when I mentioned the City of Zinn did a rare cloud trouble their pleasant and candid features.

Indeed I was tempted. At village after village where I stayed I was finding it more difficult to leave. Lovely eyes clung longingly to me as I shouldered my pack and set out again along the dusty road, always in the direction where I'd seen, through a gap in the mist and cloud, the distant prospect of a dream-like city.

The onset of winter brought my journey to a temporary halt. Snow fell for weeks, then howling winds swept across it, sculpting a pure white landscape of strange and terrible beauty, the silence broken by the thunder of distant avalanches. Roads became impassable and now I was forced to sojourn with a savage and treacherous tribe of nomads, becoming little more than a slave to them in return for a half gnawed bone and lick of sour goat's milk. I said nothing to them of my plans, nor did they enquire or seek any converse with me; and I lived and slept among the dogs that showed me more kindness. There were those among them who could have ripped me open in anger or jest, or for the amusement of their womenfolk.

Come spring and thaw I took the first opportunity to slip away, while the men were out scavenging and the women fully engaged in one of their many screaming cat fights. I followed a narrow road winding up a steep sided valley which became a rocky crevasse - nothing but bare rock and blue sky for miles. Finally I reached sheltered upland pastures, the fields bright with wildflowers of every hue, the air filled with the hum of bees and bird-song and the rushing of innumerable streams, shaded here and there by groves of alder and ilex trees. It was across this Arcadian landscape, surrounded by tender spring foliage, that I once again set eyes on the mystical city of Zinn. It ascended the slopes of the mountain on which it was built in a series of grand terraces, each buttressed by massive battlements topped with galleries and pavilions projecting out into space. There were many towers, steeples and turrets outreaching each other in splendour and elevation as they rose ever upwards, and all surpassed by a palatial building on the summit, itself surmounted by a single sky-piercing gilded spire. I could just see what I took to be cable cars moving up and down on rails that flashed in the sunlight. Lower down there were mazes of narrow streets, crooked and huddled together.

But before I could ponder any of this my attention was drawn to another phenomenon, which would indeed have been strange if I had not been prepared for it. There were dark specks whirling around and above the towers which I took to be the famous buzzards of Zinn. Though small at this distance, on the scale implied by the buildings they must have been more the size of eagles, or even larger. My eyes were riveted by them as I approached and I often stumbled, through not heeding the rutted, stony track that lead in the direction of the city. It was wonderful to see these great birds with beautiful outspread wings, circling round the dreamy towers of a fantasy city in great sweeps and curves of flight, on tenuous vanes that glittered in the sweet soft sunlight. As I approached, the realisation dawned on me that they were not birds at all but bird-like artefacts: kites indeed, flown presumably by people in the towers on cords too fine to be visible from a distance. At one point there was a sudden flash of light from one of the towers.

I came to a standstill and rummaged through my pack to find my binoculars. When I retrieved them and focussed on one of the wheeling objects even the kite theory had to be abandoned. It was indeed some kind of construction, but I could see a tiny figure poised precariously on a platform in the slender fuselage.

I moved on swiftly now, concentrating on the road and containing my interest until I could get a closer and clearer view. At last the amber walls of the city rose from the verdant uplands before me. The shadows of great wings swept across my path and I could hear creaking and fluttering as the structures strained against the wind. Looking up, my eyes were too dazzled at first by the intense light to see anything clearly, but at last I fixed on one as it passed in front of the city's massive ramparts. In proportion to the size of the machine the aeronaut working the tiller was still very small and slight. It must have been a child, a thin child at that.

I had now arrived at my destination and discovered the real nature of the buzzards of Zinn. But that discovery, like all discoveries, led only to the further mysteries. How was it done? And why? And then there was the city itself, with all its strangeness and secrets to explore. The road I trod was little more than a farm track, which turned to the right as it approached the city's walled perimeter, along the entire visible length of which in either direction I could see no opening or entrance of any kind. I continued along this lane as it seemed to follow the curvature of the walls, believing eventually I must find a way in. I came to a deep wooded valley and crossed a swift flowing brook, or small river, by a quaint little bridge. Out in the open again I caught sight of a curious object through a gap in the hedge.

In the middle of a field there was a structure of some kind: a rickety, flimsy thing put together with various bits and pieces, too organised to be a bonfire but too dishevelled to be any kind of building. After a moment's scrutiny I realised it must be one of the buzzards that had landed, and perhaps been abandoned. But then from behind it the pilot emerged, a child indeed, skinny, ragged, no more than a farmer's boy, or a street urchin. He appeared to be making some adjustments or repairs to the structure, and intent on his work had not noticed me. I advanced cautiously towards him through the gap. As soon as he saw me he jumped back, startled, frightened, as if uncertain whether to take to his heels or attempt to defend himself with the small tool he clung to in one hand. I stopped immediately and held up my hands, the palms facing out

and fingers spread, my eyes and features as open and unthreaten-
ing as I could make them. It seemed to work, and his panic gave
way to a cautious acceptance of my presence. He went back to his
task, still glancing warily in my direction. I sat down on the grass
and busied myself with undoing my backpack and sorting through
for some of the little parcels of food I'd salvaged to bring with
me.

After a long hike, food eaten in the open air always tastes delicious, and I was visibly relishing a meaty bone, washed down with
clear spring water. I picked out another and held it up in offering
to the diminutive aviator who had been tapping and setting the
trim of his machine with the skill of a piano tuner, the ruffled
heap reassuming a bird like form as I watched. He approached
quite nonchalantly now, took the proffered meaty bone and
immediately began to gnaw at it. I beckoned him to join me and
he sat down, crossed legged, still chomping at the bone. I just sat
and smiled at him, enjoying his enjoyment. He had big brown
eyes and a small head shaped like a hazelnut, cupped with dark
shiny thatch. Finally he was satisfied and was licking his lips and
picking his teeth with his nail. I handed him the bottle of water
and he took a swig. Then I pointed to myself and told him my
name: "Jason." He nodded and told me his - it sounded like 'Ark'.
I repeated it and smiled and he smiled back. We were friends.

I tried to explain that I was a traveller from a far distant land,
finding some of the words I had learnt on my journey to Zinn
were intelligible to him. I showed him a world map in my atlas,
indicating an estimated position of Zinn, then tracing back my
route by land and sea to the British Isles. He was fascinated. I
pointed to a tiny flake of green which was the Western Isle where
I lived. When I mentioned Scotland his ears pricked up and his
eyes opened even wider to take up a considerable proportion of
his face. "Scottie!" - he pronounced the syllables quite precisely.

At this point a shadow passed over us and I looked up to see a
buzzard about twenty feet above our heads. It wheeled round,
showing the full spread of its wings, disappeared behind some trees
and then zoomed towards us low and straight. Its legs dropped

and talons splayed to form skids and with wings arched like a swan's and tail dipped and fanned to act as air brakes it careered to a halt in front of us.

The skinny kid who jumped out was the same as Ark in build and complexion, and wore the same rough serge clothing of no particular colour. But this one was a girl and had a mop of blond hair. She raised her hand in a comradely salute to Ark as she approached, and seemed quite unconcerned about the presence of a stranger. I took this acceptance to flow from my easy relationship with Ark but I soon realised there was another reason.

She clearly had news of an urgent and serious nature to impart to him, and they jabbered excitedly to each other for some minutes. The one word I recognised was 'harr', harshly pronounced, like 'kharr', which meant fire. Only during an anxious pause in the conversation did Ark's attention briefly return to me. He pronounced my name for her benefit and hers for mine. 'Sulibe' is about as close as I can get to it. He pointed to the map and explained where I came from. Again the name 'Scottie' passed between them, with a measure of interest and mild surprise.

As we talked, more shadows swept over us and suddenly the air was full of wheeling buzzards, larger and smaller, some with one, some with two pilots, their hair flying and their cries shrill above the swishing and swooshing and the rattling flutter of outstretched wings. It was amazing how they avoided collisions as one by one they swung behind the trees and zoomed in to land, hauling up with folded wings in closely spaced rows. Other children appeared as if from nowhere, pulling trolleys on which they loaded the craft and rolling them off towards the wood on the other side of the field. They worked with swift efficiency, Ark and Sulibe joining them; so I got up too and was soon handed the end of a rope to tug with the rest.

Then there was a shout and everyone stopped and looked up. A single craft was coming in, losing height rapidly, its wings on fire and smoke trailing behind. We could only stare helplessly, and we could see the pilot and sense his desperation as he struggled to control his rapidly disintegrating machine. Miraculously he managed to turn on to the landing path and hold his height a few feet above the ground before a fiery wing dipped and the whole contraption flopped down and crashed into a hedge in a blaze of sparks. Children were already running up with buckets of water from the river, not for the bird which was clearly a goner, but for the smoke blacked imp who stumbled from it, his shirt on fire. I quickly went over to the group surrounding him, thinking my first-aid kit would be needed. But he'd already been doused and his charred clothes exchanged for a wet towel, and the others were helping him to his feet. He looked cheerful enough and it appeared had come to no serious harm. Everyone seemed relieved but the sense of urgency remained. When I looked round all the other buzzard planes and all the other children had disappeared into the wood, and we swiftly followed them.

One by one the kids were wriggling into a hole scarcely bigger than a badger's set. They beckoned me to follow and I felt two little hands pushing me from behind. Nonplussed I shook my head but their quiet urgency was compelling. Small hands divested me of my backpack which swiftly vanished into the earth and then I found myself sinking and my feet going the same way. Pulled from below with my arms held back behind I was paralysed by the dread of premature burial and I could only shut my eyes tight and try to convince myself I was dreaming and must wake at any moment. I felt my rib cage being crushed and then soil in my face stifling my breath and my terror exploded into flailing limbs as I fought to regain consciousness. My Dervish-like frenzy continued for at least half a minute before it occurred to me that I was encountering no resistance, so I halted, mid fling, and opened my eyes. I found myself in a dimly lit cavern full of goblins, staring at me, almost invisible except for their glowing eyes and on each little face an enormous grin.

Released from my panic attack I struggled to regain my dignity, attempted a casual smile and began brushing loose soil from my clothes. Other hands were swiftly assisting me in areas I couldn't reach. Light came from a row of fat yellow candles on a rough wooden table, with matching benches on either side. The hole I'd

come through had disappeared but there were other smaller apertures in the wall through which some were peeping out; these
admitted shafts of light whenever the watchers turned to report
to the others. Suddenly there was a note of alarm, the candles were
all extinguished and the whole assembly remained still and silent.

As the silence deepened my ears strained to catch any faint
sounds that filtered through from outside. I could just hear
the soft hush of the brook, and then there were voices, getting
louder, heavy adult male voices, and the sound of an engine. The
voices seemed all the harsher in contrast to the bird-like pitter-
patter of the children's talk that my ears had grown accustomed
to. Curiosity drew me to the row of look-out holes, at my eye
level. Ark was peering through one, standing on a stool. He
jumped down to let me look with a cautionary finger to his lips.
I put my eye to the disc of daylight, a grass fringed spy hole no
bigger that a tennis ball.

There were a dozen or so men in the field, examining the
charred wreckage of the buzzard, scanning the ground and
poking about in the hedges. They were burly men, stoutly clad in
black woollens, with shiny brown leather boots, jerkins fringed
with chain mail and close fitting steel helmets. Knives in holsters
and thick truncheons hung from leather belts studded with steel
roundels, and some carried poles with wide metal hooks tapered
to needle sharpness. Several shouldered hefty guns like ancient
fowling pieces. A Breughelesque militia indeed, but the mediaeval connotations were checked by the presence of a motor vehicle,
a box-like van that could have served as an ambulance on the
battlefields of World War One, its motor quietly chuntering. But
this was no errand of mercy. They were looking for the buzzard
kids, and if they were school attendance officers they certainly
regarded truancy in a more serious light than their Western counterparts.

Rather incongruously one soldier was dressed in the smart tight
fitting uniform and peaked hat of a modern day officer, with a
short baton under his arm, clearly from his manner and bearing
in charge of the operation. There were also two civilians among

them who from the cut and colour of their clothes and robustly porcine proportions fitted the universal stereotype of prosperous farmers. And there were dogs.

I watched with some apprehension. The search seemed to concentrate on the landing strip and the crash site. One trooper picked up the pilot's discarded shirt and after a cursory inspection tossed it into the smouldering ruins where it burst into flame. But the dogs were ranging more widely around the perimeters of the field, and even as I observed this I heard a rustling of foliage and panting breath. Then my spy hole was stopped by a long canine snout being thrust into it, and I reeled back as a blast of dog breath hit my nostrils. The beast set up a ferocious barking which almost immediately was joined by others, and the chorus swelled as the pack closed in. I looked round me, for guidance or assistance, but there was no one visible in the feeble light from the spy holes which flickered as the baying hounds pawed and snuffled at them. All had gone, except for Ark who stood next to me. It was now very dark, but he took my hand and led me away.

After several paces another opening appeared, faintly outlined by a dim light beyond it. Thankfully it was a good deal larger than the entrance to this underworld and I could pass through it on all fours, following Ark who only had to duck his head. As soon as we were through, two or three others rolled a round stone across the gap and eased it into place. It was a tight fit but they still pressed loose soil in around the edges. Then a black drape, hanging from a rail above, was drawn over. It all seemed well rehearsed and I felt a little easier now, in the care of hosts who clearly took my safety into consideration along with their own. We moved off together down a descending passageway, with earthen walls propped like a mine shaft, lit by occasional candles set in wall-mounted brackets.

We must have gone down a hundred feet or more below the surface and travelled three times that distance before the passage opened out into an enormous cavern. Judging by the structure of the rocks that enclosed it, it was a natural feature rather than another prodigious feat of juvenile engineering, though the floor had been levelled off with hard packed clay. Most of it was occupied by buzzard craft, I would say fifty at least, and there were areas where maintenance and construction work were taking place. Other children were unloading packs from the bellies of the buzzards and taking them to long tables where they were being sorted. All went about their tasks in the same orderly way, quite unconcerned about what might be happening above ground.

My guide stood beside me, with a smile that suggested he was enjoying my amazement as I took everything in. Then he plucked my sleeve in a manner indicating there was more to be seen and done and I dutifully followed him back into the tunnel. We took one of several smaller side passages that branched off this main artery. I had to bend low in it and occasionally take to my knees; it was hard hot work keeping up with the elfin figure dancing ahead of me. The gradient got steeper until we came to steps made of logs set in the earth and filled back, and then we reached a spiral staircase rising vertically in a solid wooden tube. There was a disk of daylight above us, a welcome sight indeed, reviving my strength and spirits, and I grappled my way upwards with a will.

Emerging from an opening just wide enough to squeeze through I found myself in the crown of a great ash tree, embowered all around with leafy boughs. Ark had taken up a position towards the outer edge, standing confidently on a narrow branch and steadying himself with a light grip on a higher branch, and perched nearby another lad, half hidden by leaves and the dapple of leaf shadows. There was a quick exchange of greetings followed by a gesture to remain silent, and Ark turned to gaze intently in the same direction as his fellow watcher. I crept carefully along one of the larger limbs as far as I safely could and then lay flat on it. By dint of parting a spray or two I was able to gain an outlook beyond the world of foliage, to see what was going on of such interest.

My view travelled over the tops of trees to the field where the buzzards had landed. The dogs had been pulled off and the foot patrol was now assembled along the edge of the wood, on a line corresponding to the underground chamber with the spy holes.

The van had been backed up there as well, and the sound of the engine being revved carried towards us. The next thing I noticed, to my horror, was a pipe leading from the van's exhaust and disappearing into the ground. The men stood around in attitudes of casual indifference or idle curiosity, while the two plump farmers, hands on knees, stared more intently. The scene could have been a badger cull, carried out by Ministry officials at home – but these were humans, and children! Darker images from accounts of Hitler's Einsatzgruppen hovered at the edge of my thoughts.

But murderous though the exercise was, it was clearly not going to work. The chamber had been too well sealed and very soon the lethal gas was issuing back from the row of holes, and the farmers and troopers were being forced away. The engine was switched off and a brief conference took place between the officer in charge, the farmers and the man in the van. The latter climbed out and went to the back of the van, joined by two troopers. They got inside and were lost from view for a minute, but then emerged wearing gas masks with round goggle eyes and sinister proboscises, giving them an aspect better suited to the nature of their enterprise. Two carried spades, and the other a bundle of yellow cylindrical objects attached to a coil of cord. The spadesmen shovelled vigorously and soon knocked a gaping hole through the wall of the chamber, the object was chucked in and the cord trailed back forty yards of so, to which latitude all retired. A light flashed and then a flame fizzed and sparked its way like a snake in the grass till it reached and entered the breach.

A shattering blast and roar of muffled thunder. We felt the shock wave all the way up to the top of the tree. I saw the ground lift and erupt in a spurt of soil and shattered timber, followed immediately by a landslide from the bank above, bringing trees and bushes crashing down on top.

Had the military taken the trouble to excavate and explore the chamber they might well have found the entrance to the passage leading to the great cavern. But typically they preferred the laziest and most violent approach, and the one that made the loudest bang. They could not more effectively have sealed this point of entry to the children's underground refuge – there must have been at least one other where the buzzards had been taken in. And doubtless too, as he ordered the men to pack their gear and prepare to march off, the commander, in the manner of his kind, was already mentally phrasing the report to his superiors, which would then form the basis of a press release of another successful operation against the insurgents, rebels, criminals, terrorists – however they chose to categorise their fearsome opponents.

The excitement over, my two companions now chattered happily together and Ark introduced me to the other boy whose name was Raldo. Voices from below signalled the arrival of others to relieve them on the watch. Ark and Raldo pointed to their mouths and patted their empty tummies and were soon scampering down the hollow tree trunk and back to the cavern, followed, with grunts, sweat and toil (fit though I was) by myself. Back in the cavern all eyes turned to us, but a few words soon dissipated the anxiety in them. The infantry were in retreat, the coast was clear, and it was time to tuck in to the lavish meal that had been laid out in our absence.

Boys and girls, younger and older, sat down on the long benches with no apparent order or ceremony and helped themselves freely. There were plates of cut meat and small delicious fish and bowls of salad, tough rye bread spread thick with dripping, familiar and unfamiliar species of vegetables, roots, nuts, fungi, and fruits, and tall jugs of fruit juices and sweet fresh water. Some of the smaller ones were being helped by their elders, siblings perhaps, but needed less coaxing when creamy puddings and honey glazed flapjacks were laid out.

The meal over, there was a riot of play and animated conversation. The young ones were skipping, tumbling, hiding, climbing, and playing with balls, dolls, push carts, and every form of innocent childish entertainment. The older ones paid little heed, intervening only when tears or a tumble required it. I noticed quite a few disabled children, missing an arm or a leg. They hopped around and joined in the fun quite as happily as the others and there was no sense of incapacity on their part or condescension on the part of their peers. One little girl had her right leg amputated above the knee and used a slender bamboo crutch with great agility. But she also had a prosthetic leg which she carried around with her - it was much too big for her to wear: apparently a prized possession she had somehow acquired, and hoped, perhaps, one day she would grow into.

I spotted my backpack that had been placed safely on a shelf, and as I went to retrieve it was surrounded by an excited little mob eager to discover its contents. I sat down and took out my bits and pieces one by one, explaining them as well as I could and allowing them to be handled, which was done with reverent care. My Swiss army knife was much admired, and my torch, though to conserve the batteries I couldn't allow more than a brief demonstration. My binoculars, looked through both ways, were a source of wonder and amusement and my wind-up alarm clock was another winner. Almost everything was a novelty to them, even pens and pencils and a pencil sharpener. As for my mobile phone and digital camera, the former beyond the range of any signal and both out of battery charge, they were as meaningless to my audience as they were now useless to me. Again my maps were of great interest, and there was hushed attention as I tried to explain and they to grasp their significance - the dimly apprehended wonder of lands, continents, seas and oceans stretching far beyond the world they knew. It was obvious they had received no formal education of any kind.

As I talked I felt a small warm body pressed close to mine and looked down to see the smiling face of the girl with a false leg. Her name was Aya.

CHAPTER 2

The Pool

THE CHILD was speaking to me, and I trying to understand, when Ark appeared and indicated with a gesture of his hands and eyes that it was time for a conducted tour. As well as the main hall, which also served as a hangar for the buzzards and working area where they were built and maintained, there were side rooms formed from natural cavities and alcoves in the walls of the cavern. The largest contained the kitchen where food was stored and prepared. The sleeping areas were simply piles of rugs, furs and pillows where the children just flopped down at random when they were tired. There was little in the way of privacy or personal possessions. The washrooms were on a lower level and were salubrious, thanks to an underground supply of fresh water. There were rooms where certain games were played, one like squash or fives where a ball was struck against the cave walls, which being irregular sent it in all directions. I had a go but my reactions were no match for the pace and unpredictability of it. The storage of aircraft parts and materials occupied a good deal of space, and then there was a place where animals and birds were kept: pigeons in one cage, hawks in another, and small mammals mainly of the ferret family. Though lovingly cared for I guessed they had a use and were not just pets. Finally there was a room which seemed to be for prayer, or quiet reflection.

After several bedtime signals had been largely ignored a general round up of the smaller by the larger children was now taking place. Some willing, others still protesting through their yawns and eye rubbings, they were gathered and funnelled into the sleeping areas. Little Aya came up to me and proffered her cheek for a goodnight kiss. I placed one there carefully and off she pegged with the others on her improvised crutch, with its wished for future replacement tucked under her free arm. Sulibe watched over her, and from a certain resemblance I guessed they were sisters. The sounds of romping, chatter and laughter continued for a while, then all subsided into silence. With the older ones more serious matters were now afoot. A good deal of activity centred round the craft, and I strolled over to take a closer look.

They were truly marvellous artefacts, varying considerably in size, design and materials. The body or fuselage was a light frame construction made of thin willow or bamboo rods: the cockpit having a platform for the pilot to stand on and any cargo to be stowed. Weight was obviously crucial. The head was modelled, painted and polished to resemble a raptor, with a fierce hawkish expression and menacingly hooked beak. Everything else in the machine was fully articulated: the wings, tail and each individual feather in them, and the talons could be raised and lowered like the undercarriage of a plane. An object could be grabbed in the talons and lifted forward to be secured by the pilot and similarly a package could be deposited fairly accurately in a chosen spot. This suggested that some kind of trafficking was involved.

The structures appeared to be made from almost any materials that came to hand, some natural, derived from plants and trees, some man-made, hammered out of thin metal or plastic cut from discarded household goods or waste of any kind. A complex system of ligatures controlled the trim of each feather and the angle or spread of groups that acted as ailerons. All were linked to the joy stick which had a T shaped bar on top with levers and rotating clutch controls. The wings as a whole could be 'flapped' to assist lift, an eliptical rather than up and down motion effected by locking the joy stick and turning handles on either side which simultaneously opened and closed the wings on the up and down strokes. In the larger two-'manned' machines the second crew member operated the wing rotation and loading devices. Rather like a vulture the wings were beautiful and mathematical structures when spread out and in use but when closed formed a ruffled heap which only the skilled young engineers, checking the alignments and tensions of each separate element, could decipher. The tail could be lifted, dipped, fanned or narrowed and the talons, as I'd witnessed, could also act as skids when landing.

From looking round in the construction area it was possible to get a good idea of the evolution of the buzzards. There were some dusty old birds in the dark recesses with fixed canvas wings and simple controls, and others of primitive design were set up on stands for the younger children to play and practise on. The large machines with two navigators were among the most recent, and one designed for a crew of three, the most manoeuvrable yet made, was just off the production line. There was also a class of smaller craft and these too were very elaborate and sophisticated compared with earlier models. They were made out of some light alloy scrap hammered thin and flexible and were obviously designed for speed and manoeuvrability. A shifting ballast device with a weight that could be jettisoned, and the way the wings closed tight to form the profile of a missile, suggested they were intended to swoop down from a great height with perilous velocity.

The children didn't seem to mind my presence and I watched them at work, once again amazed at their skill, discipline and application. Then I wandered over to a group that were huddled together in conference. It included Ark, Sulibe, Raldo and the one with bandaged arms, called Sorren, who had come down in flames. These, I guessed, approximated to the leadership in a free and easy society, with no formal organisation or hierarchy, and not much in the way of rules. With the younger ones they were confident, easy going and reassuring. Now they were locked in earnest debate which seemed to centre on the causes of the fire, the injured pilot Sorren gesticulating in an attempt to explain what had happened and shading his eyes with his hand. A beam of some kind, I gathered, had struck the craft. This appeared to be an unprecedented and worrying development. The name Jobu was much bandied about in a tone suggesting strong disapproval, uncharacteristically approaching anger and hatred.

It had been a difficult day and the strain was telling. Everyone was tired and the discussion was getting no further. Several were yawning and Sulibe appeared to have nodded off. Raldo roused her and we all headed towards the sleeping area, Ark drawing me along with the group. Having discovered me in the first place he took responsibility for me, in a casual but friendly way.

We entered a dimly lit chamber. Some who were already sleeping there were woken up by others who had just arrived - a relief watch I assumed. Everyone else just dropped down wherever they liked, curling up and burrowing into the bedding. Ark found me a place and Sulibe lifted her cheek for a goodnight kiss just as Aya had. There was a drowsy murmur of goodnight wishes as sleep claimed them and they became children again after the cares and responsibilities of the day. I put down my backpack and soon I too entered into the contented sleep of physical and mental exhaustion.

I awoke in pitch dark, struggling to disentangle my dreams from recent events which were no less fantastic. In a while my eyes were able to collect enough photons to make out dim outlines confirming that if what had happened so far was a dream, I was still in it. I was cold and pulled more blankets over me, and tried to compose myself to sleep again. But my brain had fired up by now and was asking questions and demanding answers.

Here was a tribe of happy, pleasant, and highly gifted children surviving on their wits, and being ruthlessly hunted with lethal intent by soldiers, apparently the regular armed forces of the neighbourhood, supported by the civilian population or at least one section of it. It was hard to accept that this death squad had emanated from the beautiful city of Zinn, but I could see no alternative explanation. Why were the children outcasts - why considered a threat? With extraordinary ingenuity they had taken to the earth and the air to evade capture but it seemed their

enemies had come up with some new device to bring them down
- quite literally. Surely it was only a matter of time before their
refuge was discovered. In short I had landed in the middle of a war
zone. A very strange war but a war none the less. A mass killing
was afoot, not as usual on ethnic or religious grounds, but generational.

For me this raised all kinds of issues. My whole philosophy was
that of a traveller: one who arrives, observes, appreciates and moves
on, but does not seek to question anything or take part in local
affairs. I identified with the place I was in for the time I was there
and it would remain undimmed in my memory, charged as it was
with all the glamour and excitement of discovery. Then it
belonged to me and I would never return to find that all had
changed, and changed as always, for the worse. The temple may be
razed and replaced by a Tesco, the grand squares and gracious
avenues buried under multi-lane highways and high rise blocks.
Even in my lifetime entire cultures and civilizations, in South
America, Africa and the Middle East, that I had lived in and
known intimately, had gone forever.

For me the traveller was a kind of poet. Memory and imagination created an ideal: it was his quest for immortality, for a world
that never changed, an abiding city. I hated the idea of growing old
and believed obscurely that by constantly travelling onwards
through space I could avoid travelling through time. I would go
on as long as I lived to new horizons, new marvels and mysteries
of man and nature, and even death would be a new adventure.
Perhaps I was already a ghost.

I must leave now, I told myself, before I get involved in this situation. There will always be wars, injustices, atrocities. What can
one person do about that? And what possible use could I be, not
even able to speak their language? There are terrible things happening all the time, but seen from outer space the Earth is still
peaceful and beautiful and to embrace the whole planet and
absorb and celebrate its beauty is the only reason for being alive.
I still wanted to enter Zinn, with its prospect of architectural and
cultural treasures. In a tribe of feral youngsters I was completely

out of place - I felt like Gulliver among the Lilliputians. But I was stuck in this cave and the problem was I hadn't the least idea how to get out.

These things went round and round in my head and I tossed and turned while all the children slept peacefully. The only resolution I could find was the thought that tomorrow in the light of day my path would be clear, and I could leave if I wished. At last I grew weary and slept again.

After my disturbed night I must have slept late. The light that shone into the cave, though faint, was the light of day, and the sound of voices and the general bustle of morning activity filtered through. I shouldered my pack and stepped out into the main concourse. A port had opened in the wall of the cavern revealing a long straight inclined passage up to an opening through which light was streaming. There was a set of rails leading up, fashioned from split bamboo and gleaming from constant use. This then was the entrance through which the buzzards on their trolleys were brought in - and hauled out too but none appeared to have moved today. The squadron had been grounded.

My hosts greeted me and beckoned me to help myself at the communal table. Everyone else had eaten but there was plenty left. I peeled an egg, ate some quince-like fruit and drank a cup of milk. I had all but decided to move on, and it was tempting to stock up a little for future need. I had no doubt that it would have been acceptable and even encouraged, but it seemed mean - ungracious. The hall was mainly empty now, with just a few engineers still tapping away and lovingly preening the great birds. Had they soared into the ether for the last time? That thought must have been going through the minds of their makers as well as mine.

I made my way up the ramp to where it debouched in mottled sunlight from the steep face of a wooded escarpment. I marvelled at the way the outer surfaces of the gates had been modelled to match their surroundings, with real bushes planted in them. A drawbridge spanned a stretch of dense brambles and descended in a tunnel through them and out through a screen of foliage to the path below. I wanted to find Ark and the others I had met to tell them as best I could that I was continuing my travels, thank them for their hospitality and wish them well. So I crossed the bridge and took the path towards the river, from which direction the sounds of children at play reached my ears. The path opened into a clearing where the river widened into a natural pool, lined with rock and lush with ferns and mosses of many varieties, before splashing down a boulder strewn race to disappear into the darker depths of the woods.

The children were skinny-dipping in the pool. The excited pitch of their voices made a constant vocal ululation. Heads of some were bobbing up and down in the bright water and others were standing along the bank facing them, plopping in and popping out again like a row of penguins at the zoo. Still others were among the boulders washing their clothes, but these too were bantering with the swimmers and making occasional forays among them. The scene brought me to a standstill, filling me with a strange mixture of delight and pity.

They were so beautiful and innocent and so much a part of their natural surroundings. The intense light reflected by the water, shining and shimmering around and between the flowing frieze of their animated bodies, looked like tongues of flame, the very life force leaping up, the unquenchable resurgence of joy and hope. What hope, what future did they have?

In a moment my presence was noticed and I was being waved to and beckoned to join the fun. I spotted Ark among them and tried to signal that I'd like a private word but children were running up the bank, coaxing and pushing me and pulling my clothes off and again I found myself not entirely acting under my own volition. My resistance in any case was weakened by the fact I had been tramping for days and sleeping rough and really needed a wash. And the water looked very inviting. So I joined the party and was soon swimming with the dolphins; but these particular mammals were mobbing me, intent on splashing and ducking me as much as possible, little Aya's and Sulibe's beaming faces among them. I splashed back, causing great hilarity, but then decided the horseplay had gone far enough and struck out up stream.

Being a strong swimmer I soon lost my escort. Pitting my strength against the swift, cool current invigorated me, and I must have swum over a hundred yards before I tired and waded up on to the shore. A couple of lads were fishing further upstream and we waved to each other. There was no one else around, so I lay down on the smooth sand, arms outstretched, absorbing the pure fresh air and the birdsong and the glorious light. Very soon I was asleep.

I was woken by the two anglers who spoke briefly and urgently, then ran off. As I rubbed the sleep out of my eyes and looked around to get my bearings I noticed some lights flashing near the top of a tree. Changing my position slightly I could see, through a gap in the foliage, a hill beyond with the road curving round it. There was some large glittering object there, coming in my direction. As it approached I realised it was another troop of soldiers on the march, the light reflected by their weapons and metal trappings. I quickly decided it would not be to my best advantage to be found naked and undocumented in an area associated with rebel activity. So I dived in the river and made swift current-assisted passage back to the pool. Alerted no doubt by their ever vigilant lookouts, the children had already gone to earth, safely concealed, I hoped and prayed, in their subterranean refuge. There was not a trace of them to be seen, but as I half expected my clothes had been washed and laid out to dry. My backpack was there too, undisturbed, with a daisy chain in the shape of a heart on top of it. I didn't need two guesses as to who put it there.

I judged it wise to keep clear of the patrol if possible so dressed hurriedly and retreated deeper into the wood, and waited quietly until it had had time to pass by. Then I made my way back cautiously to the path by the pool, and on from there to where it joined the road. The coast was clear so I continued my journey from the point at which it had been interrupted. A mile to my left the city of Zinn cut its fantastic shape out of the sky. The road broadly followed the curvature of its ramparts, with occasional detours to skirt one of the small round hills or placid lakes which were features of the terrain.

It was a rich and ordered landscape, which again seemed strangely at odds with the brutality I had witnessed. I encountered surly, glowering looks in the farms and villages I passed through, the ingrained suspicion and hostility of those who live under oppressive rule. I had no luck getting served at any of the inns I passed, although I had large denomination notes in many currencies to offer. I drank from the streams and chewed the succulent inner stems of grass but there was nothing ripe enough in the hedges yet to do more than stave off the pangs of hunger. Eventually a landlord who in better times would have been as jovial as they come, having scrutinised me carefully and decided I represented no kind of trick or threat, invited me into his own parlour and fed me well, but would accept nothing but my heartiest thanks in return.

There had to be an entrance somewhere to the city. From time to time I passed a small doorway set high up in the wall and connected to the ground by an open flight of stairs barely a foot wide. For any brave enough to risk the ascent, the nailed door at the top was as heavy and forbidding as could be imagined, and any unwanted visitor or unsolicited caller could easily be sent to his death. Beneath one of these unwelcoming portals what appeared to be a rib cage poking out of the grass gave weight to this theory. Tramping on I looked up to the heavens from time to time but the only buzzards I saw were a pair of real ones, circling above with their shrill mewing cries. Just once I saw a hawk-like shape very high up, flapping and gliding, which could possibly have been a winged child soaring free of all earthly fears. But I lost it in the sunlight before I could decide. The only humans I encountered on the road were farm labourers, on foot or driving horse-drawn wagons, and one in a rusty tractor that belched blue fumes. Happily there were no more patrols, though at some point I realised I would have to have dealings with those in authority. I felt more and more uncomfortable at the thought.

I must have walked half way round the walls of Zinn before reaching what I took to be the main port of exit and entry. On reflection it made sense for the rebels to establish their headquarters as far from it as possible, giving them maximum time to observe enemy movements and avoid surprise attacks. Suddenly the country road I was on veered away from the city to join a main highway heading directly towards it. Traffic, in the shape of an occasional lorry or bus of similar vintage to yesterday's gassing van, passed to and fro, as well as an assortment of horse-drawn vehicles and an old man on a creaking bicycle. I kept to the grass verge with my head down, ignoring all, and plodding wearisomely so as to pass at a glance for a local serf. When I looked up, after half a mile or so, I saw a checkpoint ahead, with raised barriers and guard kiosks on either side of the road. There were soldiers, lounging and smoking, and occasionally pulling a vehicle in for a routine inspection.

As I approached I felt distinctly uneasy, an unfamiliar sense of foreboding replacing my usual confident sense of adventure. But I was already under observation and it would be risky to retreat. In any case I could hardly give up now after so long and difficult a journey. I came in friendship, I told myself; I had letters of intro-duction attesting as much that had served me well in many difficult situations. One was from a cabinet minister, another from a bishop, and a third, which often proved more effective than either, from a grand master of the Masonic Order. If refused entry I could simply walk away and honour would have been satisfied. At least I would have set eyes on an unknown city - unknown in the West even to fable, and a city, I had begun to think, that was better seen than experienced. So I summoned as much *sang froid* as I could and marched boldly up to the men, whose eyes had not left me since I first came into their view.

Assuming a cheerful and casual air I looked candidly into the expressionless faces of three thick-set dragoons who blocked my path. In my own language I told them my name and explained that I had letters of introduction to present to the authorities of the city. There was no movement or response from them of any kind. Meanwhile, through the open window of the guard box to my left I could see and hear another squaddy on the phone, speak-ing in the clipped robotic phrases of a soldier of low rank replying to a superior officer. He put down the receiver and addressed the others, now in a rough familiar tone, bluntly summarising their orders with the unmistakable addition of several choice expletives. As a result the three men moved aside and one of them pointed, very slowly and deliberately, in the direction of the city. It was a step forward, but somehow it didn't feel like one.

From this point the road became an elevated causeway between high stone walls that blocked the view on both sides. As close as this Zinn lost all its ethereal magic: just a vast brutal wall stretching to the heavens and holding the visible world in its immense, impending shadow. The sky was empty, and glancing back I saw that the three soldiers had once again taken up their positions and stood motionless across the path, staring at me. There was no way back.

Above the entrance rose a high, pointed arch enclosing an iron palisade, itself surmounted by a coat of arms, menacingly jagged, cut into the stonework. The gates themselves were lost to view behind a modern brick and timber clad extension projecting outwards, with a steel framed gantry-like structure crossing the road, and with rooms or offices above and on either side. Another military reception party stood awaiting my arrival, as stolid and taciturn as the last one. This time I made no attempt at a greeting, estimating the likelihood of any kind of acknowledgment at about zero. I simply allowed myself to be escorted inside. A door was opened and I was directed into a small bare room, perhaps a cell. The door was closed, and then locked.

After pacing around a bit I realised I was in for a long wait and so might as well try to get some rest. A hard, narrow, slatted wooden bench was the only concession to bodily comfort. So I lay down on the floor using my backpack as a pillow and tried to rest and calm my thoughts. I was just beginning to wind down a little when the door burst open, one of the men came in, jerked the pack from under my head and left with it, banging and locking the door behind him. Shocked and discomfited I could only wonder if this seizure was to check my belongings or deprive me of rest. I decided the latter as they would otherwise have confiscated it at the outset. And I now noticed there were several spy holes in the walls.

It was hot and stuffy. The only window was a narrow slit near the ceiling and it was closed. I lay with my back to the clammy bare brick wall, closed my eyes, and told myself I'd been in tight spots before. Time would pass, and I'd look back on this as just another adventure, one for my memoirs. I'd done no wrong, I reasoned, not altogether with conviction, other than to be here, and I'd be happy now to leave and never return. I was as close as any Westerner had ever been to entering the unknown city of Zinn, and it was close enough. Looking round at my harsh and comfortless surroundings, I thought I really needed to be somewhere else.

It was an hour and twenty minutes by my watch before the door opened again. Two of my guards came in and pulled me to my feet, shoved me through the door and frogmarched me along the corridor into a much larger room. It looked like an office, with shelves, box files, filing cabinets, wall maps and charts, framed photographs of top brass and military parades, and centrally placed above a broad polished desk a large tacky oil painting. The subject of this was a garishly uniformed gent, with sharp twinkling eyes in a crinkly face which beamed a folksy smile of ghastly complicity at one and all.

At the desk below, facing in the same direction as the portrait but small and mean by comparison, and with unsmiling eyes behind his round, thick spectacles, sat a real life individual. His dwarfishness was exaggerated by his large peaked cap and the immaculate uniform and trappings of an officer. To his right sat another officer, this one very fat, his eyes dark slits in a puffy face, and a hatless one in plainer uniform to his left, busying himself arranging pens and papers, clearly a secretary or recorder. Facing the desk was a solitary wooden chair to which I was swept forward, and in which I was unceremoniously dumped.

"So. I see. You English," began the one in the centre. "Why you here English?"

"I am a traveller," I explained. "I came to see the City of Zinn."

"How you know Zinn? How you find? Who sent?"

"No one sent me here. I was in another country when I saw the city at a great distance. I thought it a beautiful city. I thought it would be good to go there and meet the people of Zinn."

His eyes narrowed with incomprehension or suspicion, or both.

"I come in friendship," I added hopefully.

He glanced down at my letters of introduction which were in front of him and flicked through them impatiently. "These papers, incorrect," he snapped. "You not ambassador. Why you here?"

"Friendly interest," I replied; "nothing more. Simple curiosity."

"You spy!" he barked.

"No, of course not. There is no hostility between my country and yours. Zinn is not even marked on our maps."

"Hah! Good job! You English, you Americans. Bloody imperialists. Bloody thieves. You find Zinn you send bloody bombs."

I had to admit he had a point, but replied as calmly as possible: "If I told people at home about Zinn they would never believe me. They would think I was crazy. They'd say I made it all up."

This seemed only to anger him more and he was about to spit out some other accusation when the fat officer, who had sat Buddha-like and inscrutable during this exchange, turned to him, raising his fat fingers, and spoke in a quiet voice. There ensued a discussion in the Zinnian tongue, in which the strident tones of the interrogator gradually abated, and at the end of which some agreement had clearly been reached. Meanwhile the secretary scribbled away furiously with a scratchy pen, trying to keep up with what was being said. Finally after a minute of tense silence the thin officer addressed me again.

"So. Must go. Now. Leave Zinn. Go. Not talk, Zinn - not tell person Zinn. Not come back Zinn. Never! You understand?" I understood. "You leave Zinn territory. Twenty-four hours we find you here, you Spy. We arrest. You dealt with. OK. You understand?"

I reaffirmed my full comprehension and was briskly escorted from the room and from the building. My profound relief was tempered only by the loss of my backpack and its contents. I decided to push my luck and asked the guards for its return, outlining it with my hands and pointing at my shoulder. They stared at each other, nonplussed by a development not covered within the scope of their orders. With knitted brows one went back inside while the remaining one glared at me as if I had committed some outrageous misdemeanour and was now really for it. But after an anxious moment the other returned, gripping the rucksack in one enormous fist and then thrusting it into my hands. The other raised his fist and gritted his teeth as if about to deliver a punch, but with painful self restraint released his index finger instead, and pointed, with the same emphatic deliberation as the guard at the checkpoint had before. But in the opposite direction, away from the city of Zinn. I was only too ready and happy to comply.

CHAPTER 3

A Staff Entertainment

IT WAS not until I was well out of range of the hostile glare and pent up violence of the soldiers at the gate and those at the checkpoint that I breathed a sigh of relief, and a lightness returned to my step. The highway headed due west and I decided to stay on it. I guessed it would be the quickest way out of Zinn territory, though I had no idea where the borders were. I didn't fancy retracing the long twisty mountainous road I had come by, or re-negotiating my passage through the savage tribes of the hills - or indeed the importunate hospitality of the folk of the plains and valleys. Above all I did not want to encounter the children again or get involved with their fight. I was profoundly thankful that my involvement so far was unknown to the Zinnian regime. It would certainly have condemned me and worse. If they had suspected me of having any useful information I had no doubt they would have used the customary means of extracting it.

Another possibility that occurred to me was that I might get out faster by hitching a lift. Traffic was light and there were no cars: only lorries and other commercial vehicles. But all passed me by, or responded to my uplifted thumb with an angry blare of the horn. Perhaps the gesture had another meaning to them. I tried different signals, but to no avail. By now the sun was sinking in a sea of blood and fire, filling my mind and the world with a sense of doom and departure. I resigned myself to a cold, dark and wearisome hike ahead.

I was glad to find that my stash of banknotes was still safely hidden in the lining of my rucksack and I was able to buy a decent meal of fried spicy rice with egg and chicken and some green leaves melted into it, and as much tea as I could drink. This was at a busy transport café where I was less conspicuously a foreigner, or strangers were less the objects of suspicion, than in the rural inns. It was rough and ready but gave me a welcome feeling of returning to normality. I stayed there and rested as long as I dared.

It was dark when I came out. Hour after hour I trudged on, the starry sky and the thin scythe of a moon above, the gloomy landscape on either side and the endless road before me: nothing but the headlights of the occasional vehicle to vary the monotony. First light brought me to another service depot where another meal revived my spirits. I lay down in a communal dossing area intending a quick nap but must have slept several hours as the sun was high when I left. Relentlessly the road drove on ahead through an open, featureless agrarian landscape, rising steadily towards distant woods and mountains, with nothing to measure progress but the change of light. Clouds gathered, and night fell swiftly and there were intervals between passing vehicles when I could barely see the road to stay on it. At least I could comfort myself with the thought that every step took me further from Zinn and its iron-fist custodians. "Further and further with every step," I repeated to myself like a mantra, too tired to think of anything else – "further and further with every step, further and further . . ." but not far enough.

The headlights of another vehicle came up behind me, surrounding me momentarily in a blaze of light, but instead of driving on and away this one swung in and screeched to a halt in front of me. Almost immediately dark figures jumped out of it, there were angry shouts and I saw streaks of light on the levelled barrels of guns. Then a beam from a searchlight struck me with blinding force. I froze and held up my hands. Two soldiers appeared in the pool of light and beckoned me to come forward. I might well have shown a moment's hesitation, more from shock than any intention of resistance. But in any case the next instant I was seized and dragged forward, pitched head first into the back of the lorry where I was beaten and kicked till I lost consciousness, whether from a blow or striking my head on something hard and metallic I cannot tell.

I woke up in a grimy cell – this one had no pretensions to being a room. The walls were stone, the window barred, the door was steel. There was no furniture and I lay on the concrete floor, my bones aching and my head throbbing. Painfully I raised myself, carefully testing each limb. At least nothing was broken, just heavy bruising and a gash on the side of my head now cased in congealed blood. There was food: stale bread and some kind of broth that had solidified, and water in a bottle. I drank, and then poured some water on the stale bread and gnawed it. I wondered vaguely how long I'd been unconscious.

Well, I was warned about Zinn, I told myself. Did I really expect these military thugs and that Himmler impressionist to keep their promise? I'd credited myself with a bit more savvy. But why not arrest me straight away? Were they playing games? Then I remembered the fat officer who had shown some restraint. Probably the farce of releasing me was just for his benefit. But why leave it so late? I must have been pretty close to the border.

I'd come to see a beautiful city, and ended up half dead in this squalid hole. I had to admit my prospects now looked pretty bleak. The best I could hope for was that there had been some mistake; that the boys who nabbed me were acting on their own initiative and had not been informed that I had already been questioned and released. Surely they'd get in touch with headquarters and then just kick me out. Better still they might even apologise and transport me to the border.

As I turned things over in my mind, and struggled to convince myself that this would be the likely outcome, the slots between the bars of the window grew faintly visible and grey light crept into the room. Another day was dawning, and however grimly I clung to hope I knew deep down that it would be my last. I began to hear sounds – engines starting up, voices, shouts, the general clatter of morning activity, getting louder. Then heavy footsteps outside and the sound every prisoner dreads: a key grating in the lock.

Once again, under heavy booted escort, I was marched along dank corridors and bundled up stone steps in echoing stairwells. Once again I found myself in an operational area serving as an ad hoc court room, facing a sinister dwarf in a hot pressed uniform who would say to me at any moment: "So! We meet again." Even worse, my fat friend of the previous tribunal had been replaced by a sergeant, or adjutant, not fat but very big, the wasteland of whose countenance was so devoid of humanity he might have been drafted in from some outer part of the solar system. On his other side was a man in civilian clothes whom I'd seen somewhere before, but couldn't think where.

After pretending to scan some official documents in front of him for several minutes the presiding officer looked up, fixed me with a withering stare, sneeringly relished my discomfiture, and spoke:

"So, English. We meet again."

I declined to answer and after a moment's pause he geared up to his mode of angry accusation.

"You, in Zinn territory, twenty-four hour. You foreign spy yes. You enemy agent. Yes . . . CIA," producing the last accusation as though it were a stroke of deductive genius. I explained as calmly as I could that I had had every intention of leaving the land of Zinn, but had been prevented from doing so by his men, who had arrested, beaten and imprisoned me. Ignoring my remarks and before I had even completed them he turned and spoke enquiringly to the civilian gentleman, who nodded assent.

"This man, he see you. Hah! He see you with anarchists. Hah! He see you no clothes. You go no clothes with anarchists. You pervert. Yes!"

Then I recognised the man and the ground sunk beneath me. It was one of the farmers assisting the troops who blasted the entrance to the cavern. He or one of his men must have been watching and reporting on the children's activities. "That's absolutely ridiculous," I began to protest but the prosecutor banged the table with more force than his thin arm seemed capable of and yelled "Silence!" I realised my case was hopeless and gave up. He continued in measured tones:

"Court has reached verdict. You foreign spy. Penalty DEATH. You pervert sex tourist. Penalty, DEATH. We hang you twice!"

Then he laughed showing all his yellow teeth, this accompanied by a satisfied grin from the fat-pig farmer and some ghastly simulacrum of mirth from the massive hulk of a sergeant. The merriment stopped as suddenly as it had begun and the officer jerked his head towards the guards. I was seized and dragged backwards through the door, along the passages and down the stairs and flung back into my cell.

Battered in body and spirit I lay there as I'd fallen. I was no longer alone in my cell. Another presence filled it and filled me, and obliterated me. Mortal dread. No words can describe it, and unless you have experienced it you would never imagine it. Those who babble of terror and terrorism and terrorists know nothing of it. They would be choked by their own breath and the blood would freeze in their veins if they had a moment's knowledge of it. I lay there for an hour or maybe more, shaking from fear and cold, in the ruins of my life and being, until those impulses to revive, rebuild, construct some basis for continued existence, began to stir again. I told myself, no, this cannot be right. This cannot be real. It's a farce. They are playing games. They just want to put the fear of God into me so I keep my mouth shut and don't come back. Well they've succeeded.

Another idea was forming itself in my mind. Though it all seemed so concrete and actual, none of this was really believable. The gravity defying children above a perpendicular city, the eclectic mediaeval storm troopers - it must be a dream, an hallucination, or perhaps I was in a coma. I tried to think back to where it all began, on a narrow path cut into the side of a precipice. Perhaps I fell. Yes, I was rescued, badly bruised and delirious, taken somewhere, a quiet pleasant room, cared for by kindly, innocent people. That my injuries had been replicated in my delusional state indicated I was now regaining consciousness.

Any minute I would come to and this nightmarish scenario would vanish.

I would be in a secluded monastery lying on a couch spread with richly woven fabrics in a sunny room; on the wall opposite a picture of an imaginary city built on a mountain peak; outside through the window buzzards circling in the clear bright air. Perhaps it would be at the moment of my death that I would return to the world of the living. I closed my eyes and imagined it all as strongly as I could, picturing every detail of the room and the monks and acolytes who came to see me until I fell asleep and the dream itself became a dream.

Shouts, shock, pain - it was no saffron robed well-wisher who roused me from my sleep but the moon-crater-faced and mountainously muscular centurion of the trial room, with attendant squaddies. Another forced march but this time taking a different route, entering a long passage with daylight at the end of it. There was a smell, or something more insidious, that animals detect when they are being taken to slaughter.

We emerged into a yard enclosed by high stone walls. Near the top of the outer wall was a wooden platform accessed by tall ladders. High above this against the cloudy sky, a long beam with a row of nooses hanging from it. There were several figures moving around up there. Opposite against the wall of the building, and on a level with the gallows, was a tiered stand for spectators with a door opening into it from the fort, as turrets and battlements now showed the place to be. The gallery was half filled with officers and their wives or secretaries, and others were arriving. One I recognised straight away from his manifest prominence, despite a diminutive stature, and another easy to identify was the only male not in uniform. They were chatting and laughing in a casual way like parents at a school play or sporting event. A dozen or so soldiers at ground level were also in relaxed conversation, smoking and swapping stories, bawdy no doubt, that led to gusts of raucous laughter.

I was held at the entrance for some moments until a young man finished his conversation with a group of soldiers and beckoned our approach. He stood out from the others by his good looks and engaging smile. He had fair hair and broad shoulders and a slim athletic build, and wore tight pants and a leather jerkin without sleeves, showing off his smooth, powerful arms. He returned to his conversation with his mates while I was hustled forward. At the foot of the ladder I froze, unable to take the next step until a stinging cut from a cane across my shoulders galvanised me into further action. I scaled the rickety ladder and was hauled on to the platform by a guard at the top.

The melée had now resolved itself into a row of six individuals standing on trapdoors next to the nooses, and guards, pistols in belts and canes in hand, standing behind them. The oldest was a man I would say in his sixties, the youngest a lad in his early teens. There was one space next to him remaining at the end of the row, to which I was led. My arrival seemed to draw the attention of the crowd, which now fell silent. Clearly I was regarded with some interest. Light shone on a certain pair of spectacles, and on the opera glasses some of the ladies had raised to their eyes.

The stage was set for the star performer, the young man with the fine arms, who now appeared on the scaffold. He continued to bandy words with his mates below and exchanged a jest or two with the upper echelons. Then almost without a pause he gracefully hitched the noose over the first of his victims and kicked the bolt with his boot. The man disappeared. A tremor went along the structure and the nooses twitched. In the dead silence his choking, gagging gutturals, as life was wrenched out of him, filled the whole space. Predictably the Zinnians preferred slow strangulation to a swift breaking of the neck.

The first man's death throes were soon joined by the next, then the next; swelling to a chorus of throaty gurglings and retchings; while the ropes wriggled and the whole scaffold shook and the crowd stared wide eyed and enthralled. The second from me was the elderly man, a portly figure of some dignity, wearing a suit and a brimmed hat - as if he had dressed for the occasion. The young executioner simply flipped the hat off with a flourish of his fingers before hooking the noose over his head and swinging his boot. He enjoyed his work.

The lad next to me was pale and trembling. He couldn't have been more than fifteen. My heart went out to him and I prayed for him. I cursed myself that I had never given more, never cared more; and all the love and care I had left I gave to him. For myself I decided I had had enough of this vile world and I closed my eyes, intending never to open them again.

I expected my next and penultimate sensation to be the feel of the coarse fibred rope against my neck. But instead I felt my wrists being grabbed and pulled backwards. In extremis the brain can work at phenomenal speed and I knew instantly what was happening. That ghoul really meant it when he said they would hang me twice. The first would be by the wrists, wrenching the arms almost out of their sockets in the time honoured torture method known as strappado. When they had got the most entertainment they could out of that they would hang me by the neck. I instinctively struggled to free my hands, bending forward to wrestle them from the young man's powerful grip. Then I felt a jerk under my armpits, the solid platform went from under me and my eyes popped open. What I saw amazed me.

Instead of the ground hurtling towards me it was racing away from me. I sensed a great presence coming over and sheltering me – as if the angel of death was bearing my soul away from the pitiful remains of my tortured body. But the scene below was all wrong. Instead of rows of amused, excited, gratified faces watching my writhing agonies they were all looking up at me, horrified, scowling, enraged. The soldiers were raising their firearms, there were flashes from their muzzles; and the executioner was lying at the foot of the scaffold, blood pouring from his neck. Bullets whizzed around and pinged above me. Raising my eyes I found myself peering through a wicker framework at a pair of brown skinny legs, and beyond them I glimpsed a streaming mane of blond hair. Above me the glorious wings of the great three-crew buzzard almost filled the sky.

The two strong talons held me securely as the craft lifted from its swoop and levelled, gliding above the outer fortifications, roads, barracks, depots, and on over farmland. But now we were losing height from insufficient breeze or thermal currents and the extra weight of carrying me. The second pilot, I could just recognise him as Ark, began rotating the wings and we gained a little. But without the third crew, whom I assumed had been left out in anticipation of the extra load of an adult male, he was soon exhausted and again we lost height.

We were now crossing an open stretch of pasture bounded at the far end by a wall of woodland. Here I was gently lowered and deposited on the grass, while the great bird banked steeply, skimming the tree tops, circled upwards to regain altitude, then slid sideways and away till I lost sight of it. I could feel my heart pounding. I felt scared, shaken, exposed. The horror of my recent experiences blotted out all thoughts but escape, and I ran for the woods.

Surely I would be chased. In my panic I struck deep in among the trees, with no clear idea of where I was or which direction to take. The sun was hidden behind a bulky blanket of cloud and dusk was setting in, so I could only trust to instinct that I was heading away from Zinn. I had no money, documents or anything except the soiled and blood stained clothes I wore. I must keep going and somehow get back to civilisation and re-establish my credentials, renew my resources, rest and regain my strength.

The terrain was difficult, with briars and thorn bushes and swamps and deep undergrowth, and I was parched, famished and exhausted. Only the adrenalin of flight drove me on. I hoped to find a path made by man or beast but there were none, and I was forced in all directions to avoid the denser thickets, seeking the clear areas beneath the larger trees. The wood was becoming a forest and there might be wolves or bears or wild boar but I was unconcerned. I paused only to listen for the sound of pursuit, the shouts of men and the chorus of yelping dogs. All I heard was the cry of owls and the distant bark of a fox. The gloom deepened and deepened and finally it was dark. Entangled and whiplashed, I hacked blindly on through this labyrinthine wilderness. In all my travels I had never felt so remote from anywhere, so helplessly and hopelessly lost.

Eventually I came to a shallow valley with a stream, where a little light filtered through the canopy above. I drank the water, which was peaty but refreshing, and searched around for something to eat. I found fresh herbage along the banks of the stream that looked and tasted edible, and some bracket fungus growing on a rotten stump which I supposed to be harmless if not greatly nourishing; and then some unripe nuts which were bitter but more satisfying. The food revived my spirits a little, and I felt secure enough to rest a while before continuing my journey. I stayed with the stream, paddling along it or stepping from stone to stone and it made for an easier passage than the trackless forest on either side. Not only that but the hounds of Zinn would lose my scent; no doubt they would have been given it from my rucksack. The gentle flow of water calmed me, and I continued at a steady pace, surmounting obstacles as I came to them. The night was filled with the cries and howls of wild creatures but I began to feel like a denizen myself, a creature of the dark.

Without the stream to guide me I might have gone round in circles and ended where I began. But a stream must go somewhere I reasoned, and yet I continued for hours without coming to any habitation or any sign of human presence. The sky above, glimpsed now and then, began to lighten, and a pale mist hovered over the stream. But the trees on either side seemed ever more dark and impenetrable. Fed by numerous tributaries the stream was getting deeper and harder to wade through. I was beyond weariness but I was afraid to sleep because of the cold and danger of hypothermia. I might never wake up. But I had to rest. There was a lighter patch ahead. I would make it to there and then I would rest. I noticed a dark shape on the water which I took at first to be a log. As I approached I realised it was something else - a canoe.

I came to a small clearing where the canoe was moored. At the edge of it stood a dark shed, or perhaps a miniature cottage, made of sap stained, rough hewn timber, scarcely visible against the backdrop of the forest but for a faint square amber glow indicating a window. Dewy grass surrounded it and a lightly trodden path led towards it from the mooring. I cannot say how long I contemplated it in a total quandary as to whether or not to seek help there: on the one hand the prospect of food and shelter, on the other the risk of recapture and being handed back to my persecutors. Some woodsman must live there I thought, a strong fellow I could hardly resist or escape from in my present weakened state. It wasn't hard to work out that aiding a fugitive would be one of many capital offences in the land of Zinn.

On the other hand the occupant might be someone lonely and forgotten who would not refuse shelter and a crust to a fellow outcast. Slowly the dawn was gaining strength and with it my courage began to return. After all, I had never expected to see another day. Only now did I begin to reflect on my wonderful escape and be filled with gratitude to my rescuers. It was amazing to think of the skill and courage required to swoop that great bird at colossal speed between the beam of the gallows and the top of the wall, grabbing me in its talons and at the same time flinging the hangman to his doom. The gods, or some of them at least, must be on my side.

In returning daylight the hut looked somehow benign. With a cheerful wisp of smoke rising from its chimney it seemed to belong to a peaceful, timeless world. I made my way cautiously towards it. I peered through the lighted window and saw that the glow came from the embers of a fire in an inglenook which took up one side of the room, and on a plain wooden table the remains of a meal – bread, meat, and a half full glass of what could be wine. There seemed to be no one about.

The heavy planked door had no bell or knocker and I tapped lightly on it without conviction. No one came, so I carefully tried the latch and it opened easily on to a warm interior, the firelight hinting thick rugs and cushioned seating. I tiptoed forward, thinking only to absorb as much warmth as I could through my numbed senses, drink the dark red liquid in the glass and decamp with as much food as I could stuff into my pockets.

All went well, and blissfully regaled by the warmth and wine I turned to leave. Then the glass fell from my hand and I fell with

it into the depths of the abyss. Someone was standing in the doorway. Clearly silhouetted there I saw the unmistakable outline of
my Adonis-like executioner.

Then he spoke:

"Wha the deil are ye then?" ★

★ *"Who the devil are you then?" For further Scots words see Elfie's Word Leet at end.*

CHAPTER 4

An Introduction to Fly Fishing

UNABLE to believe what I saw or heard I remained motionless - indeed could not have spoken if I'd tried. The man advanced into the room and strolled over to the fire, threw on some dried sticks and stoked it into a blaze. "Weel I trust ye'll allow me to introduce masel," he said, turning towards me. "Alseph Emmisarius at your service Sir. Scottie to ma freens." Flabbergasted I looked directly at him, his features now lit by the light of the fire. I could see that although he closely resembled the individual who was so nearly the last I would ever encounter in this world, and could have been his twin, he was in fact a different person. It was not his manner any more than his looks, for he too was a frank, cheerful, engaging fellow. The difference was as indefinable as it was profound, as between the casual charm of a warm hearted, sympathetic human being, and the casual charm of a homicidal psychopath.

Then I twigged, and the word 'Scottie' came to my mind and my lips. This must be the very one that Ark and Sulibe had spoken of when I explained that I came from part of Scotland. But what in God's name was a Scott doing here?

Before I could pursue any enquiries on this head my dazed senses returned to a guilty awareness of my own embarrassing position, caught 'snooving' in this man's house. I began to falter my apologies and explain that I was near collapse with exhaustion and hunger. He quickly put me at my ease.

"I can see th'art muckle wabbit. Gie me thae banes - there's an auld leddy in here will like the look o thaim – an' sit ye doon. I'll fesh caller fuid and dyoch for ye. Then ye'll have a gude sleep, and whan y' win up we maun be acquainting ourselves wi' ilk ither."

The gratitude I felt in return was beyond the scope or necessity of words. He went into an adjoining room and returned with bread, meat, fruit and wine. The old lady came out too, a sheep-dog with a spotty nose; and two pairs of kindly eyes watched me as I devoured the food, pausing only to ask the old lady's name. It was Credo. No sooner was I finished than a great drowsiness came upon me and Scottie made me a bed on a couch by the fire, then bade me sleep well and climbed the narrow stairs in the corner to an upper floor. As sleep came upon me the dark suspicion crossed my mind that this was a trap and I'd better make a run for it or I'd wake up to find myself back in the clutches of Zinn's myrmi-dons. But Credo's presence, curled up beside me, seemed like a good omen. So I let myself sink into a profound sleep.

I woke again, gradually surfacing from the misty depths of dreams, and lay peacefully for some time in soft rosy sunlight, not knowing and hardly caring what world I might inhabit now. Slowly my surroundings began to signify, and with their messages came memories of the recent past. From elements of light, colour and shade the room reassembled itself around me and I was back in Scottie's cheerful and homely abode.

The interior remained rather impressionistic from the absence of sharp edges and bright tones – all was rustic and homespun: rough hewn furniture, plants in pots, rows of ripening fruit and bunches of drying herbs hanging from the beams, and various tools and items of tackle. Framed leaf collages, oddly shaped and fashioned bits of bark and timber, a small creature's bleached skull, a nest of eggs and other *objets trouvés*, vases of wild spring flowers – small pale daffodils and pink geraniums – these were the non-utilitarian contents of the room. Amidst it all sat Scottie, darning a sock; it seemed an incongruous setting and activity for so fit and handsome a youth. Placid evening light beamed through the small paned window. I remarked:

"I must have slept all day."

"Aye, ye were unco forfochen, and ye'll be wanting a dook I'll wauger." And so saying he rose and went through to a back room, reappearing with a battered tin bath which he placed by the fire. Pulling on a pair of thick leather mitts from the hearth he took hold of the large iron cauldron that was gently steaming above the embers, lifted and tipped it effortlessly into the bath. Then he went to the kitchen and I heard the gush of a faucet and the hiss of cold water on hot metal; returned with this and a small block of soap and a flannel, added the water little by little to the bath, testing with his finger till a smile signified he was satisfied with the temperature.

"Forby ye'll require new cloots," he said, speaking with the same rather odd inflection which betrayed him as no true native of Scotland. "Thae here are ower sma now for masel but aboot yer size," and he patted a neatly folded pile he'd placed on a chair. In the pleasant light he was lovely to behold, having the bloom and essence of youth combined with grace in all his movements, and I had to check myself from gazing too openly. Nodding and smiling again he explained he had a little business abroad and would leave me for a short while, and with this he departed.

I had a long, lazy, luxurious bath, and must have dozed off again as I suddenly found Scottie standing over me. "Ane awfu score athort yer rig," he was saying, referring to the cut left by the cane-wielding guard. Indeed it rankled still, adding a shrill note to the now more subdued chords of my aches and bruises. He opened a cupboard and selected one from an assortment of jars, and rubbed in a cool pungent cream which gave instant relief. I thought this might lead to a question or two about how I came by my wounds, but without another word Scottie put some logs on the fire and walked into the kitchen.

I levered myself out of the bath and began drying off in front of the blaze. It reminded me of childhood, when I'd dance around warm and naked in the firelight till my mum or gran would catch hold of me and smack my bottom and tell me to put my pyjamas on and go to bed. Grown up now I had to tell myself to put on the clothes Scottie had left for me: thick twill 'breeks', woven cord belt, a cotton blouse, leather jerkin, sandals - all browns and greys. I felt at home in them, as though I now belonged in the forest.

Sounds of a meal in preparation were coming from the kitchen so I went through to see if I could help. Scottie seemed preoccupied, concentrating on the job in hand as if he'd rather get on with it himself. But I'm good at helping - seeing what needs to be done and not getting in the way or disturbing the thought processes of the master. I was happy to sit peeling and podding while Scottie mixed herbs and spices with eggs, cream and juices, trying the results as he went along. At length, cautiously satisfied, he offered me a blob on the end of his finger. I didn't have to pretend it tasted good: it tasted good. A freshly plucked fowl was then stuffed and plastered with this marinade and taken through to be put on the spit above the glowing embers of the logs. Scottie said he had to go out again, leaving me with instructions on turning the spit and boiling the vegetables. I was pleased to be entrusted with these tasks, and to be of service to my kindly host.

Like thoughtfully prepared and well savoured meals in any part of the world this one when it came was deeply satisfying. Scottie produced a bottle of wine which he pronounced 'maumie' - the meaning of which I recalled to be full bodied, ripe and luscious, a description with which I entirely concurred. He seemed quite relaxed and the talk was mainly about the food itself, the various ingredients, how cultivated and where gathered, local names for them and suggested comparisons with the fare enjoyed by the people of Scotland.

The meal over, we washed the dishes, falling now into a natural rhythm of working together, while I took careful note of where everything was put. Then we went through again and Scottie pulled two comfortable chairs to the fire and threw on some fresh logs. He produced a pair of long clay pipes and handed me one, placing a tin of tobacco on the edge of the hearth. I was never a smoker but it seemed ungracious not to partake, so I stuffed the bowl with the moist, fragrant tinder, took a spill from the fire and lit up. I have to admit it was calming and nicer than I remembered from youthful attempts to be one of the crowd; but I was careful not to inhale and drew as infrequently as possible. A close observer would have noted my embarrassment but Scottie just puffed away nonchalantly, leaving me to my own devices. Then he got up and went to another cupboard from which he took two crystal glasses and a bottle of brown liquid. "Usquebaugh," he pronounced. "I barmit it masel. Ye'll nae deny a wee gust?" Refuse it I did not, and a racier malt from the Highlands or Islands never passed my lips.

Sipping and puffing we sat for a while staring at the fire, watching the smoke billowing round the new logs and waiting for it suddenly to blossom into flame. It did, and our faces shone in the now darkened room. His carefree cheerful manner made no necessity of conversation, but eventually he spoke.

"You are welcome ma freen, but ye maun tell me yer nem and what brang ye hither."

"Jason," said I.

"Ah, and he was a wanderer too. We kep nae mony travellers hereawa, and sic as come by dinna return."

"I certainly gleaned the impression that visitors are not welcome in the city, or in the land of Zinn either. Just how far does it extend? I thought I'd be across the border by now."

"Nae borders, Jason. Zinn has nae borders."

He asked me then about my origins, as if needing to establish my precise identity and character with reference to some bizarre Zinnian system of astrology. The configuration of the stars and planets at the time of my birth was a better guide to who I was than any account of my life or beliefs. After struggling to relate the Gregorian calendar to his own time frame he seemed satisfied with the results of his calculations, and with me. Then he asked:

"But how in the deil's nem did ye come in hereawa?"

I had debated with myself for some time just how much, or how little, I should impart of my experiences to date in this benighted realm. I knew well from many a scrape that in a conflict zone it's best to know as little as possible, and tell even less. And I was still exercised by the striking resemblance between Scottie and a certain late loyal henchman of the Zinnian regime. But it was apparent that Scottie was on good terms with the rebel children and under my present helpless circumstances I had little choice but to put my trust in him. Perhaps the likeness was just a question of ethnic type. At all events I gave him a full account of my journey to Zinn and my encounter with the buzzards of Zinn. He listened with interest, and gave an occasional nod of verification. However, when I moved on to my recent misadventures his manner became more intent, and troubled. Then when I came to describe the executioner and his antics his eyes dimmed, a look of pain came over his handsome features, and he shook his head. "You know this man?" I asked.

"I suld ken ma ain twin brither," was his reply.

From this point I hardly knew how to proceed, since the account of my deliverance involved the news of his brother's death. In the circumstances it would be absurd to offer my condolences. I faltered on, attempting to be vague and uncertain of the man's fate, but he questioned me earnestly and in the end I had to tell him that his brother almost certainly perished. At this he got up and began pacing the room, his face dark and preoccupied. I said I was sorry to have to give him that news, and I'd just take a walk outside and leave him to his thoughts.

It was as though I hadn't spoken and wasn't even there, so I went quietly out into the night. I stood in the dewy grass and looked up to the circle of stars above, listening to the sounds of the forest and breathing huge lungfulls of its moist green breath. Was this the end of my stay here, I wondered. Would I have to find my way out of this wilderness alone and empty handed? I half expected the clash of lock and bolt to signify precisely this, but it didn't come. Despite my insecurity I felt intensely alive. After a while I saw a light flicker in the upstairs window and concluded that Scottie had retired, so I crept back in again, quietly locked the door myself, and crawled into bed. Credo who was sitting by the ladder and looking rather concerned came over for a pat and settled beside me. I was still OK as far as she was concerned.

I lay still in the glowing dark thinking that Scottie could not rationally defend his brother's actions or blame me for his death, but worrying that with the irrationality of powerful emotions the tender plant of our friendship had been blighted in the bud. Eventually I slept, but I was suddenly roused to find a dark shape looming over me, a head close to mine, and a trembling voice saying: "Ye maun be ma brither noo."

Next morning I tried to say something comforting and reassuring, but Scottie seemed already to have recovered his normal temper and simply replied: "I kend he wa deid. A twin a'ways kens. And I kend ye wad win hither in his stead." Best left there I thought, and proceeded to make myself as useful as possible in preparing breakfast and tending the fire.

Scottie showed me the rest of his premises, the 'but and ben' as he put it, with the exception of his upstairs quarters. There was a store room and pantry well stocked with racks of fruit and root crops and jars of preserves. This led through to a yard at the rear where there was a covered area in which logs were chopped and stacked. Various outbuildings enclosed the rest of the yard, one a general workshop with benches, vices and rows of hand tools, another a forge with an anvil, and in the others a neatly shelved collection of miscellaneous junk: anything in metal from paperclips to the rusty ruins of an old tractor. Thrift and improvisation, I concluded, were key elements in my host's *modus vivendi*. I noticed with interest one particular chart on the wall - it was a design for the wing of a buzzard plane. Pinned up next to it was an actual buzzard's wing.

Beyond the yard a green lane led into the forest. Breakfast over we set off together along it, and thus began my life in the forest. It was a bright new morning and I felt like a young man again, setting out on life's journey for the first time, full of hope and joyful expectation. It was to be the first of innumerable expeditions, alone and in Scottie's company, and in either case rarely without Credo. When I'd fled here it was a terrifying and intractable wilderness but it came to feel more like home than the country of my birth, and more like paradise than any other I had visited. Far from being pathless it was a maze of hidden passageways, often through the densest thickets and across the boggiest hollows. Their ramblings would defeat the uninitiated but once you knew the pattern and the markers you could find your way wherever you wanted, and back again by another route. If I missed my way Credo would be sure to guide me.

With Scottie on hand to explain its mysteries the forest became a rich, complex world, full of interest and beauty. The sheer variety of life was astonishing: so many species of plants and trees and shapes of leaves and shades of green and blooms and blossoms and the different scents they exhaled. The bird life was the most immediately striking, from the noisy exotic parakeets to hidden warblers that filled everywhere with their song. There were chequered woodpeckers, jays flashing electric blue, glittering finches, shadowy hawks, hummingbirds smaller than the butterflies that floated in the vibrant air, adding another layer of colour and pattern. The design and harmony and sheer exuberance of light and colour and sound overwhelmed my senses, and I walked in a dream, while Scottie, to whom it was all everyday normality, chattered away like all the rest of its inhabitants.

He could put a name to every specimen we encountered – I couldn't understand how he had lived long enough to store such knowledge. He lead me into the bushes or reeds or ferns as tall as ourselves to point out an exquisite nest of a bird or a tiny rodent, or a teeming colony of enormous ants, or the lobed combs of a bee colony in the branches of a tree, or some weird evil looking fungus which he assured me had a delicious taste when cooked with a certain species of wild parsley. We encountered friendly tribes of delicate monkeys with soft beige fur and pink faces and hands, and I was especially pleased to find flourishing numbers of a long lost friend, that cutest of woodland folk, the red squirrel. I would have needed to be a reincarnation of Charles Darwin or Richard Jefferies, and have a stack of notebooks to hand as well, to record half of what I saw. Everything was so exquisite and benign and happily indifferent to human presence.

But I thought there must also be dangerous creatures – snakes, bears, wolves, wild boar, big cats. Scottie assured me that there were all these and he would teach me how to spot the signs and how to stay well clear of them. It was only during a hard winter when their normal prey species were scarce that anything as unappetising as a fully clothed human might attract the attention of large predators. Wolves hunted in packs and big black bears came down from the north, and even white ones sometimes from even further north. The resident bears were placid and vegetarian, a relative of the panda. As for snakes, you just had to be careful where you trod.

Our first journey of about two miles brought us to a large clearing which encircled a small farm. There were bright green meadows enclosed by hedges with great trees in the corners, walled around by the darker emerald of the forest. On a small scale it had everything you'd expect to find on an old-fashioned pre-industrial farm: cattle, sheep, pigs, poultry, bees, orchards, dovecote, duck pond, and two shire horses to pull plough and cart and do the heavy work.

It was a communal enterprise worked by Scottie and his fellow foresters and their families, who all took a share of the produce. They were country folk through and through; tough, shrewd, practical, quick witted, open handed and open hearted, lithe lads with ample wives and skinny kids. Their reception of me contrasted strongly with the hostility I had encountered in the fields and farms close to Zinn. I was greeted with smiles and nods all round, and big eyed curiosity from the children, and felt instantly included in the circle. There was a constant exchange of jest and anecdote between them, in which the children held their own. I could appreciate this from the flow of eloquence without understanding a word. Scottie helped me out with the occasional interjected translation, but I resolved to attempt to learn the language myself. I could see that the humour and temper that prevailed among them was proof against the quarrels and dissentions that so often spelt the demise of communes and utopian schemes, however auspicious their beginnings. In a word, they were canny. They knew the score.

We returned from the farm glowingly happy and ravenously hungry. Scottie announced that he would 'gang kittle some truit' from the brook for our supper. I could come if I promised to be still and quiet. We walked further along the stream I had arrived by to where it was augmented by another of the same size and raced merrily from pool to pool. Scottie knelt on the bank and peered closely into the swiftly flowing current. I peered too but could see little beyond the surface glitter until I got the angle right and could just make out a dark wavering shape, and it seemed his fingers had only to dip an inch before the shape flashed away. They were canny fish too, and the larger the cannier. Then after an almost imperceptible approach brought the wavering hand under the wavering shape the hand would flash up like a sprung trap in a shower of spray, only to be found empty. After half an hour we had just three fish, barely half a pound each. By this point the need to eat something had overruled the mere consideration of quantity and we returned to the cottage to prepare the meal.

In any case there were lavish amounts of vegetables, salads and eggs all spiced up with Scottie's delicious relishes. He tried to insist that I have the fish, and I in turn to insist that he did, pointing out that without me there would have been enough. We ended up arguing about a precise mathematical division of the three little bodies into two equal portions. During the meal I asked Scottie if he'd ever thought of fishing with a rod and line, using an artificial fly as bait. It was, I pointed out, the preferred method of catching fish in his adoptive homeland.

"I ken wha ye are speaking aboot," he replied, "but I hanna had the occasion masel, or ony instruction in the art of it. Ma ain method has a'ways sufficed."

"Well with me on board perhaps we should give it a try. When I was a lad I used to make my own rods and tackle and I expect I could remember how it was done."

"And did ye tak mony fush wi' y' rod and tackle now?" he asked slyly.

"Oh yes, hundreds. Used to have to put most of them back."

Later I went to work and selected a long straight bamboo shoot. I made rings from re-fashioned paper clips, hammered the ends flat and bound them with thread at intervals of about a foot, and then a looped ring bent down a little at the tip. I greased the thread well with lard from the pantry to preserve it from moisture. For a handle I cut and peeled some lengths of elder and hollowed out the pithy core. I tried several until I found one that the rod was a tight fit in. The reel was more of a problem - it was one piece of tackle I had saved my pocket money for as a boy. I managed to find a narrow wooden bobbin in the junk box Scottie made available to me, and to screw a bead to the outer rim to make a handle. But the rings and flanges of the conventional reel fitting were beyond me. I had to bore a hole through the handle and push in a bamboo dowel as a spindle for the reel, retaining it with a large flat headed nail inserted through the bamboo tube and hammered to make a burr at the other end. Quite a few pieces of split bamboo lay on the floor and as many curses gave the air a bluish tinge before I had a sufficiently robust and free spinning reel attached to my rod. By this time I was tired and it was beginning to get dark. Scottie had already retired to his pipe, having followed my progress with amused detachment.

The following day at the farm I spent the morning banking up spuds, but my thoughts were going round like my reel on the questions of what to do for a line, how to replicate a Zinnian fly, and, hardest of all, the hook. Would any wire I could find be strong enough, and how on earth would I make a barb? Even if I had the luck to hook a fish the chances of landing it without a barb on the hook were, well, negligible. I was going to swallow my pride and ask for Scottie's help but for some reason he'd gone back to the cottage.

I remembered that twine woven from the manes of horses was used to make netting to protect the fruit from birds, so I went along to see an old man called Wulver Glodso who generally supervised the soft fruit area. I tried to explain with many a fisherman's exaggerative hand gestures what I wanted and what it was for. After much puzzlement and more patience he worked out the former at least. He disappeared into a dark and dusty shed and came out with a large bobbin of thin strong twine, blond and glistening. I tried to tell him I only needed a certain length but he thrust the whole into my hands and patted my shoulder with a smile and waved me away. Delighted with this success I couldn't wait to return and begin my study of Zinnian water flies.

When I got back what should I find but Scottie in the workshop finishing off an exact replica of the rod I had made - except that in every detail the workmanship was superior. It was my turn now to be amused, and make a poor attempt to suppress my amusement, until we were both laughing. Then we went down to the brook together to observe aquatic insect life. Like all other life in the forest it was prolific. Tiny dancing diaphanous creatures of all shades and shapes hovered above the surface of the stream or alighted on it to ride along with the current. Every so often one would disappear in a flash of silver water and silver scales. We tried to work out which ones the fish preferred. It was a toss-up between the pale pinky-brown guys and ones with a bright blue tail. So we wandered around, scrutinising the forest floor looking for feathers and discarded seed pods and leaf skeletons and any other natural object bearing a resemblance to the delicate patterns and tissues of these ephemeral creatures. We took our collection back with us and talked of nothing else over supper.

Scottie made some hooks from tempered steel in a miniature forge, hammering and shaping them on a tiny anvil with an eyeglass screwed into his eye. His resourcefulness and skill were entirely consistent with my theory that he had been involved with the creation of the buzzards of Zinn, possibly even the chief engineer. We spent several evenings together tying flies, and had a wonderful array of specimens laid out on the table, with big black eyes and mottled wings and juicy looking bodies. Scottie's were generally the more exact replicas, but I knowingly alluded to the curiosity of fish, and claimed that verisimilitude was not necessarily the key to success.

So one fine evening we waxed our lines, wound them on to our reels, attached our lures and strode purposefully down to the brook. I showed Scottie the casting technique of gathering loops of loose line then swishing it out upstream to allow the lure to float down with the current, tempting a fish to strike. The fish must have been mightily confused by some of the objects they saw floating above them. We thrashed around for some time to no avail. "They don't seem to be rising today," I observed wisely. But then to my surprise I caught one, played it and brought it in; a good three pounds it was too.

Scottie attributed my success to luck, 'a sonsie callant' I was; but he was certainly impressed, and spurred on to greater efforts. He demanded to know what fly I had used, which happened to be one of the more outlandish ones, with a tufted tail made from Credo's fur, and spent hours practising his cast and adjusting his tackle. He pressed me for information far beyond my meagre knowledge, but I was able to describe the better rods to him, ones made of varnished split cane with cork handles and fixed-spool reels. To my amazement he then produced one, even the reel with its purring ratchet and wire snaffle which could be lifted to let the line shoot out at speed then clicked back to wind it in as soon as you turned the handle. After that there was no stopping him, and no point in my continuing with my feeble instrument.

No words were needed to make his point - just a little patronising smile as he tossed a brace of bonny speckled trout on the table before breakfast. I was happy at seeing him happy, and pleased at the pleasure he got from winning.

But there was one more surprise. One morning he came down and wished me a happy birthday. I had no idea it was my birthday, having lost track of days and months, and my watch with the date on gone the way of my other possessions. But Scottie's astrological calculations had determined it and the stars had borne him out. He spent a good deal of time looking at the stars. Then he produced from behind his back my birthday present - a cylindrical package about forty inches long. I opened it to reveal a beautiful shiny rod in ferruled sections with the most smoothly rolling reel that excelled even the 'Intrepid De Luxe' I had proudly owned as a child. I could only stutter my thanks. After that we went on many expeditions together, to streams and rivers near and far, and were never short of that most wholesome of foods. And we had enough to hand out to other forester families, especially those with lots of children.

I noticed when Scottie caught a fish he'd snap its neck immediately, rather than throw it down on the ground to flip and toss
till it suffocated in the air as I had seen some fishermen do. It was
the more humane procedure, but the action reminded me rather
uncomfortably of his late and unlamented brother.

CHAPTER 5

A Shrine

SOME NIGHTS I lay awake, listening to the solitary, heartfelt outpourings of the nightingale, the distant wuthering of owls and
churring of nightjars, thinking about what Scottie had said, about
us being brothers. Despite his genuine friendship he was wary and
reticent, guarding his secrets. Perhaps sibling rivalry explained something of his attitude towards me, and I could understand his need
for a replacement for, and improvement on, the brother he had
recently lost. Whereas Zard's easy-going confidence was the out-
ward aspect of a nature as hard and cold as permafrost, the same
manner in Scottie masked a vulnerable, needy, sensitive soul.
I surmised the reason for his reticence about himself and about Zinn
was a desire to hold on to me by keeping up my level of curiosity.

I told him all he wanted to know about myself, so he was fully
aware that I was a traveller: someone who came, saw, enjoyed,
understood, and left. For me to know a place was to leave it,
but I would never fully know the forest, or Scottie. He was so
beautiful and graceful I inwardly considered him a god - a god
of woodlands, benign, if a bit touchy at times. Also he liked to
tease me. He looked at me with a kind of half smiling reserve as
if to say you're not quite ready for me to tell you that yet. And I
teased him in turn by affected indifference and displays of worldly
savoir faire.

But his mood could change quickly, one minute buoyant, confident, ready for some new adventure, the next sad and reflective.

In these he seemed to be anticipating my departure, but I sensed there was something else - his twin brother's death perhaps, but something deeper. As if testing me, or tempting fate, he'd sometimes say he could help me when I wanted to move on:

"Jason lad, aiblins I could speer oot a gate for ye to win awa frae here. Ye'll be desiring to return to yer ain hame I'm thinking."

He could put me on the Western Highway beyond the remit of Zinnian forces. His remark about Zinn having no borders meant apparently that there were no limits to its claims, only to its knowledge and power. What the Zinnians didn't know and control was unworthy of consideration.

"Look Scottie," I'd say, "I think whatever made me want to travel was in my backpack, because since I lost it I've had no desire to go anywhere, except down to the brook to cast a fly or two."

At this his spirits would revive and off we'd go.

When I reflected on all this in my nightingale-haunted nocturnal musings I realised that Scottie's claim on me had not affected me adversely, as it would have done at any previous time. It had never been part of my plan to form lasting bonds or ties of any kind. But something had changed, perhaps connected with my recent near death experience and relief at having found a place of safety, and one that was also socially and aesthetically more satisfying than any other I'd known. Whatever the reason I no longer felt the relentless impulse to cast my shadow in every land and island on the face of the planet.

After all my travels I felt, obscurely, that I had arrived. My actual home was a distant memory, and the loss of my personal possessions severed all links, and made my return, even if desired, highly problematic. I was born in the south of England and had lived in several pleasant country towns, moving on before the advancing reticular spread, like cracking ice, of a credit fuelled motorised consumerism that plundered the earth, polluted the air, and eroded the native energies and traditional skills of my countrymen. I had fled to the Celtic fringes, first Wales then Scotland, in search of a purer and simpler life, though hardly realising at the time that this migration and all my subsequent travels had been to find a peaceful existence in harmony with nature and my fellow man. And here it was. My only desire now to journey any distance from the forest and its folk was to visit the children again, to repay the debt I owed them in any way I could. And if little Aya really wanted me as her dad - well that too.

Upstairs Scottie's thoughts must have been on the same subject because the next morning he was brooding and taciturn. Eventually he came out with:

"Certie ye'll be travelling on one of thir fine days Jason."

"I've no plans just now. I like it here."

"Weel, but ye'll soon be fashed of us simple carles, being a traveller of the warld now, an we mak ye lawbor for yer living."

"I've no objection to that Scottie, and I like the folk here, and I enjoy the work."

"Aye but ye've seen sae mony countries and sic wonders in the warld . . ."

"Nothing as strange and wonderful as Zinn, and the forest, and the buzzard children. I'd really like to know how all this came about."

"Nae doot ye'll want ta tell yer fowk at hame a' aboot it. Mebbe ye'll write a buik."

"Not me! I'm no author. Travellers' tales bore me stiff. Besides, no one would believe me, and there are too many books already. The world's stuffed full of them."

"Nae sae mony buiks in Zinn ma freen."

"Really? Well there must be some, else how did you learn to speak like a Scotsman?"

"I maun hae kent some doited gaberlunzie wad come a snifting by."

So having side-stepped my queries and got more than he'd given, his mood brightened and we talked of the day ahead.

Most days were spent on the farm, and I'd meant it when I said I enjoyed the work. No two days were quite alike, and there were always new things to learn and discoveries to make about nature and husbandry, and new skills to acquire: whether the milking of goats or the scything of grass in neat parallel swathes, or the taking of a swarm of bees. Most of all I loved working with the horses, immensely strong, gentle, willing but proud. They knew their tasks better than I did, but so did everybody, including the children who derived great amusement from my first ham-fisted attempts. But I could always rely on them for a little extra tuition if I had already tried the patience of the grown-ups. For them the farm was both playground and school, and they made a natural transition from play to helping and taking responsibility.

They had several games they liked, in particular a form of rounders with, to me, inscrutable rules. Whatever I did was wrong and I always lost. To level things up a bit I introduced them to the game of football, which they took to immediately, the girls just as eager and combative as the lads. I was elevated to the position of sole authority and referee which I assumed with high dignity, even though I had never been quite clear about the offside rule.

They formed teams and even an embryo league system, but there was no idea of the girls and boys playing separately. Teams were always mixed and girls were often captains and the star players. But the days were getting very hot and on top of farm work I was beginning to find it totally exhausting to have to run around the field blowing a bamboo whistle. So I declared the football season over and the cricket season about to begin.

Again there was instant enthusiasm and commitment and talk was of nothing but scores and averages and bowling techniques. Here too the grownups began to get involved, having been content to remain amused spectators of the football contests. No doubt they observed that frenzied running all over the place was not required, but rather muscular strength and control, and a keen eye. Teams formed in three age groups, each one producing some serious and absorbing matches.

All this greatly assisted the language learning process. I demonstrated things physically to begin with and they would translate the different elements of the game into words and phrases which I could then use and develop for further explanations. To a professional cricketer the results would doubtless have been laughable, a bit like the village cricket of yesteryear, with some bizarre individual styles of play. Yet there were some remarkable displays of both bowling and batting prowess, and several outstanding characters began to emerge.

There was one all-rounder whose performances consistently outstripped all others, and that one was Scottie. He was very much the golden boy, and all the girls had eyes for him. There were several pretty girls around the farm, and one or two very pretty ones, real beauties. I rather wondered why Scottie didn't appear to show any particular interest in any of them. He was just nice to everyone. I might casually remark that a certain girl was very pretty and he'd reply, "Aye, she's a bonny lass, and a canny fielder" - or some such point that would not normally enter the reckoning between the young and lovely of opposite sex. Well, perhaps it was his usual way of playing his cards close to his chest, and I certainly had no intention of adopting the role of a nagging parent. I was happy to enjoy our daily companionship, while knowing it was unlikely always to remain as close, and as closed, as it was.

So however our day's work and play had bonded us with the group as a whole, we always returned to the cottage alone in each other's company. We'd discuss and prepare a meal, then we might kick a ball around or fish in the stream, or work on some housekeeping task or repair job together, or just sit contentedly like an elderly couple in the calm evening light. When the air chilled and the dew fell, and the bats were skittering about, we'd go in and stir the fire, and share a bottle and a light for our pipes. We'd talk a good bit then, and Scottie liked to gossip. He seemed to know everything that was going on in the lives of the others, and I came to know a good deal more about some of them than about him.

What struck me was how accepting and non-judgemental he was, a little mild amusement being his nearest approach to disapproval. But then this trait seemed characteristic of all the forest folk. They weren't jealous or quarrelsome or even competitive off the field of play; they didn't criticise, complain or claim precedence over others on any basis, even age. At the same time they were not the least bit polite, but lively, forthright, individualistic in all they said and did. They'd make serious speeches of considered oratory, paying heed to each other, but sooner or later all would dissolve in an uproar of jest and banter. And after a while it seemed to me perfectly natural to be this way, and I found myself becoming like them, even before my grasp of the language enabled me to make any useful contribution to their discussions.

But then even back in the UK I had never been a fan of the 'soaps', those long running 'real life' drama series in which people are forever in contention and falling out and letting each other down, and a constant bad tempered bitching and bickering between them is considered the normal currency of social interaction. Somehow the foresters never seemed to take anything or themselves that seriously, not from flippancy or irresponsibility but from a profound and unshakeable inner integrity: something they shared with, and was sustained by, the forest itself, and the creatures all around them. They were part of creation; there was the force of creativity, irrepressible hope, at the heart of them, instead of disillusion, dissatisfaction and denial, constant stress and endless striving.

And yet there were some deep concerns. Beyond the worries about the health of crops and stock inseparable from farming there were bigger issues, resulting in hushed conversations and furrowed brows, and a notable absence of jocularity. Scottie, characteristically, didn't immediately fill me in, carefully testing my general understanding and maturity before venturing on to this serious ground. But eventually he spoke about the fears the forest folk had for their future survival.

"We've had nae word frae the orphant bairns these twa muins. Nae bairn gleddies ha been seen, except a wee shiny ane, an ye can gie credence tae Raelk Welgis' daft wean. Forby the kilties ha' been shelling an pluffing thereawa."

A vision of the cavern blasted open, and the charred bodies of the children amid the smouldering wreckage of their cherished flying machines, darkened my mind.

"We should go there, Scottie. They may need our help."

"We canna fecht the kilties laddie, wi our spaads an hay-sneds. Syne they wad tear intae us an we chaw 'em. The murtherers hae set tae us afore ye ken, brenning hames and hanging fowk. We maun bide till they haud awa."

The only comfort I could derive from this was the thought that if the army was still operational the children were still somehow holding out. Perhaps they had found a deeper retreat. As so often when troubled, Scottie got up abruptly and excused himself, saying he had some private business to attend to. Head bowed and slow of step he would wander into the forest. About half an hour later he would return, as cheerful and positive as ever. During his absences I'd carry on with the housework, or my studies. Or else I'd play with Credo.

I'd whack a ball as hard as I could into the woods and she'd rush off in pursuit, to return with it sometimes several minutes later, panting and dishevelled. After giving it a good goring she would return the slobbery article to be belted again, in a cloud of saliva spray. There was no end to her eagerness and she never failed to bring it back, except on this one occasion.

She hadn't shown up for some fifteen minutes and after several calls and whistles I went to look for her. Searching the area where the ball could have landed I pushed through brambles into a little grove of larches, and there came across a path I hadn't noticed before. I followed its winding course till it became a green tunnel, and then suddenly opened into a sunny glade between massive beech trees. In the centre was a little structure of wood and thatch similar to the top of a well in an old fashioned children's picture book. Scottie was kneeling in front of it, his back towards me, in a devotional attitude, and Credo was sitting quietly beside him, facing the same way. It was like a Pre-Raphaelite painting of an Arthurian knight making his vows to his liege, his faithful hound by his side.

I had never questioned Scottie about his or his people's religious beliefs. Not having any religious allegiance myself I simply accepted that others did or didn't, and either way I'd found there was no reliable correlation between professing a faith, or the faith they professed, and their treatment of their fellow human beings. So I turned to go the way I'd come but Credo spotted me, picked up the ball which was lying in the grass in front of her, and came trotting over towards me, tail wagging eagerly. The movement must have disturbed Scottie who looked round after her and saw me standing there.

"Sorry to interrupt, old boy. I lost Credo."

"Ye'll never loss Credo, Jason," he said, then added on reflection, "It would be a dark, doolsome day an we pairted wi' her. Will ye nae jine us?"

He leaned back on his arms, luxuriously absorbing the sunshine. I sat down beside him on the bright grass, which was as soft and warm as Credo's fur. I took a closer look at the shrine; it covered a stone with some writing carved on it and there was an open shelf below the little pitched roof with several objects on it. These included a book, a pipe and a pair of spectacles. The book's covers were warped and the pages wavy with exposure to sun and damp. "My faither's grave," said Scottie, responding to my curiosity.

"I see. A lovely place for it. You must feel close to him here. A good man, I think, to have such a devoted son."

"Aye a gude man in feth, and a wise one. A true scholar."

"Ah yes. And those were his personal things. And the book?"

"Aye. Ane he writ hissel. A great buik."

Scottie's voice was full of pride. Clearly the memory of his father calmed and revived his spirits. He lay back on the grass with his eyes closed, smiling and basking in the genial warmth of the sun. Credo came over and licked his cheek. The mood was infectious so I lay down too, gazing up at the glorious light through pink closed eyelids, and was also licked by Credo who was pleased to be on level terms with us. Then Scottie leapt to his feet, and grabbing my hand pulled me up too.

"Come awa lad. Ye maun see for yersel."

He went over to the shrine and placed his forefinger on a many coloured wooden cylindrical object attached to the inner surface of one of the posts. After a pause he turned it a few times. I enquired if it was a prayer wheel. He nodded. "I've never understood them," I said. "How can it pray for you?" He said "It's sae ye can pray for a' as thole and pine wi'oot ye be drooned in their dool yersel." "Well that makes sense," I said, and gave the wheel a spin.

We made our way back to the cottage. Credo came along with her ball in her mouth, expecting play to resume, but we went straight in the door and Scottie beckoned me to follow him up the ladder into his private quarters. It was the first time I had entered them.

The room was larger than the others as there were no partition walls, but the ceiling sloping down almost to the floor on two sides made it seem quite intimate. It was lit only by a small dormer window, the rest in shadow. His bed was tucked away in a corner under the rafters; there was a table and a rather fine mahogany roll-top desk, an oil portrait of a white bearded sage, doubtless his father, and shelves packed with books lining the walls. Opened books and scattered papers lay on the table and desk. I glanced along the shelves at the titles. Mostly they were in an unfamiliar script I took to be Zinnian, but there was a bay of European classics: Goethe, Dante, Shakespeare, Cervantes, Balzac, Rousseau and others, and then, as I'd almost come to expect, leather-bound sets of the entire works of Sir Walter Scott and Robert Burns, and volumes by several other Scottish writers.

"My faither's buiks," said Scottie in a quiet voice. "But he had mony more."

"What happened to the rest?" I asked.

"We gied a' ower whan we cam frae Zinn. He bidit wi me here afore he deed."

"I expect these were your favourites," I said, pointing to the Scottish volumes, and taking out a well thumbed copy of *The Heart of Midlothian*.

"He loved thir buiks. He leernit me to read them as a bairn. I read them ayeways. There are twa buiks here ye maun find eese-fae and I wush ye tae keep."

He took down a thick quarto volume stoutly bound, and handed it to me. Fanning the pages I saw at once that it was a dictionary, Zinnian-English and English-Zinnian, with the

Zinnian words helpfully transliterated into English. The other volume he gave me was a translation into English of the 'great buik' of his father's he had mentioned at the shrine. He told me his father had translated it into several languages, including Latin, but it had never passed beyond the borders of Zinn, and very few copies were distributed there before it was banned. Copies were burnt in the streets. That's when father and son had to leave and take refuge in the forest.

I thanked him sincerely. The dictionary would be a great help to me, and I looked forward with great interest to reading his father's *magnum opus*. Indeed I began reading it that very night and read and re-read parts of it avidly for many nights after. Despite all the apparatus of a scholarly work, with an immense field of reference in many languages and cultures, its central narrative was pellucid in its clarity.

Scottie's father, Emmis Zarrion, had been a celebrated Zinnian philosopher. As was the custom among artists and intellectuals he Latinised his name: Emmisarius. His central idea was original virtue. Babies were born in innocence and it is entirely what happens to them after birth that turns them into thieves, murderers, tyrants etc., or men and women of virtue and honour. He believed in what he called natural society. Animals had it, even insects, but man had lost it. There was a culture of abuse handed down from generation to generation, through patterns of behaviour, indoctrination and propaganda. Tribalism, militarism, imperialism, nationalism, even religion – all were forms of inculcated and learned behaviour with the inevitable end product of human on human violence.

Organised crime, an ethos handed down from father to son, was a well documented example of a self perpetuating cycle of abuse, and he also maintained that the state itself was another, perhaps the worst. He regarded formal compulsory education as harmful and schools as unnatural societies. Education should be an open process of give and take between individuals of all ages, making that growth possible that is stunted by prescribed learning and didactic indoctrination. He draws frequently on Rousseau, and among the many English language authors he quotes, comments at length and with approval on Wordsworth's *Ode on the Intimations of Immortality:*

> *Heaven lies about us in our infancy!*
> *Shades of the prison house begin to close*
> *Upon the growing Boy.*

Another English nature mystic he calls in aid is Richard Jefferies, quoting the chilling lines:

> *The truth is we are murdered by our ancestors. Their dead hands*
> *stretch forth from the tomb and drag us down.*

Among more recent authors he notes Larkin's ironic advocacy of childlessness in *This be the Verse:*

> *Man hands on misery to man,*
> *it deepens like a coastal shelf . . .*

and he points out that Golding's children reverting to savagery in *Lord of the Flies* were not returning to nature but replicating at a more primitive level a form of adult behaviour which the naval officer, who intervenes to re-establish order at the end, represents in a more 'civilised' form.

The newborn infant is unaware of others and entirely selfish in pursuit of its needs, but that does not imply, he argues, that man is inherently selfish or that sociality is acquired through learning. It is innate, and grows as naturally as the teeth and hair. Babies do not kill each other: adults do; and precisely, he maintains, because of learned sociality with its false and partial loyalties to the group (school, gang, race, faith, nation etc.) instead of to the whole species and the all-sustaining environment.

The function of the idea of original sin was to erase natural society so that it could be replaced by a false order imposed from above. Whether in families or societies control was achieved by an inculcated sense of guilt and blame, by rules and punishments and pressure to conform. What Larkin called the 'soppy stern' approach to parenting applied also to the authoritarian paternalistic state; on the one hand sentimental and sanctimonious mollycoddling of the 'vulnerable', the pretence of care; and on the other regulations, restrictions and penalties of varying harshness covering every aspect of life. The result was a process he termed 'infantalisation', thwarting the natural growth of independence and intelligence. This condition was apparent even in the so called democracies.

Elected governments behaved in the same arbitrarily authoritarian manner as the unelected, ignoring popular feeling in the name of 'leadership' and creating the apathy and cynicism which guaranteed that elections would amount to little more than the mathematics of self-interest, and no fundamental change in the political culture could ever take place. The infantalised populace could never collectively summon the will to challenge the established order and its prevailing myths.

Emmisarius recognised that even this minimal concession to collective responsibility was preferable to the instability of unelected regimes. In unstable polities enforced order became direct oppression, which triggered rebellion. This was met with harsh reprisals that in turn sparked revolution, and a new power group set about re-establishing 'order', and the cycle repeats. In the wider field, empires and power structures rose and fell through a process of conquest, expansion, colonisation, secession, fragmentation and implosion, at which point another power entity seizes the opportunity to begin the cycle again.

Although clearly a great deal of what Emmisarius says has a bearing on politics he was not a political writer. It would be more accurate to describe him as anti-political. He didn't propose a new political system but was against all political systems, regarding the state and its agencies as entirely malign. Power like wealth should be broken down and subdivided to be shared by all and benefit all; and he proposed a direct equation between human happiness and the distribution of power and wealth. In any society the fewer the people into whose hands power and wealth are concentrated, the greater the degree of human suffering and misery. He pointed out that you only had to listen to people in the street, watch American films or read popular novels to see that everyone realises and passively accepts that corruption, hypocrisy and chicanery are the very stuff of politics.

What made Emmisarius's philosophy revolutionary, and dangerously so to his compatriots, was his belief that politics was not only an evil but an unnecessary evil, a cycle of abuse handed down from generation to generation. No one of mature intelligence and responsibility would tolerate such a process, but its function was to frustrate the collective acquisition and application of these qualities, and stifle the full development of our human potential.

Emmisarius might well be classified as a humanist. He rejected the notion that human nature is fundamentally sinful, and also the notion that it is fundamentally spiritual. He also went on to dismiss the twentieth century idea that it is fundamentally sexual, though he accepted both sexuality and spirituality as major components. Sexual passion, he remarks, consists of two separate people having two separate experiences, and without friendship it was nothing, as evidenced by the numbers of once torrid lovers daily crowding the divorce courts. Human beings were simply human and to realise their humanity to the full was their path and their salvation.

However I could see there were significant differences between Emmisarius's humanism and both Renaissance and modern varieties of it in Western philosophy. His rejection of politics and its inevitable consequence of violence went against the Renaissance ideal of the scholar, poet, statesman and warrior. Political violence, he pointed out, was inherently indiscriminate, and therefore involved the loss and diminution of human potential. Herod's purge might have succeeded in eliminating the infant Jesus, and the child killed in the latest bombing raid might have gone on to discover a limitless source of safe, non-polluting energy. He also refused to accept any separation between humanity and nature. We were kin with every living thing on earth and indeed in the universe if it held other life. Love was the root and meaning of everything. Nothing was alien, and the study and understanding of nature and the universe was inseparable from love.

CHAPTER 6

The Lessons of History

I DISCUSSED these ideas at length in conversations with Scottie. I gathered that his father's own offspring were a challenge to this theory. Alseph (Scottie) affirmed it, but Zard turned it on its head. The social instinct did not develop in him; it was simply not there. This was a form of disability like a missing digit or a cleft palate. And yet he observed that Zard, though incapable of empathy with any other living creature, including his parents, was quietly protective towards his twin brother.

He had shown a predisposition to cruelty at an early age. It amused him to take things apart, especially living things. As a child he would give his father a dismembered frog with a beatific smile on his face, and was genuinely puzzled when his father tried to explain to him that it was wrong to hurt other creatures, and to get him to imagine how the frog felt about it, and how he would feel if someone pulled him apart. Such a fate was inconceivable to him - "but I am Zard," he would say.

His mother, who adored her boys, was deeply anxious about Zard, and he seemed to have some consideration for her. At least he avoided things that he knew would upset her, though he had no idea why they upset her. She died of cancer when the twins were fourteen, and thereafter Zard followed his own path without a backward look. He joined the military and rose rapidly through the ranks. He was soon assigned to 'special duties', which included 'interrogation' and 'correction', the latter divided into

75

two categories: 'intermediate' and 'plenary'. He became the youngest and most notorious of Zinn's executioners, known as Zard the impaler from having introduced the spiking of the executed in public places for the edification of the general populace. Boiling and skinning alive were also among his innovations in penal practice.

Emmisarius never condemned or rejected Zard. The blame was not on Zard, who was what he was, but on the state, which was only too ready to exploit his condition to its own ends.

Alseph could not have been more different. A gentle lad, full of innocent wonder and delight, devoted to his parents and twin brother, ready to bestow love and friendship on all who sought it from him. He had many pets, which his brother accepted as off limits to his anatomical curiosity, and formed deep attachments even to inanimate things. He would shed a tear if some faithful old piece of furniture had to be replaced, and would carefully reassemble a broken vase. He would even try to mend some of Zard's dissections. It was as if he had inherited all the human kindness which, if equally divided between them, would have made the twins about average in their concern for others.

His sympathy for the unfortunate led him to befriend orphans on the street, and this in turn brought him into contact with the children who flew the buzzards. Though never giving up his home and joining them he was accepted as an ally and got to know them well and all their ways. He even learnt to fly himself and became a skilled pilot, design engineer and an instructor. He taught Ark and Sulibe to fly. All that he learnt about the orphans he reported back to his father, who made copious notes and in effect used his son as a research assistant.

The outcome was his father's most famous work, *On the Origins and Theory of Natural Society*, in which he used the children as an example of a society spontaneously generated outside the shaping forces of traditional and hereditary mores, forming a cohesive, classless, self-disciplined, leaderless, crime-less and mutually supportive community, in which the will and identity of the individual blended seamlessly with that of the group.

He was responsible for attaching the term 'anarchy' to a social entity of this kind. He rejected the usual connotations of the word: chaos and misrule. It meant, he claimed, precisely the opposite. Disorder, divisions, anti-social patterns - all these were products of control from above because they took away an individual's natural status, judgement, self-esteem and respect for others. The state in fact created crime while attempting or purporting to suppress it. The more it assumed oppressive parental authority the more it interfered with the natural development of social responsibility, forcing people back into selfish, infantile, pre-social behaviour. Crime, after all, was simply selfishness in one form or another - the assertion that my rights to property, to life, to what I want or need, negate yours. The more authoritarian the state the more it infantilised, and the more it criminalised. Its draconian interventions not only fostered a criminal underclass but inevitably a political opposition, which it categorised and treated as criminal, until the opposition triumphed and took its place.

At this time the orphan children were partially tolerated. They had no legal protection and were officially regarded as a nuisance, a pest that needed to be kept down. It was only after a certain great and terrible event had taken place, for which they were held responsible, that they were categorised as anarchists - those who not only rejected but were out to destroy civilised and ordered society, and all-out war was declared on them. The book was suppressed, and father and son fled into exile.

In the course of further reading and talk with Scottie I began to gain an understanding of the history of Zinn, of what it had been and what it had come to be. The original Zinnians were a group of people not defined by a geographic location or ethnicity, but by profession. They came from India, Asia, the Far and Middle East and from Europe, and they were all architects, designers, engineers and artificers at the forefront of technology in their time, and indeed the holders of many secrets long since lost. They hired their services to princes and emperors across the vast expanse of the Asian continent, and were familiar with the Americas long before Europeans claimed to have 'discovered' them. All the great inventions credited to China were of their devising, and the Great Wall itself was built to their design.

They were as adept at politics as they were at construction, riding the waves of conflict and intrigue as kingdoms and empires rose and fell. They created not only palaces, temples, pleasure grounds and cities, irrigation systems, roads, viaducts, aqueducts and waterways, but also the instruments of war, arguing a version of deterrence theory that the more widely known and deployed these devices the less likely that a single tyrannical superpower would emerge supreme. And despite innumerable wars and campaigns, for centuries an overall balance of power was maintained. That is until the arrival, possibly from another planet, of a being called Genghis Khan. The founding father of genocide, Genghis, is reckoned to have wiped out a quarter of the world's population in his day, and at the end of his life confessed he had no idea why he did it.

Genghis employed the Zinnians to build siege towers and ballistic machines superior to any then in existence, and having done so gave orders that the Zinnians be slain before they could do the same elsewhere. But the Zinnians were a step ahead of him and set about fortifying other cities in anticipation of Mongol attacks. However they underestimated the ferocity of Genghis and his men, and the effectiveness of their own weapon designs, and were forced again and again into retreat before the fearful tsunami of Mongol expansion.

Some of their number argued they should make their peace with the conqueror on the grounds that he was probably invincible, and give him their undivided loyalty; but others more persuasively reasoned that he was a vengeful man, and could never under any circumstances be trusted. So as city after city fell and was levelled to earth saturated with its people's blood, the Zinnians fled ever further and deeper into savage and mountainous regions in hope of finding some defensible sanctuary. Eventually they came to a fertile plain surrounded by forests and ringed with mountains, in the centre of which was a single precipitous granite peak, like a stray bolt from the warring gods dropped out of the sky and striking deep in the earth. They all fell silent when they saw it, as each saw in it their salvation.

Happily the region was rich in coal, iron and other metal ores, and the Zinnians proceeded to anticipate the industrial revolution by more than five hundred years. The workforce came from the land, willingly enough for the promise of protection against the dreaded horsemen of the Apocalypse. They forged colossal iron bars with flanged ends which were wedged and concreted into caves and crevices in the rock face, and tied into the outer masonry as it ascended tier by tier. Held firm by these adamantine girders an outer wall, twenty feet thick and two hundred feet high presented an impregnable barrier to any would-be invader. It was pierced by a single aperture where an iron gate as thick as a man's arm span was raised and lowered by hydraulic machinery. The space between wall and rock was partitioned into vaults for the storage of crops and water, and three bumper harvests saw most of them filled before the watchmen on the hills descried the distant approach of Genghis and his hordes. A temporary village of wooden huts was constructed on the top level and the population duly installed. All watched and waited as the glittering army approached. Genghis took one look at the fortifications and turned away.

It is hardly necessary to describe the rejoicing that followed this bloodless victory over the world's greatest warrior, or the mood of triumphant optimism that prevailed in its wake. It unleashed all the creative energies of the Zinnians, and there were no limits to the scale and grandeur of their designs for an everlasting city built on the mighty foundations they had created. The vertiginous challenges of the site only inspired them to greater heights of fantasy and exponential advances of technology, and the results were as close to the miraculous as is possible in the material world.

The outer circle of wall provided a base for a tent-like structure of iron ribs, further secured to the central pillar of rock by the same massive girders. The city literally hung from it in all directions, honeycombed into the centre, and cantilevered into space as well as up and down by ingenious funicular devices. What you saw from outside, awe inspiring as it was, formed only part of the whole. Like Escher's eternal staircase it seemed to defy the laws of geometry. At the very top the Zinnians built for themselves the most splendid palaces of all, and believed themselves lords of creation.

It may be added as a footnote, that later generations made their peace with the Mongol empire, and at Zanadu designed for Genghis's successor, Khubla Khan, a palatial residence second in splendour only to their own.

The Zinnians also set about building a model republic, a system of governance as beautifully designed and enduring as the physical city they had created. They studied classical examples, especially Athenian democracy, and anticipated many features of the American constitution. There would be no king or tyrant or aristocratic privilege, the separate powers and offices of the legislature, executive and judiciary would be carefully weighed and balanced, and the leader was to be elected for a fixed term by full adult suffrage.

The ideas were sound enough, but in reality the distinction between the mighty minds of the creators and the humble serfs who had merely supplied the labour force would not easily dissolve, even with the passing of generations. Invisible social forces ensured that people from 'good families', that is descendants of the original settlers, were preferred to the most influential and lucrative positions, and the persistence of one social divide led to others, as upwardly mobile individuals and groups contended for the patronage of the great, and to serve them in the more prestigious offices.

In theory any could rise to the top, in practice only the wealthy and established dynasties ever did, and in time it seemed only natural for them to award each other honours and titles befitting their elevated state. Eventually the concept of royalty came to be adopted – the notion of a small interrelated group of families possessing an intrinsic, indefinable quality which automatically qualified them to assume the highest offices of state. And as those at the top rose higher, those at the bottom sunk lower, and deeper layers of social deprivation and rejection were formed.

The underclass at the very bottom came to live in hopeless poverty. The only form of enterprise available to them was crime, and indeed they had produced some daring and colourful villains. These, however, no less than the numerous petty criminals, and those driven to crime by desperation, invariably ended their brief careers on the gallows. The food of the poor was unhealthy and inadequate, much of it manufactured and artificial, and death from starvation was commoner than ever admitted in official statistics. Healthcare was almost non-existent, and the few philanthropic doctors who worked in the slum areas were often attacked by the very people they were trying to help, thus supplying further evidence of sub-human depravity. The paltry returns from the unskilled labour and menial work available had to be shared out among numerous dependants, the elderly, sick, disabled, and of course the children.

Like the poor and oppressed everywhere they had large families, the average life span being less than half that of the wealthiest citizens. Inevitably this brought more scorn upon them from above as evidence of their improvidence, and proof that their condition was of their own making. The links between overpopulation, poverty and political repression are as obvious as they are denied and ignored by those who seek to profit from the resources of poor countries. But they were not ignored by the masters of Zinn, who realised that the more they oppressed the slaves the more slaves there would be to oppress. In theory, education was provided, and was compulsory from five to twelve. But state education in poor areas amounted to little more than the training of servants: a narrow, rigid curriculum and harsh work ethic beaten into children with relentless severity. Truancy was rife, and taken as another instance of depravity and ingratitude.

What with the vile food, unchecked epidemics and the gallows, it will be readily understood that there were many orphans. They lived on the streets, doing odd jobs, running errands, in return for food or a few pence hurled contemptuously in their direction. Every so often there was a clean up by the city authorities, usually in response to a new wave of complaints in the press, or a new broom administration determined to show it was not a soft touch. A royal event or a patriotic anniversary would precipitate a major co-ordinated sweep of the streets. The gutters, culverts, sewerage pipes, and anywhere else small humans could conceivably conceal themselves, were scoured.

One of the biggest operations of this kind preceded a conference on child poverty. The captured children were caged and put on public display in the hope that good natured citizens would take pity on them and adopt them. Some of the more personable ones were adopted but often for the wrong reasons. If lucky they escaped slavery and abuse to return to their life of perilous freedom on the streets. Others who remained in the hands of the authorities were put into 'care', a term that encompassed a number of institutions which in various ways and degrees inflicted physical and sexual abuse on their charges, or exploited them in the name of employment by selling their labour to sweat shop proprietors.

There were even stories of lucrative deals between the authorities and paedophile circles, and indeed of such fraternities existing within the ranks of the civil service, judiciary and police. Even more savage tales emerged of death squads hired to kill the children, and paid a bounty for each severed child's hand they turned in.

Child abuse had been endemic for generations. The children of the poor were traded like commodities by the ruling caste and wealthy merchants. Most children didn't survive into adulthood; exhaustion, malnutrition, starvation, even suicide were common causes of death. This was thought right as a way of controlling the surplus population, since the city's resources were finite. The usual attitude of the underclass was servile, fatalistic acceptance, but beneath ran a deep seam of anger, occasionally breaking out in riots and open rebellion. Such uprisings were repressed with ruthless cruelty and the grotesque executions inflicted on men, women and children alike defy description.

When seasonal labour was required in the fields the children were rounded up, organised into gangs and hired out with their gang masters to local farmers. The brutality of these overseers knew no restraint, and with blows and beatings, on top of exhaustion and hunger, many little ones gave up the ghost. The severest punishments were reserved for those who attempted to run away. But despite this some did attempt, and some succeeded in escaping, and were often sheltered by country folk among whom remnants of human kindness were still to be found. These fugitives formed a network, and developed all kinds of skills and techniques to preserve their independence and communicate with their brothers and sisters still in captivity.

At one time the nobility decided to diversify the pleasures of the chase by including children, along with bears, wolves, wild boar and foxes, among their chosen quarry. The claim was of course to rescue straying children and rehabilitate them in society, but many died of fear and exhaustion, or in the jaws of an over enthusiastic pack of hounds. Popularised by their initial success these hunts attracted large fields and crowds of excited followers, and were occasions of much conviviality. But the children soon learnt ways of evading their pursuers, and in time of turning the tables on them.

They devised all sorts of cunning traps and mishaps that quite upset the sportsmen's customary bonhomie and jollity, and in time only one group of huntsmen, hardy, resourceful and revengeful, took to the field. Like true hunters they watched and stalked their prey, planned each campaign and boasted success on more than one occasion, bearing home a small bloodstained captive or corpse in triumph.

But meanwhile their opponents were busily engaged on a plan of their own. They spent nights underground excavating, and carrying the soil through a narrow entrance, an old badger set. They dug out a sizeable cavern, the ceiling a few inches below ground level, leaving a crust of earth thick enough to bear the weight of a child and the dogs but not that of a party of mounted men. A strong runner led the field, and after a few conventional feints and dodges to disarm suspicion led the pack across the roof of the fatal pit.

The party thundered on and plunged into it. Only one who lagged behind the others was able to draw up just in time, and beheld with horror a scene from Hades, a seething mass of men and horses, writhing, groaning, screaming. He galloped off for help and by the time it arrived three men were dead, eight would never ride again, and the remainder so bruised and broken they would not regain their courage even if they recovered the use of their limbs. The hunting of children with dogs subsequently disappeared from the sporting calendar.

I learnt with amazement and horror that such cruelty and corruption could exist in a city of such ethereal beauty. I had first seen Zinn from a great distance, and imagined its people lived in a state of sublime harmony and grace. The impoverished quarters were hardly visible from the outside as they burrowed inwards to the central rock from the outer walls. The streets there were lit by gas lamps, which often failed through cuts in supply or irregular servicing. Here the factories and warehouses were located, adding their emissions to the smoke from the houses and producing a chemical cocktail which the ventilation system, inadequate and dysfunctional like the lamps, failed to vent. Buildings often caught fire and sometimes whole areas were burnt to the ground.

Of latter years the houses had not been rebuilt. People were reduced to knocking up hovels and shanty towns from whatever materials they could salvage. An underground city, a city of endless night and perpetual fog, shadowy figures with bleached fleshless faces caught in the lurid flares - the mind's eye could barely picture it.

For the fugitives out in the fields and the woods the defeat of the hunt was a turning point. It had not been lost on them that many animals burrow underground for safety, and that they could do the same. Spades and shovels could be got in night raids on farmers' outbuildings or borrowed from the labouring folk who were natural allies against a common enemy. Smallness, agility and teamwork were advantages, and sharp eyes and ears told against the crass, lumbering, bullying arrogance of their would-be masters.

It was natural also to make common cause with poachers and other rural scavengers and misfits. Information, know-how, tools and technology were in constant interchange. In time an underground network of narrow passages extended along the city walls. They trained pigeons to carry messages to comrades in the city, and developed a language of bird cries, which they imitated to perfection. Then they began to dream of taking to the air themselves as well as infiltrating the earth beneath their feet.

They watched the buzzards that circled in glorious freedom high above the city and built their nests in lofty, unassailable and precipitous places. These birds would swoop down to seize any edible morsel discarded or left unattended. Stories were commonplace of pets, joints of meat, even living infants swept away in a flurry of feathers and claws from a moment's inadvertence. The birds could evade the clumsy firepower wielded by the citizenry and were half tolerated for removing carrion from the streets. It took several generations of children to evolve flying machines in any way approaching the speed and manoeuvrability of their avian counterparts, but in time they developed their craft and flying techniques to a high art. Their buzzards could soar so high on the thermals that they became indistinguishable from the real thing. Then they could close their wings and plummet like a stone for a lightning strike out of a clear sky.

The buzzard craft were essentially gliders, having no source of power; but the complex arrangements of 'feathers', each forming a separate plane, enabled them to take advantage of the lightest breeze and rising thermal currents. The city itself produced a column of hot air on which they could stay aloft indefinitely, but confined them to its ambit as they might lose height if they strayed too far from it. The city lords little realised that the fires and furnaces of their palaces provided the agency which enabled these pestiferous brats to look down on them from a great height.

It was to the advantage of the children that they were light from their meagre diet, and tough from living on the streets. When they grew too big to fly some reintegrated into the city among their own people, having acquired the strength and skills to survive and even prosper in the adult world. They married usually among themselves and produced new recruits to the ranks of youthful rebels. Many more joined the forest communes, or became independent yeomen.

For the escaping children, outcasts of the outcast, least and lowest of the oppressed, flying their buzzards was the most liberating and exhilarating experience, giving them a rare sense of freedom and power beyond the highest of the high. But it also enabled them to provide a service to other children and their families as they could air-lift in supplies of fresh food and game from their allies in the country and the forest. Also, manufactured goods from the city could be ferried out. The poorer country folk had very little of their own in the way of metal goods: clocks, tools and utensils. The average peasant had no gun to shoot a rabbit, or his wife even a needle to darn his socks, while in the city prosperous citizens were forever replacing their possessions with the latest gadgets and designs. The rejects worked their way down the social scale; even broken and worn out things could be salvaged, or utilised for some other purpose. The children themselves needed all kinds of odds and ends to create their wonderful birds.

'Hunters' End', as the place and event became known, was also a turning point in the attitude of the authorities to the rebel orphans. They were now regarded as criminals and it was time to get tough. A raft of new repressive measures was introduced, not only against the orphans but against those who harboured or assisted them in any way. This became a capital offence. Criminal children who refused to give themselves up could be forcibly arrested by any citizen and no action would be taken if the attempted arrest resulted in the injury or the death of the criminal. At the same time a law was passed banning all flying machines, deemed a threat to the health and safety of the citizenry of Zinn.

The combined effect of the two measures was to make discharging firearms at buzzard planes legal. Many times a fusillade from a balcony or high window had brought one crashing down to a rousing cheer from onlookers, and it was customary to make a bonfire there and then of the smashed remains and throw the small broken corpse into the flames. But the resourcefulness of the children countered every move made against them. They learnt to thread the labyrinthine streets with such speed and skill they outpaced the sharpest marksmen, and then soar beyond the range of their weaponry. They were more likely to come to grief through accidents than hostile action. However their tactics remained always evasive, never aggressive.

But then came the great and terrible event. I might have seen something of it myself if I'd approached the city from the north. Part of a royal palace, a beautiful glass oriel built out from the summit of the upper wall, suddenly collapsed and smashed to the ground. Three persons of royal blood died, five high ranking officials and others, making a total of fifty-one deaths. Without a moment's delay or hesitation blame was thrust upon the airborne criminals. Several buzzards had been seen in the vicinity. The Imperial Society of Engineers produced a detailed and authoritative report based on meticulous examination of the site and wreckage to show that the criminals had used grappling hooks to perch beneath the oriel and had dug out the masonry holding the structural supports.

Only one engineer dissented, and refused to sign the report. His theory was that one of the main structural girders had shifted due to rust and corrosion caused by industrial pollutants. He claimed that inspection and renewal of the girders, immense though that task would be, had become a matter of urgency. His ideas were summarily dismissed and anyone who gave them the least credence was publicly ridiculed. He himself never worked again and died in poverty.

Once again the children were reclassified; they were no longer mere vermin, or even criminals. A new category had to be devised. Scottie had trouble finding a term harsh enough from the vocabulary of his literary mentor to translate it for me. Evil malicious invaders, mindless purveyors of violence, enemies of all civilised values, cowardly barbaric killers, inhuman nihilistic extremists: the delightfully comprehensive and convenient word 'terrorist' had not yet infiltrated Zinn's isolation, but instead 'anarchist' was seized on from a book everyone hated and knew to be evil, though very few had actually read it.

The situation required nothing less than a full military response, and the 'War on Anarchy' was declared. Zinnian forces had never before been deployed against an external force and were largely ceremonial. Rapid attempts to modernise them were required to deal with this unprecedented threat. They were reformed and renamed the Zinnian Army of Democratic Defence: ZADD. The latest military technology to reach Zinn, that of the early twentieth century, was rapidly adopted.

The pretence of care now evaporated, but rulers and media never ceased to insist that the campaign was not against children, towards whom they had nothing but love, respect and the best possible intentions. Their campaign was against 'evil'. All genuine children hated and despised the evil anarchists.

About this time a new leader was elected, though the election process was farcical and the leader effectively a dictator. This was Jobu II, head of one of the princely families. He saw the eradication of anarchy as the defining purpose of his term of office. He called it his mission. His first move was to order the construction of anti-aircraft gun positions at strategic points all over the city. But the agility of the anarchist craft gave the gunners no better success than the amateur marksmen.

The next action undertaken by ZADD was to gas the enemy's underground network of supply lines and anarchist training camps. Luckily for the children they had recently discovered the great cavern and were able to seal it off while gas attacks were taking place, and divert the gas harmlessly back into the atmosphere. So still the buzzards flew in undiminished numbers. Puzzled and dismayed at this setback ZADD began using explosives, and then developed a new weapon, a kind of ray gun which could set fire to a buzzard at almost any height. My arrival in Zinn coincided with the first successful deployment of this new and powerful device.

The children had no idea what the 'fire gun' was or how to counter it. I told Scottie it sounded to me like a laser weapon, the principle of which I attempted to explain to him. But we both agreed that this was beyond Zinnian science and the Zinnian rulers placed too high a value on their own knowledge and their historic independence to be inclined to import weaponry from despised outsiders, even if that were possible. I suggested it might be some kind of optical device using lenses and mirrors to focus the sun's rays, rather in the way as children we used a magnifying glass to burn a hole in a piece of paper. Scottie agreed it was highly possible as all the ray attacks had taken place on sunny days. I recalled the flash of light I had seen when I first approached the city of Zinn.

CHAPTER 7

A Royal Visit

THIS INFORMATION only increased my anxiety for the safety of the children. At the same time I agreed with Scottie that there was little we could do against a full scale military assault, except spin the prayer wheel perhaps. Scottie told me that the forest had been attacked in the past. The soldiers were sent in to levy taxes, execute alleged offenders and generally terrorise the people into a proper respect for their masters. But many of the forest folk had had experience of dealing with the military in childhood and knew ways of making their task difficult and uncomfortable. One of their best tricks involved the giant wood hornet, an insect two inches long, ferocious when roused, and with a hellish sting. A simple trip wire released a seething box of them and the troopers were soon pelting back the way they had come. The army had resorted to random shelling and even burning parts of the forest. But these attacks were puny against such a vast expanse of vegetation. The forest soon regenerated and then the War on Anarchy claimed all available military resources.

All this insane hatred and violence seemed inconceivable amidst the beauty of the forest and the reality of our everyday lives in it. It was like some grotesque horror story the mind rejects and dismisses into the realms of fantasy as soon as it is over. But it lingered there as a dark, foggy background to our bright and happy days together. There were times when I was not needed on the farm and went for long walks in the forest with Credo. I'd pick the berries which had begun to ripen and look out for interesting fungi, relying on Scottie's knowledge to select the edible ones. But that was just an excuse for idling around, filling the senses and mind with the loveliness of things, marvelling at the extraordinary coincidence of my life and that of the world which surrounded me. I never went on any of these expeditions without seeing something entirely new to me, a different specimen of its inexhaustible flora and fauna.

I loved to stand still and observe wild creatures unobserved myself, or at least not considered a threat. It seemed to me they were not just content, but joyful; that every movement, every moment of their lives, was ecstatic, up to and perhaps even including the moment of death. Not for them the anxiety, the stress of human life, the ceaseless striving to gain, to achieve, and never long satisfied when we have succeeded in our aim.

On one occasion this reminded me of a passage in Scottie's father's book. When I returned I looked it up and found it was in fact a quotation from one of his favourite authors, Richard Jefferies. It came from a book entitled *Wild Life in a Southern County*, the preface to which states: 'There is a frontier line to civilisation yet, and not far outside its great centres we come quickly even now on the borderland of nature.' The passage runs:

The joy in life of these animals - indeed, of almost all animals and birds in freedom - is very great. You may see it in every motion: in the lissom bound of the hare, the playful leap of the rabbit, the song that the lark and the finch must sing; the soft, loving coo of the dove in the hawthorn; the blackbird ruffling out his feathers on a rail. The sense of living - consciousness of seeing and feeling - is manifestly intense in them all, and is in itself an exquisite pleasure. Their appetites seem ever fresh: they rush to the banquet spread by Mother Earth with a gusto that Lucullus never knew in the midst of his artistic gluttony; they drink from the stream with dainty sips as though it were the richest wine. Watch the birds in the spring; the pairs dance from bough to bough, and know not how to express their wild happiness.

Reading this passage again brought a sudden thought to my mind. I'd been on my own quite a bit lately, and I couldn't explain all Scottie's absences by the demands of the farm. When I last saw him going out he was wearing a fresh change of clothes with a bright neckerchief, and had taken more than usual care with his incomparable appearance. Without a doubt he was seeing a girl, and it only remained to find out which of the local sun kissed maidens, with their dark glossy hair and adoring, adorable eyes, he had finally selected.

One evening he came in, a little flushed and excited, pouring himself a glass of wine and trying to look composed. As ever I didn't question him directly. I didn't need to. I just gave him a knowing look then ostentatiously pretended not to have noticed anything or to be in the least curious about anything I had noticed. After a few sips he turned to me abruptly and said:

"Ye'll be thinking there's a lassie in it, nae doot." Then after a pause: "Ah weel, it mebbe so."

"Do you think I'll get to meet her? If I promise not to woo her myself."

"Aye, I rede her a' aboot ye and yer pawky ways."

"Good, so can you tell me something about *her*."

"She's way aboon me."

"How so?"

"She's a princess."

"Really? What's her name?"

"Elphane," he replied a little wistfully. Then added, like a proclamation: "Princess Elphane Clariel Shahribe of the second Palatine Dynasty of Zinn."

"You're kidding."

I could see he wasn't, and continued: "Well, she's certainly found as handsome a prince as she possibly could."

"She's foon a keelie lad, and there's nae gude in that."

He was reluctant to say more rather from shyness than teasing on this occasion, and I got no further. But his mood remained preoccupied, impatient, distracted. Never one to hide his emotions he was sometimes wistful, sometimes angry, sometimes dejected, and always marking time until the next meeting could be arranged. The homely rhythms of our life together were disrupted, and I found myself doing most of the work around the place. My cooking bore no comparison to his but in any case he hardly touched his food. None of this I minded for myself – in fact was happy to repay something of my immense debt to him. But I grieved for my friend, in the throes of one of the most painful maladies that afflict the young, and not so young. Credo was also concerned for her young master, watching him with a wanly questioning look, as if to say 'what's the matter with you? Why don't we go chase a ball or something?'

A couple of weeks later he returned from one of his solitary assignations and the girl was with him, she on a white pony and he walking by her side. She didn't look at all like a princess. She was small, with short cropped mousy hair, snub nosed, freckled, with glasses and a cheeky smile. She was dressed in light green knee length culottes with a white sleeveless top and wearing flat sandals; no make-up or jewellery except for a fine silver necklace with a tiny flame coloured stone set in a silver pendant. He introduced me formally in Zinnian, and then added for my benefit, "I keppit this body smooking aboot ma bield." I bowed and said I was honoured to make her majesty's acquaintance. She smiled and turned to Scottie for a translation, which he supplied with a certain ironic edge. She giggled and answered him in a clear and pleasant voice. I heard her own name mentioned. Scottie's translation was doubtless a summary: "She says ye may ca' her Elphane." "How about 'Elfie'?" I suggested. "It goes well with 'Scottie'." She didn't need a translation for this and laughed again and nodded.

There was a charm in her voice, her manner and her smile that matched her tom-boy appearance, but also raised it to another level. The two of them clearly delighted in each other's proximity; the magnetism between them was almost palpable. Scottie gave me a narrow look in acknowledgment of my pawkiness before returning her adoring gaze and placing a little kiss on her forehead.

The visit passed very pleasantly. We had a picnic in a sunny glade by the brook. Elfie took great delight in helping with the preparations, under Scottie's gentle guidance. She was obviously used to having everything done for her. Soon finding myself redundant in terms of both the culinary and amatory proceedings I sat outside in the sun and studied my dictionary. During the meal I was at pains to express my pleasure in the fare and its general superiority to the meals Scottie and I threw together for ourselves. Elfie seemed delighted at my effusive praise while Scottie eyed me obliquely.

Then I caused great amusement to both by attempting to speak in Zinnian, using expressions I had learnt on the farm, spiced with words culled from the dictionary. Scottie egged me on to make as big a fool of myself as possible but Elfie, bless her, thinking I might be genuinely upset by their mockery, took pity on me and began to explain and teach me. Again this was a new role for her and she took to it. Outmanoeuvred, Scottie just watched as we conversed, with a hint of a withering smile. The lesson continued until I was proficient in several common expressions. She then turned and spoke earnestly to Scottie who translated as follows:

"The lassie says she wull pit tae yer han a buik on grammar as wad be helpie to ye, ye clepie skellum."

I thanked her kindly and said I'd take a stroll down the stream to see if there were any trout in the shallows, and thus left the lovers to enjoy each other's company.

When I returned they were talking close together almost in whispers, sad because it was time for her to go. They set off together, she on her pony and Scottie by her side. I watched them till they disappeared round a turn in the lane.

I busied myself then with clearing away the picnic things and other domestic chores. Scottie returned after an hour. His mood was both sad and happy, and for once he wanted to talk. He wanted to know immediately what I thought of his wee bonny lassie.

"She's lovely," I said, "and she's yours. What's stopping you?"

"Ah," he said, "it canna be. It's cauld coal to blaw. Her being a princess and a' that." He explained she was the minor daughter of a minor prince but it would still have been a major offence for a man of Scottie's rank to associate with her. Discovery of his guilt would have called upon the services of his brother's successor. I asked how he came to meet her.

"Her aunt, now, an eccentric auld body, has an estate aboot five miles frae here. Elphane bides there whan she can. Her sisters are braw stoatin lasses looking for rich husbands o' their ain rank. A' summer they'll be gallanting at feasts and splores wi' a' the gran folk an nae fash thaimsels wi' puir wee Cinderella. I ha kent her syne she war a bairn, oot riding in the woods on her wee pownie. Showed her a' the ests and bouries of the birds and beasties, and told her a' the auld tales o' ghaists and eemocks and siclic blethers daft fowk speak of hereawa. Her een gaed unco big wi' wonder and fear but I promised to proteck her frae a' the perils o' the woods and the warld. But I canna proteck her frae her ain fowk and their damnable gate."

This, or something like it, was quite an explicit speech for Scottie. It contained several clues, most notably the outspoken condemnation of Zinn, the furthest he'd gone in that direction to date. Then there was the reference to Cinderella. He'd also known who Jason was in Greek mythology and was rarely puzzled by a chance allusion of mine from the stockpot of Western culture. I longed for some way I could help, but as a fugitive myself there was nothing I could say or do.

Elphane, or Elfie as she now became, was a frequent visitor during the weeks of high summer. She was 'clocksie' in Scottie's term – lively, vivacious, funny and talkative, and she was brave, sensitive and idealistic, full of sympathy for the oppressed and contempt for the corrupt and oppressive system into which she'd been born. She refused to attend executions, was considered childish, wilful, unmanageable and unmarriageable. Her sisters were great beauties, plotting and competing in the marriage stakes, but no knight or prince of Zinn or any other principality could ever replace Scottie in Elfie's affections. It wasn't hard to understand Scottie's love for her, and for his sake as well as her own I loved her myself.

She was quite serious, and even strict, when it came to teaching me Zinnian. I thought sometimes if she had a ruler she would have rapped my knuckles. As well as the grammar she brought simple reading books for children and set me passages to learn before her next visit. Scottie found it all highly amusing and felt I was being rightly put in my place. He became more relaxed about my third party presence, especially as my Zinnian improved and he wasn't so much called upon to translate. It was a language like no other I had encountered. A linguist would have been unable to fit it into any classification. But the alphabet, grammar and pronunciation were all highly logical, so that a minimum number of rules had to be learnt, and when learnt could be applied consistently. I came to the conclusion that it was an invented, or artificial, language.

These days passed pleasantly indeed, shaded only by the anticipation of their ending, with Elfie's recall to Zinn. At least when it finally came, with all the pitiful farewells, we were required full time on the farm, and this served as a distraction from the pangs of unfulfilled love. Harvest had begun. Clattering old machinery, oiled and repaired, was once again put into service. It must have been new once but had mellowed into the landscape like everything else. Change was so slow as to be imperceptible. Then there was fruit to be picked, sheep to be sheared and honey to be taken from angry bees and extracted from their luscious combs. We loaded the carts and threshed the grain by hand, eating on the job and pouring great draughts of sweet cider down our throats. We even spent nights there in the barns, sleeping the profound sleep of total physical exhaustion. Then came the harvest feast, and the shared satisfaction of another year's work well done, and the harvest safely gathered in.

By now my conversational Zinnian was pretty good and I could take part in general talk and contribute to the more serious discussions. With my knowledge of the outside world some weight was attached to my views. News from the front in the War on Anarchy was still not good. Refugees were coming into the forest with tales of widespread devastation, torture and atrocity.

Though the anarchists had not been seen or heard of for several months there were no bodies to prove that they had been eradicated. It was generally believed they were still in hiding. In frustration the army had now adopted a scorched earth policy in order to cut off all possible support from outside and all supplies, so they would starve to death when their food stocks ran out. Even the wealthy farmers who had supported Zinn were turned off their land and relocated elsewhere, while their cattle and crops were destroyed and their farms burnt. I was asked if such terrible things were done elsewhere in the world, and had to admit it was not unknown.

And now there was a new source of anxiety. As yet it was remote, but potentially it represented an even greater menace to the forest people and their way of life than the military and their depredations. From far to the north-west reports were coming through that the loggers were back. Illegal loggers had made forays into the forest before, but Zinnian forces had seen them off. Now they had returned, and this time were not being challenged by the authorities. The local foresters had sent a deputation to Zinn but it had been dismissed with threats. I could well believe and sympathise with that.

It was generally assumed that the refusal to eject the loggers was in consequence of the Zinnian forces' full deployment in the War on Anarchy. It would have been unprecedented if they had been allowed in, or if Zinn had entered into any kind deal with a foreign organisation. I had my dark suspicions, which I kept to myself. It was not unknown, either, for states to renege on all their traditional values and policies when the excuse of 'exceptional circumstances' presented itself.

Scottie too was exercised by this matter, on top of his other worries and his general emotional state. The foresters of the north-west were asking for help and advice on any ways they could frustrate or sabotage the advance of the loggers, who were tearing their homelands apart. "I maun gang there and gie 'em a han," he told me. "I ken sumhin aboot it syne I ha' palled the briganers afen enough." At the next meeting he was asked to fulfil this request as our most experienced saboteur. He readily agreed and I also volunteered to join the resistance.

In truth I had not the faintest belief that anything could be done. One thing I had learnt about the world was that there is nothing you can do to save it. Human affairs were driven by human need, and even more by human greed. The demands of the few to possess far in excess of the many knew no bounds, and no restraint. For this forests would be destroyed, countries turned to desert or washed away by the sea, innumerable species would become extinct and people would die in their millions. The process would be far advanced before a general realisation that destroying the environment was in no one's interest coincided with the will to act, and by then it would probably be too late. We lived on a beautiful planet, but the bastards would destroy it if they didn't destroy us all first. But probably not in my time, and I had no kids.

This gloomy prognosis had made me a lifelong inactivist. I had never joined a march or written to my MP or even signed a petition. My normal reaction to the latest incursions of the greed machine was to shrug my shoulders and move on. There would still be world enough, and some place of tranquillity and contentment waiting to welcome me with smiles and flowers. I realised that this too was an entirely selfish philosophy and that if everybody were to make a stand against them the armies could be sent back to their barracks and bulldozers stopped in their tracks. But everybody never did, and the banner waving campaigners would, in due course, themselves be enjoying the benefits of the new development: speeding to the new hypermarket along the new motorway in cars fuelled by oil plundered from a ruined nation.

But none of this would pass my lips. I would go because I enjoyed travelling. I would go to support my friend, that being the only cause I had come at last to believe in, and at the end of it to be on hand to comfort him. Also it was good that a diversion had arisen to deflect the thoughts of a pining lover from the unattainable object of his desire.

We had undertaken a major expedition. Scottie estimated it

would take at least two weeks to reach the region where the loggers were at work. This was by the most direct way, avoiding the
Western Highway, but also the most difficult. So we had to spend
several days in planning our route, anticipating our needs and any
hazards we might come up against, and assembling our gear. Scottie had a small tent we could both squeeze into, and then we
selected a few basic cooking utensils and a supply of matches,
though he could light a fire without them if we ran out. We took
one rod, and a cross-bow to shoot game for the pot. The foresters
only hunted when farm supplies ran low, and rarely used firearms
as the noise might draw unwanted attention to them. We took
rope and a grappling hook for rock climbing and a good supply
of candles as we had to go underground at one point in the journey. Credo became very excited at these preparations, surmising
that a major hunting trip was afoot.

As ever, the most important item for me was a map. One of the
lads from the farm who had been about a bit was able to produce
one. I'd say it was very old, eighteenth century at least, but with
numerous over-written hand markings and annotations of routes
and settlements. It intrigued me as an accurate documentary val-
idation of a region that still, for all its immediacy, had about it an
air of dreamlike unreality. Zinn was there in the epicentre, and a
marginal cartouche showed the city in a front elevation much as
it was in the present, the absence of the jerry-built atrium being
the only conspicuous difference. Surrounding Zinn in roughly
concentric circles came first the farmland, with all the farmsteads,
estates and villages, copses, streams and lanes clearly marked; then
a vast belt of forest, in proportion to which Zinn and its fields
were like the bull's eye in relation to the rest of the dartboard.
Towards the perimeter the terrain became increasingly bare and
rugged until the mountains, rearing high above the tree line,
formed the outer rim. In the south-east the forest yielded to
pastoral plains and the gentler hills; here I traced the route by
which I'd entered. Due east the mountain ranges were packed
close, continuing to the edge of the map; and the same to the west
except for a pass which carried the Western Highway. This ran

from Zinn and presumably at some point connected it with the known world.

The north was bounded by a range of mountains called the Tash'kaherns. They were formed in a series of steep ridges like the plates on the back of a stegosaurus, and beyond them a region named on the map Ozoora. According to the dictionary the word meant vacuum, open space, emptiness, nowhere at all. I wondered idly if, had the map been larger, Ozoora would have surrounded the entire kingdom of Zinn. I guessed Ozoora was desert, or a foreign land not subservient to Zinn and therefore not deemed to exist.

The north-west region where we were headed looked the most intractable. It was as if prehistoric geo-tectonic forces had buckled everything up in that direction. In addition there was a great river that had to be crossed; it was called the Raffire. The word meant 'rage': the River of Wrath. Except for a single very fine pen line no bridges or fords were marked. The final obstacle was a southerly spur of the Tash'kahern ridges, too steep to scale, but penetrated by a series of caves. A dotted line in red ink on the map marked the passage through. Beyond the ridges lay a great basin surrounded by hills called the Looshin Levels, a region of ancient forest, I was informed, with trees of immense size and variety, and dotted with small agricultural settlements. This is where the loggers were active: it was a loggers' paradise.

CHAPTER 8

On the Road Again

AND SO we set out, along paths familiar enough to begin with, and
then on into the unknown. It was strange how quickly the forest
began, once again, to feel sinister. Perhaps it was the grim business
we were on that made us now strangers to it. It sheltered only
those whose hearts were at peace. Scottie was watchful and edgy
and Credo constantly on the alert. Only when you dwelt in a
place, content to be part of it, did it begin to reveal its secrets and
its solace.

It was late summer, dry, dusty and overblown, the year wilting
and waiting to turn; and some of its migrant spirits had already
departed to southern lands. We followed a track marked clearly
on the map that was anything but clear on the ground. I could see
it would not be a journey that went quite to plan, if any ever does.
Occasionally we came to a dwelling or small settlement where
we were welcomed and given fresh directions. We did best on
clear nights when Scottie could read the stars, and then we'd rest
in the day. There was no shortage of game, and the brooks and
tarns we came across, rarely if ever fished, supplied us handsomely.

Scottie's mood remained serious and determined, and I was
careful to fall in with it and say nothing that might weaken his
resolve. As an experienced traveller I knew that the hardest part of
any journey is the beginning, when the gravitational pull of home
is strongest, and all the securities and familiarities of home are the
more keenly missed. As you continue your sense of freedom

grows, your locus is movement itself. You belong to the journey, and deal with each problem as it comes along. After a few days we were quite relaxed, two carefree wayfarers passing by, talking more and even joking, following the yellow brick road. Except the road had now disappeared and we were hacking a path of our own through briar, bush and bracken. Our clasp knives were too small; we needed machetes.

We had one close encounter of a black and hairy kind when we came almost face to face with a bear, a towering hulk with a comically aloof but distinctly 'no one messes with me' expression. We discreetly backed away but Credo took it upon herself to act the gallant defender and approached the hulk barking furiously, ignoring our desperate pleas to come back. The bear responded with a casual sweep of its mighty paw that sent her flying like a volley ball into a thicket, with a piercing shriek. Scottie grabbed her and we ran. The poor creature had deep cuts on her flank from the bear's claws, which we bathed and dressed as soon we were well clear of the danger. She moped pitifully for hours after, more from the humiliation than her actual injuries. Scottie lectured her:

"We dinna warsle wi bears, bonny lass. We haud well wide o' sic as they."

A little later we came to a lonely cottage where an old woodsman lived. He greeted us amicably and gave us beds for the night. First he insisted on feeding us and sharing a bottle of brandy - he even put a drop on Credo's tongue to perk her up. He was a cheerful fellow, and glad of the company in his lonely life, his wife having died five years since and his daughter, the last of his brood, married and left home the following year. We talked late into the night. The next morning he showed us a road that ran clear for a good few miles, but best of all gave us an old hedging hook he no longer used. It was a bit rusty but he sharpened it to a keen edge on an ancient treadle grindstone. And so, in the usual snakes and ladders way, we journeyed on.

After a day's heavy tramping on lanes baked hard by the summer heat, or taking it in turns to wield the billhook to clear a way ahead, it was good to find a pleasant open spot to pitch camp and prepare a meal. We'd gather the ingredients on the way: leaves, herbs, fungi, fruit, nuts, roots, fern tips, even grasses, selected from Scottie's encyclopaedic knowledge of growing things. Then we'd shoot a rabbit or a partridge, or catch a bronze carp or an olive-green tench from one of the deep mysterious pools we found unexpectedly, hidden among the coverts. Scottie said they were the result of former shelling of the forest by the Zinnian army, to whom we gave ironic thanks for this unintentional contribution to our wellbeing.

Scottie's meals had lost nothing in quality or variety from being cooked on a camp fire in a couple of blackened pans. We ate ravenously. As he had not yet mastered the trick of turning water into wine we missed having a glass or two with the food, but a carefully rationed post-prandial tot from the whisky bottle went some way to make up for it. Then we'd stretch back on the warm dry grass in a state of deep satisfaction and talk of the day's encounters and adventures, and what the next day might bring. I couldn't help remarking on one occasion that he'd make someone a good husband, and it was some measure of how far we had come that this incautious remark didn't precipitate more melancholy longings for his little princess, who by now must have been immured, like the Lady of Shallot, in the high citadels of Zinn. "Weel, ah weel," he sighed resignedly, "she's nae for me. I maun beir ma birn an' gang ma gate."

We had not needed the tent as yet and slept where we lay, under light blankets, relying on Credo to alert us to any danger. The thought that if a bear came along she might just slink away, for once placing discretion ahead of valour, did cross our minds, but by this stage we were too drowsily complacent to bother. "She'll be about ready for a rematch by now," I offered.

"Aye she's a braw forritsome lassie. She'll nae lang be set oot."

"At least she'll bark and stand her ground long enough to wake us up."

"Aye, certie she wull; and I'm thinking it wad be yer turn to pluck her frae the jaws o' the baist, whilk I tak to ma heels."

Having scored the last point he fell asleep. Gazing at the vision-
ary stars above and feeling the strong earth beneath me I soon
followed, drifting beyond thought.

So the days continued much alike, and then the terrain began to
get more hilly and even less inhabited. We envied Credo's ability
to run up and down hill with the same ease as on the level, and
apparently no greater expenditure of energy. Gasping to the top
of one long slope, where she lay waiting patiently for us, we
reached a spot from which we could see something we had not
set eyes on since we left. Instead of facing another wall of foliage
or tunnel of trees we were looking at the horizon. Wave on wave
of unbroken forest spread before us through shades of green, blue,
indigo, violet and grey to the infinite distance. It was as though we
were seeing the world through the eyes of our first ancestors. It
seemed to us, as it must have to them, inconceivable that such a
vast expanse of wilderness could be subdued and destroyed. And
yet we knew that what we were seeing with our eyes and feeling
in our hearts, like the great heartbeat of earth itself, was as fragile
and ephemeral as the tiniest insect hovering in the pulsating light
of the dying year. With the leaves just burnished here and there
with autumn tints the sight was awe-inspiringly beautiful, but dis-
maying too when we realised how much country we had yet to
traverse. The distant Tash'kahern range was no more than a darker
shade of pale.

We trekked on through the endless forest. For several days we
passed no habitations and met no one but an ancient gipsy lady.
She had a small bunch of wilting herbs in her hand and asked if
we would like to buy them. Scottie immediately gave her a full silver crown for them, and she stared suspiciously at the coin for
some time in the palm of her withered hand, before sliding it into
some deep recess of her voluminous skirts. He asked where she
was going and she replied, "Ah, where the road takes me." Then
he asked her if she knew how to get to the Looshin Levels. "Ah"
she said, "by the road you're on." She seemed to be saying that
one road, or one destination, was as good as any other. In this
remote place it was hard to think of any destination she could live

long enough to reach. Then she stared closely at me, wrinkling up her eyes.

"You're not from here," she said. "Ah no. Not from here."

Then she narrowed her eyes to slits and peered still more closely at me and asked:

"Now where might you be a coming from, stranger?"

I replied I was from Scotland and waited to see how she would deal with that piece of information. Her face cracked in a smile.

"Ahh yees. Then you live in a castle." She was so pleased with this deduction it seemed wrong to correct it. She wandered off, muttering to herself. "Yees, lives in a castle. Not his road. He's not from here. Noo. Noo. A castle, yees, that's where HE lives . . ." She was the last person we saw this side of the Tash'kaherns.

More days followed of up hill and down dale. All kinds of woods we went through: sparse and spindly groves of hazel, corridors of dark pine, cathedrals of great oaks where wild boar rooted for acorns, soggy hollows of willow and alder, ferny glades where the dappled deer fled at our approach. The land rose and fell in waves, giving us more panoramic views, and a measure of our progress as the Tash'kaherns slowly materialised out of the mist like the approaching shields of a giant army. With so imposing a landmark we could no longer doubt we were on the right course.

Then the roller coaster hills began to break up into smaller ones, steep, rocky, conical, and increasingly mountainous. These were marked on the map as the Kaspan range. We had to thread our way through the valleys between them where dashing streams ran, often leaving little foothold between the precipitous banks. "We should make a raft, Scottie," I said, "and travel by water. All these streams are flowing in the right direction." "Nae sic a bad idea," he conceded. "Th'art a canny lad for ane wha bides in a castle."

We cut poles with our trusty billhook, formed a row of them and split some to brace across top and bottom, binding them together with our climbing rope. It was a bit wobbly and both Scottie and Credo eyed it doubtfully, but I assured them the rope would tighten when it got wet. I was deputed to test my own device – it was made clear that any untoward outcome would be laid at my door. I chose a wider, shallower stretch of water where the current was gentle, selected a short stout pole to punt off the banks and launched myself afloat. The craft sailed merrily along and I had a bit of a job pulling up to wait for the other two, who scrambled after me along the shaley bank.

We'd made the vessel long and narrow to accommodate all three of us but it was rather less seaworthy with the extra bodies and the weight of our kit, which we kept on our backs to avoid its getting wet or lost. Credo lay crosswise between us, ready to leap on to the bank at the first hint of trouble. We whizzed along at a good pace for the rest of the day, with only minor upsets, soaking wet, but pleased to have got so far so fast. We hauled up on a level shore for the night, and as well as a swift passage the stream provided us with a fine pair of mountain trout for supper.

The next day went just as well, though by the end of it we had to stop for some running repairs. Like the raft, my rope theory wasn't entirely watertight, though in my defence I pointed out that the knocks and shocks of rough water and narrow banks were enough to account for a loosening of the structure. We wedged in further cross braces to tighten the whole thing up and off we went again. As it joined or was joined by others the stream was becoming wilder; there were rapids and white waters to negotiate. But our confidence was swelling too. We were old hands by now, though Credo remained tense, and still looked unconvinced. Subconsciously something was starting to trouble me, a growing sense of unease – something in the air. But then we came to a fine level stretch, the sun blazing on the water ahead. It was like riding into the gates of glory.

Suddenly Credo leapt ashore and I yelled to Scottie behind me: "Quick, grab the branches!" I seized an overhanging willow branch and he piled into me, grabbing either side of me, while the raft shot away from under our feet. The bough dipped and strained, trailing our legs in the current; but held. We worked our way arm over arm along it to the safety of the shore.

"Jason, ye daft bammer. What for the deil ha' ye cast us aff?"

"Listen Scottie. What can you hear?" He listened, then twisted his finger in his ear as if to clear an obstruction.

"There's a soon in ma lug, man."

"Like a roaring sound?"

"Aye, a raering, birling soon."

Credo joined us, wagging her tail, a touch smugly. We all three edged along the narrow bank. The sun still shone blindingly on the water. The roaring sound got louder. Then a slight bend took the sun behind the opposite bank and we could see ahead to where the stream rushed forward and disappeared into space. Holding on to branches and carefully placing each footstep we proceeded to this point. The stream shot clear off the edge in a dazzling arc then plunged down the cliff face into a great river that roared through a deep-cut ravine some two hundred feet below. The water was almost all white, swirling, rearing and frothing as it plunged headlong on its course. A skein of mist hung over it, making it seem more air than water, like a condensation of blue sky and white clouds blown by the wind above a dark narrow street. For a moment we stared in speechless amazement. We had reached the Raffire, the river of wrath. "I kend that raft o' thine wad amaist be the daith of us," Scottie reflected, with a sad shake of his head.

Having at last filled our eyes and ears with this astounding phenomenon we lay down on the narrow verge and I studied the map. It was difficult to work out exactly where we were in relation to the thin line that indicated some kind of crossing over the frenzied torrent. We decided we were some way to the south, and having luckily landed on the north bank of the stream, we began to make our perilous way from this point northwards along the edge of the ravine. It was the toughest part of our journey so far. Keeping a few feet from the precipice to give ourselves a chance if we slipped, we clung to the stems of small trees and the roots of big ones, or grabbed hold of gorse bushes till our hands bled. At one point the only way ahead was round a tree that grew on the edge, overhanging the very rim, just its bare roots supporting it like a shelf. It was a moment that called for blind faith. I had not been closer to death since I stood on the edge of a scaffold. Credo made nothing of these difficulties, her confidence on land being inversely proportionate to her lack of it on water. But then she had four legs and a low centre of gravity, whereas we were upright and loaded into the bargain. The billhook tied across Scottie's back kept catching on branches but we were loath to jettison it.

As well as the slope down to the cliff edge our forward direction was also an uphill gradient. We were crawling up the side of one of the conical Kaspan mountains cut into by the ravine. When we eventually reached the top we could see how the river zig-zagged through these hills, tossed side to side by them as it raced along. Perhaps that was why it was angry, being thrust this way and that when it wanted to make straight for its destination. We could see silver ribbons where more waterfalls plunged into it, increasing the burden it had to carry on its tortuous course. It was another landscape of astonishing grandeur, but what uplifted us most about it was that, a couple of miles or so beyond, we could see the bridge. At this distance it seemed exactly as it was on the map, a line drawn across with a pen, a faint pen at that. As the crown of our hill offered a little level and open space we decided to camp there for the night.

The next day another perilous hike brought us to the bridge. It was made of slats roped together, with two side ropes tied to it at intervals as hand rails. It reminded me of any number of adventure films where the hero, and often the heroine, have to cross a rickety bridge over a deep chasm to escape their pursuers and reach safety. Inevitably a rotten plank breaks or a rope frays, resulting in yet another close shave for the plucky duo. This one however looked strong and secure, and in fair condition. The track leading to it was clear enough to suggest it got used from time to time. The only concern about the bridge itself was that the rising mist from the river made the slats damp and slippery. Care would have to be taken. The other question was whether Credo would find it a problem; that is whether she would identify it as land or water.

She soon provided an answer. She trotted across without turning any one of her many hairs. And then she trotted back, her eyes and ear signals unmistakably conveying the message: 'Come on then you pair of wimps.'

Scottie volunteered to go first. He trod carefully, testing each plank, avoiding any sudden movement, keeping perfect balance in his casual broad-shouldered way, and placing his steps in a straight line down the middle. Credo walked ahead of him as if to guide him over, and after seeing him safely landed came back for me. For the first third I got along fine. Then, in a moment's inadvertence, my foot slipped. I held on tight to the rope as the bridge pitched to one side and then rolled back to right itself. I saw the wave motion travel along the structure to where Credo was walking ahead. It tipped her sideways and having nothing to hold to she just slid off. I watched, and Scottie watched from the opposite bank, both helpless, and in utter dismay.

There was no splash where she fell, far below in water already agitated as much as it could possibly be. I just caught sight of her tiny head in the midst of all that foaming chaos, as the raging river swept her away.

I closed my eyes in shock and despair, unable to move another step. I cursed myself for my carelessness. The full force of Credo's importance to the journey, to our lives, hit me with such an impact I could almost have released my grip and followed her into the abyss. Scottie was kneeling there on the other side, his face in his hands. He would probably push me in himself - I could hardly blame him. Being the cause of his brother's death was one thing; but Credo! He'd told me that his father had brought Credo home for him from the farm when she was a pup, and she'd been his constant companion and loyal protector, and a wonderful friend ever since. Poor, poor Scottie. Condemned, exiled, bereaved, crossed in love, his friends persecuted, his home threatened. And now this. I walked over to him, hardly caring if I fell or not, and tried to put my arms round him. But he pushed me away.

He got up abruptly, flung his rucksack over his shoulder, and strode off along the path that led from the bridge. I followed, lagging behind, hardly able to keep up. The path led downwards through low scrubland, and ahead the first great plate of the Tash'kaherns, cracked and yellow like an old tooth of stupendous proportions, rose sheer to the sky. After a couple of hundred yards he flung his load down and once more fell to his knees, burying his face in his hands. His whole frame shook as he sobbed convulsively. I desperately wanted to comfort him, but his grief was turning to anger and I feared it would be directed at me. I dared not say a word, so just sat there, nearby, quietly waiting. Eventually he looked up, his lovely face dimmed and distraught with pain.

"Ye niver believed in this expedition. Ye suldna ha' come."

"I never said that Scottie."

"Ye did nae need tae tell me. I a'ways kend it. Now ye'll be thinking if we hadna come we wadna ha lost Credo."

"I don't think that way. I never say 'If only . . .' We don't control fate."

"But ye dinna believe we can do owt ta fash thae logger carles? We canna help the fowk therawa?"

"I think we had to come."

"That's nae ma question."

"No, I can't see there's anything we can do but I may be wrong. Who knows? Nothing can be predicted, nothing is impossible."

He was silent for a while and then said: "Jason, I'm nae fuil. Aiblins there's deil a haet we ca' pit ower ta clag 'em. Atweel, it's ain wappin trauchle - a 'labour o' Hercules' ye micht ca' it. I canna haud on wi'oot Credo. We maun gang awa hame I'm thinking."

"I blame myself Scottie, I should have been more careful."

"Nae laddie, onieane could ha sklytit. I could ha lost ye baith."

"I loved Credo too Scottie. She was a magic dog. You, me and her, it was like we were joined together. But now we've lost her we must be even closer. We cannot go back. That would be worse than loss, worse than failure. That would be defeat."

He didn't answer, but hugged me in his strong arms.

CHAPTER 9

Wormholes and Space

WE WALKED on together in silence. Darkness came suddenly as the sun dropped below the mountain top. Scottie fried up some left-overs of pheasant and added a few mushrooms and salad leaves. We were not hungry but it helped to have something to do. We found a little brook where we washed the dishes and the dust from our faces and bathed our feet; then we studied the map together and drank more than our usual ration of whisky. We slept fitfully. The absence of a friendly, watchful companion weighed heavily on us but neither dared speak of it for fear of jarring the other's attempts to find some peace in his thoughts. In any case it had been a tragic accident and there was nothing more that could be said. Not feeding Credo, not petting her; waking, packing up and setting out without her - every moment of the day's routine of which she had been a part would be a fresh opening of the wound. One day it would heal, but not perhaps until our lives, like hers, were sinking into the vast immensities of time.

The next part of the journey was easy compared with the last two days, along a clear track and mostly downhill. The wall of the Tash'kahern ridge reared up so steep it almost seemed to be toppling on to us. A little further along it we came to the entrance to the cave marked on the map. It was a good sized cave with enough headroom to stand up, the floor even, the rock smooth, pale, like pumice. We lit a candle and ventured in. After fifty yards or so we took a left turn as indicated by the dotted red line on the map, then came another fork which appeared unmarked. The map showed a sharp twist to the right so we took the right hand turn. Other tunnels entered from the left and right but we carried on, looking for the next feature on the map, a crossroads. Instead of this we came to a ford, which could have been the feature indicated, and continued on past other exits and entrances. By now we should be entering a cavern from which the route ran more or less directly through to the other side.

A road always seems longer when you're expecting to reach a known landmark at any moment, so we pressed on, but eventually arrived at a T junction. Obviously we had gone wrong at the second fork and would have to go back. We retraced our steps, recrossed the ford, and continued to the second fork marked as a sharp bend on the map, now to our left - except when we reached it, it went to the right and there was no fork. Exploring a little further we came to a place where there were cave drawings, or markings of some kind, on a smooth expanse of wall. Partially worn away it was hard to tell if they were representations of creatures or some form of script. What they did tell us was that we had gone wrong again.

We decided we must have diverted into one of the side tunnels that debouched into the tunnel with the ford. Coming in at acute angles some must have looked like the main tunnel on the return journey - if indeed 'side' or 'main' had any meaning in what appeared to be a maze of wormholes that riddled the mountain at this level. I speculated that a river must have drilled them out at some early stage in the earth's history, perhaps even the Raffire, since it certainly had the force to permeate a mountain, hollowing out natural faults and fissures. We made our way back to the ford, but when we reached it the stream was flowing the opposite way, and we weren't even sure that it was the same ford.

By now we were on our third candle and my mental map was as useless as the printed one. In any case I had mainly relied on Scottie's orienteering skills which were generally more reliable than mine. But they were dependent on astral bodies. He instinctively looked up from time to time and muttered "nae starns, nae starns," as if the removal of the stars were some inexplicable and unfair handicap imposed on him. At length he turned to me and said, "Deil it's a tickler, Jason. I'll be danged if I can kittle it oot." The simple fact was we were lost.

It would be tedious to recount all the advances, retreats, diversions, reversals and retracings of our footsteps that occupied the next two hours or so and consumed a further four candles. We were down to our last when we finally reached a cavern, from which a wider tunnel led straight ahead, though by now our sense of direction was too scrambled to know which way we were facing. We were exhausted, but the need to escape this infernal labyrinth was so strong we pushed ahead as fast as we could. We continued some way along this wide, straight corridor, and then we saw a light. For an instant there was hope, but then the hope wavered, like the light. It flickered and two shadowy figures could be seen behind it.

"There's someone there," I said. "They're bound to know the way." I called out to them, but there was no answer, except an echo, and an echo of the echo. We advanced towards them and they towards us, and then we froze. Had we taken another step we would have walked straight into a solid wall of shiny rock, in which we were seeing our own reflections.

We slumped down simultaneously in utter weariness and despair. The candle fell from Scottie's hand and went out. I heard him fumbling in his pocket for a match. "Leave it now, Scottie," I said. "We'd better save it. We should rest now." Once again he began to sob, heavily, convulsively. I could hardly bear it myself, to think of this young man, so full of promise, so fair of face and form, so passionate, so generous, and all the life and hope in him slowly, inexorably, cruelly crushed. And now this final impasse. I tried to comfort him as you would a child. I said, "We should rest now, Scottie. Try and get some sleep." I said we'd work it out in the morning - as if the sun would rise and yesterday's fears and difficulties would vanish like the morning mist; as if day and night meant anything in these vaults of hell. Somehow my soothing nonsensical words made a bed for his exhausted body and harrowed soul. His sobs turned to steady breathing, and he slept.

To comfort myself, and calm my own fears, was another matter. I used to say that for a traveller there's no such thing as lost. You'd always arrive somewhere, if not the destination you intended. But deeper in my mind there lurked an awareness of the void, often taking the form of a dread of incarceration. It was possible to take a wrong turn, or go through the wrong door, and end up nowhere.

The cave was darker than any dark I had ever known. There was always somewhere a slight variation in the pitch of darkness, a faint glimmering, an afterglow, some lingering emanation from our light saturated world. Eventually the eyes would detect a straw of light to cling to in the ocean of night. Here there was nothing, nor nourishment from any other sense out of which even the blindest can create a world to live and breathe in. Just the cold bare rock striking a chill into my bones. I wanted to get a blanket from my pack but was afraid of waking Scottie.

I lay still and closed my eyes. Some minute retinal impressions from trapped light still hovered like pale stardust before my sightless gaze, and a pallid after-image of the candle's flame. But they were fading quickly, and soon it made no difference whether my eyes were open or shut. It was as though the dark had entered my soul, and I was now one with it. Terror struck. I wanted to scream; I wanted to smash the darkness, tear apart the cold stone with my bare hands, claw my way to freedom. I raved inwardly, telling myself it would pass – everything passes. There has to be an end. We have to accept it when it comes.

I tried to force my reason to acknowledge the reality of our situation, and my will to accept it. 'Tomorrow' we would set out on the final stage of our journey. We would have no plan to follow, no map to guide us, no expectations, and no hope. The last candle would illuminate the shadowy walls of the cave for a while, and that was all that was left of the external visible world. We would go on in darkness, feeling our way, with no better or worse chance of finding a way out. Hunger, thirst and exhaustion would weaken us, till we were staggering along, clinging to the walls and each other. Being the older I would drop first, and insist that

Scottie went on as long as he could. There was still a chance, I would say, that he could find the exit, and fetch help for me before I went. We would then embrace briefly and say goodbye until we met again. We would die alone.

Going through this scenario in my head brought me a sense of acceptance, almost gratitude. Not just for the life I had lived but what I still had - air to breathe, freedom from pain, a little light, but above all my dear friend and companion. He was still here with me, and now I turned to him for comfort, laying my cheek against his warm shoulder. And then I fell asleep.

I was woken with a jolt; Scottie was shaking me, speaking in an urgent whisper, "Jason, Jason, wauk up man. There's sumhin lirkin in is gloup. I ca' hearken its braith. Whaur the deil is it caunle? A baist I tell ye. It's mebbe a BEAR . . ."

The next moment something warm and wet smacked me in the face, accompanied by a familiar smell. "Scottie," I said, "It's Credo!"

Scottie's match flared and my eyes attested the evidence of my other senses. Unless we were both hallucinating, there she was. Scottie's eyes were huge and dark. He threw down the match and grabbed the dog with both arms. There was such a slobbering and snuffling then, and a fair breeze from Credo's wagging tail, and Scottie's muffled exclamations . . . "mi bonny lass . . . mi bawtie . . . mi bonny canny dautie lass . . . mi braw wee freen . . ." and then a strong arm round me and more tongue slaps from Credo. We managed to find the candle and light it, and for several minutes just sat there in silent rejoicing.

Then Scottie asked how the deil would we unfankle ourselves and win awa from this weary place, and I pointed out that if Credo could find us in here with her nose she could get us out with the same organ. This started another bout of hugging and petting between man and dog till dog shook herself away and ear-signalled that that was enough of that and it was time to get moving. "We better join ourselves together, so we don't get separated," I said, and asked Scottie if there was any rope left.

"Deil a haet," said he. "Nocht but ae nip o' skainie." He rummaged in his bag and produced a length of string; then added, "We eesed a' the tow on that daft raft o' thine."

So we traced all our intricate meanderings in reverse, the latter part of the journey in complete darkness: two grown men tied together being led by a dog, and totally dependent on the dog's sense of smell for their deliverance from a lonely and desolate end. When at last the first flecks of light reached the black hollows of our eyes, the elation and the relief we felt were beyond speech.

Once outside again in the glorious light and wide open air we fell on our knees and all three drank from the little brook that sparkled along beside the cliff-side track. Then we decided to eat, rest and celebrate being alive before even thinking about what to do next. Scottie took the rod and went upstream to look for a promising pool while I foraged in the vegetable kingdom. I found a bed of watercress by the brook and the pretty coloured finches that abounded there had left me a few plump bilberries, growing in the peaty hollows among the rocks. Scottie returned with a brace of grilse, flashing in the light to match his smile, and we set about preparing the meal. Forever improvising he managed to create a sauce using oil from the fish, spore powder from a kind of giant puffball, and juice from the bilberries. The results of his culinary improvisations were either interesting or delicious, and on this occasion they were both, and lifted beyond the physical senses by the joy in our hearts.

After the meal we lay back and absorbed what remained of the sunlight before the sun disappeared behind the towering bulk of the Tash'kahern outcrop. We decided the occasion had come to drink the rest of the whisky, even though it meant being on the wagon from here on. There was always the possibility of finding some human habitation, and where there were people there was generally alcohol in some form or other. I observed for the first time that when you let your gaze travel high up into the zenith and held it there steadily you could see tiny dark bird shapes floating around. I pointed it out to Scottie who said they were eagles; sun eagles they were called because they flew so high up on sunny days, above the mountains where they lived. I said I wondered if any of them were buzzard bairns and he said he wished they were but we'd have to drink another glass or two before we could convince ourselves of that.

Also, listening intently we could hear the distant roar of the Raffire. I said that according to the map it swung in towards the Tash'kaherns a little further north. Scottie had a few sharp words to say about that 'eeseless' document, now relegated to the category of 'doited nories' of mine that had nearly cost us our lives. "What is extraordinary," I continued, "is that we haven't had so much as a whisker of rain in weeks, and that river is in full spate. I can't imagine what it's like in a rainy season." "We'll suin discover for oorsels," he replied. The rainy season would begin in a few weeks' time.

Scottie asked the question that had been on both our minds: "How in the nem of the A'mighty did Credo scape frae yon rampageous watter?" Between us we could come up with neither a rational nor even a whisky inspired solution. Scottie could only attribute it to some form of divine intervention, which led to a discussion about religion and faith. Scottie's father had been a vehement atheist but Scottie himself seemed to have some residual belief in deity, a life force that imbued everything in existence. Between the usual sallies he spoke for once quite earnestly about it:

"We dinna ken where we come frae, Jason. Life is a mystery we canna rede; nae scientist, nae philosopher, can rede life and they niver wull, cause we are part of it and nae craitur can explain itself. It comes frae somewhere else, some power or being and for the sake of a word we can ca' it God. God is a'things, a'roads, the hail universe. Everything that exists is God."

"Even Zard?" I asked, a little unkindly perhaps, but touching on the intractable problem, for pantheists, of evil.

"Zard was my brither," he replied. "Ithawise, he did nae exist."

There was a gentle lazy sense of autumn in the air and the nights were getting a little chilly and dewy, so we decided to pitch our tent. Before turning in Scottie smashed the empty whisky bottle and threw the pieces among the rocks. I asked him if that were a Zinnian custom, an offering to the god of stone perhaps; but he said it was to prevent a wee craitur getting trapped inside, as we had been in the cave. His thoughtfulness was a just rebuke for my feeble shafts of sceptical irony.

It was a tight squeeze in the tent, and being the larger and younger of the two Scottie accused me of taking more than my share of room. Credo curled up outside to protect us further from the perils and dangers of the night. I was thinking, and perhaps Scottie was too, about the miraculous change in our fortunes since the last time we lay down together. I gave heartfelt thanks to Whomever it Might Concern.

Next morning we had a big think about what to do. We quickly decided that even with Credo to get us out of trouble our caving days were over. We were creatures of light and space. I studied the despised and discredited map to see if there was any other route through the mountains to reach the Looshin Levels. I could see nothing to the south of our position, but further north there was a possibility. A narrow pass between two of the Tash'kahern plates appeared to connect with a gentler slope to the top of the range of hills bounding the northern edge of the Levels, and there was a point in the south facing escarpment where a crevasse might make descent negotiable. It was an uncertain and difficult route, with dangers of its own, and would add days, even weeks to our journey time. The only other course was to return home, but we agreed that after everything we'd been through this was not a choice open to us; well not yet at any rate.

Still aglow with a sense of freedom and reluctant to start the next ordeal we lingered in the sunshine, brewing pots of herbal tea and root coffee. We struck camp in the afternoon and set off again along the same road that brought us here, following the track that ran under the towering wall of rock. There is something about a long high wall that speaks of destiny and the fate of mankind. Unvarying, impervious, it excludes all background and context. Tiny figures move along it with no measureable progress from one point to the next. Objectives, errands, hopes and dreams are all suspended;

you neither advance nor retreat. The journey seems endless.

After a few hundred yards we came to another cave entrance. We looked at each other, thinking the same thought: that this was the one we should have taken. A series of simultaneous thoughts followed logically: this time the map would be right, we had Credo to get us out of trouble, and it would save us a long and wearisome trek. We turned to Credo for guidance. The ears were flat, the tail was still. Without a word, and with shared relief, we carried on along the track.

It proved to be the right decision. We passed several other caves that could equally have been the one our cartographer intended to indicate. It seemed the mountain was mined through with them, like a piece of wormy timber. Perhaps the passage marked on the map was a Zinnian practical joke, or maybe it was marked in red as a warning not to be attempted. The map was right about one thing, however: the River Raffire was looping towards us and we could hear the gradual crescendo of its approach. It had become a steady sonorous boom by the time we reached the point where it veered off to the north-east again, deflected by a smaller outcrop of rock like an emerging wisdom tooth in relation to the main ridge, with a narrow passage about forty yards wide between the two.

Here we found the solution to the mystery of Credo's escape, and it required no direct divine intervention to explain it. Where the river turned through ninety degrees a cleft in the rock allowed a narrow stream to divert into a pool, which stilled the current a little before it rejoined the river further downstream. By luck, and having perhaps worked her way towards the bank, Credo was swept into this fleeting refuge and was able to scramble ashore. We found her paw prints in the wet sand where she came out. Scottie was so overcome by the miracle of it he wanted to congratulate Credo all over again, but seeing another love attack coming she decided she had sniffing business elsewhere.

Scottie opined the pool looked promising to cast a fly over, which it certainly did. We took turns with the rod without a bite, and then he hooked one, a big one, and had a real fight to bring it in. It was a very odd fish, the like of which neither of us had seen before. Its metallic scales were almost black except for a pale underbelly; the fins were razor sharp and it had teeth, and two protuberances above its eyes gave it an angry expression. We agreed it was an 'ugsome fush' and put it back.

So we continued our journey north, settling in for a long hike. We had scarcely gone half a mile however when we saw a great pile of rocks blocking the path ahead. It looked at first as though there had been a landslide, but there was no loss or loosening anywhere in the solid cliff face above it. Also the fragments looked freshly cut, or torn apart, and when we came up to them we saw none of the little green and red spotted lizards that basked everywhere on exposed rock surfaces. We made our way around this obstruction and then beheld an extraordinary sight.

There was yet another entrance into the mountain, but this one clearly man made, straight as a die, large enough to accommodate a six lane highway and as high as the nave of a cathedral. We could see right through to the other side, an eye sized semi-circle of light. The only conceivable purpose for such a colossal excavation was to build a road connecting Zinn to the north-east region. But it made no sense in terms of communications, given the sparse population there, Zinn's isolationism, and the massive engineering problems presented by the Kaspan Hills. We surveyed it with mixed feelings.

"We won't get lost in this cave," I remarked. But Scottie was too awestruck by the scale of it to make any reply. On the one hand it presented us with a famous and providential short-cut to our destination. On the other it was a fearful reminder of the forces we were up against.

It is curious to note that we had never felt small walking beneath the great blue vault of day, or among the stars in the infinite night, and yet entering the portals of this man appointed space in nature we felt dwarfed and timid. Instinctively we walked quietly, and spoke, if at all, in whispers. Even Credo appeared circumspect, and nonplussed by the absence of her sensory world of smell. What smells she found, of petrol, oil or cordite, did not appeal to her. We passed several parked machines: excavators, resting their giant knuckles on the ground, and bulldozers with blades the size of a bus. There were no lights anywhere, though there were cables hooked to the walls, and no workmen. And yet the place didn't seem to have been abandoned. It was just waiting.

We had no idea what we would find on the other side, and as the eye of light grew larger we prepared our story in case we should be confronted. We had simply come from another region and were visiting relatives in the Looshin area. Scottie had the names of our contacts there. But then a hole is not something that needs to be guarded - it can't be stolen and won't stray. So we hoped to pass through unchallenged.

As the scene beyond the tunnel became visible we sensed the approach of another shock, though by now perhaps not so much of a surprise. The world had changed colour, from green to brown. Finally we stood together in the opening, some fifty feet above the Levels and connected to them by a ramp of stone surfaced with hardcore. A few shreds of vegetation clung to the foothills on either side, but all beyond, as far as we could see in every direction, stretched a sea of mud; ridged and gouged with lifted earth, pocked with swampy hollows and fragments of sky. Great track marks snaked across it, like the wakes of ocean going liners. Near and far were the ripped out roots of trees, clutching the air like the frenzied fingers of drowning men. Fires were burning here and there, sending columns of white smoke into the clear, still air. It was a scene of devastation beyond all we could have imagined, as though some vengeful Titan had hell-raked it from end to end. We just stared at it, helpless and bereft.

Scottie was the first to speak: "Och Jason lad, we ha' come aa this gate, throu aa these trauchles and tribbles now, to sauf this plantin, and there's scarcelins a boucht left t' hain."

"Right enough, Scottie old boy. They've taken the whole caboodle - every stick they could lay their thieving hands on. But where are the people? What have they done with them? Are we looking at a graveyard?"

Scottie shook his head in stunned incomprehension. Then as if in answer to my question two figures, darkly clad, came into view from behind a ridge of soil and debris: a man trudging along carrying a sack, a young lad by his side, moving ant-like across the blasted heath. We waited until they drew level with us and then walked down to meet them. At our approach the man put down his burden, glad it seemed to have an excuse to break his march. The boy edged closer to him warily. Scottie addressed them in Zinnian:

"Greetings to you sir, and to you young man. We are strangers here. We have come from the province of Sammonar to see how the world goes with you."

"Well you can see pretty much for yourself," the man replied, looking out across the bleak wasteland into the misty distance. Meanwhile Credo trotted up with wagging tale and appealing eyes to the boy, who reached down and touched her gingerly on the head. "But do tell me," continued Scottie, "all the folk who lived hereabouts - where have they all gone?"

"They left - that's the long and short of it. Some travelled south, some west, some far away to other lands. Like all the ones who get thrown off their land they moved into big cities, living in the slums and shanty towns, getting work if they can as cleaners or servants, or in the factories and sweat shops. There were over a hundred farms on these lands. Now it's just us. Twenty-five souls. My parents refused to budge. My father's a strong man - no one crosses him. And my old mother's got a tongue in her head."

"But how do you live?"

"We've got our fields and stock still. They fenced us in, but they let us search for whatever we can salvage." He showed us his bag which contained various tools, engine parts, nuts and bolts, all muddy but serviceable, as well as scrap metal. "My lad's certainly taken to that dog of yours," he continued, looking down at him.

The boy was stroking and talking to Credo who was gratefully accepting such unwontedly delicate and patient attention. He asked Scottie her name. "She's called Credo." "Credo," he murmured, "you're a nice dog Credo, a jolly nice old thing I'd say Credo." He picked up a stick to see if Credo wanted to chase it, but she suddenly pricked up her ears and then we all heard it - the noise of an engine, and looked up to see a fat wheeled quad bike striped black and yellow approaching, puttering and sputtering as it clawed and churned its way over the choppy terrain. The man driving it wore a bright yellow construction helmet and fluorescent jacket over black overalls. His intercom crackled officiously and we heard snatches of speech as he jabbered back at it: "three adult males . . . male child . . . commencing ID check . . . backup standby request . . ."

He pulled up opposite us, swung out of his seat and snapped, "ID cards please." Our companion produced two, one for himself and one for the boy. The security officer scrutinised them closely, comparing photographs with faces, and handed them back. He then turned to us. "We're not from here," Scottie explained. "We've come to visit relatives." "Right. You two shove off (to the man and boy), and you two stay right where you are and don't move a muscle."

He turned to reach for his intercom transmitter on the dashboard but as he did so Credo started barking. Squaring up to him with legs out wide, nose wrinkled, teeth bared, she barked and snarled as she had at the bear. Without a pause the guard replaced the intercom, hitched up his jacket, unclipped his holster, pulled out his gun, pointed it at Credo and fired at point blank range in the head - or undoubtedly would have done. It had all happened too quickly for us but the boy, still holding the stick, brought it down 'thwack', with all his force on the guard's wrist. He yelled out and the gun dropped to the ground. As he turned in fury to the boy his father pushed him and he toppled in the mud. The father then stamped on the gun with the heel of his boot, ramming it deep into the soggy ground, grabbed his sack and shouted "run!" We all ran.

"Keep close, there'll be more of them!" We followed our new friends as closely as we could as they dodged and darted along gullies and under banks, with heads held low. Then we stopped suddenly where a large uprooted tree stump made a cavity in the ground. The man threw his bag in and told us to do the same with our kit. "We'll pick them up later," he said, kicking soil over to conceal them. Disencumbered we made swift progress. We heard engines approaching, revving up angrily to a dissonant chorus. Soon they were round us like a swarm of wasps. We caught glimpses of them riding over mounds and flashing past gaps as we flattened ourselves against banks or lay low in ditches.

Heaven knows how we avoided capture, but at length we reached a belt of bushy heathland on the rising slope of the Tash'kahern scarp with good cover, and too rough and steep for the quad bikes to come after us. We followed a narrow winding path, slowing down to a quick march as the sounds of danger melted away. About thirty minutes later we emerged again on to the Levels. The static ocean of mud still spread out in front of us and to our right until it was lost in mist, but to our left there was an island of green, surrounded by a high security fence. We approached it and entered through a hinged panel in the steel mesh.

Chapter 10

Under Siege

WE WERE walking along a country lane, wheat stubble on one side, sheep grazing on the other. "We'll be safe here," said our guide.

"But they'll know where to find us won't they?" Scottie said. "What's to stop them coming here and arresting us?"

"This is my father's land," said the other. "They won't cross his boundaries."

"We haven't had time to introduce ourselves yet," said I. "My name's Jason Brockhurst, and my friend here is Scottie Emmisarius."

"Leevil Prendis," he replied. "And this is my lad Tamon."

"Credo and Tamon have already been introduced." I added. Indeed they were walking side by side like old companions. Credo eyed me with a look that said, "I'm with my new friend now but don't worry, it's purely diplomatic. I haven't deserted you two."

"Scottie," said Leevil. "I've heard that name. Didn't you once fly with the buzzard children at Zinn?"

"Yes I was with them," said Scottie, "man and boy."

"We used to see them here from time to time. But not one's been sighted for going on a year now. They say the ZADD's been cracking down hard on them."

"They have, and we don't know what's become of them."

"I expect that's why they've turned a blind eye to the loggers," I offered. "Too busy beating up on a bunch of kids."

"Not this time," Leevil replied. "The Zinn bosses invited the logging company in. They came here in their smart suits and uniforms, with their flunkeys and all. Called a public meeting. Explained we'd be better off if the forest was clear felled. More land for farming. They said it was just a consultation and no decision had been made. Zinn was a democracy they said. Wanted to know if anyone objected. One lad did and started a protest group. We haven't seen him since."

"That hardly surprises me," I said. "And now the forest has gone and the farmers have gone, what happens to the land?"

"Sold!" He replied.

"But who to?"

"To themselves of course. It's all going to be divided up into big estates, owned by the lords of Zinn and run by their agents. We could stay and work for them as labourers and servants for a pittance, half of which would go on rent for our cottages. We sent a delegation to Zinn to protest. They said the consultation process had taken place and a decision had been reached. Then they told us in no uncertain terms to clear off, or we'd lose more than just our land. That's when everyone started to leave."

"They're bastards," said the boy. "We hate them, don't we Credo?" The latter as good as nodded.

"Now lad, watch your tongue."

"I want to join the buzzard kids Daddy. Why can't I? I could go back with Scottie and Jason."

"No lad, it's not safe. The soldiers would kill you."

"I'd kill 'em back!"

"The boy's got spirit, I must say," Scottie commented.

"Aye, and plenty of it. Takes after his granddad."

"How come they didn't throw your father off his land as well?" I asked.

"He owns it - he's got the title deeds. The others were just squatters, though they'd been here for generations. He owns land across the mountain as well and we could move there. But we stay just to spite 'em. 'Thorn in their flesh' he says."

"He sounds like a great guy," said Scottie.

"Aye. He's been around in his time. Been a soldier and a miner and a gambler. Made a pile of money. And that's not all he's got," he added thoughtfully.

By now the farmhouse and buildings were coming into view. With a row of tall poplars to one side, cattle grazing in front, an orchard and hedged-in garden, it all looked homely and decent. I was very curious indeed to meet the master of this establishment, whose raised hand could stop the march of progress in its tracks.

We entered by the back way through the dairy and the kitchen where we were immediately mobbed by a bevy of excited children. Credo was made more fuss of and introduced to the other canine occupants. That seemed to go well. Leevil introduced us to his wife Maribe, and brothers, sisters and their wives and husbands: too many and difficult names for me to remember at the first hearing. Warm smiles and handshakes were exchanged. Then Leevil recounted our meeting and our adventures, and especially Tamon's heroic part in the proceedings. This was greeted with delighted applause and a round of big embarrassing hugs and kisses from Maribe and the other women. The news was immediately carried on small bare feet through to the parlour where the old man and his lady held court. We could hear an enhanced and already mythologised version of it being put together by several narrators, to a cackling response. Then Leevil ushered us through to be introduced in person.

Procter Prendis and his wife Peglin were not at all what I expected. To start with they were small - they wouldn't have made ten feet end to end. Then they had not a tooth between them. He was wiry in build and with steel grey hair slicked back and small piercing eyes in a craggy face, and she plump, white haired and jolly, but sharp with it; warm heart and will of iron. They were as friendly, welcoming and affable as could be, drawing us in and making us instantly part of their circle.

"Come on in lads, come on, sit ye down, there by the fire, make yourselves comfortable. Well now. We've got a fair draught of cider on tap. Ye'll have a glass. Sure ye will. Come on you lasses there, fetch the gentlemen glasses." Glasses were being placed in front of us and filled with the radiant liquid almost as he spoke, along with bowls of nuts, and fruits and shortbread. We raised our drinks. Scottie proposed a toast to Procter and the whole Prendis clan, wishing them all good fortune and health, and I added a special toast to young Tamon and his gallant action in saving the life of our dog Credo. Then we both drank long and deep, till the fire shone through our glasses and our eyes and the old oak panelled room reeled a little and all the faces blurred into one happy smile. After all we'd been through it was a moment of bliss, and an overwhelming sense of arrival.

"Well now," said the old man, "what a do you had with those rascals. And that villain pulls a gun on you - the damn cheek of it. I would have given him a knock." He punched his fist in his palm with surprising energy to demonstrate the point. "And these lads come all this way to see us. I'd have kicked him too," added Mrs Prendis, with no less assurance. She took a hazelnut from the bowl and cracked it in her gums. "And young Tamon, come here my boy, you did well my lad. Your old granddad's right proud of you; we're all proud of you. Quick decisive action - that's what does it. Fast thinking, instinctive reaction. Just the thing. You'd make a fine soldier. But you make sure you always fight for good honest folk, not for those thieving swine that go a tearing and rooting up other folk's livings and gobbling up other folk's goods."

Tamon having been duly praised and admonished the children were shepherded out. Leevil and his brothers came in, pipes were lit and the brandy glasses charged. It was time for some serious patriarchal deliberations.

There was much we were keen to learn from our hosts but their curiosity about us was just as strong and naturally took precedence. They'd had no news for months and wanted to know about affairs in the capital and about the war against the rebel outcasts. But there was little more we could tell them than they already knew or had gathered for themselves. Jobu's rule was becoming more oppressive; he had declared all out war on the children and any who supported them or sympathised with them. There had been many executions and heavy bombardment of rebel areas.

I told the story of how I had been saved from the scaffold myself in a courageous strike by ace buzzard aviators, which had also ended the life of Zard, the regime's chief executioner. I fled to the forest where I met up with Scottie, Zard's twin brother but an opponent of Zinn and also a fugitive. We had lived and worked happily together but my rescue had been the last known flight of a buzzard plane. The military campaign had been intensified and it was not known if the children had been killed or were still holding out somewhere. Powerless to help them we had decided to travel here when we heard about the new threat from the loggers, to offer what support we could. Clearly we had arrived too late.

"Aye," assented the master, "the whole Looshin vale cleared from one end to t'other," endorsing his words with a wide sweep of his arm. "Nothing left but rats." "And them as go on two legs as well as them on four," added his good wife.

Then we were asked about our journey and all the incidents that had taken place. Scottie did most of the talking. Generously absent from his narrative was any hint of criticism where my competence and contributions were concerned. In fact he seemed quite proud of me, and even had a good word to say about the raft. Also absent throughout was any reference to his doomed affair with a Zinnian princess. Apart from it being too sore and personal a matter for him to wish to speak of we had agreed to make no mention of it to anyone as disclosure in the wrong quarters, however unintentional, might have serious consequences.

Our experiences in the caves provoked some animated debate on whether or not there really was an underground passage through the mountain. Some believed it and cited incidents of individuals who had entered from the Levels and had later been heard of living on the other side. But others told stories of people who had gone in armed with an authoritative map and an adventurous spirit and had never been seen or heard of again. "It sounds to me," I suggested, "like one of those beliefs we call urban myths."

"And why 'urban'?" asked Kombard, the eldest and a confirmed sceptic. "Country folk are full of such nonsense."

"I suppose it's because some of these tales are so convincing that they are believed even by townsfolk, who are supposed to be more cynical and sophisticated."

This comment was greeted with somewhat dry and dismissive mirth. The people of the forest did not regard themselves as naive. They implicitly thought of themselves as knowledgeable, shrewd, honest certainly, but not without cunning when called for. They made no claims for themselves, theirs was simply the normal and proper condition, and they quickly saw through the pretensions of others.

At the same time they lived close to nature, and had an instinctive, non-scientific understanding of nature's wonders which made them open to mystical experience. It was their fundamental assumption that they were civilised, though they would not have used the term, and that is how I saw them. I had known various self-proclaimed civilisations as well as my own, the validity of the claim being as a rule inversely proportionate to its unquestioning assumption, and the claimant's readiness to use violent means of promoting it.

When at length we came around to speak of the fate of the Levels the mood was understandably more sombre. In past times there had been numerous raids and incursions by maverick loggers but they had made little impression. The foresters had many ways of making life difficult for these invaders. Their machines got bogged down or wouldn't start; their saws were shredded by pieces of metal embedded in the timber. The loggers hired heavies to protect their equipment but eventually Zinnian forces would show up and drive them off. But now the Zinnians had entered into an agreement with a large, modern logging company and unveiled plans for what they termed the 're-designation' or 'redevelopment' of the land. The Company deployed much larger and more powerful machines, protected by armed guards, and the forest began to disappear at an alarming rate. They used a method of dragging or harrowing with enormous chains which ripped out everything in their path. Stands of massive, ancient trees collapsed like dominoes.

Then came an army of men wielding chainsaws and wearing

helmets and ear muffs and protective clothing. From dawn to dusk the wailing, shrieking noise alone was enough to drive people from their homes. They rigged overhead cables called sky lines with a travelling carriage to which half a dozen tree trunks at a time could be hooked, then lifted and conveyed to the collection points as if they weighed no more than matchsticks. There they were seized in the giant claws of mechanical grabbers, loaded and carted off in convoys of trucks. It had started in early spring when the trees were opening their first fresh green leaves, which would also be their last.

In recalling these distressing scenes old Mrs Prendis was especially voluble and vituperative. When all the men folk had either been arrested or given up in despair she had organised the women into picket lines, lying down in front of machines and hurling abuse at the loggers which could be heard even above the frenzied lament of the chainsaws. Then a young woman had been killed, crushed by a bulldozer in what one side claimed was an accident and the other a deliberate assault. An inquiry, assisted by the Company's powerful legal team, decided it was an accident.

By now families were beginning to leave and Peglin's support was ebbing away. A handful of die-hards remained, cordoned off, in silent protest. In the end Procter had tried to lock Peglin in, but she escaped and went forth single handed, waving a ragged banner like a tiny sail on that great empty sea. Eventually she collapsed from exhaustion and only then could be returned safely to her home and her bed. She could be said to have carried her banner, as the last batsman standing of a defeated cricket team is said to have carried his bat.

Procter had had his own battle with the invaders. The Company offered to buy him out for a paltry sum. His refusal triggered a further series of accidents. His boundaries came under repeated attack from careless operators of heavy plant, and others claiming to be unsure of exactly where the boundaries were. This led to incursions into his woodlands and even on to his fields. It then proved necessary to use explosives in an area close to the farmhouse. Safety considerations required a curfew and close escort of anyone leaving the premises. Rocks and debris flew over, pelting the farm yard and buildings.

Having been himself an artillery captain and a quarryman Procter decided to give the boys a lesson on safety. It had been their custom to encircle a piece of woodland, driving all the wild animals into it, and then organise a glorious hunt. They'd turn off their engines and take out their shotguns and soon be blasting away at terrified creatures as they were forced to break cover. They didn't even bother to remove their earmuffs and made so much racket with their yells and fusillades they hardly noticed a few extra bangs in the background. When they returned in triumph with their bag they found three very expensive machines were smouldering heaps of shattered metal.

Of course the Company realised who was responsible. They could have issued a summons and started legal proceedings but the old man knew that their insurance only covered accidental loss, and not 'acts of war', including sabotage. They had to invent a story about a design fault in order to claim compensation.

Then came a visit from the Company's chief surveyor in an altogether more respectful and conciliatory frame of mind. The boundaries were agreed and a fence erected, more to keep the loggers out than the farmers in. To clarify his point further Procter and his sons went round the perimeter in broad daylight placing cylindrical objects under a shallow covering. They were only empty cases of landmines, but ever watchful observers with field glasses would have no way of knowing this. Clearly that other resource which Leevil had alluded to, apart from money, was Procter's knowledge and possession of explosives, and demonstrated willingness to use them in defence of his property. The price he was offered for his estate began to rise dramatically.

A further concession was the easing of restrictions on movement outside the estate. However the Company insisted on issuing passes to young and old alike and checking them on every occasion even though the holders were known by sight. It was a way of still putting pressure on the family and inducing Procter to settle.

Peglin again was the principle narrator of all this, Procter contenting himself with a growl or chuckle as he sipped his brandy and puffed his pipe, till almost disappearing in a cloud of smoke himself. She was proud to celebrate her husband's prowess, but they were divided on one point, clearly an old bone of contention. Peglin wanted Procter to go on the offensive, blow up more plant and send the varmints packing. But Procter shook his head.

"Nay lass, I would never risk a life. Those boys just get whatever work they can to support their own families. When you're young you don't think of the losers and there's always loss for gain. And it's dangerous work - there's been a tidy few killed and many injured. It's the bosses, the politicos and money men you have to reckon with. It would take some mighty force to push them back."

Peglin mumbled and cracked another nut, but she could not gainsay the master. Nevertheless she was fiercely firm on one thing. No one would take or drive her from her home while she lived. She was staying put.

Talk of explosives led to some discussion of the enormous hole that had been blasted through the mountain. A special outfit had been drafted in to do the work, and Procter admitted it was a highly professional job. The implications of the tunnel were worrying however. Clearly a major road link was intended connecting the Levels with Zinn. A 'gateway project' was the official expression attached to it. It would split the forest and make it easier for the Zinnians to subdue and control its inhabitants. Some argued it heralded a new attempt to wipe out the independence of the foresters, and the declared policy of leaving no hiding place for rebels supported this. Others held it represented no more than a transport corridor to convey the produce of the Levels to the capital. If the whole area was farmed the quantities would be considerable, and certainly enough to end the shortages of recent times. Another view was that that the project would take years to complete, if it ever was, given the ruggedness of the terrain. Procter himself didn't pronounce on this matter, retreating into his cloud of smoke from which a few testy gutturals and expectorations emerged from time to time. I noticed that in general he was reluctant to commit himself and content to let others do the talking. "He's keeping his powder dry," I thought.

Then Peglin struck up on a topic of burning interest to myself and Scottie - food. We'd nibbled as much as we decently could from the bowls on the table but now felt a strong need for a more satisfying repast. She must have noticed this as she interrupted the flow of conversation to declare:

"Now I daresay these gentlemen haven't had a proper bite to eat all day and we've had our supper before they came. They must be starved, poor dears, and we've been giving them nothing but talk talk talk, and that never filled anyone's belly." There was a general murmur of assent, and the meeting broke up. We were conducted back to the kitchen where a rich pottage from the hob was dished out and placed in front of us with thick slices of coarse sweet bread trowelled with salty dripping and an array of cheeses of varying colours and textures, delightful to eye and taste. Others watched to receive our approval and relish our pleasure.

It was well past the children's bedtime but a special dispensation was in place in view of an event as exciting and exceptional as the arrival of visitors. For the beleaguered Prendises it was as though we had journeyed from another planet. The meal over, we were plied with questions and story requests. We did our best but by now we were tired and drowsy, so with promises of telling more tomorrow it was agreed that it really was time to call it a day. The farmhouse was already full to bursting, but space was found for us in a high attic, up narrow stairs and along winding passages.

Under the dusty rafters all was plain and simple in the shadowy candlelight. A stuffed fox glared at us from a dark corner. But the beds were deep and downy, for us a luxury beyond words. We slept long and peacefully. I had one pit stop, treading as carefully as possible on ancient creaking boards towards the loo. A little window there gave out across the farm, the meadows and hayricks and slumbering trees, in the chaste moonlight a calm, immemorial pastoral scene. And out beyond was like the cratered surface of the moon itself, stretching far away to starry horizons. It felt very strange to be in this homely, human place, enclosed as if in a space capsule surrounded by a cold, alien universe.

The next morning Scottie and I agreed we would spend a few days with the Prendis family to rest and revive our strength before the return journey. With the rainy season coming on we could not delay our departure too long.

But life at the farm was pleasant, and we lingered. The logging was over as there were no trees left to fell, and road building or infrastructure work had yet to begin, no doubt delayed with weather prospects in view; and perhaps operations would be suspended to the following year. Occasionally the noise of an engine might burn a hole in the peaceful quiet of the day. Sometimes one of the Company's helicopters, used to ferry out injured loggers and now just keeping an eye on us, clappered noisily overhead.

The farm was well stocked and provisioned for the coming winter and most of the year's work was done. The men were out cutting hedges and bonfires were burning along the headlands. Occasionally they went on foraging trips beyond the fence to the sites of former settlements, looking for useful odds and ends in the absence of access to suppliers of manufactured goods. The sites were clearly marked by the flocks of crows and kites that gathered there, these being all that was left of the forest's teeming bird life. The men still followed traces of familiar lanes and byways and referred to places by name that weren't places any more. These ghostly remnants would also disappear in the next phase of development.

Procter had obtained passes for us but we declined to take part in these expeditions. We preferred for the duration of our visit to focus on the farm and the hearth, to enjoy their comforts and tranquillity, and to avoid even thinking about the weird and gloomy landscape of despair all around us. It was a self-sufficient world, without all the wonders of high technology and the facilities and choices it offered, but without the stresses they entailed.

Scottie as ever was much in demand, especially with the opposite sex of all ages. He spent a lot of time with the older ones among the grandchildren, in their teens, and it was good to see him with people closer to his own age. I was happy to entertain the younger children with stories of my adventures in many lands. But there was one lass, about seventeen, who seemed to prefer to sit with us, and at the same time to hold herself apart. She had large dark eyes, a pale complexion, and an unruly mane of dark chestnut hair. She was the only girl I had so far encountered who was not instantly drawn to Scottie, and she hardly glanced in his direction. Though perfectly polite to him and everyone, and willing and good natured, she was unmoved, and just went quietly about her work. And somehow everyone deferred to her; even Procter and Peglin seemed flattered by her attentions. Her name was Maralese. She was strikingly beautiful.

The Prendises would have liked us to stay with them for good, and by now we'd left it rather late to get beyond the Raffire and the Kaspan Mountains before the rains descended. Scottie was now keen to stay on till the next spring. But we couldn't stay forever and neither, in reason, could they. Cut off from all contacts and communications how could they survive, physically or mentally? The young people would have to move out into the world – find work, careers, partners, lives of their own. If Procter had other estates beyond the mountains the simple solution was to move there. He must know the score. But the old girl's refusal to budge was a problem. Not even he could shift her. Did they have to wait for her to die? She showed no intention of doing that either.

One sortie into no-man's-land recovered our belongings which Leevil had concealed along with his own booty during our escape from the guards. The map was damp and creased, and much the worse for wear. I spread it out carefully on the floor of the attic and once again studied it closely. I tried to work out the route that had brought us here and to see if there was an easier one to return by. Maps so often seem wrong, or inaccurate, but it's usually our ground level perception that's at fault. There were things about the topography of the region that seemed to me not only remarkable but illogical, as though everything didn't quite connect with everything else. Somehow it didn't make sense.

CHAPTER 11

Big Bang Theory

BY NOW THE year was on the turn. We had enjoyed a long period of gentle autumnal calm, of 'mists and mellow fruitfulness'. The bronze- and copper-smiths had been at work in the woods with soft hammers. The maples shed their leaves on the grass like yellow cloaks, and the last red and purple fruit ripened and rotted on the orchard floor, hollowed by wasps. The morning mist rose on the Levels like the ghost of the departed forest. Then gusty winds and light fresh rains blew in our faces; leaves were flying and trees unravelling. Unhindered now by a maze of foliage the air-stream passed full sail across the waste, while above the clouds massed and darkened in endless procession.

Every day flocks of migrating birds were arriving. Majestic swans and cranes and long chains of geese and wildfowl winged their way in silent passage across the great expanse, occasionally descending to a lifeless pool, then moving on. Small driven bands of winter thrushes and finches swerved and darted as if confused by the disappearance of their age-old winter quarters – without so much as a bush to cling to. Many flocked to the farm which became a bird watcher's paradise for a couple of weeks, so great was the variety. But a winter's supply of berries soon disappeared and there were not even enough worms for the large numbers of snipe and woodcock that filled every copse. These too came and went; everything was on the move. We had left it too late to leave ourselves, but our thoughts were in turmoil.

One of these restless days I woke early and took a walk round
the farm. I found a different path to my usual ones, following the
line of the mountain due south. Passing through a spindly wood
I arrived at the terminus of the boundary fence. From here I had
a long clear view southwards across the Levels, though mist still
hung in the hollows. Some long grey dim shape out there puzzled
me - perhaps a spit of rock. As I stared into the distance something
I did recognise edged into my peripheral vision. It was a large pair
of binoculars held towards me by a horny hand. I turned and
found Procter, beside me. He stood there, gun under his arm and
feather in his hat, no higher than my shoulder but grimly powerful, a gnarled old countryman with something too of the Nordic
troll about him: small but dangerous.

"Procter," I said, "you came up quiet. I'm not usually surprised
that easily." He grinned, a kind of leering scowl, and said, "Take a
closer look." I put the glasses to my eyes and focussed the lenses.
The thing that resolved itself through the clearing mist sent a chill
down my spine. It reminded me of a journey once across the plains
of the Vistula, coming to a point where I could see the long flank
of Auschwitz-Birkenau, the high tensioned fencing and guard towers, and the curve of the rail line that had brought so many
doomed souls there. To make the resemblance more unnerving
there were rows of long buildings spread out beyond the wire.

"What the hell is it?" I asked. "Some kind of prison?"

"No, there's no one there lad. Just a few guards."

"But what's in those buildings?"

"Packed full of heavy plant - shovels, tractors, yarders, grabbers.
Big buggers too. Make what we've seen here look like kiddies'
toys."

"For the road building I suppose."

"That's what my boys think."

"But not you."

"Nah. That's logging gear."

"But . . . I see. I see what you mean. That's what the tunnel's for.
You think they're going to start logging on the other side."

"I don't think it lad. I've got contacts. Company's bought a concession to clear the whole lot through to Zinn."

"That's surely not possible. There's the river, and the Kaspan range . . ."

"They'll cut a road through the hills and drag 'em later, if they think it's worth their while. They'll rip it all out like they have here."

"You mean all the farms and settlements - your place - and ours?"

"The whole god-damned shooting match. And fast two. In two years time the forest will be a memory."

"That's mad!"

"Makes sound economic sense, and sound military sense too. They get millions from selling the timber, and millions more from growing cash crops. Could even plant some more trees - 'sustainable forestry' - very kosher. They flush out all you anarchists and trouble makers, buy modern weapons, give the army and police pay rises - they're untouchable."

"So that would end Zinn's international isolation?"

"Not even that. It'll be wrapped up tighter than before. 'Globalisation' - what does it mean? You can move money, you can move goods, but you can keep people just where you want them. And keep them down."

I gave Procter the glasses back. I'd seen enough. There was silence for a while. Then I said, "But you haven't told your people." He shook his head. "If you know the world's going to end it's best to keep quiet about it."

"Why me?"

"Well, Jason my lad, you've got a life somewhere else. I just wanted to warn you in good time, so you can make plans, and take care of yourself and Scottie. There's no future for him here."

"And what about you and yours?"

"The old girl will never move, and me and her don't have that long to go. We'll hang out here. The rest will have to emigrate. At least I can give them something to start over. You and Scottie too, you're part of the family now. If you need help you know where to come."

"You're a good man Procter. You don't deserve any of this."

"Happens all over, my boy. As you well know."

We walked back towards the farm in silence, my mind racing. The scale of destruction was so colossal, the human consequences so tragic. Surely something could be done in a world order which claimed to be just and humane. But Procter was right. Such claims were illusory and I knew it. There was no appeal and any thought of a legal challenge had to be summarily dismissed. "Perhaps Peglin was right," I said at last. "You'd have to blow up all their machines. But you'd need a few shed loads of dynamite for that." The old man chuckled. "Let me show you something my friend."

He took me through the stables and outbuildings to an old stone barn, with narrow slit windows and mossy roof, that looked abandoned. He took a bunch of keys from his pocket and opened the double locked steel door and we entered a small dusty office. There was a desk stuffed with papers and a shelf with a few shabby files and crinkled manuals and catalogues piled on it. He unlocked a drawer in the desk and took out a brass key with which he opened a heavy door made of bronze in the further wall. Then he asked to inspect the soles of my boots to see if there were any steel studs. We entered a dim interior space divided into shelved bays like an archives repository.

The shelves were filled with wooden crates and cardboard boxes stamped or stencilled with numbers, symbols, warnings, and the word EXPLOSIVES in many languages. Procter opened boxes at random, explaining the nature, purpose and power of their contents, handling his specimens with loving care like a collector. Then there were fuses and detonators, batteries and reels of electric cable, and various canisters and other sinister looking objects.

There was no mistaking Procter's pleasure in the mere possession of this fearsome armoury, carefully acquired and assembled over many years of his freebooting, hazardous career. I found myself nodding in appreciation and admiring as if I were being shown a fine collection of Dresden china, but at the same time pondering 'to what end?' He was a generous man, even towards his enemies, and as far from being paranoid or homicidal as could be, and yet he had amassed enough explosive material to supply the world's rebels and resisters for many decades. Finally I blurted it out: "Procter, what in God's name are you going to do with this stuff?"

He grinned his toothless grin and replied:

"Well, there was a time when I thought problems could be solved with high explosives. That was long ago. The more I got, the bigger the problems got, and the more complicated. I would never take an innocent life. There is no cause in the world worth a single innocent life. It's taken me a lifetime to realise that. Now all this is just an old man's folly. You wouldn't think anybody could get sentimental about explosives, but it's all got memories for me. It will all go when I go."

I returned to our room where Scottie was still asleep, took off my boots and lay down on my bed fully clothed. I was deeply troubled by what I had learned from Procter about the impending fate of the forest and its people. A mood of anger, frustration and grief possessed me. That old impulse to turn away and move on came back to haunt me; to cut loose from this doomed and hopeless situation. It seemed that any place on this planet where I found rest, where I wanted to belong and be a part of things, would be the next to be torn to shreds before my very eyes. And no power on earth could put a stop to it. It appalled me that so much destructive force was wielded by so few, so lacking in wisdom, intelligence or humanity. Were it not better there were still gods men feared in rivers and mountains and forests? We all die anyway. Nature claims us one by one, and surely in the final end will brush aside the entire mass of our arrogant, insolent race.

And then what about Scottie, sleeping so peacefully, dreaming perchance of his love. How was I going to break the news to him? It was all very well for me to gather up my load and my losses and move on again, and again. He truly belonged here. The people loved him and he knew the forest and its ways and its creatures so well. I thought of his cottage and the things he treasured, and his father's grave. I couldn't imagine him in any other place or situation. He would simply fade away.

Credo was curled up between my bed and Scottie's, close to the door to protect us. Seeing I was unhappy she came over and sat by me in mute sympathy. "Well at least we've still got you, old girl," I said, stroking her head and fondling her silky ears, and recalling her narrow escapes from the bear, the guard and most amazingly from indomitable fury the River Raffire. I thought back to how we had felt when we lost her, and then in the caves, in utter darkness, of the despair and annihilation of spirit we knew then. There can be miracles I thought. Sometimes nature just needs a helping hand. A wire was flashing in my head.

I noticed the map was still lying on the floor where I'd left it to dry, and it came to me what the topographical oddity was that had been puzzling me. In an instant it all fell together, like the tumblers in a lock.

I picked up the map, went over to Scottie's bed and tried to wake him. He turned over with muffled Scotts objurgations.

"Wake up Scottie, I've got something important to tell you," I insisted, shaking his hunched shoulder.

"Losh man wha the deil is't ye'r blouterin aboot."

"I've got to tell you something Scottie, It's really important."

"Is the hoose brenning?" he asked, not even opening his eyes.

"No, no fire, but . . ."

"Weel it ca' bide a wee," and he snuggled down again into the bedclothes.

I put my hand over his mouth and nose and whispered in his ear "It could be urgent Scottie. Wake up." He jerked upright shaking his head and rubbing his eyes. Then he saw the map I was holding.

"Oich, Jason, that eeseless caird o thine. I a'ways kend ye wad gae gyte wi' it. And wha blethers is it telling ye the noo, sae clamant ye maun roust me frae my bed lik ae doited haveril wi a ye'r fiddle-fyke."

I waited patiently for Scottie to rub the sleep from his eyes and exhaust his vocabulary of brotherly abuse. What a gift is sleep I thought for the young; to go down so deep and bury all your troubles. It took a little while for him to gather his faculties and give me his full attention. Then I put the case to him:

"I had a talk with Procter this morning. He told me some bad news. So bad I couldn't think of any way of breaking it to you."

"Feth, Jason, is the warld aboot t'end."

"Pretty much Scottie, for us at least. Apparently the Zinnians have sold the logging company a concession to fell the entire forest, including our home and the farm. Everyone we know will be turned off, and it'll be even worse for us as we're wanted men. There's no doubt about it either. They've set up a big depot in the south, full of all the plant and machinery they need. And that tunnel they've drilled through the mountain is to take it all through. The size of it tells you how big the machines are, and Procter reckons they'll clear the whole forest in a couple of years."

I watched poor Scottie's face dissolve into that childish look of helplessness I had seen before in the cave. As then, it tugged at my heart so I hurried on to the more hopeful, or at least the 'ghost of a chance' part of my narrative:

"But Scottie, I've thought of a plan. I think there's a way we can stop them, literally in their tracks. The answer's in this useless map here." Scottie's expression hovered between hope and despair. I was sitting on the bed, and Credo had come up and sat beside me, looking up at Scottie, as if to support my case.

"Do you remember that conversation we had after we lost Credo?"

"Aye, I mind it."

"You accused me then of not believing in our expedition to help the Levels folk to drive out the loggers. And then you admitted yourself it would be almost impossible. Do you remember the expression you used to describe how difficult it would be?"

"I canna say I do."

"You said it would be a 'labour of Hercules'. Now the thing about old Hercules was that though the tasks he was given were very difficult he came up with clever ways of doing them. In the country I came from they called it 'lateral thinking'. One task he had was to cleanse the stables of King Augeas."

"I ken that well eneuch. He sindered the rin of a burn."

"That's it. There's your answer. We've got the strongest fiercest burn that ever was here, and when those rains come it will be even stronger. And then there was something Procter said before, like 'it would take some mighty force to push them back'."

"But how wull ye accomplish it Jason? Wi' yer bare hands?"

"Well now, there was something a little bit strange after we'd crossed the river and were heading towards the mountain. It didn't register at the time - we were overwhelmed at the loss of Credo. We went downhill. Normally when you leave a river bank you go uphill as water always finds the lowest course. If you look at the map here you can see why."

I spread the map out on the bed. I traced with my finger the course of the Raffire, how it drained the western forest and the Kaspan hills and was heading towards the basin of the Looshin Levels only to be deflected by the first series of plate-like outcrops that characterised the Tash'kahern mountains. These formed a kind of natural aqueduct which carried the river northwards, to sink eventually into the empty sands of the Ozoora region, or whatever lay beyond the edge of the map. Then I pointed to where the river almost reached the high wall of the main mountain ridge, and where it had overlapped its bank to form the pool from which Credo had escaped. But the main current was deflected northwards again, passing the entrance to the loggers' tunnel and entering a narrow gorge further up. All that was needed was to blast a hole in the bank by the pool and block the gorge higher up and the river would plunge down to the face of the rock, roar through the tunnel and flood out into the levels. At the very least it would make the tunnel unusable, but it could well spread out and make the ground too boggy for the machines to cross.

Fully awake now and wide-eyed Scottie took it all in, and came up on cue with the obvious problem: how in the devil's name would we get our hands on enough explosives. So I described to him Procter's extraordinary collection of materials and equipment right here on the farm. He blinked his bright eyes a couple of times to allow this sudden influx of dynamic information to fully take possession of his faculties and then leapt out of bed, all lithe and lissom in his naked beauty, pushed his hands through his fair hair and pulled on his shirt and pants. "Come awa then laddie. We maun gang speak tae the gude man."

We found Procter in the room he called his study. There were more guns on the walls than books, along with stuffed trophies of the hunt. The rest of the wall space was filled with photographs, mostly family ones. My rapid glance took in one of a barefoot young lass on a beach with fishing boats and fishermen mending their nets, unmistakeably Peglin for all the years between; and it was easy to pick out young Procter from a group of lads, work-men at some pit head or quarry, from his diminutive stature and cocky smile. Old Procter sat at his desk, a battered filing cabinet with one drawer open to its side, examining some documents through thick horn-rimmed spectacles. He peered quizzically up at us as we entered, his eyes enlarged by the lenses.

I pitched straight in, spread the map out in front of him and explained the plan. His response was to open a drawer in the desk and take out a bunch of folded maps, check through them and select one which he then opened and laid on top of mine. It showed the area in question on a much larger scale and greater detail, rather like an Ordnance Survey map, and judging by the symbols and captions at the foot also intended for military use. Procter replaced his spectacles with a magnifying glass and for sev-eral minutes he and I both studied it closely while Scottie, with his aversion to inert, two-dimensional representations of the liv-ing universe, idly inspected the guns and other objects in the room. I was interested to note that the labyrinth of caves was shown, at least in part as some passages ended in dotted lines and others were added in pencil. The position of the loggers' tunnel had also been pencilled in. After intense scrutiny Procter put down the glass and I was suddenly thrust half way across the desk by a powerful slap on the back:

"Lads," he proclaimed, swivelling his chair sideways to take in Scottie, "I congratulate you. This is a truly diabolical plan. It's been staring me in the face and I didn't see it. Peglin said you boys would bring us good news, and that lass, you know, is not often wrong. But there are a couple of problems. She's one of them, but I'll have to sort that out myself. We've got to evacuate the farm and all the stock and rig this whole thing up before the weather gets too bad." As he spoke he went over to a small wardrobe by the door and took out a thick overcoat and a scarf. Scottie helped him on with the coat and he continued:

"First I have to go and talk to the Company. They've been pushing me to sell for long enough now so I should be able to get the terms and conditions we need." So saying he marched out of the room, hardly waiting for us to join him. Scottie managed to find a spare coat and pair of boots in the hall and we tagged along as he strode down the lane towards the main exit gate, Credo trotting behind. A wild energy seemed to possess him.

"But how are you going to get to Company headquarters?" I asked, breathlessly.

"Don't worry, my taxi 'll be along."

"The other thing that's puzzling me," Scottie chipped in, "is where exactly we are all going to move to?"

"Have another look at the map, lad, a bit further up," was the brief reply, and not a very pleasing one in Scottie's case. Finally we reached the gate and Procter turned to us:

"You boys have done your bit for now. To be honest, you've pulled a blinder. Take some time off. Go fishing. Soon as I get back we'll talk again, and start planning." So saying he was off, a lonely figure trekking across the pathless waste, his scarf and coat tails flapping in the breeze.

Wondering what he meant by his taxi we stayed and watched as he receded, in that immense space such a tiny figure for all our destinies to be hanging on. Then we heard a familiar noise, the loud, busy prattle of an engine, and saw one of the Company's hornet-like quad bikes buzzing across the plain towards him. The driver dismounted and challenged him, and a brief exchange ensued. Procter produced no ID card but the guard's manner became suddenly deferential. He ushered the old man into the passenger seat, climbed in, throttled up and drove away.

"It's nae muckle he's latting on tae," Scottie remarked as we strolled back.

"No indeed, he plays his cards close to his chest. But he seems to have worked it all out in no time, unless he already had something in mind."

"God alane kens whaur we'll a' flit tae, and the baists and a'things. The bodach's ither estate lies ain fortnicht's mairch awa. We wad a' be drooned afore we winnit there. And the auld leddy says she wunna move."

"Well Scottie, you could always look on the map, like he suggested, to see what he has in mind."

Scottie gave me a sidelong look, and then said sweetly: "Ye ca' shaw me Jason, ma brither."

We returned to the study where the maps still lay spread on the desk. I traced the cliff-side path north from the tunnel, and just under a mile further came to a place where a short track diverged, cut into the mountain. Where it came to an end fine lines, some printed and some pencilled, indicated another cave system. I pointed it out to Scottie. "We'll hold out there I guess till the weather improves."

We decided to take up Procter's suggestion to go fishing. For some days we had done very little but talking, eating and drinking and playing with the children. It always seemed to me there was no happier life than that of an old established farm and its people. There is always work to be done, sometimes long and hard, and the benefits of good work are directly felt in bodily comforts and wholesome fare. But there is always time for talk, and a never ending fund of good humoured jest and anecdote. It is true that in the present case the experience was clouded with nostalgia for a vanished past and anxiety about an uncertain future, but in such congenial company, young and old alike, the spirits could but rise and banish care, for a while at least.

We were now fully recovered from the trials of our journey and were beginning to feel the need for something more in the way of fresh air and exercise. We walked to a pond that was some distance from the farm buildings. It was a dark and deep pool, trees crowding to its edge, that had not been fished for many years. We had borrowed coarse fishing tackle, sturdy rods, floats made of painted quills in corks, hooks on cat gut weighted with split shot. Scottie fished from a small jetty and I found a relatively clear spot not far away where a mossy willow trunk leaned out from the bank. We sat for hours without exchanging a word, in perfect communion and contentment.

A light breeze ruffled the water and the float seemed to be sailing on a surface rippling with the interplay of light and shade in ceaseless motion. It didn't matter how long you waited for a movement of the float not caused by the wavelets, a sudden run or twitch or plunge. It might never come but you could watch it forever, until you were one with the water and the light, the reeds along the water's edge, and the woods all around.

It was already starting to get dark before we realised we had stayed too long and should be getting back. We had only caught two fish but they were a good size, a carp and a bream. By the time we had packed up and walked the first half of the journey the sun had gone down. Smoke from the farmhouse chimneys came into view, and then the lighted windows. It was a homely and welcoming sight, but the welcome we received went far beyond what was proportionate, either to the success of the expedition or our period of absence. Procter had returned and broken the news to his family and we were greeted as heroes and saviours.

There was a profound relief that outweighed the sadness of leaving the old place. The stalemate was over; that unspoken sense of a surreal afterlife that had hung in the air had evaporated. Now there was hope - the possibility of a new life and the satisfaction of getting even with those who had destroyed the old one. Anxiety remained, but of a different kind, constructive and energising. Everyone was keen to start planning the move. The children were wild with excitement.

At supper we were served the fish we had caught, delicately cooked with fresh herbs and a nutty sauce. The others had to be content with yesterday's stew reheated. Afterwards we talked to Procter again in his study. He had got exactly the terms he wanted from the Company. The sum he would receive for sale of the farm was a handsome one, but more importantly the conditions he had laid down for his leaving it were accepted.

He and his family were to have at least two weeks to vacate the premises and remove their stock and belongings. In their comings and goings for this purpose there were to be no checks or hindrances, and they would leave via the tunnel the Company had drilled through the mountain. The money and title deeds were to be exchanged and the deal concluded at the end of this period, or before if the move was successfully completed sooner. The farm was not to be entered by the Company as old Mrs Prendis had not consented to leave until her eightieth birthday, five days after the expiry date. On that day he and his sons would remove all the mines and booby traps they had planted around the estate, and they and Mrs Prendis would make their final departure.

The Company were delighted with this settlement, not only because it meant that they had secured and could now clear the entire area of the Looshin Levels, but because they believed they had pulled a fast one over their old adversary. They assumed he would be moving to his other holdings on the far side of the Tash'kahern range, where they would in due course be paying him another visit.

We retired that night feeling a good day's work had been done, and that if we achieved as much progress every day we would soon be masters of the universe.

CHAPTER 12

Exodus

THE FOLLOWING day a party set out to the caves to see how much space was available and how they could be adapted as temporary living quarters. The group consisted of Procter and his sons, daughters, sons- and daughters-in-law, and their older children. Scottie and I volunteered to stay behind to look after the younger ones and keep Peglin company. The decisions and business involved in the move, we felt, were domestic and farming matters and as guests we should just make ourselves useful in any way we could. Maralese also stayed behind to look after the very youngest while Scottie and I organised games and activities for the rest.

Scottie's forte was devising things from the miscellaneous junk lying around in the workshop. He got them in teams making miniature steam turbine engines from tins with pin holes, to see which one would run the longest. And then together they made a jet boat on the same principle. Rooting around I found a thick rubber ball, probably from a stop tap in a cattle trough, and there followed one of the craziest games of football in the history of the sport.

From time to time I popped in to see Peglin and take her a drink, or whatever she needed. She was quite content to sit in the sunny window seat, knitting winter jumpers for her grandchildren. She talked about them and the family as if nothing unusual were taking place, or ever could to disturb the immemorial order of the farm. I mentioned I'd seen a picture of her as a young girl

in Procter's study and that started her on her childhood memories as a fisherman's daughter, and how she'd first met Procter
when she was gutting fish with a gang of other girls. He was full
of life and fun and everyone loved him, but he'd picked her out
straightaway and said it with his eyes. Her hand had slipped and
she cut herself and he'd taken her aside and lovingly bandaged
the wound, and they'd been bound together ever since. It was a
touching story, but it also troubled me because her lifelong loyalty
to Procter was now in conflict with her vow never to leave the
farm. She saw my concern and said:

"Now my dear, you mustn't worry about Procter and me. He's
a good man, and we've always found a way through our troubles."

"We're all dependent on Procter now," I said. "It's a big responsibility he bears."

"He'll do what's right, you can be sure of that."

This exchange led me to probe a little further. I said how much
I admired her courage in standing up to the loggers. "I'm an obsti-
nate old biddy is what you mean," she grinned. "No," I insisted,
mentally comparing her indomitable spirit to my own defeatism.
"But there's one thing about this whole logging business that
really puzzles me."

"What's that my dear?" she asked. "I may not be as wise in these
matters as the old fellow, but I've got a brain in my head and have
plenty of time to think about things while I'm knitting socks for
the little'uns."

"Well it's this. Why would the loggers go to all the trouble of
blasting a great corridor and building a road through the mountains to cut down all the forest on the other side when they could
just approach by the Western Highway? And if we do succeed in
flushing them out of the Levels what's to stop them doing that
anyway?"

She was silent for a moment and I wondered if I had trespassed
too far into the speculative world of affairs. But then she screwed
up her eyes to gimlet points and put the matter to me quite clearly,
in her own way:

"Jobu. Now he's the boss and what he says goes. But he's careful, and he's cunning, and like all bullies he's afraid. There's them as thinks he didn't come to be master by fair means. And there's them who thinks there's no harm in the lads and lasses as fly their bird machines and there's worse ado in Zinn than that. And then there's them as thinks there's no harm in the forest folk as keeps themselves to themselves and says good morning tidy when they go hunting and riding there and offers a drop and shows 'em the way. So Jobu takes just one little step at a time. He says just the Looshin – the people are hungry, we need more food. Then he says we need a road to bring it in and come and go. Then it'll be we need this bit for that reason and that bit for this reason. And all the time he's using the cash to buy people off and get the army behind him. And when the time comes that it's all a mess he says we'll scrape the plate clean and there's no one left to gainsay him. Now if all them great bulldozers and God knows what were to come a roaring and rattling down the Western Highway and stopping all the traffic, everyone would see what he's about and would nip it in the bud. They could nip him out. That's the way of it."

It was a comprehensive reply to a question I hadn't wanted to put to Procter, just in case, unlikely though that would be, he didn't have it covered.

The party returned in animated discussion, which continued through the evening. For once there was no cooked meal and we contented ourselves with bread and cheese and cold meats and pickles, and any amount of ale to wash it down. Instead the table was covered with notes people had made and a large plan showing the spaces available and to be allocated for various purposes. There was a row of bell shaped caverns, the largest of which, all agreed, should be reserved for the horses, and sections of the boundary fence could be used to enclose the entrance. There were indications that the caves had been inhabited before, and an inner chamber had a scorched area on the floor below a natural funnel that vented through a side shaft to the open air. This would be the kitchen and general living area.

Then there was a lot of debate about the allocation of the remaining chambers according to age, sex and family units, and a compromise was eventually worked out. The spaces were all connected by tunnels, and other tunnels wandered off into the interior of the mountain. These were cool and would be handy for storage of provisions and such possessions it was decided to take – a wagon load for each family it was agreed. Beyond this it was decided to seal off the caves to prevent straying or adventurous children from getting lost.

Finally someone said but what about Jason and Scottie and I said we'd be happy to hang from the ceiling with the bats. That didn't go down too well with some of the younger children who had been frightened by older siblings with tales of vampires, so it was quickly decided that we should sleep in the kitchen, keep the fire in and half an eye open for any untoward creatures of the night. Credo and the other hounds would also keep guard.

Procter absented himself from debate on the finer points and walked out in the evening light. Having had a preliminary reconnoitre of the site of operations I guessed his mind would be working on the problems it presented and selecting the materiél required for the job.

It was by now, I supposed, mid to late October by the Gregorian calendar and the weather could turn nasty at any moment, making work with explosives and electrical equipment in the open air very difficult, if not too dangerous to contemplate. I was restless too, and stayed up with Scottie till after the others had retired. I could see he was tired so I sent him to bed to get his beauty sleep and said that I'd wait for Procter. I sat for some time watching the last glowing embers in the fire fade away, wondering what all this was leading to. It reached the point where I started to doubt the reality of everything around me and happening to me and then to doubt if I was real myself. So I got up stiffly, put on a coat and went out into the keen air to find the old man.

He was in his devil's kitchen as I suspected he would be, or rather in and out of it as he heaved boxes and crates of stuff on to a wagon drawn up outside, a carthorse harnessed between the shafts. We worked together for a couple of hours without a break, loading the wagon, covering it and parking it in a barn, and then bringing out, loading and parking another. After we'd put the horses in the stable with some fresh hay and water I was exhausted and even Procter was showing signs of wear and tear, mopping his brow with a grimy towel. There was a smell of frost in the air. "We'll ship this lot out at first light," he said. "Get some kip in the parlour and I'll rouse you."

I lay down on the sofa and was soon asleep. It was still dark when Procter woke me. I got up quickly, put on my boots and coat and went through to the kitchen. Kombard, the eldest, and Leevil were there, dark and muffled, and there were guns on the table. Cold air blew in through the open door, where the first grey light could be seen beyond the tracery of trees. The wagons were already brought up; I could hear the clink of the horses' hooves and the creak of straining timber. The other three picked up weapons and filled their pockets with ammo from a box on the floor, gesturing me to do likewise. Noting my slight hesitation Leevil said, "Don't worry, it's just a precaution." I smiled at him and at myself, thinking I've seen enough Westerns to know that you don't take a wagon train of explosives through hostile territory unarmed. Kombard found me a thick woollen hat and a scarf and we went out into the harsh dawn air where the horses' breath was steaming, as was ours.

We clambered up on to the driving boards and put our guns on the covers behind us, ready to hand. Procter and Leevil led off and we trundled after, taking it at a steady walking pace. About half way down the lane a small dark figure flitted from the bushes and leapt aboard beside me. I looked down and saw Tamon, his eyes big with entreaty and finger on his lips. I didn't think Kombard had noticed until he said, "Well then young man you'd better hop off when we get to the gate or I'll warrant your granddad will have something to say, and your father maybe take his belt to you." "Hold on," I said, "this lad's useful. He clouted a guard and saved our dog's life." "OK Jason but you'll have to square it with 'em. I've said my say. It's your call." We passed through the farm gates out on to the bleak expanse of the dawn washed Levels, that

graveyard of ancestral memories that seemed mine now as much
as theirs, and as dreary and dismal a sight as I had ever beheld.

Tamon's rites of passage soon came to be tested. The track we
followed was miry and rutted and the horses were straining under
the heavy load. We had to dismount, with one of us leading and
the other guiding from the tail to avoid potholes. Then we got
stuck, and the others drew up and came back to give us a hand.
Tamon tried to dodge round the wagon but Leevil spotted him
and yelled "Come here you young rascal I told you NO you were
NOT coming," and grabbed him roughly by the collar. I was
about to stick up for him, but this time Procter interceded, and
held up his hand. "Leave him be son. If he wants to be a man and
work with us we'll soon give him a chance. We'll see what he's
made of." "Aye but his mother will worry herself to death," said
Leevil. Procter smiled and shook his head. "Come on my boys,"
addressing us all including Tamon, who was quietly waiting to see
if wrath would descend upon him. "Men must plough and
women weep." And so saying he returned to the leader and we
hauled onwards.

For a good hour we toiled across the Levels. Procter had told us
to keep a sharp lookout for any sign of the company's men who
might get wind of what was going on. All was quiet until we were
within sight of the ramp to the tunnel and we heard the sudden
yammering crescendo of an approaching helicopter. Procter
immediately halted and stood up on the driving board, training his
binoculars on the intruder. It banked and veered away, and was
soon lost in distance and silence.

The ramp was a heavy haul but the tunnel itself was level and
firm. The horses' hooves echoed and re-echoed weirdly as we
plodded steadily towards the growing semi-circle of light. Once
through, the ground was rocky and there were some steep lifts,
but the going was good and we soon reached the spot that Procter had chosen to stow the goods. It was a small detached cave
about eighty yards from the blast point he had chosen to block the
river, this a narrowing in the gorge with overhanging cliffs which
he'd pointed out to us as we passed. The cave was a good six feet

above the level of the track so two had to lift the crates and two drag them in as each wagon was brought up. Tamon led and steadied the horses who were responsive to his gentle control.

We found a rock pool to water the horses and left them to forage while we shared the sandwiches and flasks Leevil had brought for us. Then it was agreed that Kombard and I should return with the wagons, leaving Leevil in charge of the gear and allowing Procter more time to recce the site. Again there was a battle of wills over whether Tamon should be allowed to stay. Procter said he could make use of the lad and I promised to reassure Maribe that he was safe, but not wishing to challenge Leevil's parental authority further we left the decision to him. After a moment's grim thought his rigid features eased a little and he chucked his son under the chin.

"All right my boy, but you stay close to your granddad and do EXACTLY what he tells you." The boy gave his dad a grateful hug. Kombard was already waiting in the first wagon so I climbed up and took the reins of the second and we rattled off. Mostly downhill and unloaded, the journey back was easy enough. After days of unsettled weather a pale sun had risen, the last glimmer of summer, giving Procter the precious opportunity he needed.

Back at the farm everything was being turned inside out and upside down. Several marital and generational debates, some heated, were taking place simultaneously about what favourite, necessary or indispensable articles must be taken or had to be left. Poor Scottie was in the thick of it, being asked to decide, at the point of arrival, whether the pink or the blue dress suited the hussy best. He berated me for deserting him. I reminded him of the abuse I had received the last time I had tried to rouse him before he had completed his natural sleep cycle. We made it up over a cup of tea and slices of fruit cake. Then he was called away to help with the repair and recommissioning of a retired wagon, more congenial work for him and a welcome relief from arbitration.

Having had so little sleep and already done half a day's work I pleaded the right to retire and recoup my strength. I hardly slept but pretended to be fast asleep when Scottie came in so that I could kick and curse when he tried to wake me. Tamon had come panting back with a list of more gear that Proctor needed - rope, clamps, rags, tins of grease, more reels of cable, tarpaulins, with details of where to find it. And not forgetting food and drink. We were to load the cart, harness the cob and make all speed.

Tamon didn't wait but ran off again before his mother could catch him. I remembered my promise and reassured her as best I could. The problem was not just Tamon going but others wanting to go as well, and the unfairness of it. Edging out of maternal earshot I whispered that they would have to do really hard stuff if they came. "Like what?' they asked dismissively. "Like walking on a tight rope across the Raffire," I replied; whereupon the crowd of eager volunteers somehow melted away.

Scottie and I loaded up, Credo jumped on board, and we took the journey at a brisk trot, arriving at the designated flashpoint in under an hour. Procter and Tamon were on the opposite side of the river, crouching on the rock. Procter was tapping with a hammer, listening, and putting in markers here and there, explaining it all to his eager apprentice as he went along. We waited, not wanting to disturb their concentration, until he saw we'd arrived and shouted across to us to bring the stuff we'd brought up to the footbridge where they'd meet us. So we drove back along the route that had brought us to the Levels, past scenes of disaster and deliverance, till we got to the bridge and waited for the others to arrive. Also troubled, no doubt, by recent memories of the scene, Credo lay low and still in the back of the cart.

With a slight allusion to my previous performance on the bridge Scottie insisted that he would take the gear over himself, piece by piece. I was happy to concede a point in exchange for this exemption. When Scottie returned from the last load he told me Procter's instructions were to drop off the rest of the load at the storage cave and then that Leevil should return in the cart and try to instil some order into proceedings at the farm. Too much attention was being given to personal effects and not enough to provisions, and the logistics of survival in the caves and the journey ahead. Then there was the problem of stock: it couldn't all be taken.

I was to be on guard duty and told to pick up a whistle and Procter's field glasses from the storage cave. I was to check the tunnel from time to time and keep my eyes and ears open for any sound of a vehicle or helicopter, and blow the whistle if I noticed anything suspicious. And I was to be on hand if anything more was needed. Scottie and Tamon would stay with Procter.

I returned to the storage dump to pick up Leevil and drove him to the far side of the tunnel, where he took the reins and we parted. I stayed there some time, taking a good look across the Levels and scanning the heavens. Nothing moved. Just bland everyday ordinariness, as though nothing ever would or could happen but the passing of time.

I walked back, picked up the food hamper we'd left at the entrance and took it to the cave. I moved a couple of crates to where they were out of sight and then sat and listened, trying to filter out the noise of the river from any incongruous sound, concentrating so as to become sensitised to whatever else was happening. Then I went back to the operational site to see if I was needed there.

I could hardly watch. All three of them were hanging on ropes just inches above the racing current which seemed to want to leap up and drag them in. Scottie was leaning back, his feet almost touching the water, to put his full weight on an auger which he was turning to drill into the rock. After a few grinding turns he'd take the drill out, strap it to his belt then unstrap a long chisel and a lump hammer, insert it in the hole and pound with mighty force. Tamon was half way inside a narrow fissure, reaching into it, while Procter supplied him with tubes of dynamite which the boy rammed in deep with a wooden pole. Procter then grappled sideways and handed Scottie dynamite and a detonator fuse to put into his completed hole, whereupon he began drilling another about a foot further, and Procter abseiled up again to refill his pouch. I yelled over to ask if there was anything they needed. He shook his head and glanced up to signal for me to keep up my watch.

Fearful of heights and feeling a little queasy I was glad to be dismissed. I went along to the cave entrance which was the optimum point for seeing or hearing any unwelcome approach. It occurred to me that the piles of rock from the excavation presented an obstacle to the river's smooth entry into the tunnel but could be turned to advantage if all shifted and banked up to one side. I walked down and had a look at the various mechanical shovels and diggers parked there. I found one unlocked, lightly dressed lovelies adorning its interior, and another even had the keys in. Feeling I'd made a more positive contribution than just keeping watch I went back to my post, rested, waited and listened, perhaps for a couple of hours. Then I saw the three dynamiters approaching, Tamon now walking with the same swaggering confidence as his granddad. The latter gave me the thumbs up sign as he came up. "So far so good," he said.

We went back to the cave and tucked into the contents of the hamper. I'd never seen Scottie so exhausted. He lay back with closed eyes pouring water over his dusty face and into his mouth. Little Tamon began nodding and Procter made him a bed of coats to rest on. "He certainly cut the mustard," I said. Procter nodded. He at least seemed to be going strong still so I told him my idea about banking the rubble at the tunnel. It met with his approval but the wiring had to be done first while the weather held. He took a grubby notebook and stub of pencil from his pocket to explain to me how it was all supposed to work. The object was to throw as much rock in the river as possible at one go. Too little, the river would push it aside, and taking it out one layer at a time, as in quarrying, would attract the enemy's attention before the whole job was completed. The method was to make a semi-circular row of insertions as far down the rock and deep into it as possible, and the same on the top surfaces so as to send in simultaneous horizontal and vertical shock waves. The result would be to unseat and dislodge hundreds of tons of rock and tip them into the gorge, and the presence of loose shaley seams in the rock structure made him optimistic of this outcome.

But there was a chance of an airblast, sending out fragments of rock in all directions and a massive, unabsorbed shockwave without penetrating the inner core. Given the quantity of dynamite they were packing in this could prove lethal within a range of a hundred yards.

Taking in this grim scenario I asked about the second part of the operation: collapsing the bank so that the river could diverge into the tunnel. The demolition side of it, I gathered, was relatively simple as there was a weak point in the ridge that held back the river and the backsurge from the blockage would increase the force of the current pushing against it. The problem was insufficient cable to stretch right back to the cave, so a second detonation station would have to be set up.

Leaving the other two to get some rest Procter and I boarded the cart for a tour of inspection. On the opposite side of the gorge was now a row of plugged holes and crevices connected by cable. All the connections were heavily taped and wrapped in greased bands. We went on to the tunnel and I showed Procter where the rocks could be shifted to deflect the force of the current. Then we continued to the sharp bend in the river where a pool had formed and looked at the base of the ridge. It was deeply fissured and Procter had already crammed it with explosives, the fuses poking out ready to be connected to the main line. Undoubtedly the river would have broken through here itself in the course of time, but we needed a flood, not a leak. Finally we crossed the footbridge and walked up the other side to inspect the day's work. A corresponding semi-circle of drills and fills had been made on the level surface at the top of the cliff, and a short shaft further down had been packed for good measure. Procter checked all the contacts and then we threw branches and gravel over the site so nothing would be visible from the air.

By now the pheasants were settling to roost and the first owls hallooing their doom laden prophesies from the darkening woods. Walking back we plotted the next day's proceedings. Procter and the other two would stay overnight to make an early start and I would return to the farm to tell them all was well, and get Kombard and Bilder to come out in the morning to help with the rest of the preparations. I would follow later with the first wagon train carrying food and other essentials to store in the inner caves. By then, all being well, the bulk of the engineering work would be finished and we could concentrate on setting up the encampment. We parted company at the mouth of the tunnel and I trekked back along the trail towards the farm.

At the farm operations were proceeding more smoothly, and I took advantage of my redundancy to the proceedings to take a bath and get a good night's rest. The men left early and by noon I and three wives were heading out in a train of four wagons laden with provisions. We rolled up to the caves where we were joined by Scottie and the others who helped with the unloading. Procter and Tamon were not to be seen so I went off in search of them. All the drilling, filling and wiring had been completed at the gorge, the plugs now forming a broad grin, and a cable had been thrown across the river (calling on Scottie's casting techniques I learnt) and running up to the operations cave. Further along, mid way between the two blast sites, the second detonation point had been set up, caged in with weld mesh from the farm boundary fence. Inside I found Procter and Tamon crouched on the floor staring into a box with a maze of multi-coloured wiring in it.

"Hell of it is," said Procter as though I'd been there all along, "I've had to use every scrap of cable I can find from all over the place and none of it matches up. Colour coding's all different . . . army rubbish . . ." After staring at it, poking and muttering for a full minute, he replaced the lid and screwed it down. He pointed to a plug at the end of the cable stretching up to the blast point and said, "If I've got it right when we connect that plug we're in business and ready to go. If I've got it wrong we're dead." I felt a sudden emptiness inside and even Procter for once looked uneasy. "You two push off," he said, but before I could move Tamon picked up the plug and shoved it in the socket, squeezing his eyes closed as he did it.

Silence.

Procter wiped his sweating brow with his sleeve. He eyed us both fiercely. "Not a word," he said.

Over the following days the exodus continued, the wagons plying to and fro carrying out stocks of meat, fruit, preserves and vegetables, barrels and bottles of drink, medicines, furnishings, timber, tools, personal effects, and as the living quarters took shape, family members themselves. The small children were lifted up, dressed in their warm coats and woolly hats and clutching favourite toys or dolls like wartime refugees. Procter never returned to the farm, so I asked what he wanted of his own. Apart from his clothes and a box full of photos and documents, there was only his collection of guns. All the farm equipment had to be abandoned except the wagons themselves; the horses were also needed for the journey on. Then there were pets and a few individual favourites among the livestock considered *hors d'agriculture.*

As for the rest of the stock it would have been impossible to drive it all the way to the distant estate which was the final destination. Slaughter would have been kinder than to abandon it to the floods or the loggers but no one had the heart. After much debate we herded all through the tunnel and on to higher ground where there was forage and shelter among the trees, with two wagon loads of hay, and left the poor creatures to take their chance in the wild.

The only remaining, and unspoken, problem was Peglin. Procter seemed to have some solution in mind but no one was quite sure. I went in to see her from time to time and she seemed quite content, and willing to talk about how the move was going as if it had no bearing on herself. I was the last to leave, and looked in on her again before doing so. I didn't like to say goodbye as it would have implied, or confirmed, that she really did intend to sacrifice herself on the altar of her sublime obstinacy - and that this was acceptable. "Well, be seeing you again soon," I said cheerily. "Aye, in this world or the next. Take care my dear," was her not altogether reassuring reply.

It was rather hoped than assumed that Procter would come back with her after he had been up to Company headquarters to collect his money and hand over the title deeds. But when this day came, he returned alone.

CHAPTER 13

Fire and Water

THE SKIES were darkening menacingly and intermittent rain had made heavy work of getting the last wagon loads through. Everyone was anxious now to settle into the new family abode, and there was all the bustle and excitement of a camping expedition. The womenfolk were re-establishing domestic order while the men relaxed after their exertions, taking a drink or two and contributing when required or ordered to do so. The children were at a high pitch of excitement and everyone was keyed up in advance of the big bang. Procter asked Leevil and Kombard to go out and recommission two of the machines parked in the tunnel and shift the waste rock at the mouth of the tunnel to form an embankment, thus sealing off a return to the estate. "And what about our mother?" said Kombard. Procter replied:

"You know I could never abandon her. Let us just say I have made what arrangements I can. I believe - I hope and pray - she will join us later. But there's too much at stake for everything to founder on one old woman's tenacity. That's all I can say about it for now. You'll have to trust me, and her, and fate."

On the first night of full occupancy there was a thunderstorm and it was clear that the season of rain had finally arrived. As soon as the children were in bed Procter called a conference and explained that the blasting would take place at first light; with the risk of damp seepage it could not be delayed any longer. The children were to be kept in their beds and Tamon was to be tied to his if necessary. "I've used a hell of a lot of dynamite," he said, "and there is an element of risk. If I don't come back Kombard, my eldest, will take my place as head of the family. Now I need one assistant." All the brothers and Scottie put their hands up. Procter looked thoughtful for a moment, then turned to me and asked my opinion. I said, "If there is an element of risk, and I'm sure it's a very small one, Scottie is too young to die, and your sons and son in law have got family responsibilities. There's one person here with no dependents; a useless wanderer, whose crackpot idea this was in the first place. You have to choose him." Procter eyed me shrewdly and nodded slowly. "I'll wake you," he said. "The rest stay inside and keep everyone else inside."

Procter didn't need to wake me - I hardly slept. In truth I was far from easy about the outcome. I had seen too much of the constraints and complexities of the operation. We were too close; there was no margin for error and no plan B. I got up, dressed, and went through to the cave entrance. Procter was sitting there staring out into the dark. Did he ever sleep? I pulled up a chair and sat by him for some time, listening to the steady roar of the river. It had rained heavily in the night and the world, inside and out, seemed too impenetrably dismal for any enterprise ever to be succeed.

My existential doubts were gnawing into me again. Was Procter having second thoughts? He wasn't giving anything away. He seemed to have turned to stone. Then, without the rest of him moving, his arm swung robotically towards me holding a hip flask. I took a swig and handed it back to him. Then I must have nodded off because I woke up with a start and there was light, or some feeble substitute for it, filling the cave mouth and defining the now familiar scene in front of me. Procter was on his feet. We put on heavy waterproofs and boots and set off without a word.

We reached the explosives cave and climbed the ladder into it. A wall of empty crates weighted with rocks had been built across the mouth with a narrow observation port. Procter removed a tarpaulin to reveal an old fashioned plunger-type detonator with cables running into it. "You take this one," he said. He handed me a pair of earmuffs and told me to lie down flat, and continued:

"When you hear my whistle put on the ear muffs, press the green button, then push the plunger down slow and steady. If nothing happens push the red button and wait."

"Right, got that," I said.

"Good man. Don't do anything till you hear the whistle. About three minutes."

Procter left and I peered through the gap in the crates towards the neck of the gorge. The bare rock, glistening wet and black, seemed utterly impervious, the muted thunder of the river below constant, imperturbable. I felt deep down that nothing would or could happen. The world is as it is. The course of things cannot be changed, at least not by me. But even while this was going through my head I was repeating the drill to myself: whistle, earmuffs, green button, plunger; whistle, earmuffs, green button, plunger; whistle, earmuffs, green button, whistle ... "My God that was the whistle. What's next? Green button, no – earmuffs . Stay calm. Start again. Whistle – had that; ear muffs – put them on, green button, press, now plunger – slow, steady."

Something clicked inside the box and staring out I could see fire inside the guts of the rocks, darting out. Everything cracked and split apart. For a second I thought I'd been electrocuted. In slow motion I saw the cliffs of the gorge unfold and rocks the size of lorries just lift and hang, and then a sonic boom and white water rearing up and fishes flung high into the air like flames in the reflected light of the fire. Then the counter shock wave from Procter's blast hit me and I blacked out.

When vision returned the scene framed by the observation port was unchanged, but for one detail. The neck of the gorge had disappeared and been replaced by a circular funnel half filled with broken rock. There was no sound. I realised I still had the ear muffs on and took them off and heard again the noise of a great mass of water in motion, but now more distant. I got up, feeling shaky and light headed, dusted myself down, and carefully descended the ladder. The whole area was covered with dust and splintered rock. I looked down the track in the direction of the tunnel and saw the distant figure of Procter, standing on top of the embankment facing away from me.

As I walked towards him and the bend in the river came into view I saw that the level was low and the surface calm. I passed the sandbagged wire mesh cage, dusty but intact. The noise of water grew louder at every step and I thought Procter hadn't heard my approach until I had clambered half way up the rocky slope. Then he turned and held out his hand to help me up, with the widest grin I had ever seen on his or any face. We would have had to shout to hear each other but words weren't necessary. The river now was tumbling over rapids where Credo's pool had been, rushing up almost to our feet in a great gurgling whirlpool before rolling into the tunnel, filling up to almost half its height. A mighty back slap from Procter might have precipitated me into the torrent if a fierce firm handshake had not accompanied it.

His euphoria was also mine. For the first time in my life I felt powerful. I had played my part in something fundamental and consequential – I hardly knew how to express it, a primal event, a creational happening. And it felt entirely right. The river of wrath was angry no more but jubilant, pouring into the Looshin Levels, its true destination. For millennia it had been curbed and deflected, condemned at last to failure and oblivion. Now it would bring life back to a desecrated land, and then through the south western pass spread its generous waters to the fields and pastures and plains beyond. So many people, young and old, strong, wise, honest, beautiful people, who asked no more than freedom from want and oppression and to live and love in peace, would rejoice at this day.

For a brief instant the immutable laws had been suspended: mountains moved, water flowed uphill, and fishes flew in the air.

Everyone was up when we returned to base. The blast and tremor would have roused the dead. They were all waiting at the top of the ramp and we raised our four thumbs skywards as we approached. There was cheering and waving and the children and dogs came running down to meet us. The weather seemed to have taken its cue from our activities, distant flashes and rolling thunder indicating more rain was on the way. Despite this everyone wanted to go down and inspect the blast areas and see the river flowing into the tunnel. Some already had their boots and oilskins on.

But Procter would have none of it. He made everybody go inside. As ever he was thinking a stage or two ahead in the game. Besides which, we were ready for our breakfast. Scottie came over and hugged me. I could see he hadn't slept and his fair features were drawn with unwonted care, now overlaid with relief. "Ye were a'ways a sonsie callant," he confirmed. I had so many kisses and handshakes from them all my dizziness began to return. Procter grappled my hand again. "We did it son." "Yes," I said, "we did, but we've raised hell." He replied with his sly grimace: "Hell is there to be raised."

After a hearty breakfast cooked on our open fire Procter addressed the whole tribe and outlined his concerns. "Some folk are bad losers," he explained. "We don't know whether we've winged them or fatally wounded them yet, but either way we can expect retaliation."

"Company or Army?" Kombard asked.

"Either, or both. We have to stay here till the rain eases and it's safe to move into the open. We're well armed, our position is defensible, and it would be almost impossible for them to get men on the ground for a month at least."

"They could fire on us from the choppers," said Leevil.

"That's the risk. Even random firing could go through these screens and hit someone. We have to have a constant watch day and night. Any sign of danger the whistle blows and everyone moves back into the main storage cave. We'll need a door in the back wall."

The rest of the day was spent on these arrangements. A guard box was built with observation ports in three sides and a glass panel in the roof made from scraping the foil from the back of a mirror. A guard duty rota and an evacuation plan were worked out. We walled up one of the small cave openings with rocks to make a pill box from which it would be possible to observe even under fire. I took an evening watch but had nothing to report, except that the rain was getting heavier.

The next day Bilder was on guard and the whistle blew. We all heard the noisy flap flap of a helicopter coming directly over. Everyone retreated into the catacombs except, as agreed, Procter and myself, who took up our stations in the pill box. The machine veered to the right, circled and came in low, hovering over the tunnel entrance then moving up and hovering over the collapsed gorge. Then it came up and drew level with us, its scything rotors battering the caves with noise and air waves. The horses were whinnying and clattering their hooves in the stalls. We could see the crew, one at the controls and the other with glasses trained on us. Then it lifted away and disappeared. They'd seen everything now, we agreed.

Day after day the rain got heavier till it was coming down in sheets continuously. Seen from the guard box the river had now risen above the embankment and flooded back up into the gorge and was only forty yards from the start of the ramp. Inside the mountain too, water was flowing above and below us. There were drips and puddles everywhere and it sounded as though all the taps had been left on. Keeping warm and dry became a daily struggle, and it was easy to see why previous cave dwellers had moved on. Luckily the fire flue stayed dry, and we had laid in a good supply of dry timber to burn.

This was a wearisome and worrying time, keeping our spirits up and the children amused. Morning lessons were organised; otherwise there were books, pets and games, and endless stories. Even I was getting to the end of my stock, though certain favourites seemed capable of endless repetition. No one knew how long the rain would last. It had been known to continue through to winter, when it changed to snow. Apart from letting the dogs out and brief sanitary operations we stayed put.

Two weeks passed. Still there was no let up, and it was getting cold. Any sense of triumph had long since evaporated. Dullness and lethargy took possession of our souls. It was hard to bestir ourselves, as night and day blended in universal gloom, and the endless boom of the river and pelting of the rain slowly wore us away. Procter was saturnine and taciturn. He spoke only to insist on the rota being kept up, though most thought the likelihood of attack had long since passed. If the Company had been forced to give up what good would attacking us do them?

There was even an element of questioning and silent dissent in some quarters, mixed up with anxiety about Peglin's fate. Had the old fellow got it right about the Company's intentions and the need for this drastic solution? Scottie and I held firm to our faith in him. The only other solid loyalist was Tamon, and the four of us shared most of the guard duty as the rota began to slip. Without exercise or work or external stimuli all was sad and desultory. We were just going through the motions of being alive.

One morning the rain eased and the sky lightened a little, though still overcast. Tamon was on guard duty, Credo keeping him company, the rest of us huddled around the fire waiting for a pot of porridge to boil, like savages round their cauldron. Then the boy came running in blowing the whistle as loud as he could. "Granddad," he said, "there's a big one coming." Procter leapt up and roared at everyone to get back - into the store cave, open the door and right back as far as possible. I made towards the pillbox but he grabbed my arm and pulled me back with the others.

The noise of the helicopter came up loud and menacing, drowning out every other sound. Then another sound obliterated that, and sense itself: a sustained ear-splitting hammering, like a rock drill but heavier, faster, and a metallic shrieking descant. It seemed to be punching its way closer to us every second, and we instinctively retreated into the darkness, pushing the children in first and putting our hands over their ears. The dogs whined and crawled into hollows and behind rocks. It came and went in a wave, lasting perhaps two minutes but seeming to go on and on. Then came a barrage of violent explosions and smoke and dust forced us further in. We remained motionless, in the choking blackness, hardly able or daring to breathe.

After several minutes of silence the air began to clear a little. Procter tapped my shoulder and he and I went together through into the living quarters, scarves covering our mouths.

Through the murk still hanging in the air the sight was horrifying. The screens were smashed to pieces and everything was ripped and torn to shreds, blackened and smouldering. Clothes, toys, dolls, all in rags; furniture, utensils, battered to pieces and even the cauldron in fragments, its contents spilled on the fire. The walls were scored as though some giant beast had clawed them and shells lay everywhere. We stamped out the burning debris and went along the passage connecting to the livestock cavern, dreading what we would find. The wire mesh fence had been slashed open as if with a maniac's blade and the eviscerated remains of the horses and other beasts lay in a lake of their own blood. We stood and looked and turned away. The Augean stables had returned to haunt us.

When we went back into the kitchen the others had already come through, moving around listlessly, poking among the wreckage as though something might still be salvaged. I followed Procter to the entrance where he scanned the heavens. "Will they be back?" I asked.

"I doubt it. It was a surprise attack. They wouldn't have expected anyone to survive."

"If that was a Zinnian ship we're in trouble."

He shook his head. "Nah. The Zinnians are bastards all right but they're medieval bastards. The Company must have hired it, or called on their friends. Which means either they're still in business, or they're prepared to throw good money after bad for the sake of revenge."

We went back into the kitchen and he announced:

"Right my boys and girls. Time for another pow-wow. Find somewhere to sit down without setting your arses on fire and listen up." They settled themselves as best they could around the walls, but not Kombard and Bilder, who remained standing; between them they measured at least two and a half foot higher than Procter. It was clear their rebellion was about to come into the open. Kombard spoke:

"First of all, Father, perhaps you could explain to us what has just happened."

"Certainly, my son. We have had a visit from an Apache heli-copter gunship, an American warplane, armed with rockets and a rapid firing multi-barrelled machine gun – one of the most lethal war machines ever devised."

Kombard replied with stern dignity: "Father, you know we hon-our you and always will. But Bilder and I, and perhaps Leevil too, feel you have made bad decisions and led us astray. We are trapped in these miserable caves surrounded by the charred ruins of our lives. If we try to escape, that thing could come back and tear us to ribbons. We cannot reach our mother, and she may be dead. The children are terrified out of their wits. We believe it is time for a change of leadership. The fact is you started a war, and you've lost it."

Procter replied in equally measured terms: "Kombard my son. I am proud of you and all my children and grandchildren. You will make a fine leader, but your time has not yet come. You know nothing of war my son, and I am glad of it, and pray that you never will. I pray that none of you will ever have to see what I have seen, or do what I have done. But I will tell you one thing about war: the winner is the one left standing. I ask you all to trust me just one more time, and to follow me one last time. And we will find out who the winner is in this war." Then after a pause: "Those in favour?"

Tamon and the other childrens' hands went up straight away, followed by the adults, one by one with increasing hesitation, and then Leevil and Bilder, and finally Kombard.

"Right. Fall in my gallant comrades," said Procter, "and we'll get started." He marched through to the store cave and rooted around for his chest of documents. He dragged it out, lifted the lid and sorted through till he found what he was looking for. It was a map, which he spread out on the top of the chest. Then he opened another of his crates, prising up the nailed lid with his knife. All watched and waited. He got out a tapered baton with a thick greasy looking top, and then took a box of matches from his pocket, struck one and held it under the greasy top. After a few seconds it lit up into a bright flare. Holding this over the map he scrutinised it for several minutes, then folded it and placed it in his pocket.

"Right," he said. "I want volunteers to be torch bearers." There was a chorus of young voices, "me," "I will," "let me," "please Granddad." Procter lit six more torches one after the other and handed them out, and then handed out unlit ones to all the others who had not been forcibly removed from the muster by their parents. "You lot will have to take over when the first ones burn out," he explained. "And no messing around with them!" So saying he raised his torch and led the way into the darkness, and all of us, and the dogs as well, followed trustingly in his footsteps.

In the lurid torchlight the caves receded ahead of us in a weird succession of ghostly gothic vaults and arches. The smaller children held tight to their parents, while the eyes of the older ones were big with wonder, and a sense of their responsibility as torchbearers. In marked contrast to mine and Scottie's wanderings in the caves Procter seemed to know exactly where he was going, taking a left hand fork or a right, or drawing us in Indian file through a crevice barely a foot wide, without a moment's hesitation. We hiked on for about half an hour. The flares were burning low and red and young arms beginning to droop when we turned sharply and saw up ahead a tiny jagged disk of daylight. A cheer went up from the leaders, and passed down the line. The disk grew larger and brighter and it was not only daylight but something we hadn't seen for an age and lifted up our hearts.

Sunshine.

Then Procter suddenly stopped and turned round. "Squad HALT!" he barked. "No one moves, no one speaks, till I give the order to advance. Understood?" So saying he walked forward towards the light. I had to admire his grasp of practical psychology. This game of soldiers and then the business of giving the children the torches - already the shock of recent events was fading from their minds, and their grandfather's protective authority and control re-establishing itself. For several minutes Procter stood there alone, gazing into the light. Then he raised his arm and waved it from side to side and turned to us and yelled, "Forward men." We came out on a broad apron of rock and the most wonderful sight greeted our eyes.

A great expanse of water spread before us as far as the eye could see. In the remote distance a pale grey ribbon could be mountains or clouds. Gulls flew over on their long white wings and here and there were little flocks of wild duck bobbing on the crisp wavelets. Swans too were sailing by, and a crested grebe plopped in to reappear quite some distance away. Then little Taminee said "Look Granddad, there's a boat." "Why so it is. I wonder who that could be?"

Far out beyond the shadow of the mountain, on a glittering sea of diamonds, we saw the silhouette of a boat. Then it came into the dark water, heading fast towards us with strong sweeps of the oars, although it was a large boat with a canopy over the bows and the rower was a small dumpy figure with white hair shining bright as it caught the sun. Then a chime of voices: "Look it's Grandma, it's Grandma, Granddad, it's Grannie Peglin."

Peglin came in close then feathered the oars and swung round to face us side on. "Well there you are you land lubbers," she said, "you've missed all the fun. I saw it all. I never laughed so much in all my life. The water came up so quick they didn't get a single one of them great engines out. Truck loads of men came in splashing through the wet and mud and started up the motors but they all got stuck in a great jam before they could get out of the gates. They were up to their waists in water and had to climb up on the roofs till the helicopters could winch them off. I rowed down there and saw it all and they saw me so I shook my fist in the air and waved my old banner at them. All them big iron engines with their great grabbing arms and jaws, they're all drownded now and gone forever. You should have seen it!" She gave a victory whoop and once again raised the banner with "STOP THE LOGGING, SAVE OUR FOREST" in bold crude lettering.

Procter turned to Kombard and said "Well now, son, there's your winner." In reply Kombard simply put his arm across his father's shoulders and gripped him in a gesture of affection and support.

Peglin edged in and threw up her painter and was pulled in and helped up. Procter took her in his arms like some battle worn king of ancient legend embracing his fair lady of the lake. "Well lass," he said, "you were born in a boat so I put one all ready for you with stores and a cover. I knew you'd get in it soon as your socks got wet." Peglin chuckled and then she took the rope from Tamon who was still holding it and spoke some ancient ceremonial words in a strange language and placed her hand on the prow before consigning the boat gently to the waves.

The expired torches were also tossed into the water and Procter lit up the ones carried by the relief torchbearer detail. We took a final look at the great, glorious sea we had created and which in a year or two would be teeming with its own life.

It was a happy, chatty, jaunty mood in which we made the return journey, very different from the one in which we'd come there. Trammis, a torchbearer of eight, asked me what 'sonsie' meant as he'd heard Scottie call me this. I told him 'lucky' and he said, "We've all been sonsie, haven't we?"

Back in base camp we made a fire from the rags and shattered timber lying around and baked potatoes and sausages which we ate with pickled preserves, cheese and fruit. The larder cave was out of the line of fire and we still had a good supply of food. We found a pan which was only dented and not punctured and used it for a brew of tea. The fate of the horses and other animals was explained to the children and they were told not to go into the stable as it was an unpleasant sight, and soon the kites and vultures would be crowding in for the feast. This of course acted as a challenge to the bolder ones who sneaked in to take a peek, and carried back grisly descriptions to their more timorous siblings.

After the meal we all went out to enjoy the sun and view the altered landscape. The river came up within a few feet of the ramp and filled its old bed as far as the barrier. It had flowed up to the edge of the high ridge as far as we could see and a glassy swirling vortex, like an enormous plug hole, marked the point where it issued through the tunnel; and no doubt it had also found the passage through the natural caves that we had failed to find. 'Where Alph the sacred river ran, through caverns measureless to man.'

Words remembered from school days long ago came back to me.

The rest of the day was spent in preparation for the journey to the family's estate in a distant part of the forest. We would set out at dawn. Scottie and I would travel on from there to our own home and the life we had before. We brought out all the remaining stores and goods, but the journey was going to be an arduous one, having to carry everything on our backs. Then Scottie came in with the news that one of the wagons was repairable. Parked in an alcove it had escaped the bullets, and the blast damage to the side planks could be made good. So we could load everything on and pull and push it along ourselves. Whether this would be possible over rough terrain was open to question. At all events we got everything ready and planned as well as we could, Procter spending a good deal of time with his maps working out the easiest route. It only remained then to search around for enough usable bedding to keep ourselves warm and comfortable for our last night in the Tash'kahern caves.

Then a crisis. The nightly headcount was short by two. Tamon and his younger brother Reld were missing. We scoured the caves and then out and yelled into the rapidly fading light, Procter blowing his whistle. Five or six big vultures launched themselves in a flurry of feathers from the slaughterhouse that had been the stables. Another sat on the bare rock, its great wings draped like a canopy over its back, seemingly too gorged to move. Then the two culprits appeared, little figures legging it from far up the track to our left. Anxiety turned immediately to anger, without seeming to pass through relief in Leevil's case, as he shouted threats of dire reprisals.

Breathless, the two lads came running up the ramp: "Guess who we've found, Dad?" "You'd never guess." Leevil was in no mood for guessing games, but Procter held him back. "You'd better tell us boys before your dad gets his hands on you." The boys stopped in their tracks and said in unison "We've found Klibber and Klebbo." This meant nothing to me but it had a wonderfully pacifying effect on Leevil and everyone else. Procter and four men set out immediately, carrying ropes and led by the two boys.

The others thought it very amusing not to tell Scottie and me who Klibber and Klebbo were, and we didn't find out till the party returned, leading the two sturdy black draught oxen that had been used for ploughing on the farm.

CHAPTER 14

Rolling Home

WE SET OFF at first light. The smaller sleepier children were found spaces in the wagon and carried out in their bedding. The rest of us felt somewhat subdued and unreal in the hesitant dawn, anxious, but glad to be reunited with Peglin, and hopeful for the future. The weather promised cold but bright.

Klibber and Klebbo were harnessed up with stertorous trumpeting and bellowing on their part which seemed to say that they were pleased to be back at work. Procter strode ahead, wielding a great staff like a diminutive Moses leading his tribe out of exile. We headed north along the wall of the mountain. The track, cut off by the empty gorge of the Raffire, followed the only direction possible, and the woods on the other side were in any case too dense and swampy to penetrate. Fear of a further attack kept us on the alert, and we sheltered briefly, scanning the heavens, in caves and hollows along the way. But all was quiet, and the rising sun helped to restore our confidence. Soon we were strolling along as casual and carefree as any family outing, giving the children rides on the wagon, with talk and laughter going round from group to group and Peglin in full spate, re-living the glory of the loggers' defeat.

Days followed without major incident, settling into the steady rhythms of living on the move. The trees gave way to low scrub and thorn bushes, then to windswept moorland of gorse and heather, and then dark tundra broken with craggy outcrops. The nights were cold, and we huddled together in shelters made from the tarpaulins Procter had used to cover his detonation circuitry. Where the ridge ended and the track turned into the mountains we found a way down into the valley of the river and followed that. It had been worn smooth by the current and we made good progress. But we were still travelling north and needed at some point to turn off in a south-easterly direction.

Eventually we left the river bed and followed a trail that led north-east. It took us into a dry empty region with more mountains beyond, but Procter stayed on this road despite there being tracks that led off to our right, more in the direction we needed to go. He seemed to have some plan in mind, something up his sleeve as ever; and his judgement had been too recently vindicated for any further questions to be asked.

"There she is," he said at last, grounding his staff and bringing us to a halt. We looked ahead and saw tin clad ramshackle buildings perched on a rising slope a couple of miles away, spectral in the dusky light. On tall sketchy stilts a shute descended to a cluster of buildings below, cubed in the sun's oblique rays. "Sapphires," he continued. "I made a fortune out of that place."

"I don't see it, Dad," said Leevil. "What use would sapphires be to us now?"

"Precious little, Son. But there's something else there that might come in handy."

Zinnian sapphires, he told us, were the finest, largest, purest and rarest in the world and commanded high prices, but it was thirty years now since the mine was abandoned. It had been undisturbed ever since and had that feel of a place suspended in time, as though the work force had left only yesterday and the echoes of their shouts and whistling and the tramp of heavy boots had only just faded into silence. A half filled dumper truck, a shovel thrown in the grass, everything was just as they left it, preserved in the cold clear air. The children convinced each other that the place was haunted, while the dogs sniffed around for lingering scent traces of long departed predecessors. The rest of us were just glad at the prospect of spending the night for the first time since we left the farm with a proper roof over our heads.

We moved into the brick built office block and mine manager's house. A shelf full of vellum ledgers contained records of production from the day the mine opened to the day when it was decided it had nothing more to yield. Work sheets and load manifests lay scattered under a thin layer of dust. We fired up the old range and cooked a meal on it. We ate at a table. We found warm bedding and Procter and Peglin actually slept in a bed.

A study day in industrial archaeology, we assumed, was not the primary intention of this visit; nor even on Procter's part a trip down memory lane. The next day we waited for some announcement from out leader, but none came, or at least not one that explained what he had in mind. He simply informed us that he and the men folk had some serious business to attend to that might take several days, and the women and children were to see to domestic matters and their own amusements. This aroused considerable protest from the women and children, ironic and dismissive on the part of the former, wounded and vehement from the latter. "It wouldn't be safe for the young 'uns," Procter insisted, "and as for you ladies, well, let's say it's just not your kind of thing my dears." This stirred Peglin into action.

"I'm surprised at you, Procter Prendis; you were never one to take that high and mighty attitude where us women were concerned. And there's not much you men can do that we can't do just as well, or maybe better." A murmur of agreement to this. "Lord's sake Procter you're turning into a bossy old fool to say such daft things."

"Nay lass, nay," he protested, for once a little abashed. "Let's just say we've been through some troubled times of late and yours and one or two other birthdays and the like have gone by the board. I can't promise anything now but we've got a person among us here that knows a thing or two about certain matters, and with his help I thought it might just be possible to do something like, to level things up a bit. You just take it easy for a day or two and we'll see if we can't come up with summat."

You could see Peglin's mind working on this mumbled

pronouncement for a moment or two, screwing up her eyes. Then she grinned. "Well you are an old fool, husband, but a romantic old fool. That's all right with me though, and I expect with the rest of us." More murmurs of assent, but not from the older children whose sense of injury was if anything enhanced by this exchange. Procter addressed them with regained authority. "Now my lads and lasses, you've been champion all through these troubles of ours but this is heavy work and not safe for you. And I may even have to sack some of the men!"

This last comment went some way towards assuaging youthful pride. "Now we don't want any accidents, do we! Will you promise me to stay away from the place we'll be working?" Reluctant nods and assurances given, Procter jerked his head in the general direction of myself, Scottie and the brothers. We followed him outside, with no more idea than the others of what was in store. Credo followed cautiously, hoping her membership of the works party would go unchallenged.

Procter led us in and out of the jumbled buildings, past a row of miners' cottages in their faded colours, and then across an open space towards a detached pair of sheds clad in corrugated iron. He produced a key, which it required some effort to turn in a rusty padlock securing a heavy steel door, and ushered us inside. It was almost dark, but for dust-bleared skylights admitting a few feeble rays and revealing dim forms of massive wheels, pistons and cylinders. But the smell alone, a rich concoction of oil and rust and coal grit, was enough to tell us we were in an engine shed. The first job was to wake a generator from its slumbers. Procter topped up the tank and Kombard yanked the starter rope. Not so much as a mutter, so Scottie cleaned the spark plug and after a few more hefty pulls the engine fired a couple of times, emitting a cloud of black smoke. The next pull and it cleared its throat and was popping away nicely; Procter threw a switch and the lights flickered on. As we looked around at an array of weird and antiquated rolling stock he at last revealed his hand.

He explained that after all the hardships we had been through, alarms and stresses that in his view women and children should not be subjected to, he wanted for their benefit especially to complete the journey in comfort and in style. A railroad led from this depot to his estate. Part of it was built in the distant days of Zinn's industrial past, and built to last, using hardwood sleepers and granite ballast. He had built the spur to here himself, and could vouch for it. And he had instructed the caretakers of his estate to keep the line clear. There were the two engines we could see here, in working order when the mine closed, along with the trucks and stock vans, and in the other shed an item he had picked up cheap in a scrap yard some half a century since.

He led us through to show us a thirty-seater carriage of the old Zinn Imperial Railway, the spread-eagle coat of arms still visible on its flank. It was built of solid mahogany from roof to floor, and inside beneath the dust of ages we could see the luxury of its plushly upholstered and bronze fitted interior. "Sound as a bell," Procter assured us, "but as you see it needs tidying up a bit."

Procter went on to say that he'd long cherished the dream of getting the line working again and now the opportunity had arisen because we had Scottie, whose reputation as an engineer, a pioneer of aeronautical design, was well established. Scottie was to be the director of the project if he was agreeable, and we were all to take our orders from him.

The young man in question had been looking around him wide-eyed since we came in. "Well, I think we could give it a go," he said. "Best take a look at those engines though." We went back into the main shed and studied them. Although they bore an overall resemblance to the steam locomotives I was familiar with from my own country and in other lands, it was clear to me that they were quite unrelated, the products of a parallel evolution which had nevertheless come up with the same basic format of tender, cab, boiler and firebox. But the pistons pushed forward to drive wheels at the front; the other wheels were the same size and had grooves rather than flanges, and the whole works were boxed in with steel panels with only the cab and tall central smoke stacks projecting upwards. They had the rock-like immobility of seized up machinery, sequestered relics of a vanished age. We all waited patiently for Scottie's feasibility verdict.

We discussed it doubtfully among ourselves for a bit while Scottie scouted around to see what tools and equipment were available. He came back with a can and a box containing hammers and spanners. First he brushed the triangular bolt heads on the side panels of the larger engine with liquid that smelt like a mixture of petrol and paraffin, and then found the right spanner and gave a steady pull at one of the bolts. It didn't budge, so he took a hammer and tapped the arm of the spanner a few times, repositioned the spanner and then pulled again. "Here let me take a go at it," said Kombard, but Scottie shook his head. "Old metal is strong but brittle," he said. "It could break like a biscuit. You have to be gentle with it."

Sure enough after a little more persuasion it yielded and came out clean. He went away again and came back with a pot of paint and a small brush. "This is essential," he said, "they're all different." He proceeded to mark all the bolts and their positions with numbers and the position of the panel in relation to the frame it was mounted on. Then he found more spanners and hammers and got us all pulling and tapping away at the rest of the bolts and in a short time we were able to prise and ease the panel free. It was a small initial success but a sense of feasibility began to take hold.

Scottie asked Procter to wire up a spotlight and with this he climbed into the machine and could be heard tapping and testing things inside. He emerged smudged and dishevelled to deliver his findings. "It's in reasonable condition - nothing broken, but it's all pretty solid - sealed up with rust and hardened grease. We could try steaming up and having a go but there's a risk something would break. The alternative would be to strip it all down, clean and oil and reassemble." "How long?" asked Procter. "With luck no more than a week." Glances were exchanged all round, turning to nods. Procter said "OK lads. Job on."

Long days of hard work and happy industry followed. We worked singly or in pairs or as a group, each contributing his strength and skill and leaning on the strength and skill of the others, so the group became more than the sum of its parts. Somehow the most intractable problems got solved, or bypassed in some way, and gradually the whole machine came apart like an expanded diagram. Scottie sketched and labelled everything: rods, levers, valves, gears, and went crazy if anything got moved before he had recorded its exact position. He was masterful when it came to lifting heavy parts with block and tackle from the gantry; with a constant, urgent mantra of "Steady," "Take the weight," "Mind your back," 'FINGERS!'' "Let it come," as a ton or more of cast iron was guided safely to rest. We came to have complete trust in him.

It was satisfying to work with abrasives on some blackened archaeological lump of metal until silver glints appeared and a precisely engineered component emerged; then rub it with an oily rag till it gleamed with renewed purpose. I was happy to be given simple cleaning jobs and to be sent to fetch the sandwiches from the house, to resist sly questions and lay false trails.

After hours of physical effort and mental concentration, lunches and tea breaks were times of blissful relaxation and of jestfully uninhibited conversation. When we returned in the evening for supper we had to be more circumspect, but by then we were too tired for anything but to eat and sleep. Luckily the most essential lubricant for engineering works, beer, was in good supply, a pair of musty barrels having been discovered in a basement.

Thanks to Scottie's mechanical grasp and organisation the reassembly went like a dream. Everything clicked, slotted and settled back into place. The panels were bolted back. A smooth oily polish reflected from every surface. What had been a rock ready to sink in the earth was now a bird, ready to fly. Next we tackled the carriage, swabbing, scraping and brushing to remove years of dust and grime. There was not much making good required, and beeswax and linseed oil brought life and light back to dull parched woodwork. The soft leather upholstery responded to a mixture of fats and oils which Scottie prepared.

We opened the big doors on to the track and hitched up Klibber and Klebbo to haul the carriage out. We all had to push as well to shift the inertia, but it rolled smoothly once the oil worked into the axles. Then we serviced two wagons, one for extra coal and one to take all our gear, and a stock van for the oxen, and assembled the train in a siding ready to hook up to the locomotive. We filled the tank with water and the tender with coal but we couldn't steam up without giving the game away. So the time had come to make the presentation, trusting to luck and to Scottie that the loco would actually work. He appointed me to ride the footplate with him and we lit the fire while the others went to fetch the rest of the family.

The fire was building up and the first hissing of steam audible in the escape valves. Scottie was tapping the gauge and testing the control leavers. "Do you actually know how to drive this thing?" I asked him. "Aye, middlins I ken it," was the not quite satisfactory reply. I shovelled more coal into the now roaring furnace and slammed the door. Clouds of steam began issuing out and filling the shed so we could only dimly make out the line of folk waiting at a safe distance to see what would happen. Scottie pulled the cord and gave two shrill sharp toots of the whistle. "We gang awa then laddie," he said, pushing one leaver and hauling with all his weight on another.

There was a mighty grunt and a shudder went through the whole body of the beast, a metallic scraping, screeching sound below, then another shuddering thrust. Suddenly light was shining down on us. We were outside, and moving, and gaining speed with each blast. "Can you stop it?" I yelled. Scottie was too busy wrestling with the controls to answer. Once again we were enveloped in steam, and a squealing noise filled our ears as the wheels protested against the brakes, mad at being deprived so soon of long denied mobility. We ground to a halt some distance along the track.

Now people were running up, laughing and shouting. Scottie leaned out and waved majestically. The children had to be physically restrained from scrambling in. "Hey Scottie, Mr Sonsie, let us ride, please Scottie, go on Jason . . ." But we had to get out to change the points so we could back into the siding, so ignoring all the adulation Scottie reassumed his leadership role, ordering everyone back well clear of the track and all children under strict parental restraint. "We've got to reverse now and this is the really hard bit," he explained. "If we get it wrong we could wreck the carriage."

He asked Procter to see us back to link up the coupling, and we climbed back in. We had the devil of a job getting into reverse. "She," as it had now become, just didn't like the idea and we had to inch forward and keep trying, juggling the levers before a loud clunk and violent jerk indicated we had either succeeded or bust the gear box. Scottie, who was quickly getting the hang of it, gently increased the piston pressure and we moved slowly backwards while Procter yelled out the distance as the gap closed. With a foot to go we shut off the power and applied the brakes and felt a satisfying 'clop' as the hook dropped into its harbour. Scottie immediately shifted into forward, this time without protest, and we took up the strain, moving the carriages forward on to the main track before releasing the steam and rolling to a halt. Finally we gave another toot on the whistle and shook hands.

It was now time to let everyone explore and admire, and congratulate the team. Scottie was raised even higher in stature by old and young alike and I basked in some reflected glory. It wasn't really possible to say whether we'd succeeded in keeping the women and children in the dark or if they were just gallantly pretending to be overcome with surprise. But whatever the case they were certainly delighted.

It was mid morning, a fine day in prospect, and no time was lost in loading up and preparing for the journey ahead. Klibber and Klebbo were settled in their van after bringing the waggon up, with plenty of dry bracken for bedding. Our belongings and remaining stores were loaded in the truck, along with buckets to replenish the boiler, anticipating there'd be no shortage of water along the line. In the carriage itself quantities of prepared food and drink along with books and games were laid in for the journey, and we found our own rations neatly packaged and placed in the cab. Someone said, "What about the waggon? We can't just abandon it. It's all that's left of the old place." "A good waggon too," Zaric added. We hoisted it on the gantry and loaded it into another truck, which we pushed out and coupled to the end of the train.

And so we said farewell to the sapphire mine, briefly reawakened from its long sleep, and we climbed aboard. Scottie and I took up our stations, shovelled more coal into the furnace, blew the whistle and shut the valves. With mighty snorts and blasts of smoke and steam the train pulled forward and was soon chuffing busily along at a measured pace. Credo was curled up in a dark corner of the cab, nose between paws, looking up with upside down eyes.

I don't think I'd felt such unalloyed excitement and cloudless optimism since I was a child, riding in the little train that runs along the beach from Fairbourne to the Barmouth ferry. Deep down I knew that peace was a bubble in a dark murky sea, but for the moment the world was kind and wonderful and hope as high as the distant peaks of the Tash'kahern Mountains. Scottie too seemed pleased and happy, checking his dials and leaning out to scan the track ahead. It certainly seemed as firm beneath us as Procter's report had warranted, but we held to a leisurely pace to be on the safe side.

There was a good view all round across the craggy moorlands. We saw herds of bison and deer, and an eagle, startled from its prey, flapped wildly above us. Over the top of the tender we could just see through a small window into the coach, where the passengers were in all attitudes of relaxation and enjoyment.

"This is jolly," I said to Scottie. "I always wanted to be an engine driver."

"Ye were ayeways ane ambitious drochle I'll be boon."

Credo crept over and put her chin on Scottie's knee and gave her tail a hopeful wag.

"Weel ma bawtie. Hame agane soon."

"I expect you're looking forward to getting back yourself Scottie."

"Aye. There'll be muckle wark tae be done afore the snaw sets in."

"I always find it strange coming back to a place where nothing's changed after so much has happened to you. But then you get into your old routine and all your adventures are just a memory, or a dream."

"We are sic stuff as drames are made on," he replied, with an arch little smile in my direction.

"Couldn't have put it better myself. But there are good dreams and bad ones. We'll have sweet dreams about this trip."

Scottie checked the controls and I threw some more coal into the hungry furnace. Then we sat on the little wooden fold down seats and tucked into our sandwiches, and gave Credo the meaty treats that had been thoughtfully included for her. We talked mainly of home: what calves, foals or babies might have been born; whether this or that crusty ancient had yet been laid to rest with his forefathers, or a certain wilful beauty chosen yet from her retinue of despairing suitors. We could be back in time for the ploughing competition, a highly contested event and one in which my attempts were expected to add a comic element to an otherwise serious affair. Then there was the football season to organise, where, as the game's undisputed supremo, I would reassert my authority. I was hoping this general chat would open up some thoughts from Scottie about his own future. There had been barely a mention of Elfie since we set out, and now he said nothing. I didn't want to raise it directly for fear of disturbing some inner process of healing, or perhaps denial.

The other unspoken matter between us was the fate of the buzzard children. It had always remained in the back of my mind, a persistent and insistent presence whatever else was going on. Now it was one small but sombre cloud in the vast blue sky above us. Recent events had if anything deepened the wound. I had been surrounded by families, and Scottie too would undoubtedly marry in due course and become a father. And those children, the little girl Aya especially, and her sister Sulibe, had wanted me to be theirs. They needed me then, they might need me now, but now might be too late. Either way I had to know. A resolve began to form in my mind amid the bustling, puffing, pumping heartbeat of the engine and the rattle of the couplings. Whatever the risks, and even if it meant missing the ploughing competition, I would go there and see for myself. And I would go alone.

Surely there was never a more wonderful railway journey in the entire history of this transport of delight. The sheer grandeur of the scenery silenced us and we could hardly keep our eyes off it to tend the engine. The line ran along ledges in the sides of precipices, leapt across ravines and spanned wide valleys on bridges of such slender and mathematical construction that we seemed to be riding through the air. We had faith in our destiny as you would in a fairy tale. Spread far below us the woods were dark even in bright sun from the recent drenching of rain, with flashes of autumn colours still clinging here and there, pale yellow and amber and blazing scarlet. There was water everywhere, rivers in flood, cataracts plunging hundreds of feet, raging rapids and pulsing streamlets.

"Where streams of living water flow, my ransomed soul He leadeth." Once again some old remembered words kept running through my mind. My eyes drank in and heart filled with the glory of things, as the first men must have known and felt in nature the divine will, and being part of the natural world, possessing and belonging.

We had travelled a good two hours before we saw our first habitation, an isolated crofter's cottage; and then up ahead through the tunnel of trees we saw a cluster of houses and barns, with platforms beside the line and derelict station buildings. We blew the whistle and steamed to a halt. People appeared in doorways and windows and looked up from their work and their gardens in astonishment. It was the first train to arrive in decades. As we all got out to stretch our legs they came up to greet us. News of the flooding on the Levels and defeat of the loggers had already reached them and when we told them our story we were welcomed as heroes. Young men took Scottie's and my buckets from us almost by force and continued filling the tank, while we were guided with others to the village hall. A feast sprang up from nowhere and there were speeches and toasts and presentations. We did these celebrations the justice we could without offending our hosts but in truth we were all anxious to continue our journey home.

Scottie and I went back to work up steam while Procter rounded every one up and we bade farewell with promises of future reunions. The idea of restarting a regular service for goods and passengers had been eagerly discussed. Wherever there were habitations we had to take it very slow and watch the line as excited groups gathered to wave and cheer. We waved back and blew the whistle but rolled ahead. Then we had a long run where the line was clear. We stopped once in an isolated spot to replenish tank and tender and light the lanterns as dusk was falling, and then we steamed onwards into the night. Bewildered creatures on the track again slowed our progress from time to time.

It was after midnight and the lights had been dimmed in the carriage when we passed beneath stone portals festooned in ivy and suddenly there was openness all around us, dim fields visible under the light of the stars and a slender moon. In a little while we saw buildings and the rail terminus up ahead. Scottie blew the whistle and eased down the pressure, and we came gently to rest on the buffers.

CHAPTER 15

Affairs of the Heart

DARKER THAN the surrounding night a low, rambling, many gabled house stood before us, embowered in foliage. Peglin led the main party up and the menfolk followed after putting engine and oxen to bed. Dim lights already glimmered in a few of the small heavily framed windows. Inside the candlelight made everything seem darker: sheeted furniture, massive planks, heavy stone and panelled walls and thick dusty hangings figured with obscure designs. Mentally exhausted from so many impressions and emotions of the journey and recent past we did little more than camp for the first night, after hot drinks had been made and the brandy bottle passed round. Next day was bright and cheerful and neighbours had begun to call before we had shaken the sleep from our eyes.

Just from sleeping, breathing, eating and talking, human presence soon brings life and warmth back to the deadest habitation. It was a time of resurgence for the Prendis clan after their many trials. What with friends and tenants and their families coming in and offering their services, and the societies of children and young people rapidly expanding, the place was soon resounding from basements to rafters with lively interactions and purposeful activities. While the women folk set about bringing order, cleanliness, comfort and charm to all domestic interiors the men serviced the entire infrastructure, replacing or repairing anything damaged or decayed in the fabric and restoring the plumbing and electrical systems, the latter still a rarity in Zinn. And when the house was deemed habitable there was the farm and the estate to take in hand. Procter and his sons did the rounds, assessing and discussing the state of things and resolving what steps needed to be taken.

As you'd expect Scottie was in the thick of everything, in respect both of his practical and social skills. Again he seemed to know all the new names at once and was on the easiest terms with everyone. We had agreed we would stay only so long as we needed to rest and recuperate before continuing our journey home, but now he seemed reluctant to move on, and I had no wish to curtail the pleasure he was getting from his usefulness and popularity. Then, as the condition of the household prospered, my own suddenly worsened. I grew weak and feverish. Medical advice was called in and I was ordered to bed on a diet of bread and milk and vegetable broth.

I was given a pleasant room, simply furnished with a few pieces of plain rustic furniture, a rug on the polished floorboards and a cast iron fireplace where a fire was lit. There was a picture on the wall of an elf in a misty woodland clearing, and another of a ploughman with his team, driving a furrow straight towards the sunset. They imparted, or I invested them with, a sense of timeless serenity. The iron framed bed was high, deep and soft and gave me a view, through the small low window, opened for fresh air, of a paved terrace with stone urns and lawn sloping down to trees with water shining between them. Scottie brought me my meals and tended the fire, and told me the news of the day, and others looked in from time to time with gentle words of comfort and concern. Credo came often to lie on the rug by my bed and look at me with sorrowful eyes. I felt like a complete fraud.

It was like being ill as a child: the unwonted attention, the guiltless idleness, the whoozy dreamlike euphoria as I drifted in and out of sleep. The hum of voices and sounds of work that occasionally reached me while making no demands on my attention soothed me with a sense that all was being taken care of and everything said that needed to be said.

Nights though were more troubled, and at times I was delirious. In my dreams I seemed to be a mentally disabled person being cared for, protected, as I moved through scenes and encounters beyond my understanding. I was keeping my eyes shut to screen out incomprehensible or intolerable things, and then when I tried to open them I couldn't. I remember crying out "Mummy I can't see. Help me, I'm blind." But even in the midst of such terrors I knew that it would all vanish and evaporate with the morning light and that by midday I wouldn't even remember any of the people and places, known or unknown, that had been so real to me. Yet there was one scene that did linger, and troubled me.

In a few days I felt fine, but took advantage of the solicitude of my carers to malinger a little longer. This was not entirely self-indulgence but partly a desire to give Scottie time as well to reach a point where he wanted to return to our own modest home-stead, which must by now be looking sadly vacant and in need of attention. He seemed though in a buoyant, almost defiant, mood, as though he'd reached some major, self-liberating determination. The thought crossed my mind that he had decided to stay for good and make his home with the Prendises who had so taken him to their collective heart. But one morning he came in and finding me up and glowing with restored health, declared:

"Ye daeless sloonge, Jason, I ca' see ye're braw and bonnie the noo. We maun gang awa laddie and tent tae our ain wee abaid."

To have Scottie berating me in broad Scots again was a sure sign I was fully recovered. "For my part," I replied, "I'd be only too happy to get on our way. The Prendises are good folk and it's lovely here, but there's no place like home. And it will be good to see our friends there again."

"Aye, an pleuch kempan an a gemm or twa o 'football' I rackon."

"We might even see Elfie again," I ventured. But there was silence. I was standing by the window looking out at the terrace. Without turning round I said:

"I had a crazy dream, Scottie, while I was sick. Maralese was out there on the terrace, in the arms of her lover. They were kissing strenuously, passionately. Well that isn't strange, she's a beautiful, bewitching girl for sure. But the weird thing is, the lover was you."

Again there was silence. I turned to see Scottie sitting on the bed. His face was flushed. He looked up at me wide eyed with an appealing, helpless look. "I don't understand," I said. "I know you love Elfie."

"I love her, Jason. And I wull a'ways love her. But I canna mairry her. I canna touch her. I may niver set een on her agane."

"But she loves you too, Scottie. Don't underestimate her courage or her cunning. She'll find a way to you as she has in the past."

"This isnae bonnie Scotland, Jason, land of romance. This is Zinn. They wad prison her; they wad see her deid afore they wad gie her leave to wed sic ain main carle as I."

I had to acknowledge the force of this, and began to think it was foolish and insensitive of me to reopen a wound that all this time my friend had been striving to close. And yet another impulse was telling me that after what we had achieved in the Levels anything was possible.

I had come to form such a positive idea of Elfie. She was one of those people who make little impression on first meeting but who dwell in the mind's eye and develop in memory and reflection. She was quirky and funny and yet serious in a childlike way. There was a freshness about her, and for all she was cute and canny, an essential purity of mind, and an innocence of the heart which is the most precious of all human qualities. Maralese was all woman and no child, sensuously and self consciously a beauty. She should have been the princess – an exotic summer bloom rather than a spring flower. Even in the intimacy and squalor of our time in the caves and under violent attack she had never wavered in her self-possession and faultless manners.

Once I'd chanced upon her washing under one of the caves' natural showers, in her naked loveliness. Her hair, which she'd cut shorter, was tied up on the top of her head, with a little off-centre tuft which shook as she moved. I had never seen a lovelier woman, as strong and soft as silk. Beauty is in the assemblage and rhythmic harmony of the parts – you cannot itemise it. Of course I should have withdrawn immediately but I could not help gazing in pure admiration. Yet there was something in the toss of that little top knot which told me she could be trouble.

On another occasion in the tents when we were heaped together I found her sleeping next to me, deeply and sensuously asleep with her breath on my shoulder. As any man would I thought 'supposing she were mine', but the folly of the notion dismissed it the instant it formed, and I found myself wondering if she would ever belong to anyone except, supremely, to herself.

Scottie sat there looking so forlorn I went over and sat beside him and put my hand on his hunched shoulder. "Well, Scottie, you may be right. I just thought we might give the Fates a little longer to see if they come up with a solution. How far has it gone with this lassie? Are you engaged?"

"Trystit? Troth I canna say the noo. Naither tane or t'ither."

"It seemed to be going pretty well out there on the terrace. I had the idea that you'd reached an agreement – and I can understand it. She's a lovely creature."

"The bonniest lass I ever set een upon, forby couthy and gracie in her disposition. I wadna find a better wife neither kinder kin in aa the wide warld."

"So what happened, Scottie? What went wrong."

Scottie shook his head and was silent for a while. I'd never seen him so crestfallen. Eventually it came out that in the sharing of confidences he had let slip something about his relationship with Elfie, a lady of high rank, the one asset Maralese lacked. "She wurna speak to me, Jason. She's sae displeased and angered at me." Well there's the thorn, I thought; mentally comparing this reaction to what Elfie's might have been if Scottie had confessed a former love to her. It was a wretched position he was in now, between two lost loves, thwarted by circumstance in the first instance and then by his own candour. And I was concerned that knowledge of the liaison with a princess of Zinn had leaked. So I said:

"Perhaps I might speak to her, Scottie. She could hardly refuse, and she can't leave you in limbo – there has to be a yes or a no. And maybe she's thought it through by now. And we have to ask her not to speak of Elfie to anyone else. We should sort it out before we leave." Scottie looked at me wistfully and nodded his assent to this proposition. "It wull be ain sorraful wayganging after aa our stours and heroic deeds," he reflected.

I had warmed to Procter so much, and come to place such complete trust in his judgement and integrity, that I discussed Scottie's problem with him in private. I told him the story of a prince in my own country who married a beautiful woman but had already given his heart to another, and all the troubles that came from that, ending in their divorce and the death of the princess in a tragic accident, which some even thought was not an accident. To my surprise he already knew something about it. I said I realised it would be a happy day for him and his family if Scottie were to become part of it. Procter grinned his grisly toothless grin, which no stranger would have recognised as a sign of his benign generosity of spirit.

"Scottie will always belong to us whether he marries us or not. And the same goes for you Jason. We are comrades in arms are we not, and if we never set eyes on each other again you will always be in our hearts. As for the girl, yes, speak to her. I know she likes you and respects you, and she'll give you an honest answer. I would never interfere in my children's or grandchildren's choice of partner, but I'm always prepared to give an honest opinion myself if asked. If she and Scottie do make a match they'll have my blessing and support, but Maralese is a fine young woman and won't lack for suitors if it doesn't happen. Perhaps she just feels she needs more time herself - her life has been sheltered and she needs to see more of the world. But whoever marries her will have his work cut out. It will be a career in itself."

Scottie and I got all our stuff together and were ready to go before we announced our departure. We were not much in the mood for more festivities but it was impossible to escape a lavish supper to mark the occasion. In the event we couldn't be other than cheered and uplifted by all the expressions of praise and gratitude and regret at our leaving and good wishes for our future happiness and insistence on keeping in touch - and it was agreed that this very day should be the occasion of an annual reunion.

Just about everyone, young and old, made a little speech

recounting some particular moment in our adventures they would always remember us by. It was clear that for the youngsters Scottie was the hero and role model while I was a kind of comic side kick. They'd picked up on Scottie scolding me in the Scots tongue, and in particular the word 'sonsie'. I explained that anything I had managed to bring off was the result of pure sonse. Finally Procter made a speech saying it was a lucky day indeed when we came into their lives and we would always remain in their hearts and proposed a toast wishing us all happiness and success and good fortune in all our future doings.

When it was all over I found a moment to tap on Maralese's door. She greeted me and ushered me in with her usual composure. The room, lit only by two candles and the light of the fire, was so choice and ordered and arranged in its furnishings and ornaments it was like a shrine. She beckoned me to a seat by the fire and sat opposite me. The deep soft shadows of her face in the glow of the fire gave it such mystery and almost unearthly beauty that I found it hard to address her. My mentally rehearsed phrases of introduction and reassurance failed on my lips, so I spoke directly and to the point:

"Scottie has told me about yours and his relationship and is deeply upset and confused at its having faltered, or come to an end - he isn't sure which. As he tells me you are unwilling to speak to him on the matter I offered as his friend to ask on his behalf. Should he accept that the affair is over, or has he any grounds to hope that it may at some later stage be resumed?"

The girl remained silent, and I was beginning to feel ill at ease, until finally she spoke:

"I assume he told you the reason for my coolness."

"Yes. He told you about his love for a princess of Zinn. He has known her since she was a child and they are in love. But because of her position it can never come to anything. Her parents will insist on her marrying someone of her own rank and it is quite possible he will never see her again. He undertook this expedition partly to put her from his mind and has tried his utmost to do so. Since we left we have hardly spoken of her."

"But has he succeeded in putting her from his mind?"

"Perhaps not entirely - not yet."

Then surprisingly she smiled, disarmingly, and said:

"I must apologise to him, and to you Jason for being the occasion of such a difficult assignment. I admit my pride was hurt by his confession and I failed to see how honourable it was; and it was wrong of me to react as I did and leave him in such uncertainty. Please tell him I'm sorry. The answer is I think quite clear from what you have said. We both need more time, me to grow up a bit, and him to recover from what seems a hopeless love. I suggest we should both be free now to go our own ways and follow our fortunes in love. But if when we meet again in a year's time we are both free of all other claims on our affections, then for my part I would be more than happy to continue our courtship."

"Well that does seem entirely fair, and I'm sure Scottie will think so as well."

"I really am very fond of Scottie and you must know how grateful I am to him and you Jason for all you have done for our family. You are our saviours, and I bless you both."

"Thank you my dear. I'm entirely reassured by your candour. There is just one other thing." She smiled again and said:

"I can reassure you on that as well. I don't even know the girl's name, and I will speak of her friendship with Scottie to absolutely no one at all."

At this she rose, and I did too, and she kissed me on the cheek, and I was too stunned to do anything but mutter my thanks again and retreat awkwardly from her presence. I went down to see Procter in his office before retiring. He poured us both a stiff nightcap and I told him about my interview with Maralese. We both agreed she had spoken very handsomely and the result was satisfactory. If Scottie had the ghost of a chance with his princess he was free to pursue it. Equally Maralese, who would likely travel abroad and perhaps attend a foreign university, would be free to take up with any stricken prince who might fall at her feet. Honour would be satisfied and there would be no hard feelings.

We went on to discuss our travel arrangements. Procter furnished me with a new map and pointed out the best route, following the bed of the old railway, which was still fairly clear, until it crossed a green lane, a drove road heading towards Zinn. Some thirty miles along this a footpath opened to our right which would bring us home. He offered us horses - a pair of sturdy cobs which would be ideal for the terrain. I declined however, saying we preferred to return as we'd come, on foot; and knowing that at present Procter could ill afford to spare the beasts. I said that we'd leave early, at the crack of dawn, as we'd said our fond farewells and received every good wish that could possibly be bestowed upon us. Procter nevertheless added his again, and so we parted.

Scottie was already asleep when I returned to our room, and Credo looked up with her eyes without raising her head from her paws. As usual before setting out on a journey I slept very little, checking through a mental list of everything that was needed to cope with every predictable eventuality, and feeling that inner tension of anxiety and excitement at taking another step forward into the unknown, or back to past scenes that may no longer be the same. I roused Scottie in good time and we climbed into our gear, augmented by the abundant provisions that had been prepared for us, and went out into the cold misty air.

It was the first hint of dawn, the presence of trees, in their immemorial stillness and vastness, more sensed than seen; a moment at the beginning and end of time that precedes creation, and yet speaks of all histories.

As I'd expected, Procter was there waiting to see us off, standing at the top of the embankment above the course of the abandoned line. We both embraced him briefly, without words, and set off side by side. Reaching the first turn after about a hundred yards I glanced back. The light was better now and I could see Procter still standing on the ridge. It may have been the dense atmosphere or a trick of perspective, but he seemed about ten feet high, his hand raised in a final salute.

We marched along for a few miles in silence before stopping to sink our teeth into fresh egg and salad sandwiches and pour hot coffee from the flask. For all it had been such a warm, intimate, exhilarating experience living and fighting with the Prendis clan it was good to be alone together again, sharing a meal, feeling strong and happy in each other's company. It was clear where Scottie's thoughts had been as he asked me why I'd never married.

"I've often asked myself that. Caution perhaps. Fear of losing my independence, or just plain selfishness. I suppose I have never fallen madly enough in love."

"It's nae ower late for ye."

"Did you have anyone in mind?"

"The lasses like ye mair than ye ken, ma fier. Forby Maralese hersel has an ee til ye. She well kend ye wur takking tent o' her dooking in it cove, ye radgie hinkum."

"She knew I was watching her – my God I never realised. How embarrassing. Still, I've been called worse than a peeping Tom in Zinn. But I assure you it was purely aesthetic appreciation on my part, Scottie old man. I'm no rival to you there I promise you."

"I trow ye be ane o' thae puir chiels as be contentit wi' companionship."

"I suppose so. And as far as that goes I suppose I'll have to be content with you."

In my own thoughts I had been pondering the next journey I would undertake, back again into the malevolent sphere of that magnificent and merciless city of Zinn. I'd been so long away from it in thought and space I'd begun to wonder if I'd simply dreamt it, and the buzzard children who had towered aloft above it in their precarious freedom. It would be wonderful to discover it was all the product of some delirious fantasy and I could settle down for good with Scottie and our friends there and the Prendises and the wife and family he would doubtless acquire sooner or later. I would relapse happily into becoming a genial old buffer amusing his bairns with my preposterous tales.

We spent three nights under canvas and by the end of the fourth day were on the drove road, within striking distance of home. Our route skirted several settlements and we met and conversed with a few of the local folk, going about their business in the woods. We were frequently asked if we'd heard about the flooding of the Looshin Levels - it was clearly the hot topic of the hour. Here they had no idea that we were responsible for it or that it had been brought about by any human agency. A great bolt of lightning was said to have pierced the mountain - the sound wave had travelled immense distances. Perhaps it was an earthquake. At any rate it was a natural disaster, as doubtless the logging company were claiming in order to get insurance on their losses.

It occurred to me that the gunship attack was not revenge, or only revenge, but an attempt to remove all witnesses to the contrary. At any rate we had no wish to put the record straight as it would only have held us up to have to tell the story and be drawn into further congratulatory celebrations. And it would be better for everyone if the Zinnian overlords could pass it off as a quake rather than an affront to their authority on the part of the foresters, to which they would feel bound to retaliate and exact reprisals in some way.

The days were shorter now. The light was failing and the temperature falling and we were hungry, but eager to get home. We decided to make our last meal in the open air and then press on and sleep in our old beds again. We were already in familiar territory and our path was clear. Scottie had gone to gather a few sticks for a fire and I was laying out the groundsheet and preparing the ingredients when a figure emerged through the dusk. It was an old lady, rotund and bulkily clad in dark bedraggled skirts. I recognised her by what she was holding in her clenched hand before her face became clear. It was a bunch of wilted herbs.

"You'll be wanting some of these for your pot, Sir," said she; and in the next instant she recognised me. "Why bless me, it's you again. Still skulking about these woods are you? I thought you'd be away by now to yon castle of yours. You're not from these parts - oh no. You're on the wrong road here I reckon."

"Indeed," I said, anxious to be rid of her and her nonsense. "We both have a long way to travel." I fished out some coins from the bottom of my rucksack and handed them to her in return for the herbs, which I placed with the other ingredients, and busied myself as busily as I could chopping and peeling in the hope that she would wander on in her endlessly maundering meanderings. But she showed no inclination to leave and every inclination to continue her witless discourse.

"You'll not have heard what's been happening hereabouts, you being a stranger from a castle far away. There's old Lember Baldo's barn been burnt to the ground, and the great oak by Braggin's Cross be down, and Cammise Sarabar is with child again and the Looshin Levels be flooded out and young Allus Dorkle fell off a hay rick and broke his leg; my word, such things you'd never think could happen, you being from foreign parts . . ." The list of news items, all of equal importance to the news bearer, droned on and on and I stopped paying attention and almost ceased to hear when something she was saying struck me like a blow from a pick handle. "What was that you said? - I'm sorry I missed that bit. A young princess?"

"Oh yes, dear little thing. As used to ride her white pony about these woods and was right kind to folk and wished us the time of day, bless her, not like the rest of them stuck up gentry and their hoity-toity womenfolk. Poor little thing. Ah well it's always the best that go first. They do say God takes them back as is too good for this sad old world. Well He couldn't like me very much to leave me traipsing round and about these old lanes forever and ever and having to listen to all the folk's worries and troubles, and then there's Widdis Plendergard, Plefth's brother, as used to keep . . ." "Please, the girl, what happened to her?" "Well I told you that. It's like I said. Fell she did, off her pony. Broke her poor little neck. Snap! She's gone. And then that Widdis Plen . . ."

"Look, you must leave now. I'm sorry, I don't mean to be rude but my friend will be back any minute and he'll . . . he'll be angry because I've been listening to you and not getting the meal ready. Thank you for telling me the news and for the herbs and I'm sure God likes you a lot but I really must ask you to go along now before my friend gets back."

"Ah well I can see you've no time for a weary old body such as I but then you're not one of us are you now. Oh no, not this road, lives in a castle he does, oh yes, far away, far, far away ..." I could still hear her sighing voice after her dark shape had merged into the crepuscular gloom; and no sooner had it done so than Scottie came along from the other direction, threw down a bundle of sticks and said, "Troth, Jason, it's gude to be ganging hame and I'm sae blithe to be thinkin we'll soon be doon-sittin by our ain hairth smuiking our pipes agane. Shuilie 'we'll lift a cup of kindness up for the sake of auld lang syne'."

My brain was reeling with the news of Elfie's death – it could only be Elfie, and I had to force myself to eat a hearty meal and share Scottie's jocund mood at the prospect of our imminent return home. He soon saw through my pretence and berated me soundly for an 'ourie doolsome soor-lik bodie'. I did my best to pass it off.

"I'm always this way at the end of a long journey," I said. "A sense of anticlimax I suppose. It comes of being a perpetual traveller. But don't worry about me Scottie. I'll be right as rain in a bit. Just bear with me while I think things through and I'll soon be myself again."

So we packed up our gear and continued on our way. The night was frosty and clear and the moon and stars shone brightly on the little track we both knew well that led directly home. It should have been a moment of triumphant euphoria – 'mission accomplished'; but instead my mind was in a turmoil of grief and doubt.

As the news was common knowledge I would have to break it to him soon; and there he was, striding along, whistling and swishing the bushes with his stick and chatting to Credo in pointed mockery of my sultry silence. I could not bear the thought of seeing him cast down again. Would it be better to let him find out for himself and pretend ignorance? No, he had always kept the affair secret and it would be worse for the news to come out in some casual, thoughtless exchange. I had to be there with him and break it as gently as possible and have prepared whatever comforting thoughts I could conjure up. But not tonight – I had to come to terms with Elfie's death myself first because I loved her, for her own sweet sake as well as my dear friend's. But how could I get through the happy homecoming scene and the whisky mellowed fireside reminiscences and future plans glowing in the boles of our pipes and wreathed in clouds of tobacco smoke?

The long-term future was even more daunting than the immediate impasse. I make no claims to any great depth of insight into the affairs of the heart, but even I could see how foolish it would be to think Elfie's death would solve the dilemma posed by her inaccessibility and his feelings for Maralese. If Elfie had been married off to a Zinnian lord and gone on to live her own life he could perhaps have got over her and reclaimed his. Now he would be enslaved to her idealised memory for ever. He might even see her death as punishment for his dalliance with Maralese. Her loss would keep his passion alive and kill any other. I foresaw a loveless, childless future, with a man who lived only in the past - a man I too loved and would never leave. I could only pray for him in my heart. And pray for us both.

We came now to the little clearing in front of Scottie's house, seen there under the night sky just as I'd seen it for the first time - it seemed an age ago. Then Scottie suddenly froze, and his arm fell like a pole across my chest, bringing me also to a halt. Almost instantly I realised that the déjà vu was too exact. There was a dull red glow in the window, and a wisp of smoke from the chimney. We stood rooted there in baffled silence but Credo carried on towards the house, her tail wagging. Scottie called her back with a low whistle but she ignored him, trotted up to the door and began tapping it with her paw.

After a moment the door opened and a silhouette appeared. It immediately crouched down and hugged Credo whose tongue slappings of its face were clearly audible. It was a small shapely female silhouette and Scottie was already running towards it, turning into a silhouette himself, and then the two shadows were locked in each other's arms, becoming one. I allowed a few moments for this communion to take place and then stepped forward myself to offer my heartfelt greetings to The Princess Elphane Clariel Shahribe of Zinn.

CHAPTER 16

A Legal Argument

IF SCOTTIE was joyfully surprised to find Elfie in his house, how ecstatically amazed was I to find her in the land of the living, and discover that rumours of her death had been scandalously exaggerated by that gossiping peripatetic crone I'd had the misfortune to encounter. Credo was bounding up and down in excitement and my heart was bounding too inside me. Elfie burrowed into Scottie's broad chest and he held her so tight the two of them seemed to be morphing into one, but she managed to lean out for a second to place a kiss on my cheek. For a while we were just too happy to speak, and then Scottie said with unconscious irony, "When I saw the light I thought there was a ghost in the house."

"Do I look like one?" she said. "I think I might be."

"Well," said I, "that kiss you just gave me didn't feel like a ghost's."

"They say you die if a ghost kisses you," she replied.

"But we're not dead. We're alive! Alive!" I said, "All four of us. It's wonderful, astonishing – we're alive, alive, alive . . ." and Credo barked in choric response to my exultation.

"My God," said Scottie, "he's finally lost it. He's over the edge. You'd never believe it but he was as miserable as sin half an hour ago."

"I told you I'd perk up," I replied. Then Elfie said:

"We had all better try and calm down a bit as we've got lots of catching up to do. I was just making some hot chocolate when you arrived so if you boys would like a mug we could all sit down by the fire and tell each other our news."

To this we heartily assented. Elfie skipped off into the kitchen to prepare the drinks, Scottie threw a couple of logs on the fire and we sank down in the sofas and stretched our legs in blissful comfort. Where we'd expected a cold, lifeless interior, reproachful of our absence, all was warm and cosy and dusted neat and tidy, and radiant with Elfie's presence. She came in with the tray of drinks and Credo who had gone into the kitchen with her emerged with a tasty bone and sat between us on the rug, with warmth, food and the assembled pack around her in doggie heaven. Elfie sat as close to Scottie as was physically possible and said, "You must have had such adventures all three of you - you must tell me everything. Is it true you flooded the Looshin Levels and drove the loggers away?" Scottie replied:

"We'll tell you every last detail, but the lady first! I must know how you came to be here and if ... well, if ... how long you can stay?"

I was glad Scottie insisted on hearing Elfie's story before we told ours as I was agog to know how she came to be unattainable one minute, dead the next, and then the next alive, bright eyed and bushy tailed, right here in front of our eyes. Elfie snuggled up to him and said, "I'll never leave you again Scottie. Never, ever," and a tear rolled down her cheek. There were more heartfelt exchanges of this kind, too mawkish to record. I sat and sipped my chocolate, staring into the fire where the rise and fall of empires and all the glory and chaos of human life passed before me. And then Elfie told us her story:

When I got back to my aunt's after seeing you last there was a message waiting for me to return immediately to Zinn. An escort was arranged and by midday next I was back at home. Mother was in a great flap and everyone was rushing around in panic and confusion except my father who had shut himself up in his library. "What on earth's happened?" I asked.

"Really Elphane, you live in your own little world without a thought for what might be occurring at home or if you might be needed sometimes

to lend a hand. Surely you've heard your sister Zarielle is going to be married?

"News to me," I said. "Who's the lucky man?"

"Oh I despair of you, child - Prince Baldark of course. And Jobu has proclaimed the wedding is to be in ten days' time to coincide with the victory celebrations." You'll know this Scottie, but Jason might not, that Baldark is Jobu's favourite nephew, and heir apparent. Zarielle was spending most of her time at the Palace and was in a permanent swoon and my other sister was away on a hunting trip with Lord Jashmin and his family and is engaged to one of his sons so she couldn't possibly be summoned so I was brought home to help. Not that Mummy really needed me - she could get all the help she needed and had engaged this madly flamboyant fantasy wedding creative designer person who was flouncing around waving his arms and rearranging the whole place and ordering everything at colossal expense, and Daddy was refusing to get involved and really Mummy just wanted someone to talk to and calm her nerves. Well of course I did my best.

Anyway in a day or two we managed to get things more or less in order and everyone knowing what they had to do and had contrived to bring the maestro down to earth a bit, but all this time I was very sad because I was missing my Scottie and thinking how unfair it was because I could never marry the man I love. I was having a little cry in my room when Mummy came in and saw me and asked me what the matter was and I didn't say anything but she realised and said "Never mind darling. Your turn will come soon enough. There are lots of young men who really like you and once we're related to Jobu you'll be a bit of a prize I can tell you." This only made me cry even more and I said I'm in love with a man who's worth more than all of them put together, and she said "Darling that's wonderful. I knew someone would take an interest in you sooner or later. Tell me who it is it, I'm dying to know," so like a fool I told her. I blabbed it all out and her eyes went hard as steel and her voice went cold.

"Elphane!" she said. "You must put this nonsense out of your head immediately." And I just cried and cried and she said, "I really can't be doing with this, on top of everything else I've had to deal with. It's so selfish of you. I'm going to have to talk to your father about this and insist that he beats some sense into you. You'll be the ruin of us all."

So saying she marched out and I just sat there sobbing and wishing I was dead. About ten minutes later she came back and said "Your father will see you now." I do like my dad, he can be quite fun sometimes but he's very strict and won't stand anyone stepping out of line. "I'm really for it now I thought." I crept along to the library and tapped on the door. "COME IN" boomed his voice from the other side so I stepped in and stood there trembling like a naughty schoolgirl. He was sitting at his desk by the window all dark and angry. "SIT DOWN" he said.

"NOW, GIRL, WHAT IS ALL THIS ABOUT. YOUR MOTHER SAYS YOU'VE TAKEN UP WITH SOME ROUGH FELLOW. WHAT IS THE MEANING OF IT?"

"He's not a rough fellow Daddy he's a lovely kind generous man and a perfect gentleman and I love him and he loves me and I don't want to marry anyone else."

"AND THE FELLOW'S NAME IF YOU PLEASE?" he said taking up his pen and I said, "Daddy I can't tell you."

"HIS NAME?" he repeated. "Scottie . . . I mean Alseph . . . Alseph Emmisarius." He began writing it down then stopped half way and said, "Did you say Emmisarius?"

"Yes Daddy."

"The son of the philosopher Emmisarius?"

"Yes Daddy, that's the one."

"How extraordinary," he said. "I was just reading all about him and his brother in his father's book. A most remarkable book. And you've met this young man, you know him?"

"Yes Daddy."

"And you say that you and he are in love and you wish to marry him? This isn't some childish fantasy of yours is it?"

"No Daddy. I met him when I was a little girl and used to ride in the woods at Auntie Mordrid's and he told me wonderful stories and all about the creatures in the woods and we've been meeting ever since."

"Well that's really interesting. You must introduce me next time we're over there - as soon as this damn wedding's finished with. He helped in his father's research you know. A very intelligent young man by all accounts."

"Oh he is Daddy, I'm sure you would like him and have some very

interesting conversations with him. So I can marry him after all then?"

"Good heavens no, child. Tut, tut. That's quite out of the question. Besides I don't think I could stand another wedding."

"But Daddy it wouldn't be at all the same I promise you. We'd get married ever so quietly in the forest, just a few friends and you and Mummy of course."

"My dear girl, you know how the law stands on these matters. It's forbidden, and there's an end of it."

"But isn't reading his father's book forbidden as well?" I asked all innocently.

"I'll read whatever book I damn well like in my own library I'll tell you young lady."

Then I stood up and said, "And I'm my father's daughter and I'll marry whatever man I damn well like and no one's going to stop me." And I started to walk out but he called me back:

"Well, well, indeed. Spirited I must say. But you have a point my dear. Never let it be said I can't take a point. Hmm. So you are really determined to marry this man?"

"Yes Father, determined."

"In that case we have a problem, an interesting problem and one which I shall enjoy finding a solution to. Leave me to think it over and come back in about an hour."

"But what shall I tell Mummy?"

"Oh God, tell her anything for now. Tell her I gave you a good hiding and you've seen sense."

I ran upstairs to my room and I was hugging myself and jumping up and down I was so happy and surprised at what Daddy had said and even more at what I had said. Then a bit later Mummy came in and she was all sympathetic and apologetic now saying how hard it was to be a parent as I'd understand one day and sometimes you had to be cruel to be kind and deal firmly with things before they got out of hand and how she and Daddy really loved me and had my best interests at heart and all the usual stuff. She'd spoken to Daddy she said and he would see me again as soon as I was feeling better and she was sure he would say exactly the same things as she was saying. So after a while I went down to the library again and he had some big fat law books on his desk and was peering at one of them through his eye glass: "Rum thing the law, my girl, rum thing. It appears that while it's totally illegal for you to marry young Emmisarius, there's no law at all against your BEING MARRIED to him."

"That doesn't make sense Daddy, how can I be married to him unless I marry him?"

"Quite. The reasoning appears to go as follows. No person of your rank and dignity in their right state of mind would conceivably wish to marry a person of lower status. Either then you are insane, in which case you are ineligible for marriage and it would be annulled, or you have been deceived, seduced, drugged, or compelled by force to consent to marriage. Ipso facto your seducer is guilty of the offence of rape, whether or not sexual intercourse has taken place. The marriage would be annulled and so, I'm afraid, would he. However if you are legally married to that person you will have gone through a process and ceremony designed to test your sanity and consent in a public place before impartial witnesses, the law stipulates at least twenty, entitled to veto the proceedings on valid medical or legal grounds."

"So it's like I said Daddy. If we just get married quietly . . ."

"HUSH child. Never interrupt a legal argument. It has form, like a poem. Now where was I? A secret marriage would be out of the question. It would not conform to the legal requirement for the banns to be read and for it to be recorded and published in Zinn. As soon as that happened the cat would be out of the bag, if you'll pardon a non-legal expression, and the weight of the law would descend on you both like the wrath of the gods. Now then. The publication of the banns can be carried out either by the parents or guardians of the couple in question, or by the couple themselves, to take account of the possibility the former may be deceased. So you and Emmisarius can publish your own banns."

"But he hasn't actually asked me to marry him yet because he knows he can't. And he's gone away now and I can't get in touch with him." Daddy thought about this for a moment and then asked:

"Are you absolutely sure he wants to marry you?"

"Yes I am. Absolutely."

"Hmm. Well I don't see that's a major problem. You can publish the banns on behalf of you both and it can be formally recorded and made known."

"But then he'll be arrested and executed and we'll all be disgraced and . . ."

"Be patient child. Be patient. The next step is the most important. As soon as the declaration has been made public your mother and I adopt a time-honoured procedure known as the 'riding accident'. We announce that the Princess Elphane suffered a tragic accident while out riding and is, alas, no more. All our friends will send us their condolences but they will know perfectly well what this means. 'Riding accident' is a euphemism, a . . . well . . ."

"I know what a euphemism is Daddy."

"Oh, yes, of course you do, quite so. It will be taken to mean you've lost your senses, broken the rules, and been sent away somewhere to a private institution where you will receive appropriate care and will not be heard of again. In some cases I fear even the private institution may be a euphemism. At any event: end of story. BUT, you will have published the banns and will now be free to gather your trusted friends together and become married, at which point the law cannot touch you. It may never even become known. If it did I would not escape censure but to be perfectly frank with you I don't give a damn." I practically gasped at this.

"You're so clever Daddy, you've worked it all out. But you'll come as well, won't you, to the wedding, you and Mummy, and you'll come and see us and meet Scottie and his friend Jason the traveller from far away who I know you would love to meet and have conversations with, and all the other people we know in the forest who are good-hearted honest folk. You promise me Daddy . . ."

"Of course my dear, of course. To tell you the truth I was intending to move to the country in any case. I've had about as much as I can stand of that idiot Jobu and his stupid 'war on anarchy' - a moron besotted with an oxymoron. And as for that oaf Baldark your sister's marrying, God help us all when he takes over. I'm thankful my dear, thankful, that at least one of my offspring has had the sense to fall in love with a man of character, and I look forward very much to shaking him by the hand.'

I ran over to him and started kissing him madly but he gently pushed me away and said:

"Elphane my child, before you get too carried away I must tell you there is one serious drawback to all this that may well give you pause. If and when you marry this man you will lose your rank as princess, and it would be illegal for me to make any gift or bequest to you at any time. You will become, to all intents and purposes, a common person." And I replied: "Daddy I don't mind or care in the least and I will be more than happy to be no longer a part of the Zinn aristocracy and all its cruelties."

"Quite right my dear. Just as I expected. Now you'd better run along and carry on stopping your mother from becoming totally hysterical and that lunatic popinjay from spending every penny I've got. As soon as this ghastly business is finished we'll remove to the country and set things in motion."

After that Mummy mistook my tears of joy for tears of contrition and she carried on being ever so nice to me and I was ever so helpful in return. The wedding and victory celebrations were the biggest event in Zinn for years. Absolutely everybody in the aristocracy was there and a public holiday was proclaimed and there were street parties and bands and military parades. You would have heard about it if you hadn't been so far away. The ceremony and reception at our place went off splendidly to Mummy's great relief, and then the main festivities took place in the golden oriel of the high palace. You can see for miles through the crystal windows and I looked out and thought of you out there, far away in the mountains or the forest, wandering lost or in some dreadful danger and wished I was with you and Jason and Credo, all of us together.

I have to admit that my sister looked stunningly beautiful in her shimmering silk dress which seemed to shine with its own light inside. I always envied her beauty but I didn't envy her her husband, a poor specimen in my view, even in his red and gold uniform an apology for a man compared to my Scottie. And then oh dear all the speeches and addresses that went on and on and the wedding feast with course after course and the toasts and then the evening ball and all the time people were saying to me 'Never mind Elphane, your time will come' with their pitying looks and thinking 'poor thing she'll have to wait I expect, she'll be lucky if anyone can be found.' I was just about ready to drop and said to Mummy "Can we please go home now?" And she said "Of course not darling we must stay to the end. Why don't you dance like the other young people?" "It would help if somebody asked me" I said, and was about to be scolded for my cheek when Daddy cut in with "Really ma'am, can't you see the girl's had as *much as she can take. It can't be easy for her with her sister getting all the attention. You and Amarel stay and I'll take her home. You can say she's not well." And so saying he swept me away and the coach was ordered and off we went and he said "Well if you could have stood any more of it I certainly couldn't." And then I fell asleep on his shoulder.*

Well, after all the fuss was over and the happy couple had departed on a round the world honeymoon tour the rest of us packed up and went out to the country, and no one knew besides Daddy and me that we wouldn't be coming back. It was only when his books arrived in several cartloads that the penny dropped. He summoned us and Aunt Mordrid to his newly furnished library and announced his intention to stay and assent to my marriage in his voice that must be obeyed. Aunt Mordrid and Amarel thought it was all quite a lark but Mummy looked very miffed. Later she said to me, "Well Elphane you are a sly little thing aren't you, I only hope your father knows what he's doing and we won't all become a laughing stock. It's a good thing we are staying on the estate and don't have to endure the comments and condolences of our acquaintances in the city. At least your two sisters have chosen partners who will bring honour and respect to the family, so I must be grateful for that. And as for you, child, I only hope you don't come to regret throwing away your rank and inheritance and that this young man of yours is everything you and your father believe him to be." And I said "You will meet him won't you Mummy and see for yourself how nice he is and come to our wedding and give us your blessing?" And she said "I suppose I'll have to if you father commands it," but then seeing how upset I was and starting to cry again she put her arms round me and said she loved me and only wanted me to be happy and I said I loved her too and was sorry I'd always been so much trouble to her, and she said I'd understand her feelings when I had children of my own, and then she kissed me and I could see even though my tears that she really did care about me despite all her worries about what people think.

So the plan was carried out and the marriage announced and then the riding accident took place and the people on the estate thought it really had and news got around and I had to hide. I stayed in Amarel's room and she brought me my meals and the news and she was really friendly and interested like a proper sister. No one knew except my parents, Aunt

*Mordrid, and Molder, my father's faithful butler. There were rumours of a
great flood where you and Jason had gone and that you were coming back
so one dark night I rode over here. Daddy wanted to escort me but I said
I knew the way very well and would be quite safe because if anyone saw
me they'd think I was a ghost and run away. He said that was a good
point. So here I am and I've been here on my own for nearly two weeks
and I was starting to think you might not come or had been killed by the
loggers or the soldiers or had decided to live somewhere else and had fallen
in love with a very beautiful girl and I would stay here till I died of grief
and loneliness and shame. And then I heard Credo whimpering and
scratching on the door.*

At this point in her helter skelter narrative Elfie disappeared again
into the embrace of her lover and only muffled words and sobs
were audible. I was touched myself, I have to say, as well as entertained by these glimpses of domestic normality among the ruling
caste of a ruthless empire. It was thus, no doubt, in Nero's Rome
and Hitler's Berlin. When she had regained her composure and
dabbed her eyes with her hankie and said she was sorry to be such
a baby I suggested we should leave our story for another time as
it was late, and we were tired from our journey and we were all
exhausted from the emotional outpourings of our homecoming.

Two beings more wedded in body and soul than Scottie and Elfie
it would be hard to imagine, and it might be expected that Scottie would now bear his beloved away to his bed. But I had lived
long enough in Zinn, and with Scottie in particular, to know that
moral and marital codes were strictly observed, except perhaps
among the lowest of the low. Elfie did retire to Scottie's bed, but not
with him. I reclaimed my old sofa bed and he made up another,
Credo absorbing the last heat from the fire on the hearth rug, and
it was not long before deep and contented sleep claimed us all.

It was in fact only possible for Scottie and Elfie to sleep under
the same roof because of my presence as a witness and chaperone,
and the first thing that had to be arranged on the following day
was for her to move in with a respectable family in the village
until the ceremony had taken place; and it would be brought

forward with as much speed as possible. We made our way to the village where we were greeted with something approaching rapture. The whole community gathered in the village hall to hear our story, or rather stories, for there was the tale of Scottie and Elfie's courtship and engagement to be told as well as the saga of the Looshin Levels.

Scottie on both accounts was the recipient of wagon loads of congratulations, admiration and good wishes. Elfie was not unknown in the forest, and much liked as the only one of the lords and ladies who occasionally came there who was not 'stuck up'. The fact that she was now prepared to cast off her rank and privilege to marry a humble forester raised her higher in general esteem. The only ones a little less than delighted at the forthcoming nuptials were certain village maidens who had hopes in Scottie's direction themselves. But this was compensated for by the satisfaction of several young men who were glad to see their chief rival removed from the field.

The village was served by a peripatetic priest. He had visited recently and was not expected again for several weeks, so a messenger was dispatched to request the services of another, a genial man who had ministered among the poor in Zinn before retiring to an area bordering the forest. The ceremony was to be a very simple one and take place in the glade where Scottie's father was buried. The requisite number of witnesses would be made up by members of the Shaldar family who had taken Elfie in, the village elders, Scottie's closest friends in the neighbourhood, Elfie's parents it was hoped, and possibly her aunt and sister, and myself in the honoured position of best man.

The reception would be held in the village and everyone was invited. Elfie had already been taken over by the village ladies who would attend to her dress and deportment, and pass on their collective wisdom regarding the married state. Scottie saw very little of her in the days leading up to the ceremony.

However the three of us were together for one rather delicate mission. It was decided best for us to go in person to invite Elfie's family. They could meet their future son in law and the ice could perhaps be broken, or at least a little melted, before the ceremony itself. We rode over one crystal clear morning, a journey of about two hours on horseback, feeling somewhat subdued and anxious about the encounter ahead. Elfie talked brightly enough but it was obvious that she too was uncertain of the outcome. Parents were unpredictable beings. Even her father might have had second thoughts.

There was a moment of light relief when I pointed out to Scottie that as far as I knew he hadn't actually proposed, and she had not accepted his offer of marriage. He immediately dismounted and knelt beside Elfie's pony and formally requested her hand. She tossed her head and rode on disdainfully and he ran after her pleading, imploring piteously. Eventually she drew rein and with a show of weary reluctance gave her consent, and offered the tips of her fingers to be kissed.

We came to the high stone wall that surrounded the estates. There was a small gate to which Elfie had the key. I suggested that I should go ahead and announce the arrival beforehand as they would be quite unprepared, and this suggestion was eagerly accepted. Elfie unlocked the door and I passed from one world to another.

I was taken aback by the scale of everything: rolling parkland as far as the eye could see with great majestic trees and stands of fine timber, and, except for a few cattle on a distant rise, not a creature in sight. A mile or so ahead of me lay a shimmering lake, and beyond it, through a vista of trees, what I can only describe as a stately home, a dream-like edifice of pearl grey stone. I made my way across this ordered, empty landscape, the path joining the main gravel drive which, rather than deviate to skirt the lake, spanned it at its widest point on a well proportioned bridge of many arches. Crossing the broad carriage concourse and ascending a sweep of marble steps to the pillared portals I tugged on a massy iron bell-pull and heard a hollow clanking far within.

After several minutes a door panel creaked open and the tallest, snootiest butler I have ever seen looked down upon me with undisguised contempt. "Your business?" he demanded. I explained with as much dignity as a man of my small stature could summon that I was there to herald the approach of the Princess Elphane and her intended, and would he be so kind as to inform her parents. "Your name?" I told him and the door closed. More minutes passed before he returned and I was ushered in to a vast dim baronial hall and led through dark panelled corridors to arrive at length at a door which looked too heavy and shut ever to open.

My guide opened it none the less, stepped in and closed it firmly again, and I heard my name pronounced with that degree of scorn which only headmasters can command when addressing some small quaking offender. I was then shown into a room which was by contrast bright and cheerful, with blue and white decor and a view of the lake and the park. An elderly man, well built with strong features dressed in fusty tweeds and a somewhat younger woman in grey velvet, with the remnants of beauty in her care-worn countenance, stood facing me by the window. The Prince strode forward, extending his hand.

"BROCKHURST, my dear fellow, it's good to meet you. My wife, Esolday. WELL. I understand you have conducted two young people here who have a certain announcement to make. I think you'll find us prepared for what is to come. Absolutely no need for you to go back for them - I'll send someone out, and in the meantime I trust you'll join us in a glass of something that will raise our spirits to the occasion. Esolday my dear, if you'd be so good."

So saying he opened the door and fired a volley of sharp instructions at the butler whose responses were now gravely subservient. Meanwhile the lady turned to a side table and poured dark liquid from a decanter into tall crystal glasses. She asked me if I thought the weather exceptionally fine for the time of year. I explained it was my first year in Zinn so I had no basis for comparison. "Oh dear, I quite forgot. But your Zinnian is excellent." "I have your daughter mainly to thank for that," I replied. "Oh really," she said. "How interesting. Do take a seat."

We both sat rather stiffly in chairs by the window holding our glasses. In a moment the Prince joined us and took a swig from his, which was a signal for us to take a sip from ours. In contrast to his wife's edgy hauteur his manner was entirely relaxed and reassuring. He began by asking me bluntly, as a man of the world, my opinion of young Alseph Emmisarius, and would I recommend him as a son-in-law. He insisted that I be entirely frank. In reply I said that the Princess had just complimented me on my proficiency in the Zinnian tongue but I had yet to find words adequate to describe my regard, affection and admiration for my dear friend.

"And how long have you known him?" asked the Princess, frostily.

"Well Ma'am," I replied, "perhaps no more than six months, but in that time we have lived together, worked together, travelled together and faced almost certain death together. I can vouch for his courage and generosity. And his feelings towards your daughter are the finest and tenderest you could imagine." "My word!" said the Prince with a hearty laugh, "you could almost be married to him yourself." "I was going to add," I said, "that I would be unwilling to give him up to anyone else but your charming daughter." The Prince continued:

"My dear sir, you have said enough on that score to satisfy me. And if I may speak for Esolday, I am sure she will come round to my way of thinking. I am usually right, am I not my dear?"

"I think you are used to being right," she corrected.

"Point taken, my dear. Point taken. In any case I was already disposed in the young man's favour by the account of his childhood and upbringing in his father's book. You've read it of course Brockhurst. In my opinion Emmisarius is the greatest philosopher Zinn has produced. The greatest, without question."

"His views are certainly radical," I replied, "and perhaps in some respects not entirely practical."

"You touch a nerve sir, you touch a nerve. Of course you are right. The way I live and my family and my people live, is entirely at odds with his prescriptions. I am fully aware of it. But it would be very difficult for me to attempt to conform to them, and quite pointless. I can do small things of course, in the management of my affairs, and ensure the wellbeing of those for whom I am responsible. But I recognise that the world I have known must change, and will change. Not suddenly, and I greatly hope not violently, but through broad and gradual recognition of those fundamental truths that the great Emmisarius has laid before us."

"The banning of the book in Zinn and embargo on its export cannot be assisting that process," I remarked.

"HA! You'd better not get me started on the follies of the current administration. I am regarded, Sir, as a loose cannon, and I have been told to moderate the expression of my opinions not only by our leader, but more formidably, by my wife."

"Well if you're not prepared to upset the apple cart why go on about it?" chimed in the lady in question.

"A fine thrust my dear. A fine thrust. I was going to add that the best way to get a book noticed is to attempt to suppress it. But Esolday is right. I am what I am, and the rest is just talk. But it is to the young we must look for change, for new and exciting possibilities; to the young who question conventional thinking, and on whom the grip of age old habits of thought and behaviour is less rigorous. And that, Sir, is why I regard with interest, and indeed with favour, this initiative of my youngest daughter who is prepared to give up all this (a sweep of his hand taking in the house, the estate, and the entire principality) for a new way of life - simpler, closer to nature, more true to the human heart."

"I see," said the Princess, who had glanced out of the window during this exposition, "that our young redeemers are now approaching."

Minutes later the butler reappeared and drew breath to make his announcement, but the Prince cut him short. "All right Molder, that will do. Just show them in if you please." They were hardly in the room before he had stridden across it to embrace Elfie and shake Scottie warmly by the hand with every expression of pleasure and welcome. But it was the Princess's reaction that most interested me, and I watched her closely. Without being able to see the joints in question I would say she went weak at the knees.

Scottie, as I might already have mentioned, was an extraordinarily handsome man, tall of stature, broad of shoulder, fair of face, with fine eyes and firm lips, and with his easy natural grace and attentive, unassuming manner the effect he had on women of all ages was palpable, if unconscious on his part. Introduced to Esolday he said no more than that he was delighted to meet her, but as he raised her hand to his lips I was certain, without having a finger on her pulse, that her heart missed a beat. Momentarily those elements of girlish beauty that still haunted her face came to life again. She quickly reassumed her *noblesse oblige* manner, but never quite convincingly and there was a hint of perplexity about it. Perhaps she was asking herself how a mere prole could be so princely in bearing, or perhaps wondering how her wayward urchin of a youngest daughter could have captured this god and brought him down to earth.

CHAPTER 17

Consummations

ONCE IT WAS clear that the mission had been a success we could relax and enjoy the lavish hospitality offered by the house of Shahribe. Scottie in any case was perfectly at ease and seemed as much so in this environment as in the lowly dwellings of the forest folk.

On the way to the dining hall we passed through chambers filled with the most splendid artefacts, objects carved, inlaid, painted, gilded, and bejewelled with exquisite art and craftsmanship, from the smallest ornament to panoramic pictorial tapestries of historic events and hunting scenes and august ancestral portraits. The Prince and Princess paid not the slightest attention to any of them, nor paused once to point out something of particular beauty or interest. It was simply unquestioned normality for them to be surrounded by treasures that had cost generations of dedicated genius, toil and skill. I surmised that their effortless acceptance and acquisition of Scottie, once they had set eyes on him, had something to do with this assumption that anything of exceptional quality had its natural place within their sphere of existence.

The rest of the day passed very pleasantly. We were joined by Elfie's aunt Mordrid and sister Amarel. The sumptuous setting and obsequious serving of lunch made the fare seem more special than in fact it was - but then we had called unannounced. Elfie was so pleased and happy it was a delight just to watch her as she passed from one to another in animated chatter and unrestrained hugging, then flitting back to Scottie's side as if to say 'yes he really is my man', while the man in question, at the centre of attention, was calm and modest, without a hint of self-consciousness.

Mordrid was a tough, forthright, commonsensical old spinster who had taken Elfie under her wing as a waif of a child and, it transpired, was in her confidence regarding the affair with Scottie, of which she heartily approved. Amarel, a handsome athletic girl, came in flushed from a long ride. She was less able or bothered to conceal her reaction to Scottie than her mother. She looked at him, and then at Elfie, and then at him again, her eyes getting wider each time. I saw her and Elfie in a girly huddle together and took a shrewd guess as to what they were giggling about.

With the Prince on cracking form, not a dull moment was possible. An admirable conversationalist, he was ready to expound his views but also to question and listen, to concede a point and provoke contradiction. While the ladies inspected the gardens he showed Scottie and me the one room he did take a passionate interest in, his library. Books were everywhere in careless profusion, and he would dislodge a pile to retrieve one and throw it open in front of us; and it might be some finely printed and brilliantly illustrated or illuminated, and richly bound volume of great antiquity such as gloved hands alone would reverently touch in the British Library. His copies of Scottie's father's books led to a deep discussion between the two concerning some finer points in the texts, and the Prince's eyes positively blazed when he heard that Scottie was in possession of the seer's unpublished manuscripts. "We should edit them, my dear Alseph, and publish; at my expense of course. As soon as all the fuss has died down we must get together."

By now it was getting a little late in the afternoon and the Prince and Princess invited us to stay the night. We were mindful however of the anxiety our failure to return would cause so we gratefully declined, stressing the need to attend to the wedding arrangements. "God help us, all that bother again. But it's getting dark already – you'll at least allow me to arrange an escort." "Sir," replied Scottie, "the forest is my home. And you have graciously consented to entrust your daughter's future protection to me." "Indeed, dear boy, sound points. Till we meet again then, on the happy day."

So with handshakes and kisses we mounted and rode off. At the bridge we turned to wave, and the four noble Shahribes stood at the top of the marble steps waving back, while behind them, in the gloom of the doorway, stood Molder the butler, like a disconsolate spectre.

The happy day, when it arrived, was blessed with pleasantly mild weather, a wistful memory of summer. It was usual for a spell of such weather to come between the heavy autumn rains and the rigours of winter. With the bride's appearance spring was again in the air. Silk and satin gowns from many wardrobes had contributed to a pink and white creation with tight fitting bodice and cascading train, and as many greenhouses had contributed to the floral adornments and bouquet. She walked as in a dream; indeed without her glasses she needed the steady guidance of her father's arm. And she was a dream, an ethereal being; among her numerous bridesmaids, all in pretty dresses and bedecked with flowers: a queen of the fairies.

Scottie was attired in what for the foresters passed as Sunday best: white linen shirt, drab waistcoat with brass buttons, cord trousers with shiny leather belt and gaiters; a bright red silk necktie the only concession to colour. It was a garb that suggested yeoman-like independence. The benign old priest led them through the responses, spoken in clear unfaltering voices in the still air; and blessed them, as only the wise and gentle can, as one who passes on the gift of life itself.

We were all surprised and delighted by the appearance, just as the service began, of two additional witnesses: Leevil Prendis, and his brother in law Bilder.

Back at the village a band of foresters, in similar gear to Scottie, had formed a guard of honour, with raised staves making a corridor through which the couple entered the hall. Proceedings began with the speeches, which were briefer than those I was accustomed to, but all the principles were expected to say a few words. My soundings indicated that more in the way of candour than humour was called for, an act of witness rather than a performance.

The Prince spoke first, and pronounced himself a doubly convinced Emmisarian, first from reading the works of the great philosopher, and second from meeting his son, whom he was honoured to have now as his own son, and who represented all the social virtues of which Emmisarius wrote so eloquently. He repeated his profound belief that the false divisions that separated mankind and set them against each other would one day pass away, and the young would lead the way in this peaceful revolution. Esolday said that she of course bowed to her husband's wisdom in all matters, while not always agreeing with him, but in this instance she had been swayed by Alseph's personal charm and his obvious devotion to her daughter. Elphane, she confessed, had been a difficult child, and she may at times have been over strict with her, but the love between them was never in doubt, and never stronger than it was at present.

My own contribution consisted of a few reminiscences of key moments in my friendship with Scottie, especially the circumstances under which we first met. If he could be so generous, I opined, towards a destitute and fugitive stranger, how certain was it that he would always treat with loving care the one he loved as deeply and passionately as ever man loved woman. Aunt Mordrid said that despite her frailty Elphane never lacked courage, and never gave up. After a tumble from her horse she always got straight back on again, and she was sure it would be the same with her marriage. Amarel said she wished she'd gone riding in the forest as a little girl and if there were any more lads like Alseph hiding there she would be pleased to meet them.

Elphane spoke in her clear flute-like tones. She thanked her parents for her upbringing and said they had only been as strict as she had deserved, and her dear Aunt Mordrid for helping her and teaching her so much and her sisters who had been so patient with her childish ways and she hoped would be as happy as she was in their choice of partners. As for Scottie, everyone in the forest knew how caring he was and he had been unfailingly kind and good to her since they first met. Her debt of gratitude was as infinite as her love, and she would spend the rest of her life repaying it.

Finally Scottie rose to his feet. His merits, he declared, had been greatly exaggerated by previous speakers, and as his good friend Jason and his friends in the village knew, he was not always as even tempered and patiently understanding in his disposition as had been alleged. However in one point these eulogies had been spot on, and that was his love for and devotion to Elphane. Even as a little girl she had touched his heart because of her outgoing love for all living creatures. She would carefully lift a half drowned worm from the footpath and place it safely in the moist soil, and at one time his house was full of the wounded birds and animals she had found in the woods. Even snakes and toads and suchlike – they were all her friends. Such a tender concern and love for life itself had seemed to him, in a hard and cruel world, a precious and fragile thing, and roused in him the strongest passion a man could feel, the impulse to protect. Love of the marrying kind, of man and woman – that came later, but rested still on the firm foundation of his recognition of a beautiful soul, and his desire and determination to protect and cherish that soul for the rest of his life, and if need be, with his life.

There was a great round of applause and sage nods of approval from the elders. Everyone had spoken well. The party started immediately. Doors burst open and huge plates and trays of food were brought out from the steaming kitchens and laid on the tables. Sparkling wines and fruit juices and foaming ales followed. There was no order to proceedings, no place settings or anything to limit free movement and the flow of conversation. The bride and groom passed among the company receiving tributes of esteem and well-wishings from all. The Shahribe family were made especially welcome and drawn into the circle of communal happiness and shared good will.

The Prince needed little drawing in, and his strong voice could be heard here and there in active conversational engagement. I was somewhat concerned about him, and for him; and felt that on this occasion it fell to me to keep within earshot and steer the conversation where necessary. He was, as he'd said himself, something of a loose cannon. There was a general agreement now among all the foresters to say nothing about the Looshin business, and allow the belief or agreed fiction that it was a natural disaster to prevail. Of course the Prince would not wittingly betray the foresters but he was fearlessly outspoken, and his own position could be exposed as well as theirs.

For the same reason there was also an injunction, applying to young and old, not to publish news of this marriage beyond the present company. Those who believe that conspiracies by large numbers of people are impossible as someone is bound to spill the beans would be surprised to know how many can keep a secret, and for how long. The Zinnian leadership was currently celebrating victory in its 'war on anarchy', and the least provocation they could be given to convert this triumphalism into a 'war on forestry' the better.

Not mentioning the war was particularly tricky when Leevil and Bilder joined the Prince's conversational circle. However we entered on safer ground in talking about the fabulous railway journey from Procter Prendis's sapphire mine to his eastern estate. The idea of reopening the railway right through to this area and running both passenger and goods services had been much talked about and found in the Prince a vigorous supporter. It would "raise the level of life," he insisted - "raise the level. And bring together the elements of a scattered community. It was in my view a mistake, gentlemen, a serious mistake, to allow the old imperial railway to fall into decline."

I was relieved, none the less, when the Prince and his party announced their early departure, pleading the long journey home. It would certainly not have been possible to accommodate them in the forest in the style to which they were accustomed. They made their affecting farewells to their daughter and her husband,

and retired to their coach amid general and genuine good will.

After this came music and dancing, led by Scottie with Elfie melting into his arms, still in her dream. But soon they also were allowed to retire and rode off side by side in the moonlight to the little house where they would now live together. I had made arrangements to stay in the village as it would be right for them to have the first night in the marital home entirely to themselves. Although I had yet to announce my intentions I had decided not to return to live there before setting out on my journey to find the truth about the buzzard children. I was also waiting for an opportunity to talk alone with Leevil and Bilder, who had to leave the following day.

In the glow and euphoria of the occasion it was hardly surprising that no one had asked the question that had troubled me since I first saw them among the group of witnesses. I could see in their eyes that they had not come for a celebration, and their true reason for coming had been put out by the event they had walked into. There was no way that the news could have reached them, and they in turn have reached us, in time. By now I had decided that the answer to this question was the answer that I feared. Procter Prendis was dead.

When at last the opportunity of a private talk arose Leevil told me the old man had increasingly left the management of the estate to Kombard and spent hours sorting through his precious chest of documents, burning the midnight oil. One morning he was found sitting peacefully in his chair, seemingly asleep, but beyond all waking. Envelopes addressed to every one of his children, their spouses, and grandchildren lay neatly set out on his desk.

It was only when these were opened that the full extent of his possessions became known. At a time when the Zinnian government was selling off great tracts of virgin forest he was in a position to buy, and he bought everything he could lay his hands on. The estates became a trust, with Kombard in overall control, but everyone had a stake. Among the many individual and personal gifts was one to Maralese of a bursary to study fashion design in Paris. His guns were distributed among the menfolk. All of them were objects of fine workmanship, but there was one of crude making which he left in trust for Leevil's son Tamon. It was the rifle he had been issued with when he joined a militia fighting in the resistance to the Japanese invasion of the East, and came with the injunction that it should only be fired in a just cause.

A fund was set aside for the development of the estates and another for the reinstatement and extension of a rail service to link them. The remainder of his cash assets, still a very considerable sum, was bequeathed to his wife Peglin, to be disbursed in life and in death according to her own wishes. In a letter addressed to Peglin and the whole family he requested that once they had laid him to rest they should not mourn his death, but rejoice in his long and wonderful life, in which the crowning joy had been their loyalty to him, and their love.

I thanked the two men for making the long journey here to tell us this news and their discretion in withholding it from Scottie on this occasion. I would pass it on as soon as it seemed appropriate, and I knew he would join me in sending Peglin and the Prendis family assurances of our profound sympathy and love and good wishes to them all. Procter had made the longest and most courageous journey of all, from a gainer to a giver, and from a warrior to a man of peace. His life and example would never fade from our memory. Before we parted Leevil took from his bag and handed me two packages, one addressed to Scottie and a bulky one addressed to me.

I lodged with the family of one of the elders, and after we had discussed the day's proceedings, and agreed that it was a glorious one in the annals of the village, I was glad to be alone again in my room. When it came to big events my social stamina was not great, and at some point in them a sense of my loneliness and separateness returned, and a hankering for the road ahead. I was thinking about Procter, who increasingly had become in my thoughts a kindred spirit, and a point of reference. But now he had travelled on ahead of me. Would we meet again? – I wished I could believe it. And somewhere at the back of my mind I could hear the shrivelled voice of that crazed old woman: "Not your road, oh no, not this road. You're not from here."

In contrast to such vague, other-worldly visitations, Procter's bequest, in its solid material reality, sat on the table in front of me, provoking my curiosity; and to dispel any further wandering thoughts I decided to open it straight away. Half of its bulk was made up of Procter's field glasses, wrapped in tissue paper. I remembered the weight and balance of them from that time he had appeared out of the morning mist and handed them to me to scan across a ravaged wasteland and see the emerging menace of the enemy encampment. I would say they were old when Procter acquired them, but a fine piece of optical workmanship none the less, and made to last.

Then in a stout leather box there was a numbered sequence of maps, the complete set from which he had produced the one that covered the area of our operations. The scale was large, and the detail precise, and a quick run through them showed that they covered the entire region encircled by mountains, with the city of Zinn at the centre. But I could find no clue to the location of this land in relation to the world as I knew it. Beyond its perimeters, there was simply white space.

The next item in this treasure trove was a soft leather bag which contained a handful of uncut sapphires, ranging in colour from white to an intense blue. I'm no expert on gem stones but from their size and purity I would guess their value was considerable. Finally there was an envelope containing a document and a letter from Procter, in a bold florid hand, which read as follows:

My Friend and Comrade, I salute you from beyond the Grave. No gifts from me could express my Gratitude towards you, or the Warmth of my feelings. Nevertheless it is a Pleasure to me that I can bestow on you these few tokens of my Esteem, in memory of an inspiring Partnership, and a great Deliverance. The document herewith is a Zinnian Freedom, a kind of Passport. It is not Sovereign against every injustice and indignity this iniquitous regime can inflict upon its Citizens, but it will at least protect you from Arbitrary Arrest, and it will allow you to answer any Charge openly in a Civil Court. It will also allow you to leave Zinn whenever you wish, although it is My Wish and Hope that you will remain with us, and continue your protective Care towards Scottie and his People, and towards my own Family, for which our debt to you is beyond words.

Remember me, my dear Friend as one who loved you, and now for all time, with every Blessing, bids you

Farewell.
Procter Prendis

Despite my tiredness from the day's festivities I hardly slept that night. It was a time when past, present and future, sadness, happiness and apprehension, made equal and insistent demands on my emotions. The generosity with which Procter's gifts supported me, and tender eloquence with which his words released me, made me mourn him the more. But his work was done, and all was well.

There remained my plan to seek out the buzzard children. Now was the time to address myself to it and make my preparations, but my resolve was attacked by fresh uncertainty. Talk of victory celebrations in Zinn suggested they were beyond help, and was I not needed here? On the one hand there was the proposal to re-establish the railway to link and strengthen the communities. And then the alliance with Prince Shahribe opened up diplomatic possibilities. Outspoken and out of favour he might be but he was the father in law of Jobu's right hand man and intended successor. No doubt the Prince was not alone in his views, and there were other liberal elements in the Zinnian establishment, voices reasoning: "Look, we've had our war and our victory. Perhaps now's the time to start mending a few fences and building a few bridges and attending to a few root causes here and there." Such a spirit, if it existed (and it often does after a bout of savage reprisals) might result in legitimising the foresters' settlements and allowing them a degree of independence. I was well placed for an initiative of this kind. Perhaps this was my path.

I slept finally in the early hours and woke mid morning.

Scottie and Elfie had both insisted that I should still live with them after their marriage and my idea of not returning to the cottage until my fact finding trip was over, like the mission itself, was losing ground. Besides, I had to see Scottie to tell him the news of Procter's death, and hand over the package entrusted to me. So I thanked my hosts for their hospitality, gathered my things, and made my way over to my former home. I found Elfie alone in the kitchen, washing up, and dabbing her eyes. "Not tears already!" I said.

"I'm so happy, Jason, it hurts. I can't stop crying."

"Perhaps the problem is you didn't get enough sleep last night," I suggested.

"I don't know what you mean," she said, blushing.

"Well I've never been married myself you know, but I have heard the first night can be quite exhausting."

In reply she hit me with a wooden spoon. And then she said, "But Jason, there's something I really must ask you."

"Honestly I'm not the one to ask. Perhaps one of the married ladies in the village . . ."

She raised the spoon again and looked as menacing as she could, which wasn't very.

"Where is he anyway?" I asked.

"He's gone to his shrine. He likes to meditate there, and talk to his father. And say some prayers."

"Well you're doing really well Elfie. It took me weeks to find that out, and then only by chance. What was it you wanted to ask me?"

"He uses these funny words, and I don't know what they mean."

"I see. What words has he used?"

"He calls me 'hinny', and his 'dautie', and 'bonny lassie'."

"Well you don't need to worry about those words. They mean 'honey' and 'pet' and 'lovely girl'."

"But why doesn't he talk in his own language?"

"Well it's a bit complicated. When he was a little lad his father introduced him to the stories of a writer called Sir Walter Scott.

Scott lived in Scotland when ordinary folk still talked in a language called Scots. Scottie of course has never been to Scotland which is far away. But he liked the idea of Scotland and learnt the Scots language and that's how he got the nickname Scottie. Does that make any sense?"

"Sort of. But I still can't see what makes him want to talk in a funny language."

"I wondered that too. I think the reason is that Zinnian is so formal. Whatever horrible things the Zinnians do they always speak in a sort of official, correct way. Perhaps it's to make the horrible things seem perfectly normal."

"I'm ashamed at what my people do. Such cruelties."

"You're not responsible for them, and you've turned your back on all that."

"But I can't bear to think about it. And I'm so happy, and I think what right have I to be so happy when there is so much suffering? And children too." More tears began to sparkle in her eyes.

"My dear it is your duty to be happy. Every bit of happiness you have and every bit of happiness you give is a blow against the tyrants and the torturers. You mustn't let them kill your happiness. They kill because they are dead themselves. Be alive, be happy Elfie. Always be happy."

"Oh Jason, you say such good things. You make things right."

"If I do, that's what makes ME happy."

She smiled now and said, "So this Scottie talk - he can say things to me he can't say in Zinnian?"

"Yes, that's it. Like 'bonny.' It means lovely, pretty, attractive, good natured, cheerful, and all of them in combination. It's the sweetest word a man can use to describe a woman. There's no word like it in Zinnian, perhaps not in any language. It's a romantic, poetic language, and it's also an honest one. You can really call people names in Scots, and put them bang to rights. It's full of words which mean fool, wretch, idiot, rogue, and so on."

"But how will I know when he's calling me something nice and when he's calling me something bad?"

"Well I think the best thing would be for me to teach you some of the words. I'm not an expert by any means, but I did live in Scotland for a time. It would only be repaying you for teaching me Zinnian."

"Your Zinnian's really good now. No one would know you were a foreigner."

"I'll write out all the words I know and their meanings and you can learn them secretly and one day you can surprise him by answering back in Scots."

"Thank you Jason, that would be lovely. I want to hug you."

Without waiting for permission she ran over and circled me with soapy hands and nuzzled her tear stained face against me, and almost involuntarily I placed a little kiss on the glossy crown of her head. Just as I did so Scottie appeared in the doorway.

"Deil tak me an I canna step oot a blink but ane gyte gallus dig-got is a mirding wi an dauting ma ain."

"Are those bad words?" she whispered.

"They don't come much worse," I whispered back.

"Oh dear. I've got you into trouble."

"I think you might be in trouble as well Elfie."

Scottie strode across the room and grabbed me from Elfie's embrace and pressed me to his chest. Then he reached out an arm and hauled Elfie in and we all huddled together, Credo with furiously wagging tail leaping up and adding to the melée.

CHAPTER 18

Aftermath

THE DAY continued in joyful communion and complete idleness, but for the leisurely preparation, eating and clearing up after a meal, bringing in wood for the fire, and throwing sticks for Credo. We talked non-stop. I asked about their plans, and whether they intended to go away, but as I expected they had no desire to do more than be together in this peaceful place and share each other's thoughts and lives. It was a delight for Elfie to be mistress of her own home, though but a dolls' house by comparison with the scenes she was familiar with, and Scottie had done enough travelling to satisfy him for a good while to come.

There was much to say about the wedding and the guests, in particular about Prince Shahribe's ebullient performance. Esolday was judged to have coped well with social transplantation, seeming neither aloof nor condescending. Mordrid like the Prince was fine just as herself, immediately identified and accepted as a 'character', while Amarel found herself challenged by young people every bit as bright and lively as her own set, if anything more knowledgeable and a good deal less conventional in their attitudes. Elfie said how pleased she was that Leevil and Bilder had come, and to hear more tales from them about the great expedition. While she was talking about this I saw a puzzled frown forming on Scottie's face. "It was good to see them," he said. "But I can't imagine how they found out the wedding was taking place, or how they got here in time unless they flew." This was my cue.

Scottie was shocked and upset to learn of Procter's death, and Elfie upset on his behalf. I had been somewhat more prepared as I had seen a man setting his affairs in order, and reflecting on the course and fruits of his life. I told them he had died peacefully, and in peace. I told them too how he had distributed his land and other property among his descendants, and had left me his field glasses and maps, and a valid passport in case I was arrested again. Scottie remarked rather ruefully that the maps had certainly fallen into the right hands.

He told Elfie that Procter had been like a second father to him, wise, generous and dependable, despite his rough exterior. He was sorry she would never meet him and said we must go over soon to share their loss and give them our good wishes in person. It was too late in the year to travel now, I said, and the two of them really needed a settled time together; but we would certainly go as soon as spring arrived. In the context of bereavement the thought of spring, a new year and a new life together, was cheering for us all.

As we talked about Procter and our exploits together I wondered at what point and in what way Scottie would enquire if any small token had been left for him. I had yet to meet a human being who, however sincere their grief, was utterly without a mercenary or acquisitive thought when a rich person close to them had died. After the conversation had gone on for some time I now realised I had met not just one, but two. The idea that they might, or should, or would have liked to receive some material benefit or memento had clearly not crossed Scottie's or Elfie's mind.

"Oh by the way," I said eventually, "I almost forgot. Procter left something for you as well. It's in my bag I think. I'll go and get it." I fetched the brown paper package and handed it to him. With a slightly blank and puzzled look he broke the seals and unwrapped the contents. Inside was a bundle of documents, some new and some written in sepia ink on ancient parchment, in a crabbed legal hand with many a flourish and faded rubrication. Scottie looked through them blankly, increasingly perplexed.

"I've no idea what all this is Jason. I can't understand a word of it."

"I tell you what Scottie, why don't you and Elfie go for a romantic stroll in the woods and wade through drifts of leaves together while I try and work it all out. I might need to borrow some of your father's dictionaries and reference works."

"Hae aheid laddie," he replied, lapsing into his familiar manner. "For a' the trees are bare and a cauld braith in the air I'd suiner walk in the wuids with ma bonny lass than fash masel kittling oot thir dusty auld scrieves." Elfie gave me a special little smile when she heard the word 'bonny', and the two put on coats, gloves and scarves and went out arm in arm.

It was a good two hours before they returned, flushed and laughing. I already had tea on the go, and was milking over some eggs in the pan with hot sizzling fat. We ate heartily and Scottie seemed to have forgotten all about the documents that I'd laboured over for most of the time they were out. Then his eye caught one I'd left unfolded on the floor, an estate map, and he asked if I'd been able to make any sense of those dreary old papers. "Certainly have old man. And what it comes down to is that you are now a laird." He laughed, and then stopped laughing when he saw I wasn't joking.

"What's a 'laird'?" Elfie asked.

"It's a landowner, like your father," he explained gently; then less gently to me, "Och lad, wha haivers the noo are ye bletherin on?"

"It's just like I say Scottie, those dreary old papers make you a laird, and a rich one too." He glared at me, with a mixture of perplexity and rejection. Elfie looked concerned.

"Some twenty years ago now," I continued, "this part of the forest was sold off by the Zinnian authorities in twelve lots, named after the months of the year. That's why this area is still called Sammonar (September in Zinnian). All but one of the lots were purchased by the Zinnian nobility, like Elfie's father's and aunt's estates. They were cleared, renamed, and turned into fields and parkland, with mansions built on them. Sammonar was the one that no one was interested in - it was too wet and wild I guess, so Procter bought the title deeds, and he's now made them over to you."

I picked up the map and pointed out the shaded area bordering the Shahribe estates and stretching a good ten miles in both directions, including the cottage, the farm, and a sizeable tract of virgin forest. "The other thing he's left you is a stack of government bonds, worth a tidy sum at face value alone, and probably as much again with accumulated interest."

"But Jason," he said quietly. "I don't want to be a landowner, and I don't want to be rich. I'm happy as I am. We share things here. You know that. It was very generous of Procter to think of me, but it's not what I want."

"I do know that," I replied. "And so did Procter. He explains it all in a letter. It's just a precaution. Till now you had no legal entitlement to live here, nor did any of the villagers. The army or the loggers could come and boot you all out, like they did in the Levels. But they couldn't shift Procter because he had the deeds."

"I doubt if a few bits of paper would stop them if they had a mind. They'd force us out one way or another."

"Right, and that's what the money's for. You can hire lawyers to defend you, and if it comes to you being forced to leave and move to another country, at least you'll have the means to set up home there and not end up in slums, or camps, or shanty towns like so many refugees and displaced people. Procter was just thinking of your interests, and thinking ahead as he always did."

Scottie brooded, still not entirely convinced; and then Elfie said, "Jason's right Scottie. Procter was a good man who really cared about you. We just need to put the deeds away somewhere safe and we needn't tell anyone about them, and we'll just carry on the same."

"Aye, well yes," he said with a sigh. "I just don't want things to change. Everything's just perfect exactly as it is. But who knows what may come? Bad things happen in Zinn." Then he got up and said, "I'll just go out and have a think about it.'"

He put his warm clothes on again and went out into the dark

with Credo. Elfie said, "He's gone to talk to his father. I'm sure he'll be all right." She'd been sitting between us both on the rug by the fire, and now she moved closer to me and laid her head against my leg. "Will you stroke my hair please Jason?" she said. "I like having it stroked."

"Elfie dear," I replied, "you're a married lady. Any stroking to be done is your husband's job. You can't just go from one to another like a kitten."

She laughed. "Don't be silly. You're his best friend; he wouldn't mind, he'd like you to."

"But what about my feelings? It would be awful if I fell in love with you."

"Have you ever been in love Jason?"

"Not for a very long time."

"Well there you are. You're completely safe. I just need you to calm me. I'm so excited, but also I'm fearful. Such bad things happen, like Scottie says, and you seem to understand and explain them."

She pressed closer to me and I felt the tension in her. I put my hand on her shiny poll and let it slide smoothly down to her shoulder, flicking the soft, warm little ear half hidden in her hair. The tension disappeared.

We both stared dreamily into the fire and then I said, "I don't have all the answers you know Elfie. There's something that's been on my mind that perhaps you can help me to decide."

She looked up enquiringly. I told her all about my first coming to Zinn and my encounter with the buzzard children, and about the little disabled girl Aya and her sister Sulibe who had in some unspoken way adopted me as their father. I told her why at the time I thought it best to leave, and then in flight from the soldiers had met up with Scottie who had taken me in. I left out my arrest and narrow escape from death at the hands of Scottie's brother, knowing how deep and painful her distress at Zinn's brutalities. But I said that my experiences in fighting the loggers had convinced me that sometimes you can stand up to the bullies and despoilers of this world and I'd come to regret my decision to leave the children. I felt now that I should go there and see if any of them were still alive and if I could help them in any way. If they were dead at least I could mourn, and try to come to terms with my regret, and my guilt at having abandoned them."

She replied, "Oh Jason we really want you to stay, and I don't know what you could do for them. But I see you have to go. You must go or you will never be at peace. Perhaps if you could find the little girls you could bring them back and we could look after them here."

"Yes you're right. I must go. I will go. But I don't know how I'm going to tell Scottie."

"I'll tell him for you. I'm sure he'll understand. I'll tell him tonight. But you will come back won't you?"

"This is my home now and I will do everything in my power to return. I promise it will be the last journey I make on my own."

All this time I continued stroking her hair, but now I retrieved my stroking hand and felt in my pocket for the little bag of sapphires there. I opened the drawstring and spilled them into my palm where they glowed in the firelight.

"They're lovely," she said.

"Procter gave them me. He was thinking if I ever needed money I could sell them. I'm going to take just one, this lovely deep blue one, with me, and if Aya and Sulibe are gone I'll leave it in the grass by the stream where I last saw them. Aya left my clothes there with a daisy chain in the shape of a heart. I want you and Scottie to keep the rest for me until I return. If I don't, I want you to have them."

"You're more precious than any gems to us Jason. But I'll do as you ask. I'll take them upstairs now and put them somewhere safe; and I think I'll go to bed now. Scottie will be back soon. You won't keep him up talking will you?"

"I'm sure I couldn't if I tried."

She gave me a little smack and then a kiss on the cheek and off she went. Just before climbing the ladder she turned and said, "You won't forget to write me a list of Scottie's Scottie words will you?" I promised I wouldn't.

Scottie came in a few minutes later. I could see immediately from his manner that he had come to terms with Procter's bequest and his easy going, upbeat mood had returned. He came over and patted Credo who had settled by the fire in the warm spot left by Elfie. Then he ruffled my hair and clapped his hand on my shoulder, before walking over to ascend the ladder, muttering "Laird he ca's me. Aiblins Laird o' Dumbiedikes on his doited pownie ..."

I sat there staring into the fire and stroking Credo, as I had Elfie a few moments ago. I was wondering why I had changed my mind again about undertaking a dangerous and probably futile journey. Perhaps I *was* afraid of falling in love with Elfie. Perhaps I already had. Certainly she did something to me, something subcutaneous. At this very moment she was in Scottie's bed and in his arms and I asked myself if I was, even in the tiniest, remotest degree, jealous. I had to admit I was not. I felt only happiness for them and wished them absolute, unblemished and unending bliss in each other's bodies and souls. I realised it was comforting Elfie that had brought the thought of Aya and Sulibe into my mind again. Elfie had her strong handsome man to protect her but those poor little mites had no one. We cannot help everyone but there are times when we are chosen. Their claim on me was valid, and therefore sacred.

The next morning I was up early, thinking about the journey and what I would need, and putting my things together. Procter's maps were a timely acquisition, I thought, and I laid out in a chain the ones linking my present location and my projected destination, marked as Marchenor. My route lay in a south-easterly direction crossing the Western Highway, and as all roads like this one radiated out of Zinn there was no direct way, just a maze of local byways, many no doubt disused and overgrown. I'd better take that old billhook, I thought.

I was still on the floor poring over the maps when Scottie descended. He stood looking down at me for some time, his expression unresolved - troubled, hurt, resigned. "You really must go." It was neither quite a question nor a statement.

"I'm sorry Scottie, my dear good friend. I want everything to be perfect too, but this worry of mine about the bairns runs through me like a flaw. They took care of me, and I left them. And then they saved my life. I have a debt and must discharge it before I can lay claim to any of the happiness you and Elfie give me."

"But ye'll come back? Promise me ye'll hasten back."

"If I can; if I'm spared. And I promise then I will never go away on my own again. For the rest of our lives we will travel together."

He joined me on my knees and we embraced briefly. For a few moments he was helpless in my arms, but then I felt his strength and resolution slowly return to him.

"Weel sae be it, ye maun gang yer gate bonny lad." Then glancing at the maps he said, "Y' wurna gang faur wi thae auld cairds Jason. A' the roadies be shiftit."

"I was rather afraid they would be, and my compass is long gone. It'll be a difficult journey."

"Nae laddie, there's a bonny airt an ye ken it." He was smiling now. "Come awa, I'll shaw ye."

He put his thick coat and his boots on and beckoned me to do the same. We stepped out into the cold crisp air. A white hoar frost misted the grass; the trees beyond were black and comfortless. Every nerve rebelled against a journey even as far as the stream whose muted babble was the only sound. We pulled our coats tight round us as walked over to it. The tethered canoe was riding on the stream, just as I'd seen it when I first arrived - it seemed like years since. Scottie prodded it with his foot.

"There's yer airt," he said, and then continued in reply to my questioning look, "An ye fallow this wee burn it will tak ye tae anither, and thereawa tae anither, and then anither muckle braider, and teeming forrit tae ane bonny watter, and the rug will cairry ye onwards and onwards till ye win by the puil, where the bairns were a'ways dooking and splashing ye ken." The memory was indeed poignant.

"A canny road," I said, thanking Scottie for telling me this, and for the use of his canoe. But it occurred to me that it would be a lot easier to go than to return by it.

The rest of the day was spent in planning and preparation.

Scottie rigged me a crawl-in tent and waterproof sleeping bag, a little oil stove and a lamp and supply of fuel. Everything had to be on as small a scale as possible not to overload the boat. He said it was lucky I was a 'droich', which I protested was a gross over-statement, or understatement, of my trim build and spare proportions. Elfie concentrated on nutrition - cooked meats, cheese, preserves, dried fruit, oat and rye bread, again as much as possible into as small a space as possible. I had travelled long enough to acquire some survival skills, and picked up from Scottie a good deal of local knowledge as to what was edible in the forest - roots, berries, fungi and so on; and then there was my fishing rod with flies, floats and tackle. I stowed Procter's field glasses and my Zinnian passport, in case I fell foul of any patrols. I also smuggled in a map of my destination region.

I asked Scottie and Elfie to let me leave quietly; to slip away first thing so my going would seem, as I intended it, just a brief inter-ruption in our lives together. I would like to go to bed early and leave early and say goodnight and goodbye at the same time as any kind of send off would only make the parting harder, more significant. So we all retired after supper, and I spent an hour or so compiling a word list for Elfie, which I hid in a place we'd agreed on, then lay down and tried to sleep.

I'd be fine, I told myself, as soon as I got started. I'd spent most of my life travelling in my own company and I'd soon get back into that way of things, adapting to circumstances as they arose, trusting to luck. The problem was I couldn't envisage any good outcome to the journey. Except perhaps to find absolutely noth-ing, and persuade myself that none of it ever happened.

Then everything got rather strange and sad, and it was only after a conversation with Procter about digging an underground passage beneath the battlefields of the Somme to find his long lost family that I realised I must have slept. But sleep had not eased my fears and forebodings and the only thing was to blank them out, and do what I had to do.

It was still dark as I made my final checks. Most of my stuff was already in the boat. All was silent above, but Credo woke and regarded me with perplexed and sorrowful eyes. I hugged her with all the reassurance I could summon in my hollow, anxious heart. "Take care of them, magic dog," I whispered, and stole out as quietly as possible.

Just as I unhitched the rope and was manoeuvring into the main stream I heard a window open, an audible click and a creak, and then the stillness was broken by Scottie's voice, ringing out loud and clear. He was not addressing me but the forest:

"Hearken to me," he was saying, "tent tae ma words, aa ye wuids and shaws and aaken trees and craiturs that bide in thaim. Jason is ma brither, ma fier. He is ae braw bonny lad, and wise and douce. Shuilie he loved me, forby he gied ye his love, and saufit ye frae yer faes, sic as wad hae spulyied an wrack'd ye. I ca' upon ye ta keep and proteck him and presser him frae hairm. Return him sauf tae me, ye gods and spreerits o' the forest that haud its saicrets and sacred places. Be ye feal tae him as he war suifast tae ye . . ." His words faded into silence and darkness as the swift current carried me away.

I said amen to Scottie's prayer and added my own for him and Elfie, my two babes in the wood. Concentrating on avoiding the rocks and overhanging boughs that emerged suddenly from the darkness helped me to focus my thoughts on the task in hand. And then creation began again, with the slow return of light, and with it new hope and new courage. Surely even on my last day dawn would not fail to work its miracle for me. As the stream was swelled by tributaries, and light silvered the road ahead, I could relax, leaning back on the loaded stern, and glide forward with just a dipped paddle here and there to guide my course.

There was much to see and enjoy. I passed singing trees, evergreens full of tiny birds, wrens or titmice, and in the leafless trees the nests of birds that summer foliage had hidden were now visible. There were wildfowl and waders that took no more heed of me than a passing log, and herons and kingfishers. The clear water teemed with fish, big ones deep and dark, spined, speckled or barred, and shoals of silvery tiddlers darting and flashing here and there. Water rats plopped into the stream as I passed, otters streaked and swerved, their sleek heads skimming the surface; shy deer came down to the edge to drink.

All the joy of wild nature surrounded me as I raced effortlessly on, but I could not outpace my inner fears, the undercurrent of anxiety. It was a dark business I was on and I felt the curse of the ancient mariner, condemned by my origins and my history. Nature's grace and bounty were forfeited long since – it was not my road. That wandering baggage and her nagging chant floated again into my mind.

The first two days of the journey passed without problems or incidents. I had been well provided for. The tough hide skin of the canoe coped with occasional scrapes. I kept a sharp lookout ahead for any obstacles or dangers, remembering our narrow escape on the raft in the Kaspan Hills. I dragged the canoe overland to avoid rocks and rapids, and on one occasion to circumvent a damn built by a colony of beavers. Nights were still, cold and frosty under the blaze of stars.

All my cooking and sleeping arrangements worked perfectly and I was as cosy as could be, but how I missed my two friends, and Credo's warm fur and watchful eyes. On the second day the forest began to peter out and I could see light and space beyond the screen of trees. Then came open farmland, with no cover but the river banks, and I began to feel exposed. The current was slower now and I had more work to do with the paddle, but it was easier to draw into the bank from time to time and peer ahead through Procter's powerful lenses.

The fields were vast and empty. Here and there a lone tree stood among shorn stubbles that swept to the horizon. Cloud-like flocks of finches, buntings and sparrows rose and settled, and rooks were walking around, prodding and poking, with the same rocking gait as farmers. Some distance away a group of women were gleaning: dark shapeless figures bending wearily to their toil. It could have been a scene from my youth, except the pheasants I saw in the stubble were golden and not copper coloured. And another scene, a group of children pulling turnips from the stiff, sticky soil, watched by a heavily built man wielding a long cane, reminded me I was in Zinn.

The main object of my surveillance was to spy out the Western Highway well in advance. It was late afternoon when it came into my field of vision, a line drawn with a ruler across the undulating ploughlands, bounding the horizon. There seemed to be more traffic than before, and larger vehicles. A convoy of heavy trucks moved slowly along it towards Zinn. I decided to take advantage of the cover provided by a small copse to have my evening meal, and wait for darkness before approaching the highway. The river must be channelled beneath the road and the chances of being seen from it in daylight were probably not great; but after my previous experiences there I was averse to taking any risk.

As night fell I paddled cautiously towards the high embankment where the headlights came and went, throwing menacing arms of light and shadow far across the fields. I realised I must have been long away from what calls itself civilization, in spirit if not in time, for a mere highway to become a fearful object of oppressive power. In the culvert the walls shook as another convoy rumbled heavily above. I held back until it had passed before slipping out the other side and paddling swiftly on. The highway was out of sight and earshot before I moored my vessel and pitched camp for the night.

The following day the river took me into a more pastoral countryside, settled and populous. My first human contact was with an old man fishing. I came round a bend and he was there before I could think of any way of avoiding him. I took care not to cross his line and bade him good morning as airily as I could. He responded in like manner and seemed in no way concerned or surprised at seeing me. Soon there were other vessels: rowing boats, coracles, and wherries loaded with hay or other produce, and the river ran through farms and villages, past wharves, warehouses, orchards, inns and gardens. As my presence attracted no attention I just sailed on past, with the occasional wave or greeting.

But once I did take swift evasive action. The river skirted a road for some distance and I saw lorries approaching, grey khaki, chunky lorries with high, narrow slit windows, and I pulled into the reeds by the bank, peering through them. Packed with soldiers they lumbered by, and above the roar of the engines was the noise of the soldiers singing. They stood in close formation chanting in unison some triumphalist anthem, their voices harsh, heavy and loud. I noted they were now wearing regular camouflage battle fatigues and carried semi-automatic weapons, though they still had the same round steel helmets like halved ball bearings.

The near encounter with Zinn's new model army was not the only reminder that I was not boating pleasantly on the Thames or the Severn. Zinn itself now became a fixture on the horizon, thrusting through the early mist and glistening in the noonday sun. All the magic and romance I'd seen in it or invested it with at the beginning had vanished. It was now a harsh, alien artefact, a malign presence, gleaming with cruel, implacable, all-pervading, all-seeing power. Its subjects were not hearty independent countrymen but small, uncomfortable people, with no aspiration but to be permitted to stay alive until they died of natural causes.

I remained in a state of high vigilance, but the following day passed without incident in the same busy, riparian setting. The next day the weather changed and the landscape too. It got much colder. There was ice in the still water among the reeds and the water filled hoof prints where cattle came down to drink. The sky darkened to a greenish grey, threatening snow. People became scarcer, rootless, poorer - gypsies, mouchers, tramps, homeless families in makeshift dwellings. The fields were untended and choked with weeds and empty barns and cottages stared out across them, dark vacant doors swung open, and windows like hollow, sightless eyes. Crows hung over ruined farms and dead trees spread like roots into the air.

As I paddled on through this day and into the next, the scene of desolation turned gradually into one of devastation. Scarcely a building was left standing, walls tattooed with bullet holes and blasted with shells or burnt to the ground, whole settlements razed, as if some maniac with a giant blowtorch had been let loose. There were now no people to be seen. Fields were churned up, hedges and woods smashed or burnt, tree stumps splintered like matchwood; tyre tracks everywhere, the roads obliterated and marked only by the wrecks of farm carts and vehicles.

At one point I had to crawl and drag the canoe beneath a barbed wire entanglement that crossed the river and stretched from one bare horizon to another.

I made for a small copse, one of the few left standing. The whole land seemed deserted now, but in case there were watchers still, it would provide some cover for me to rest and heat a little food and coffee on my stove. I'd hoped these small comforts would revive my spirits but there was something about the place that sent a chill down my spine. I explored a little beyond the bank and saw in the soft grass beneath the trees what appeared at first to be wasp-hollowed fruit. I stopped dead in my tracks when I realised they were the skulls of small children. And there were things hanging in the trees unknown to botany.

Returning to the bank something else caught my eye. A bit further downstream I saw there were stone parapets on either side of the river where a bridge must have been. I walked past these and a little further I came to a pool. The muddy banks, stiff with frost, were bare and open to the bleak wintry sky. There were crushed cans and cigarette packets and broken ammunition cases and the charred circle left by a fire. The pool itself was partly choked with some other debris, half sunken tangles of sticks and rags and wire, set in ice. Then I realised that I had reached my destination. This was the children's bathing pool, and I was looking at the pitiful remnants of those ethereal artefacts, the buzzards of Zinn. Seeing again in my mind's eye those small bright faces, full of light and laughter, the sadness overwhelmed me; and I wept like a child myself.

CHAPTER 19

Trial

I KNELT down in the grass beside the pool at about the spot where Aya had left my clothes. With my pocket knife I cut the stitches of a little pouch I had sewn in the lining of my coat and took out the sapphire, and placed it there in the grass. My eyes were filled with tears and I squeezed them closed, but then I felt a sudden tightness round my head and I could see nothing but darkness when I opened my eyes. A sharp voice yelled "Get the knife!" My wrists were seized and twisted and my arms forced backwards. The knife fell from my grip and I felt the cold muzzle of a gun against my head. Then another voice, "Kill him Vark, blow his head off. He's a spy." "Stab his eyes out," said another. I reeled back as I felt the pressure of a blade point against the blindfold. "Pitch him over, we'll cut his balls off first and then we'll rip his tongue out." Someone else laughed. Then the first voice spoke again. "Shut up the lot of you. We've got to take him in for interrogation. Tie his wrists. Tarvis, Kruxel, you go and find his belongings and see how he got here. Drack, you run ahead and tell the Leader we're bringing in a prisoner. The rest of you get him up and get him moving."

I was dragged to my feet with kicks and curses and bundled forward with thumps and prods, which increased as I stumbled and lost my footing on the rock strewn, rutted ground. "Take his blindfold off you idiots so he can see where he's going," came the voice of command again. It was ripped off and some of my hair with it, accompanied by a heavy blow on the back.

I couldn't open my eyes until the initial shock and pain passed. When I did they confirmed what my ears had already told me. It was not a detachment of Zinn's merciless soldiery that had seized me. My captors were children. They were clad roughly in furs and animal skins and their faces daubed with frown marks and tiger stripes in grey, black and ochre paint. All were armed, the captain with an ancient matchlock gun and the rest with knives, spears and clubs. I'd guess their average age was ten. I tried to say something. "Shut it!" rapped the captain and another cracking whack from behind knocked the breath out of me. "You'll get your chance to speak later."

We made our way in silence up the bank to where the cavern had been. The landing strip had disappeared and the ground was cratered with shell holes filled with ice, staring up like ghastly eyes. The cavern itself had become an ice lagoon ringed by steep cliffs. The spread-eagled disintegrating wreckage of buzzard planes had been attached to a section of wall, like a gamekeeper's gallery of kills.

We followed the rim for some distance and then came off at a tangent and descended into a hollow where a few trees were left standing and there was a ground covering of bush and briar. A mile or so along this valley we came to a bank with two upright props and a lintel supporting what appeared to be a disused mine shaft. The captain produced an old miner's helmet made of brass from his kit bag, struck a match and coaxed the wick into feeble flame. He put the helmet on his head and led the way into the tunnel. The walls were ridged and serrated, hewn from slate or compacted shale, the roof held up by sagging beams, black wet grit on the floor. The faces of my escort flared like demons in the dim flickering light. Then the tunnel came to an end, hollowed as though the tunnellers just gave up at that point.

The captain put his hand into a narrow slit and there was a sharp click. He pushed near the edge of the barrier with his gun butt and the whole end section unsealed itself from an invisible incision and swung inwards. We filed into a wider corridor where another joined us and whispered a lengthy inaudible message to the captain. The door was sealed behind us and we continued in silence for some time. After passing several side shafts we entered one which led to a heavy wooden door with a small iron grid at child's eye level and a hatch near the bottom. It opened on a cell which the captain's lamp momentarily revealed to be about five feet square, hacked from the same razor edged rock and completely empty. I was pushed inside and fell headlong on the serrated floor. The door was banged shut and locked behind me.

Sore and shaken, my arms still pinioned behind me, I struggled to my knees. A sharp projection from the wall dug into my back. I felt it with my fingers and then rubbed the rope ligature backwards and forwards on it till the strands parted. A small victory. As I couldn't sit or lie on the jagged floor without discomfort I took off my thick woollen coat, a present from Scottie, and doubled it to make a mattress. It occurred to me that my incarcerations in Zinn had got progressively worse, and now I was like Jonah in the gullet of the whale.

A feeble beam of light still shone through the aperture in the door, and grew stronger, throwing a grid pattern on the opposite wall. I could hear muffled voices outside. They continued for a while and then there was silence, as though a decision had been reached, and seconds later the key grated in the lock again. Three guards burst in and beat me again with their clubs. I was dragged out across the cheese grater floor into the corridor where I was held down and the clothes pulled off my back and buttocks and the next moment I was being thrashed mercilessly from all directions. Maddened by the intolerable pain, I struggled and managed to turn over but before I could raise an arm to defend myself I was slashed across the face, opening the flesh of my cheeks. The flogging over I was flung back in my cell; the door slammed and the lock clunked again in its socket with heavy finality. The shadow pattern faded from the wall, the light in the aperture disappeared, and there was silence.

My bones were raw with pain and my eyes filled with blood. I was too shocked and broken to move and lay there helpless, moaning. I can't say how long it was before I attempted to move. I slowly eased my clothes back over my lacerated body. Feeling around I found the coat and curled up in it in the least painful position I could find, too absorbed in my suffering to think about anything. I lay there probably an hour or more before my mind refocused and I tried to compose my thoughts and reason out my predicament.

Who or what were these imps of hell that had laid hold of me with such ferocity? Could they be in any way related to the gentle, hospitable buzzard children who lived here before? Could a harmonious and peace loving society have been transformed in less than a year to a band of bloodthirsty savages? But it was not the first time I had seen the effects of massive force by an overwhelmingly superior military power on a defenceless population. The evidence of such an onslaught here had been only too clear in the latter stages of my journey. That these were the same children, or their successors, who had welcomed and accepted me with such open-handed and open-hearted kindness when I arrived in Zinn was not only possible but probable. And given the visible evidence of hideous cruelty and brutality against them it was less probable than inevitable.

And what of my prospects now? Surely there must be some here who would remember me, and could vouch for me as a friend. Once I had a chance to speak to someone higher up the chain of command than the foot soldiers who grabbed me I would be able to establish my credentials. Beyond that I had no idea what course of action, if any, would present itself.

What was their agenda - survival? - resistance? - retaliation? Clearly the Zinnians had now vacated the war zone in the belief that they had removed or destroyed all opposition - indeed all human life. For the survivors, perhaps a mere handful of them, surely the only course was to remain invisible, and as and when possible migrate or be evacuated to regions where they could be helped to return to normal society. I knew that in warfare as in other forms of extreme abuse the abused, who became abusers themselves, can be and had been rehabilitated, as in certain cases of rescued African child soldiers. But whatever their plans were I doubted if anything I could propose would influence them now. They were desensitised, radicalised and organised. At least if I could find Aya and Sulibe I could take them back with me to the forest. Thus I turned things over in my mind, but more to keep at bay the fear, pain and darkness that threatened to engulf me, than in realistic expectation that events would fall out in accordance with any line of reasoning or calculation.

The heat generated by my recent experiences began to wear off and the chill damp of the floor penetrated through to my flesh. I stood up as high as I could, put my coat back on, and cautiously worked my limbs and shook myself to keep my circulation and my spirits flowing. I closed my eyes, which were aching from the weariness and futility of straining for the faintest essence of light. How long would they keep me here? My impatience and frustration grew more acute as doubt began to eat into me, and I approached the precipice of fear.

Hours passed. I divided my time between rest and exercise and tried to blot out the present, thinking of good times past. But the instant claimed me, with all its urgent, feverish speculation, the imperative of action and the tyranny of sensation like millstones without grain grinding each other. In the caves with Scottie we had each other and we could still move onwards, however hopeless the journey became, and would have done to the end. Now I was trapped inside this hole, inside myself. I was utterly alone and helpless. I could do nothing but breathe. Panic seized me. I grabbed the grill and shook the door, yelling and screaming through my pain, and went on and on until my voice grew hoarse and my arms were weak, but still I moaned and tugged feebly at the immoveable iron. I cursed my breath for keeping me alive in this pit of horror, and then a wave of self pity and infinite sadness came over me. I curled up on the floor, squeezed myself into a foetal ball, shaking, sobbing helplessly.

My mother was holding me in her arms. I could smell her milk. We were in the Anderson's shelter. She sat on the low steel sprung bed, the oil lamp hissing, talking to Dad, worried about her brother who was in the Met. and her mother who wouldn't come in the shelter. Hitler wouldn't get Granny out of her own bed. Dad was trying to reassure her, saying the raid was over. My sister was playing with her doll. "Why is Jason crying? Why does he keep crying?" Mother held me tight and looked down at me and Dad looked at me as well. "He was born with all the worries of the world," she said.

I awoke with a start and the horror of my situation again burst in on me. I clung as long as I could to the dissolving images and presences of my dream, and voices reclaimed from the gulf of time. They belonged to a lost world, also one filled with fear, but precious now beyond all imagining. I longed for my mother to kiss me. Did she ever kiss me? But Elfie had kissed me – by the fire, and again when we said goodbye. Soft as a flower. It was good to think of her and Scottie together. There was peace in that thought.

But the mill of the mind was grinding again; I was breathing still and my life was killing me. Another wave of panic came and I raved and roared and would have wrenched the door from its sockets and smashed it to pieces if psychic energy could translate into physical force. I slumped down again, hugging myself, shivering; and then light did appear. I watched with amazement as it dimly filled the square and then a brighter shaft shot through the hatch below followed by a thin arm. It placed a bowl of something and a bottle of water and an empty bucket. I tried to say "Who are you? Please let me speak to you. I must speak to someone," but my voice came out as a feeble croak. The hatch snapped shut and the light went away.

I didn't know if I was hungry or thirsty or needed to relieve myself. My body was just a dull ache, devoid of appetite or impulse of any kind. I crawled forward to investigate these offerings. There was some kind of soup in the bowl. It smelt unpleasant. I tried some on my finger and it tasted unpleasant: gloopy, lumpy stuff. I drank the water which was cool and refreshing and felt good in my throat. Then I heard a noise - a kind of rapid sipping slurping noise, and I put my hand to its source and felt warm fur, following its arched contour with my finger until it became bristly and ended in a point. The rat took no notice of my touching it but continued gobbling away. I could imagine its bright beady eyes and its twitchy nose as it chiselled away at the fatty lumps. "You're welcome to it my friend," I said. "Be my guest."

I felt a little better then. It was not death I feared but timelessness, eternal nothingness, and this place was so like it I could slip into eternity without knowing. To be, but to be nowhere; to see, but see nothing, staring with vast eyes into the eternal void. We need time. Without time there are no beginnings or endings, departures or destinations, no events of any kind. Without time we cannot even die. Eternity is hell enough without the fire. Fire is an event. Pain is an event. The hell of the theologians is a ridiculous invention and the world's torturers have discovered there is more terror in sensory deprivation than in any invasive or corrosive physical assault. The coming of light, the attending, however minimal, to my needs, and especially the arrival of the rat, all told me I was still part of the living, dying world and not the world of living death - of eternity, non-entity, the abyss.

Food came regularly - I guessed daily. Sometimes there was bread, which I ate, but no more than a finger lick of the soup passed my lips. The rat was a regular visitor at mealtimes but didn't seem to understand that these were occasions for conversation as well as feeding. To delay his scurrying away I placed little bits of bread around the place he'd have to spend a few moments searching for, and I could interpret the brief pauses between courses as comments or replies. The conversation was still rather one-sided but I did gather he lived in narrow seams and cavities in the rock strata with his friends and family and that he had found a way into my cell that he was keeping secret from the others because if he told them they would eat all the food themselves - the rats!

The food, the water and the rat cheered and revived me a little. I decided that this one meal of the day was breakfast. Then I would exercise my battered frame with its various appendages as well as I could in the space available. Then I went to work. I had found a few loose chunks of rock and with these I bashed away at the most jagged areas and sharp projections of the floor and walls, and then

used the chippings to fill in the hollows in my 'bed' area with a
raised 'pillow' at one end. Thus every day produced some small
improvement to my quality of life. After a while I was able to lie
down with my coat on and stay warmer longer without loss of
comfort. I would fold myself up into the smallest bundle possible
and hide, secure in my own interior world. Happiness, I decided,
consisted of having good things to look back on, absorbing and
satisfying activity in the present, and good things to look forward
to.

The good things I looked forward to were sleep and dreams. I
cannot say my dreams were always pleasant, in fact sometimes they
were so bad or scary they would wake me up. Even the good
dreams had about them an air of indefinable sadness, the wistful
haunting melancholy of far off days and long lost causes. Railways
were a recurrent theme – waiting forever on the platforms of
abandoned stations, graveyards of weird and antiquated engines, or
escaping by train on magical journeys through fantasy landscapes,
leading to home and peace.

And then there were war dreams, desperate attempts to evade or
hide from terrible forces, crossing minefields, hunted down by
fearsome aircraft, bristling with turrets and machine guns,
and sometimes being a soldier myself, marching and killing, blasting everything and everyone. But even in these the prevailing
emotions were fear and sorrow.

All kinds of people from every period in my past life would turn
up in the oddest of contexts, and though they were no more than
ghosts of their former selves they were still company, and were
more forthcoming than my friend the rat. The only dreams bad
enough to wake me were those in which I lost my footing on a
high building or was hurtling towards a brick wall in a car, or
those in which an irremediable situation had come about, a dreadful mistake or an inconsolable loss.

My dreamscape ranged across the whole of my life, and not only
the remote past put the immediate present. In one I was escorted
to a court room here to be put on trial. The room was hewn out
of the ragged rock like my cell but was very high, and the walls

were draped with thick woollen coverings. I was placed in a high enclosed dock, like a pulpit, a row of guards with spears below. The audience sat in tiered rows directly opposite me and consisted of the same feral characters who had arrested me, sitting there scowling in their war paint, girl savages as well as boys. There was no jury. To my right, facing the judge, were two lecterns on raised plinths where the counsels for prosecution and defence would stand.

All was grim and grey except for the bench and the judge's throne which was surrounded by a blaze of colour. There were hangings of scarlet silk and blue satin trimmed with gold braid and pieces of tapestry and embroidery, and furled flags on either side; but it was rather a hotchpotch like something from a fairground or a circus, and the flags were crudely painted.

The judge entered from behind a screen. She wore a dress of rich purple velvet and had a sort of crown or helmet on her head. It was gold in colour and rose to a crest in which were inlaid bright coloured shiny squares of glass. She was a nice looking girl of about twelve who would have stood out from the other scrawny kids even without this extraordinary garb by her plump well formed figure and an air of cosseted privilege. She seemed very pleased with herself and adjusted the balance of her helmet from time to time with delicate hands. She did not once turn to look at me, in my wretched state, and indeed, with her head raised in a queenly way she seemed only to address the air in front of her.

She informed it that the prisoner in the dock was charged with the heinous offences of espionage and treason for both or either of which the punishment was death. Death, she reminded the court in her sweet childish voice, would be inflicted by means of earth, air, fire or water; that is to say by burial alive, precipitation, burning or drowning. She would decide which one was appropriate to my case. Then it all got confused and I was back in my cell. Ark was talking to me. He was my counsel. His speech was rapid and urgent and I couldn't follow it. My replies were garbled. I gathered my case was hopeless and then I woke.

For the most part the dreaming state was far preferable to being awake. Reality was to be avoided as much as possible. For one thing my bucket was rarely emptied and the place stank. I was filthy and my face and body encrusted with scabs of dry blood. As the people of my dreams became godlike, ethereal beings, I became loathsome, like Kafka's insect man, lurking in my hole, my segments slowly articulating. Panic attacks still came but I let them happen, knowing they would pass. Everything would pass, as it should, and there would be an end.

I held on to my dreams as long as I could and I kept my eyes closed most of the time to assist the dreaming process. The time between sleep and wake was the best as the conscious mind could mould the material of the unconscious, and I could live entirely in myself and create an inner life. The actual world, when it reclaimed me, was a dreary, cheerless, hopeless place, ruled by hard circumstance and heartless people.

Life then, of a kind, was possible, but that life was ebbing away. The voices became more distant, the scenes more remote, the faces of loved ones grew vague. The distinction between states of mind became blurred and I babbled even without the excuse of the rat's company. In my delirium Ark was often there – though I couldn't see him I knew his voice. Concerned and anxious he talked continuously and in minute detail about the case. I couldn't follow him at all but it seemed to be going from bad to worse. The prosecution had produced damning evidence; the judge had made unpropitious comments. There were references also to 'the Leader.' The Leader was angry and wanted me condemned.

I didn't really care much about the trial – it all seemed a bit farcical. I wanted to talk about the old days and the buzzards; and what became of little Aya and Sulibe. Ark became such an insistent presence that I began to entertain the possibility that he was really there. In a rare moment of lucidity I decided to test this hypothesis by reaching forward to see if I came in contact with a warm human rather than cold mineral substance. To my surprise my hand came to rest on a small thin shoulder. "Ark," I said, "is that really you?"

"Of course it's me Jason. Please listen and try to concentrate. The trial isn't going well at all."

"It's good to see you Ark. Or touch you rather. I was beginning to wonder if I'd ever meet up again with any of my old friends here."

"Jason you won't be seeing anyone much longer the way things are going. They found a Zinnian passport in your belongings, and an ex-army pair of binoculars and a military map. I told them you were with Procter Prendis and Scottie Emmisarius and helped to defeat the loggers but I've got no evidence. They think you made it up to save your skin."

"You're saying there really is a trial? It's not something in my head?"

"Jason, I've got something for you. But don't tell anyone."

Ark was whispering now quite close to me and I felt his hand nudge mine. He guided my fingers to the thing he was holding and lifted it towards my face. I smelt it then - brandy. I took a little sip. It burnt my throat and jolted my senses. It had been so long since I was fully awake and alert in present time it felt strange, but exhilarating. Ark started on again about the trial and how the Leader had it in for me but I stopped him and said, "Look Ark, I really need some background information. Things have changed a lot since I was here last. I can see you took a hell of a pasting from the army, but some of you escaped. What happened to you? What is this place? And what happens now?"

"It was terrible. I can't describe it. The bombardment. Day after day, night after night. You couldn't rest, it shook you to pieces. Kids were going crazy. The little ones were all quivering and moaning and some just went to sleep and died. They were the lucky ones. Some tried to run away but they were captured and tortured. Jason, they used loudspeakers so we could hear their screams.

"The pilots decided to form a resistance and die fighting. We fixed blades to the buzzard wings and crashed on the soldiers and we killed some of them. I hit a truck full of soldiers and it rolled over. I was flung out and landed in a tree and managed to escape.

It didn't do any good; the shelling just got worse. Our Leader, who was the only other suicide pilot who came back, rallied us and made us dig new tunnels and forced us to work when we were defeated and exhausted and just wanted to die. One of the tunnels struck through into a mine shaft and we discovered this whole network of them and an enormous hole deep underground. It's an old slate mine. We hid here till the shelling stopped. They blasted through to the old cavern and thought they'd killed everyone, and then they went away."

I took another pull from the brandy bottle to keep my grip on reality as this vision of hell unfolded.

"Sulibe," I said. "Where is she? Is she here? And her little sister Aya?"

"Sulibe is dead," he said firmly.

"And Aya?"

"She's dead too. I'm sorry. I know she loved you. She was the first to be captured. It was just after you left. She was playing with the others when there was an alarm. They all ran away like rabbits but she went back to get her leg. They caught her with one of their long hooks."

I felt sick with anger, pity and despair as the scene flashed in front of me. And there was I feasting and fishing and enjoying the comforts and pleasures of our life in the forest while these helpless innocents were pleading for mercy and screaming in agony. My hatred of their killers was engulfed by the loathing and revulsion I felt towards myself. It was more than I could stand and I took a long swig from the bottle. Everything went fuzzy and I passed out.

When I came round Ark was still there but it must have been a later occasion because this time he had brought me food - meat and fruit and oat bread spread with dripping. He fed it to me as though I were a child. "How are you feeling now?" he asked.

"Terrible," I said, "and I've got a headache."

He gave me some fresh water to drink, was silent for a while, and then I thought, poor Ark, he's trying so hard to help me. For his sake I must try to be helped. So I said, "I'm sorry Ark. What with being left to rot in this hole for so long I'm not really myself. You've been a good friend to me and I will make an effort now with this trial."

I could sense the dark place where Ark was crouching brightening up again. He asked me lots of questions, about the Looshin Levels, Procter, Scottie and his marriage and relations with the house of Shahribe. I didn't understand why he needed this information but was happy to tell him all about my adventures. Then he said: "Well, we've got a new recruit."

"That's good," I said.

"And he's got a gun!"

"Now that could come in really handy."

"Yes, we've got fifteen all together now, and nine of them work."

"Rounds?"

"Yep, some of them too."

"But Ark, seriously. You don't imagine you can take on the Zinnian army do you? They have modern weapons now - guns that can fire hundreds of rounds a minute. And there are lots of them and only a few of you."

"We're getting new recruits all the time now. We've got tunnels that go right under the walls and kids are joining us every day. We'll fight inside the city as well as outside and take guns from the soldiers we kill. The Leader says we will win in the end."

"And when is this new war due to begin?"

"Very soon. The Leader will kill Jobu and then it will start. But I shouldn't be telling you all this."

"Why not?"

Ark replied with a little hint of mischief in his voice: "You haven't been acquitted of being a spy yet."

"And when will that be?"

"The final judgement is tomorrow."

"But I haven't even been in court yet, unless I've been too sick and confused to realise it. I haven't been asked if I'm innocent or guilty of the charges."

"That's not our system here. The accused is only present at the beginning and the end. The judge hears all the evidence and cross questions the witnesses - I could have called you as a witness but I don't think you would have done yourself any favours. In the final session the prosecution and the defence make their concluding submissions and then the judge asks you if you're innocent or guilty. You have to be very careful then because if you say you are innocent and the judge finds you guilty the punishment will be a lot worse."

"What's worse than death by fire, earth, air or water?"

"If you pleaded guilty you'd be allowed to choose. Air's best because it's quick. Get some sleep now, you'll need to have your wits about you. I'm still hopeful I can get you off but you never know how these things will turn out."

Ark collected up the remnants of my meal and put them in his pocket. "Don't tell anyone," he whispered. Then he shouted through the grill and a guard came and released him.

I didn't sleep at all. I couldn't stop thinking of Aya. Such a sweet, brave, innocent child, in spite of her situation and disability and the pain she must have been through; so full of hope and ready to give me her love and asking for mine. And then falling into the hands of those brain-dead killers. The terrible things I had seen in the copse burnt into my mental vision and lacerated my conscience. It was unthinkable, unbearable. Could I have prevented it? Perhaps not but I would never know.

I may have done some good in my life, but in the end I had betrayed myself, and there was no way forward. In any case what did I have to offer the survivors? What good would my pacifist ideas be to them? Diplomacy, negotiation, reconciliation, forgiveness, justice? Try that lot on Pontius Pilate or Genghis Khan. The children would fight and die as millions before them, and no one would even remember them. I could only laugh, with hollow laughter, that a few weeks ago I was thinking of building bridges.

Now I just wanted to go back into myself, into that world of imperishable essences I had so recently been taken from; to return to my own beginnings. There was a place where we would all be together, where we had never been apart. I had lost my way here.

This was not my road after all. In my heart I was already dead and the physical process of dying no longer held any terrors for me. The reappearance of light in the tiny window of my cell brought only a weary acceptance of more, yet more, absurd business to be gone through before I could be at peace.

CHAPTER 20

Judgement

THE GUARDS came in, the same ones as before, with their spears and clubs, and bound me again. Ark was with them, his presence no doubt acting as a restraint on their inclination to use me as a punch bag. It was the first time since my return I had actually seen him - in the wavering torchlight the same little nut brown Puck-like figure with big dark eyes I remembered from our first encounter. I tottered and stumbled, despite Ark's attempts to support me, till it occurred to the captain that I was not likely to make a break for it or attack him and his boys and he instructed one of them to support me on the other side.

A series of tunnels brought us to a gallery overlooking a vast cavity, sparsely lit with torches, like the auditorium of an old fashioned Odeon cinema that seemed so immense to me as a child. On the floor deep below us there were fires burning, their smoke making a layer of cloud which a gentle air current carried away into dark space at the far end, if there was an end. Beneath the cloud I could make out shacks and tents, laid out in streets like a shanty town, and figures moving about.

I was steered into one of the side openings in the gallery and found myself in the courtroom, which was exactly as I had seen it in what I thought was a dream. My hands were released and I was helped up into the dock, holding tight to the edge to stay upright. The public seating facing me was packed. This time I think only a few of the children had their war paint on, but their faces were a blur.

There was a buzz of excitement when I appeared before them, and then a court official called for silence. Ark and the prosecuting counsel, wearing dark gowns, entered first, stood on their plinths and placed their papers on the lecterns. Ark was a diminutive figure compared with the other lad, who was tall and wore glasses. The psychological disadvantage was so obvious I wondered if it was deliberate. I had formed the impression that this Leader of theirs, whoever he might be, was pulling all the strings, and perhaps like Stalin at his show trials watching proceedings from a secret observation post.

The judge then made her radiant entry, settled herself comfortably on her throne and adjusted her crown. She raised her chin and gazed vacantly in her queenly way and there was complete silence. Then she condescended to lower her head slightly and nod in the direction of the prosecuting counsel as a signal to begin.

The case against me went as follows:

"When the accused first visited our community in the spring he was welcomed as a friend and shown our secret quarters, and our aircraft, in which he took an extraordinary interest. He left the following day and went straight to Zinn and was seen to enter the city with a military escort. It was soon after this that the Zinnian Army began shelling, and concentrating their attack on our former headquarters. After further dealings with the military at Fort Rossak he turned up at Sammonar, where out gallant friend Alseph Emmisarius gave him lodging. He too was deceived into thinking the accused an ally when in reality he was spying for ZADD.

"He accompanied Emmisarius to the Looshin Levels, and it was fortunate that he was unable to communicate with his masters in time to frustrate the glorious success of Emmisarius, and the late hero Procter Prendis, in driving the loggers out of the Levels. However, immediately on his return to Sammonar, he visited a Zinnian prince, the father in law of Baldark and related through marriage to Jobu himself. And what purpose could that visit have had other than to report his findings and receive new instructions?

"My learned friend the counsel for the defence has proposed several bizarre explanations to fit these facts; facts that point so obviously to the accused being a spy. He claims that he himself, and another who cannot now confirm his story, rescued this man from the execution platform at Fort Rossak. Such a daring and dangerous manoeuvre might have been undertaken for a loyal and valuable colleague, but for a mere passer-by, on such brief acquaintance - is it credible? Then he claims that the accused actually assisted and took part in the operation to flood the Levels. Well, what would an undercover agent do? Show his true colours by refusing to help? And then the final absurdity - the suggestion that his visit to the Prince Shahribe was in connection with the marriage of Emmisarius to the Prince's youngest daughter. Is it not as inconceivable that Emmisarius should have contemplated such a union with a scion of the hated enemy as that a Zinnian Prince would have allowed it to take place?

"Finally he turns up here in Marchenor. For what purpose would he, or any person, come here, a war zone, a devastated area, a scene of death and carnage, other than to report back and satisfy the ruthless tyranny that employed him that their work had been successfully completed? But we do not need to rely on speculation and conjecture. We have hard evidence. This was found in his luggage - a Zinnian passport, signed by the Notary General, and this - a pair of field glasses of the very type issued to the Zinnian murderers. And if that was not enough we have here (flourishing the document in his finger tips) a map of this region prepared by the Zinnian War Office.

"And then there was another object we found. He appeared to have dropped something, and was bending down, looking in the grass, obviously distressed, when he was apprehended. We searched and found this - a sapphire of great value which our expert has told us could only have originated from a Zinnian mine. Your Honour, what could it be other than a reward for betraying us to our enemies? He is a spy and a traitor. The blood of our fallen comrades is on his head. In their name I call upon you to condemn him to death."

The judge seemed very pleased with this presentation, and smiled her approval. Then she turned and looked down at Ark and enquired: "Do you have anything further to add?" Ark puffed his chest out and spoke in a bold, confident voice:

"Indeed I do Your Honour. What we have heard is nothing but supposition and innuendo. Consider. The accused is a traveller from a far distant country. When he first visited us he had only just arrived in Zinn and spoke hardly a word of our language. I was the first person he met here, and I could see straight away that he was a friendly chap, and a complete stranger. When and by what means could he have been recruited by the Lords of Zinn to spy for them, and what use would he be as a spy if he couldn't even speak Zinnian? When have those high and mighty Lords, so confident of their supreme ability in all affairs, at any previous time employed a foreigner for any purpose whatsoever? And were we so foolish in those days of innocence as to nurture a viper to our bosom?

"He came here merely as a traveller, a sightseer, and for that reason alone went on to visit Zinn. Naturally he was refused entry and warned to leave the country on penalty of death. He attempted to do this but the army arrested him anyway on the Western Highway. Ironically they too accused him of spying, but spying for us. He was condemned to death and about to be executed when I was able to assist in his rescue. I trust my reputation and my record here will vouch for the truthfulness of my witness.

"As for the flooding of the Looshin plain, it is well known that he played a leading part in that operation and at considerable risk to himself. He would not have had to send messages to Zinn to frustrate it; he simply had to pass word to the logging company whose agents were everywhere.

"As for the visit to Prince Shahribe, my client assures me it was to discuss the marriage of the Prince's youngest daughter Elphane to Emmisarius, and that the marriage has now taken place and is a matter of record. My learned opponent finds the idea ridiculous, and it is certainly remarkable. But what would be both remarkable and ridiculous is that a spy in the service of the Zinnian High Command should report to Shahribe, a known dissident, out of favour at court, and now in voluntary exile at his country estate.

"Finally we come to the return of the accused. It is a personal matter of which he is reluctant to speak, but it has to do not with enmity or ill intent towards the people here, but his love and concern for us, and for two in particular. You may find this hard to accept, but I find it hard to accept that a spy would travel into enemy territory carrying documents and a piece of equipment that betrayed his true allegiance. The objects produced as 'hard evidence' were all bequeathed to him by the late Procter Prendis in token of his esteem for a true friend and comrade in arms. The passport was simply to protect him from summary execution by his enemies, who are also our enemies.

"This man should be honoured among us, instead of which he has been treated with cruelty and contempt - which is only too evident from his appearance. I call upon Your Honour to dismiss these spurious charges and clear his name, and welcome him here with the respect and hospitality, and the gratitude he deserves."

Although my mind began to get a bit fuzzy during these long speeches I had to admit that Ark had defended me well, especially given my uncooperativeness and poor attitude towards the trial. It seemed surreal to me, Lilliputian - I couldn't be entirely sure I wasn't dreaming still. The judge nodded briefly in acknowledgment of Ark's speech, and invited the two counsels to stand down. Then she spoke herself, and it took me a moment to grasp the fact that she was speaking to me.

"You have heard the arguments put forward by the learned counsels for prosecution and defence. You have been charged with the crimes of espionage and treason, both or either of which are punishable by death. How do you answer to the first of these charges: espionage?"

"Not guilty, Your Honour."

"And to the second, treason."

"Guilty."

An audible gasp from the entire assembly followed my utterance. I saw Ark's face looking up at me, perplexed and distraught. He immediately mounted his stand and addressed the judge. "Your Honour this man is not in his right mind. He has been beaten and kept in solitary confinement in total darkness for almost a month, and fed with vile food which would barely keep a rat alive. You cannot accept his plea."

"If I accept the first I must accept the second," the Judge said calmly. "Please return to your seat." Then she turned gracefully and beamed her blue eyes directly at me. "Have you anything to say in explanation of your pleas?" she enquired.

"Your Honour I have. I wish first to thank, profoundly, my dear friend and advocate Ark, who has made every effort to assist me and present my case. Everything he said in his submission is true. I have done nothing to harm or endanger your people, or the people of the forest. It was I who devised the plan to create a flood in the Looshin Levels, and I, with Procter Prendis, who risked my life to carry out the great explosions that brought it about. And I know all about Scottie Emmisarius's marriage because I was his best man." Pausing briefly to steady myself I continued:

"But it is also true that I left you, after being welcomed among you with great kindness and protected from a ZADD attack. I reasoned at the time that I could be of no help to you, but I have come to see that this was no excuse for my desertion. There was a small girl here called Aya, who appealed to me for protection. I left her too, and I came back here to find her and her sister. When I learnt that she was dead, and how she had died, I realised I had betrayed not only her but myself, and my life was meaningless. I accept the sentence of death, but I have a last request: that it be death by water, and at the bathing pool where I last saw them. I put the sapphire there in their memory, but I bequeath it to you now to raise funds for your defence. Let my own life be a token of my boundless grief and contrition."

The judge looked at me with unblinking gaze and lips slightly parted throughout this speech. Indeed I surprised myself at my eloquence, which left me faint and gasping for breath. She remained silent for some time and finally rose to her feet and spoke quietly: "I accept the prisoner's submission. Let the sentence be carried out according to his wishes without delay." She turned and disappeared behind the screen.

The guards took me down and I was immediately accosted by Ark, almost in tears with grief, anger and disbelief. He insisted I should withdraw my plea, and he would go straight to the judge and demand a stay of sentence until I had recovered my mental clarity. I said, "Dear Ark. I am so sorry. But I am tired, and I can no longer be at peace with myself."

"But you're doing it again," he almost yelled. "You're leaving us. We need you. You can help us. You defeated the loggers."

"That was a different kind of war. No one was killed. I'm a pacifist. All I see is one war leading to the next and it goes on and on. You have to break the chain. But that's no use to you where you are in the process; you've got to fight or die. You have a war leader - ruthless, cunning, determined, from what I've gathered. You can sell the sapphire and buy guns. You can hide and strike - look what you've survived so far. You're tough and resourceful. You can hold out and your time will come. I just hope your humanity survives as well and you don't turn into your enemy. Remember the old days Ark, and be true to them - all the good times together and building the great birds and the joy of flying up there, shouting in the wind. I pray they will come again my friend. Remember me, and keep the faith."

I could say no more as my strength was failing. We embraced, and Ark clung on to me, until the captain of the guards, respectful now, gently drew him away. Realising I was too weak to walk to the pool they strapped me to a stretcher and carried me. I felt relaxed, dreamy, and happy to be on the last stage of my journey through this vale of tears.

I had a wonderful surprise when we came out of the mine shaft into the open air. After weeks of near or total darkness the light was intense, and the more so as it had snowed heavily. I had to shield my eyes to begin with, but then peering through my fingers saw the sky above was the purest blue. A pair of buzzards,

avian ones, were circling up there, their cries piercing the still air.
The deep covering of snow had blanked out all the violent despo-
liation of war, with delicate trees still standing here and there, like
dark feathers. I felt my body shaking but I was insensitive to cold,
or any physical sensation. I was simply absorbed and transported
by the beauty of the world, passing before my astonished eyes. It
may have been an hallucination, but I fancied I saw another
raptor, a child buzzard, drop like a stone from the blue and disappear beyond the white horizon.

The gentle rocking of the stretcher lulled me and I slept. I was
woken by a knocking, hacking sound, and low voices. After a
while I realised we must have arrived at the pool, and the lads
were cutting a hole in the ice. For the first time I felt some apprehension, but I told myself it would soon be over. The shock of
the cold would probably kill me before I drowned. I'd already
done the difficult part of dying and been close enough to death
to believe that after the storm of pain and fear, and yet before
negation, there came a moment of peace, and that might last forever in its own dimension. I would break through that final barrier
into the heart of light, and come face to face with the ultimate
truth that had been manifested to me in all the love I had given
and received.

They lowered the stretcher and lifted me out and took off my
clothes. They were so gentle now, leading me across the frozen
surface, careful not to slip. I stared down into the black water at my
pale, wavering reflection. I'm already a ghost, I thought. Then the
image shattered and I felt myself seized by a terrible crushing grip
and the light went out in a flash as if a fuse had blown.

And this time I really believed I had made it over to the other
side, standing in the water by the shore of the river Jordan where
an angel, tall, beautiful, radiant, stood with her arms outstretched
to receive me. Soft watery light surrounded her, and her attendants stood at a respectful distance. But the vision lasted only a
few seconds and then I found myself on the ice again, and the
angel only seemed tall because she was standing on the bank above
me, and because she was wearing something on top of her head.

I rubbed the water from my eyes and there stood the judge, looking at me, a bruised, wasted, naked man, and her bright blue eyes were smiling now. A warm blanket was thrown round me and I was walked forward over the ice to take her hands and step on to the bank. She said "Your sentence has been revoked. You have been acquitted."

I was dazed and dazzled beyond any comprehension of this; my only coherent thought was that at least I'd had a bit of a wash. Attendants gathered round me, and shielding me with blankets rubbed me down and dressed me in warm new clothes and boots and a fur coat. Then I was ushered forward to take a seat opposite the judge in a kind of double seated sedan chair. It was lifted, and away we went.

The judge took her crown off and laid it on her lap. "That's a fine crown," I said.

"Yes it's nice isn't it? I had it made specially. Do you like my dress, (opening her coat to remind me of it)?"

"I do, very much."

"I thought the trial went very well. I so liked your speech at the end. Do you think it went well?"

"Indeed, and I think you handled it with great dignity. You really are a very fine judge."

She smiled with pleasure at this compliment and proceeded to chatter away amiably with all the innocent vanity of a twelve year old girl. In response to a few polite questions she told me her name was Zandolay, and that she was the only daughter of a wealthy barrister. They had lived in a beautiful house and had everything they wanted, but one day her father disappeared; her mother believed he'd been killed by the government for defending an anarchist. She started a campaign for women whose husbands and sons had disappeared, and then she too died. They said it was an accident.

Zandolay was taken in by her aunt and uncle but they treated her unkindly and she ran away. She joined a group of anarchists and came with them to live in the mines. The Leader appointed her as a judge because of her legal background and because she had the right qualities. She talked about the nice rooms she had been given and how she had decorated them, and about her various privileges, and I half listened while trying to regain some grasp, however tenuous, of my own circumstances and mental state.

Eventually I asked her if she was in a position to divulge the reason for my unexpected acquittal.

"A boy came to see me immediately after the trial. He had been in the audience. He had only recently joined us, but he had come from the forest and knew you well. He testified that everything that you and your counsel had said was true, and spoke highly in your favour. His name is Tamon, a grandson of Procter Prendis, so he had firsthand knowledge of those events."

"Really! Tamon. But his parents must be very worried about him. I hope they know where he is."

"I am sure they do. He brought a gun with him too."

"Yes, it belonged to his grandfather. He's a brave lad, a real asset. But I was guilty of treason, wasn't I?"

"Yes. I discussed it with the Leader who was not willing to revoke the sentence, but had a mission to attend to and said I was to decide as I was the judge. I ordered my carriage and came out to the pool, thinking it would all be over and the Leader's wish would have been fulfilled. But it took a long time to cut through the ice."

"So it's because of you that I'm still alive."

"And the ice," she added.

We were now approaching the entrance to the mines. Zandolay said, "I see your friends are waiting for you. I will leave you in their charge and say goodbye until we meet again. It has been a pleasure to converse with you."

"For me too," I said, and raised her hand to my lips. She smiled again and tapped the roof of the carriage to signal a halt. Two of the guards who had been escorting us helped me out. They all clapped me on the shoulder and shook hands as if to say "No hard feelings old chap," and then followed the sedan as it disappeared into the mouth of the cave. I stood there, irresolute, and opposite me stood Ark and Tamon. Ark's expression was both reproachful and smug.

"Well you didn't get away this time," he said. Tamon seemed to have grown a little, certainly in stature if not much in height. He came over to me and put his arms round me. As I released him Ark came over too and gave me a nonchalant hug.

"Well, what now my gallant comrades?" I asked.

"We're to look after you," said Ark, "and make sure you don't get into any more trouble."

"I'll do my best."

"Anyway you must be starving."

"I suppose I must be."

I looked up to the heavens and absorbed as much light as I could into my body and whole being before once again entering the chthonic gloom of the mine shaft, Ark in front and Tamon behind me.

We wormed our way through the tunnels that seemed to go onwards and downwards forever, until at last we reached the great chasm and the gallery. This area was the centre of operations, and also the living quarters of the high command. We passed the court room again and what I took from its imposing and colourful emblazonments to be the entrance to the judge's apartments. Ark's quarters, which Tamon now shared with him, were simple and comfortable. They were lit by candlelight and a fire glowed in a fire basket beneath a copper hood, the fumes ducted away I suppose wherever and however the smoke from the village below was dispersed. There were rag rugs on the floor and some on the walls where there were also pictures and designs of buzzard planes in rustic frames, and portraits of Ark and his friends all signed with a big Zinnian 'A'. I recognised a face or two, but could not see Aya or Sulibe.

A low table in front of the fire was surrounded by a semi-circle of seats covered in cushions and furs. Hot food and cool wine were brought in on a tray by an attendant, and we sat by the fire enjoying them for some time in silence. I couldn't take much as my stomach had shrunk, but what I did consume was good and reviving, along with the cosy surroundings and the company of friends. Behind the surface of the bizarre succession of events I still felt that emptiness and worthlessness that had led me to seek the ultimate escape. But then I thought: we do not decide our coming or our going, and if I had to stay in this unconscionable world some while longer I had best make the most of it and try and be of some use.

After the meal we talked. I began by asking Tamon how things were at home, and if his parents knew where he was and agreed to it. All was well, he said, and he had left a note. They would never have consented. He was very sorry about causing them anxiety and he was setting up lines of communication by pigeon post so that he could keep in touch. But there it was. He had to do what he had to do. It transpired he'd been around for a couple of weeks, unaware of my detention until my appearance on the last day of the trial. He was already well in with the Leader who had made him virtually second in command. His contribution of a useful firearm was the least part of his value. He was quick witted, inventive, alert, focussed, and developing a tough, almost ruthless mindset.

Procter Prendis had taught him secrets of the art of war derived from his own experience and the writings of Sun Tzu. Tamon saw great potential for evasive warfare in the network of tunnels, which he already knew intimately and was extending below the city walls. A hard task master, he quoted Sun Tzu: "Bring them together by treating them humanely and keep them together with strict military discipline. This will ensure their allegiance." Operations would be subterranean and the force would remain invisible. It would be a war of provocation and attrition, fought on both sides of the city walls.

Ark's role was now less active. An ace pilot from the days of flight and only survivor apart from the Leader of the suicide attacks, he was now an honoured veteran. Originally the buzzards were not designed as weapons. They were flown to escape capture and for the pure joy of flight, but had also been used as transporters. The swoop that killed Zard had been the first lethal use.

As well as the kamikaze crashes the Zinnian light ray weapon had taken its toll. The rest I supposed had been destroyed when the cavern was blasted open. But it seemed that Ark's skills might be redeployed at some future stage as the Leader had ordered a new generation of craft built on the lines of the razor hawk, small, fast, agile: a deadly weapon for surprise attacks on key Zinnian personnel.

Listening to the two of them talking tactics and strategy like seasoned warriors, but with childish enthusiasm, I came to a more positive view of their chances of survival. But is seemed to me a recipe for endless, self-perpetuating war, in which any values worth fighting for would die, if they weren't quite dead already.

My own position was a puzzle to me. I couldn't leave again, even if I were permitted. I had made it quite clear that I was a convinced and resolute non-combatant. On the subject of warfare we just had to agree to differ. And they accepted this, but they still seemed to want me, and need me, perhaps as a father figure or token adult whose mere presence was enough to authorise these activities. The only alternative solution I could conceive was evacuation to the forest, assuming that would remain a place of safety; but the numbers involved were much larger than I had thought. And the logistics of such an operation were at present beyond me. I could do nothing but wait and let things take their course, in the hope that some opportunity would present itself.

I was starting to feel sleepy and hazy again, 'doited', as Scottie would have said, and asked if I might retire. Tamon hugged me again, still a child beneath the panoply of a war lord. Ark showed me to my room, which was small, neat and comfortable, with the same soft wall hangings and floor coverings, and a bed that nearly filled it. The rounded ceiling reminded me again of the Anderson's shelter. Ark lit the candle on a small bedside table and then he hugged me too, his little head pushed against my bony chest. It was a tight, possessive hug, and I patted him gently to reassure him of my renewed loyalty.

My physical wounds had started to heal and my raw conscience was relieved a little by the thought that I was being given a second chance. After he had left and I had started to undress I noticed another of Ark's portraits on the wall. The subject of this one was me. I saw a man with keen black eyes in narrowed apertures, dark hair flattened back and receding between two fingers of weather-beaten flesh, strong hooked nose, high cheekbones, somewhat feminine mouth and weak chin; a visage of no particular type or character, not handsome or distinguished in any way, and one that could belong anywhere. He'd also managed to suggest my slightly hunched posture, from years of humping a backpack no doubt, and a desire perhaps to pass by unnoticed, and unremembered.

Though recognised and familiar, the individual in the portrait seemed to be someone else – or perhaps there was no longer a 'me' to correspond with it. Having so recently and entirely abandoned my life it seemed in no hurry to return to me. Beginning with my strange conversation with Zandolay what I said or did, my whole existence now, would somehow depend on and be activated by others.

I also realised, comparing this image with the one I'd seen mirrored in the ice pool, that I stood in need of a haircut and shave. I made a mental note of it as a short term goal. On the other side of the bed was a shelf with a vase containing some evergreen fronds and sprigs of holly with bright red berries. Beside this was a thick, quarto-sized book which I took down and examined. It was a complete works of Shakespeare, translated by Emmisarius. As I flicked through, my eye picked out several familiar passages quaintly and precisely rendered into formal Zinnian: '...When the blast of war blows in our ears, then imitate the action of a tiger. Stiffen the sinews, summon up the blood. Disguise fair nature with hard favoured rage ...'

But my own sinews were giving way as I read it, and my eyelids drooping. I put the book back on the shelf, blew out the candle, and went to sleep.

CHAPTER 21

A Messenger

IT MUST have been mid afternoon when I retired and mid morning when I woke. Ark and Tamon had gone, leaving a note saying there was food and hot water and if I needed anything else I should ask an attendant at the gallery guard point, and that I should just keep the fire in and take it easy till they returned. On the table there was bread, honey, fruit, milk, and bowls of tea and porridge I could warm on the fire. I did my best to eat as much as I could, and then explored the apartments, peeking behind the drapes which served as internal doors. Ark and Tamon shared a room which was as untidy as you'd expect a boys' room to be. Books, papers and drawings were scattered on the beds and floor. And there were constructional and deconstructional projects in various stages of completion and incompletion. The only unusual feature was that they all related to war, real not make-believe war, and the weapons of war.

The plumbing arrangements were primitive but decent. In the bathroom there was a tank set in the wall with a fire beneath it. The fire had gone out but the water and the room were still warm and I enjoyed the almost forgotten luxury of a long lazy soak. Ark had left me a razor and scissors and clean shirt and underwear. I really didn't deserve such a friend. My body was still mottled with purple and yellow bruises and criss-crossed with scar tissue, and I doubt if I weighed eight stone. But when I'd finished my toilet I felt refreshed and comfortable, and not entirely unpresentable. I busied myself for some time with washing and tidying up and seeing to the fire, and I reset the fire in the bathroom to relight when the boys came back. After working in the tunnels or whatever they'd probably appreciate a bath. No doubt I could have commissioned a servant to do these tasks but I wanted to do something after so much inactivity, and having things done to me; and I didn't feel in a position to start giving orders.

With myself and everything put to rights I relaxed in front of the fire and began reading *Twelfth Night* in Zinnian. I found myself translating bits of it back into English from memory as Zinnian prose, even in Emmisarius's hands, was rather heavy. The book was heavy too and after a while it dropped beside me and I dozed again. I was awoken by a light tapping on the door. I got up and opened it and there was a girl in a pretty dress standing there. She was holding my rucksack and said, "I'm returning your belongings to you." In the dark doorway I couldn't see her clearly but recognised her voice. It was Zandolay, the judge. "Would you like to come in?" I enquired. "I could make a cup of tea." "Thank you," she said. "That would be very nice." I showed her to a seat by the fire and she placed the rucksack on the table. "Everything is there," she said. "But we've accepted your offer of the sapphire towards the war effort. I know a dealer in the city who will give me a fair price." "That's excellent," I said, putting a pan of water on the hob to boil.

We sat in awkward silence for a moment, and then I said, "No cases to try today then?"

"Oh no," she said, "This is a rest day for me."

"Yes, for me as well. I've been ordered to take things easy. I certainly hope you're not often called upon to pass the death sentence."

"Oh no. Yesterday was the first time. The worst sentence I had to pass was a flogging for a boy who was caught stealing things. But mostly it's a reprimand or a minor penalty. The children are very well behaved on the whole, and Tamon has greatly improved morale and discipline."

"I take it then you were not responsible for my misfortunes."

"Oh no. You were treated very harshly indeed. I'm so sorry, but the Leader's instructions were very precise. We have complete faith in our Leader."

"I hope I shall have the honour of meeting your Leader at some point."

"Yes indeed, I trust that may be possible."

"Good. In my life, Zandolay, I have been blessed with great friendships and some love, as well as much indifference and mild contempt. But I don't think I've ever been an object of hatred. It perplexes me. Ah, the water's boiling I think."

I made and poured the tea and handed her a cup. She thanked me and sipped discreetly. She really was a very pretty child, with perfect manners. I thought it wise to steer the conversation into calmer waters. I told her about my adventures in the Tash'kahern mountains and the Looshin Levels with Scottie, Procter and the Prendis clan. She was especially interested in any anecdotes relating to Tamon: how he saved Credo's life, and risked his own abseiling down the gorge of the Raffire to stuff dynamite in the rock crevices; and how he kept watch at the caves when the others had given up and spotted the approaching helicopter gunship. Her blue eyes were wide with wonder and horror at the ferocity of the attack. She certainly had a soft spot for that young warrior. Then I remarked:

"Ark's apartments are very comfortable, but rather plain. I expect yours are really splendid."

"I do my best to make the chambers and my own rooms as nice as possible, and the children are very kind. They bring me things from the City and things they've made themselves and I like to encourage them. But you must come and see for yourself. I have some business in the morning but perhaps you could join me for tea in the afternoon."

"I would like that."

"Oh good. Then I'll send someone for you. We are neighbours now after all."

For the rest of the afternoon I read and dozed, or simply relaxed and reflected upon my life, past, present and to come. I thought especially about Scottie and Elfie - would I hear of them or they of me again? They seemed so distant now. But they were happy, whatever else was bad or wrong, and I had played some part in their happiness and had left them with good memories of me.

The boys returned in high spirits. Food was ordered and fruity wine splashed into tall glasses. Tamon talked freely of his day's work designing the tunnel complex and motivating the work force. He explained that he had to provide for the possibility of one or more of the exits being discovered. He was laying false trails, setting booby traps and ambush points where their limited fire power could be used to greatest effect. He was selecting his ground and preparing the battlefield in accordance with the principles of Sun Tzu. And it was essential that every soldier knew the tunnels intimately and exactly how he or she would be deployed. "I'm almost starting to feel sorry for the Zinnians," I said, half in jest.

"But Jason, you can't possibly have any pity for those murderers after the things they've done."

"My dear boy, terrible things have been done and I fully understand that you need to use every means at your disposal to secure victory over an army that can commit, and a society that can underwrite, such atrocities. At the same time many individual soldiers of theirs will be young lads whose heads have been stuffed full of propaganda and make-believe and all kinds of patriotic rubbish from an early age, and have been recruited, conscripted, indoctrinated and desensitised long before they're capable of thinking for themselves. They are victims as much as those they kill."

Then Ark cut in with: "You have to kill the ones responsible; strike at the head. That's why the Leader is planning a hit on Jobu."

"And how can the Leader do that?" I asked. "Jobu will be encased in layers of security."

Ark grinned, shook his head and said nothing. "Come on Ark," I said. "Don't forget I've been acquitted of espionage!"

"Well I shouldn't really tell anyone but everyone knows. We

were able to save two aircraft when we came to the mines, the big three-crew raider eagle and the little razor hawk. They were the last to be built and the fastest and most manoeuvrable. The leader and I have been working on them to improve the accuracy of the dive trajectory and recovery angle. We reckon we can get it sharp enough to go in and out of a small internal courtyard which Jobu crosses every day before breakfast to go for his morning swim. We've been practising non-stop for weeks. We marked out an area the size of the courtyard and used a sack full of loose dirt and rabbit droppings to represent Jobu. The razor hawk gets about 80% success rate, but that will only kill Jobu, and Baldark would cover up the cause of death for his own ends. The Leader wants to use the raider eagle to grab him and lift him up and spike him on the pinnacle of the highest spire of Zinn so everyone can see him and they will know who killed him, and they will know who rules."

"That should put a stop to the victory parades," said Tamon.

"And it will make a start to a new and bloody war in which hundreds, thousands even, will be killed and tortured," I rejoined.

Ark shook his head again. The Leader is set on it. We're getting close to 60% success rate with the raider."

"But if you're the co-pilot you could refuse."

"In which case the Leader would go ahead with the razor hawk and I'd end up in the dock facing a treason charge and dear sweet Zandolay would have to perform her solemn duty of condemning me to death."

"But I'd defend you Ark. And I'm well in with Zandolay now. I had tea with her. And if I couldn't persuade her I'm sure Tamon could."

This got a laugh from them both, slightly embarrassed, I thought, on Tamon's part. And so we fell to talking and joking about less dire and intractable matters, and played a few games of cards and drank more wine and retired in a state of mildly euphoric recklessness.

Over the following days I saw Zandolay quite frequently, usually in the afternoons as she was busy in the mornings. Formal trials were rare events, but children were sent to her for some minor misdemeanour or breach of military etiquette. As many were orphans or came from difficult backgrounds she was careful and patient with them, giving guidance and advice rather than handing out punishments. I learnt all this because she liked to talk about her cases. She was a mother figure to them, loved by boys and girls, younger and older alike. Her approach to military discipline was certainly different from Tamon's, but the two together were an effective combination.

Supplies and booty of various kinds were constantly being brought in from the City, and anything fine or precious like an ornament or piece of fabric or some delicacy to eat, was invariably presented to her by an adoring acolyte. Consequently both the chambers where she and her secretary worked and her own rooms were luxuriously, if somewhat eclectically, appointed. She showed me some lovely examples of Zinnian craftsmanship, notably a carved ebony screen of interwoven foliage in which the different birds of the forest were presented with such detailed accuracy I could recognise most of them.

Then there was a beautifully embroidered wall hanging depicting the city of Zinn in all its glory surrounded by an arabesque border showing the fields and the forest, with all the birds, animals, fish, fruits and crops in brilliant colour. It was an image I'd seen somewhere before which I took to represent one of the guiding principles of the founders of Zinn, of a harmonious relationship between city and country, and between civilisation and wild nature. Recalling the devastation of the Looshin Levels and the blitzing of this area it was clearly an ideal which had now been abandoned.

The days of leisurely convalescence continued. Though my appetite didn't recover and I continued to lose weight some of my energy returned, and when not reading, entertaining or being entertained by Zandolay, I liked to stroll about the gallery and look down at the busy life in the valley below. I was soon on friendly terms with the guards and attendants and some of the other officers who lived there. Ark had brought me more books to read, classic works by Zinnian authors in prose and verse. The poets especially impressed me, their lyrics having the same purity and precision that characterised Zandolay's art works. These too were reminders of what Zinn had once been.

Among the pile I found another work by Emmisarius, this one quite short, no more than an essay, which was surprising given the title: *The Arc of Becoming: Reflections on Creation, Existence and the Destiny of Mankind.*

I had certainly drawn the conclusion that Emmisarius was a convinced atheist, but reading this pamphlet I realised it was not so much God he was against as organised religion, which he saw as another manipulative and abusive tribal power structure. The concept of a creator certainly entered his speculations, but only as a concept, or a symbol. One of his fundamental axioms was that reality extends beyond our perception of it. It was self evidently absurd that a species descended from the apes a split second ago in cosmic time should comprehend, or have the ability to comprehend, the totality and meaning of everything. The progress of science was simply the discovery of ever greater mysteries.

He saw the universe as an ongoing act of creation: a becoming. He took Darwin's idea of evolution to a cosmic level. Existence was not an absolute given but relative, a matter of degrees and movement from lesser to greater or a lower to a higher state. He illustrates this by assuming the role of the creator, taking a blank sheet of paper and a sharp pencil and making a tiny dot on it. This represented a universe of zero dimensions. To human perception such a universe would be invisible and inconceivable. If the dot is extended to a line, with length but no width, we have a one dimensional universe, but still theoretical as far as we are concerned. Only when the artist shades an area do we have a work that exists for us as a visible fact, but even this ceases to exist if we turn the page to its edge. The artist has to gum several sheets together, creating a third dimension, for his work to be visible from every viewpoint: to exist.

Of course even the tiniest mark made by a pencil is in reality a block of solid matter, and anything less than three dimensions does not exist, other than as concept, for sensory, physical beings like us. And even the three dimensional universe does not exist for us unless, like us, it exists in time. As Einstein observed, time is the fourth dimension.

Thus we have a solid, tangible, continuing universe, but even this cannot truly and fully be said to exist unless something or someone is there to observe it, to affirm its reality. In other words the evolution of life, and with it the development of sensory organs and neural processors, is necessary for existence to become complete. In this model of existence consciousness is the fifth dimension, but the consciousness of animals, birds, insects, even plants, of their environment, is all that is required.

In the evolution of the human species Emmisarius sees the unfolding of a sixth dimension, for humans are not just aware of their surroundings for the purposes of survival but able to reflect, question and discover. Our consciousness expands beyond the life force imperatives. We seek to create beauty and harmony; we search for cause, meaning and purpose in things. We pursue ideals like justice and truth. We are capable of love beyond self, beyond fear. Our spirituality is located in this higher dimension and flowering of existence. For Emmisarius the question 'does God exist?' is meaningless because God is existence, in the highest form we can conceive and aspire to. God did not create the universe: the universe is the creation, the unfolding, of God.

Thus evolution of life, and human life, are not freak cosmic occurrences but central to the creational process. Humankind is the torch bearer of existence, and as such the bearer of an immense responsibility. Emmisarius was by no means confident of our ability to discharge this responsibility, given the countervailing forces of human greed, arrogance, destructiveness and stupidity. Every day and everywhere truth, honour, grace, integrity, hope, innocence and loveliness of mind and heart are betrayed, corrupted, crushed. Zinn's history was example enough. What is learned or re-learned by one generation is forgotten again by the next, and this inability to adapt is the surest sign of evolutionary failure. Evolution proceeds by trial and error and for Emmisarius humanity will almost certainly be consigned to the latter category.

We are unhappy transitional creatures, incomplete, imperfect; caught in the net of dimensional becoming. As a race we submit to the idiocy of politics and fail to make the connections implicit in the works of musicians, artists, poets, scientists and saints. It would take no doubt many millennia for a more intelligent life form to evolve, but the universe is not short of time. And life may also be evolving elsewhere in the cosmos. Strange, he observes, that it never occurs to science fiction writers that we might be the aliens.

Every step in this progressive dimensional enhancement of existence represents a quantum leap, an exponential expansion; but is mathematically impossible as however many times you multiply zero by zero it will never produce a value. Emmisarius deduces from this that universes of less than four dimensions do in some sense exist, even a universe of zero dimensions. In a highly speculative passage he anticipates the 'big bang' theory, proposing that all the energy and matter in the cosmos originated in something infinitesimally small – in other words a singularity. But he insists it would be wrong to suppose that the universe began at a point in time, progressed by stages to the present and will continue to expand, contract or change in any way. That is an illusion of humanity's time-dominated viewpoint. There is no beginning or end, and time is only one dimension within the totality and harmony of existence, which is by definition simultaneous and co-eternal. It is here he draws on religious thought and mystical insight. 'I am Alpha and Omega, the first and the last.'

I was struggling to take all this in when there was a quiet knock on the door. I was surprised on opening it to find not Zandolay or any other child, but a tall young man. He had to stoop to enter and altered the scale of things by his height. Weight loss and confinement had brought me closer to the children in physical stature, but this young man was deferential and child-like in his attitude towards me. There was something familiar about him and something troubling as well. He introduced himself as Eldis Komash and I invited him to take a seat and share a brew.

"You don't remember me," he said, "but I remember you. I'll never forget you."

I looked at him more intently and my feeling of unease increased as I did so. "I heard you were here," he said, "and I wanted to thank you."

"I'm pleased to have done you some service, but you'll have to remind me what it was."

"You didn't do anything. There was nothing you could do. It was just something you said that helped me at a critical moment."

He was dressed like a forester and had a thick scarf round his neck. I noticed he hadn't removed it despite the heat from the fire. Then it came to me.

"I'm delighted to see you," I said, "and amazed to see you. I thought you were dead." He was smiling now, and I took his hand and shook it warmly. The last time I had seen Eldis Komash he had a rope round his neck and was plunging from the high scaffold at Fort Rossak. "My dear boy, you were the last victim of the notorious Zard. But how the deuce did you survive?"

"I thought I had died. I was choking. It was horrible, indescribable. Then I was falling again and I lost consciousness. The swoop that killed Zard and rescued you must have cut my rope and I was knocked out by the fall. When I came to I was lying in a heap of naked corpses all thrown together, men, women and children, with terrible wounds and staring eyes and gaping jaws, our legs and arms all snarled up. In a gap between a rib cage and an armpit I could see other heaps the same, like haystacks, and across the clearing was a digger digging a trench and a bulldozer shovelling the bodies in. Nearby there was a lorry, with its tailgate open and a load of corpses it had just dumped in a pile behind it. It was parked in front of a filthy shed and loud voices, swearing and laughing, were coming from it. As there was no one in the lorry I guessed the driver was inside the shed.

I managed to crawl out of the heap and across the ground and under the lorry, and then I somehow wedged myself into the chassis, gripping the rusty metal so tight my fingers bled. Then men came out, two I think, still roaring with laughter and shouting back at the ones in the shed, and got in the lorry and slammed the doors. The engine started up and the prop shaft shuddered, the whole thing shook and fumes were everywhere and we were bumping and lurching over rough ground. It was torture. We went over a corpse and its guts splashed out all over me. Then we were on a smoother road and I could tell from the shadows we were in the forest, belting along. What with the dust and noise and fumes from a leaky exhaust, and grit pelting me and a sharp ridge ripping the length of my back, my strength and endurance were failing. Just as they gave out we slowed down to go through a ford and I let go. I sank into the cool soothing water and lay there as long as I could hold my breath. When I sat up I saw the lorry disappearing in the distance."

"That's incredible! What happened next?"

"I got into the forest before I collapsed and blacked out again. I was woken by a lantern shining in my face. It was a hunter who found me and he took me back to his cottage where he and his wife and daughter looked after me and nursed me back to health."

"But that's wonderful, I'm so pleased for you and I'm so glad you came." I poured us both a mug of tea and just stared at him for some time in amazement and pleasure. Then I asked, "But why were you condemned to death in the first place?"

"I was a pilot myself as a boy. Then when I grew up I still kept in touch with them, helping with supplies and carrying messages. I got caught in the blockade. But I'm still with them; in fact I'm helping Tamon set up a pigeon post. He says communications and supply lines are the key to success."

"Indeed, I'm sure he does and I'm sure they are. But tell me Eldis, have you any news of the Sammonar region?"

"Yes, I came through there on my way here. It's not all good news I'm afraid."

"Why, what's happened? Scotty ... Emmisarius, and his wife, are they all right?"

"Yes, they are well. But you will know that Mrs Emmisarius's sister married Baldark. The couple went away on their honeymoon but returned unexpectedly. Some say it was because Baldark was afraid of plotting behind his back in his absence. That was probably part of the reason but he and his wife had had a blazing row. She wouldn't put up with him openly flirting with other women. She came back to her parents' home and then it was announced he was divorcing her, having hired false witnesses to say she had been unfaithful to him."

"She's better off without him in my opinion."

"But worse was to follow. One day armed police came and smashed their way into the Shahribe mansion. They shot the old butler and arrested the Prince and took him away. It was published that he had links with anarchy and he was charged with high treason. Baldark had been spying on him for some time. The Princess hired a legal team and they were able to secure the Prince's release on bail, but when the Princess went to collect him from the police station he had been so badly tortured she could only recognise him by his coat. He died soon after."

"That's terrible. He was a good, kind, honest man. It seems there are no depths of depraved cruelty to which these bloodsuckers will not sink."

"The Prince was tried posthumously and found guilty, and as he could no longer forfeit his life he was condemned to the loss of all his estates and possessions. The family was left utterly impoverished, with only the clothes they stood in, and sent into exile. The estate was given to Baldark in recognition of his patriotic conduct in exposing a traitor, and he has now installed one of his mistresses there."

"But what has become of them? Esolday, Zarielle and Amarel?"

"They were taken in by the foresters. Princess Esolday lives with her daughter Elphane, but a new home is being built for her close by. The grief and shock of these events almost killed her too, but she is said to be receiving every attention and making a slow recovery. Scottie paid for Zarielle to go abroad to study. She is in Paris where she has met up with another Zinnian girl, related to the Prendis family, already famous for her looks and talent. These two beautiful and mysterious creatures from a place that doesn't seem to exist have attracted something of a cult following. There can be no doubt they will find rich husbands."

"In Zarielle's case a better one I hope."

"She could hardly find a worse."

"And what of Amarel?"

"She's staying with the Prendis family and is walking out with one of the young men. She's a bold, healthy outdoor sort of girl and has really taken to forest life."

I invited Eldis to stay, but he had urgent matters to attend to, and a long distance to travel. Before he left I asked him, if he were in Sammonar again, to call on Scotty and Elfie and tell them he had found me in good health and spirits, living with the children and at their service; to give them my warmest greetings and also to convey my sympathy to the Princess Esolday. He promised to do this and bring back news of them when he returned.

Finally I asked him what it was I had said to him on the scaffold at Fort Rossak. I remembered feeling great pity for him, a young man about to meet such a hideous and untimely end; but I couldn't remember saying anything. He replied, "You were about to die yourself, and yet you turned to me and said, 'Have courage my friend. God is merciful'."

"I really said that?"

"Those were your words."

We embraced and parted. I was pleased that I had given some help to another in dread circumstances, but still puzzled by the words I had spoken. At that time I knew little Zinnian and the Deity didn't normally fall within my terms of reference. I had never been a religious man but I had travelled the world and realised that as a privileged and protected Westerner it was easy for me to dispense with religion. For the vast majority of my fellow human beings life was meaningless or intolerable without faith. Religion may be the opiate of the people, but it is a prescription drug, not a recreational one.

Later I told Ark and Tamon about this encounter and the news it had brought. Tamon said that it was the first time that the cruelty of the Zinnian regime had been directed against one of their own. It marked an escalation of the reign of terror. Jobu was a tyrant now, for all to see, and Baldark's teeth were growing longer and sharper by the day. "Do you agree with me now," he demanded, "that we have no choice but to fight?"

"I do, Tamon, but a war of evasion and survival. It won't be long before Baldark cuts Jobu's throat, and only a matter of time before someone cuts his. Think sideways. Play the long game."

He seemed to take this on board, but Ark once again put in that the Leader would never be dissuaded from the planned impaling of Jobu on the crowning spire of his palace, city and empire. That would truly be poetic justice. Nevertheless I ventured to hope that Tamon might have some influence with the Leader, who was leaving so much of the tactical detail to him.

Later, alone in my room, I turned all these things over in my mind. I was disturbed by the news from Sammonar, not only by the sickening brutality towards a good hearted, forthright, honourable man, but that those same dark forces had made a move closer to my loved ones. Suddenly their position seemed fragile and exposed. I desperately wanted to be with them, but reasoned that if there was anything I could do for them, for us all, it would be from here. I wondered if I would ever get to meet the Leader, and urge caution and cunning, rather than confrontation. I had made further tentative enquiries but it had been made clear to me that an interview would be granted only if and when the Leader chose.

The next day I was agitated and no longer content to read and rest in recuperative idleness. I had no visitors to distract me, and felt it unfair to burden my companions with my anxieties when they needed to relax after their work. In any case we weren't likely to get any further on the subject of the conduct of the war. The day after that was going much the same way until tea time, when there came Zandolay's familiar tap on the door. I opened it but she didn't come in. She stood there and said quietly, "The Leader will see you now."

She escorted me to the end of the gallery, then down some steps and into a tunnel lit by torches that led away from it. At the end was a heavy doorway guarded by two warriors with their furs, spears and painted faces. They opened the door and stood to attention when they saw Zandolay. She took me along another tunnel to another door, which she opened herself and peered in, and I heard her whisper my name. Then she ushered me through and closed the door behind me.

It was dark inside, with shadowy hangings. There was no furniture at all except a low table with a single candle on it, and a square object, a soft padded bag like a cushion case; behind this a scatter of cushions and rugs against the wall. A little girl was sitting there, dressed in a plain hessian frock. She had a wide-eyed pixie face and a mop of blond hair. I recognised her immediately. Sulibe.

CHAPTER 22

Vengeance

SHE SAT STARING into space. I stood there waiting for her to acknowledge or notice my presence, but she remained motionless. "Sulibe," I said quietly. She replied in a hollow voice without moving or changing her expression:

"Sulibe is dead."

"That is what I was told. So you are now 'the Leader'. Well, the penny drops. But Sulibe is alive enough still to hate me, and hates me enough to want to kill me. And I don't blame her. I hate myself for deserting you."

She looked up now and stared at me with stony contempt. Then she looked down at the object on the table. "Open this," she said.

I stepped over, picked it up and undid the buttoned flap. There appeared to be some soft pale leather inside. "Take it out. Open it out and hold it up in front of you."

I did as she said, and almost fainted. It dropped from my grip and I knelt down and tried to gather it up, but tears were blinding my eyes.

It was a small human skin, with only one leg, and a round hole in the centre.

Sulibe reached and took it from me, folded it carefully and returned it to the cloth case. Then from the lining she produced a folded sheet of paper and handed it to me. "Now read this." I unfolded the sheet and read as follows:

My Dear Zulibe,
I enclose, with my compliments, all that remains of your late sister, Aya. I have had her carefully preserved by an expert tanner, and I placed her on my bedroom wall as a memento of the pleasure she gave me. But she looked lonely there so I thought I would return her to you until such time as you can join her. It won't be long I trust.
Yours very truly,
ZARD

I closed my eyes and tried to hold on as the moral axis of the universe reeled violently from side to side. Zard was a psychopath, I told myself. They exist. They have no love, no sympathy, no human understanding. They sometimes do terrible, horrible things. Men of power and greed have always used them and use them still. But the victims – little Aya, so innocent, full of love, full of joy, and Sulibe . . . I turned to her. The same hard empty gaze. I wanted to comfort her but she said, "Don't touch me. Stay just where you are."

I stayed there, kneeling, with my eyes closed. "My dear child," I said at last. "There are no words to express my grief for Aya, or for you, nor my regret that I had taken a course that made it impossible for me even to have a chance of preventing this terrible thing. But you surely cannot blame me alone."

She replied in the same dry unchildlike voice. "Not you alone. I blame Zard first, and I killed him. I didn't go to Rossak to rescue you but to kill Zard, and I didn't even know it was you that Ark lifted. Then I blame Jobu and he will die soon. I wanted to kill you too. I wanted you to suffer first, as I suffer. Every minute, every second I'm in hell thinking of my poor sister, the terror and the agony of her death. How could anyone endure such a fate, let alone a little child?"

"But I was ready to die, and you could still have me killed."

"I know that. But it's no good. You accepted your guilt and you made your peace. You would have died in peace and I wanted you in hell with Zard, and Jobu . . . and with me. Where was I when Aya was having the skin torn off her body by that bloodthirsty maniac? I only pray that I can find peace in death, but I intend to sell my life dearly. You've escaped me, and I hate you even more for that. You've got nine lives like a cat, and everyone loves you. You turn everyone - Aya, Ark, Scottie, Tamon, even Zandolay. It was she who went out to save you. I couldn't give a damn whether you lived or died. I'd done my best. But you won't turn me, I tell you that."

"And you will never make me hate you, Sulibe. I cannot hate. There's too much hatred, it's like an ocean. But I am the shore where the ocean ends."

"Sulibe is dead."

"I have to call you something. 'Leader' is just a title. And besides, you're not my leader. Do you have another name?"

"My name is Vengeance."

"Well it suits you. Vengeance then. Do you not think it might be possible that Aya didn't suffer as much as you think? In the first place, she might have been dead or unconscious when he did that. The wound in her stomach, I may be wrong but that could have come from the weapon they used to capture her. Of course Zard wanted you to think that he'd skinned her alive and she died in torment. But even in that worst possible case her suffering would have ended and there would have been peace. And she would not have been alone then. You would have been with her, and every-one who loved her.

"I remember once visiting an old professor in a country ruled by a dictator. He, the professor, had criticised the regime. When I left and he was showing me out we found the body of his son lying outside his door. The boy had been horribly tortured. But the old man remained strangely calm. 'Look at his face,' he said. Despite all disfigurement, it was at peace."

"Are you telling me everyone dies in peace - even Zard would have died in peace?"

"Zard was already dead. Aya was full of love. The only thing that lives is love, and love lives forever. God is merciful."

"God does not exist. If he did I'd hate him for letting all these cruel things happen. Only a fool would believe in God and you're not a fool and you don't believe in him."

"Well no, I don't; not in the way people think. But I believe that to say 'God is merciful' is to say something true that cannot be said in any other way. God is love; human love and divine love are the same thing. God knows his own and gathers his own, and you and Aya will never be apart. I have been close to death myself and I can tell you, in the end there is mercy."

"You're trying to turn me. You're trying to stop me hating you. You don't want me to kill Jobu and you've turned Tamon and got him saying it's a bad idea. But you won't succeed with your God stuff and your peace stuff. Jobu will die tomorrow if there's a clear day and a light wind and the chances are I'll die too and so will Ark. And I will be happy, if only for an instant. You and Tamon can have it all to yourselves then. There's no more to be said. GUARDS!" She shouted with surprising force and the two, who must have taken up positions outside the door, entered immediately.

"Take this man away. Hang him up by his toenails and stick needles in his eyes." The two lads stared at her and at each other. "Oh just take him back to his room for now. I'll deal with him later."

I was marched back along the tunnel and released into the gallery. Zandolay was there waiting for me, looking anxious. "How did it go?" she asked.

"Not well Judge. Not well at all."

We went back to Ark's apartments and I told her about the interview, and what was said. She was troubled, divided as she was between her love for, and loyalty to, the Leader and the justice of slaying Jobu, and the fear that so conspicuous an act of defiance would lead to bloody and indiscriminate reprisals. More innocents would suffer. On top of this was the real possibility that the Leader and Ark would themselves be killed. "Perhaps I should try to speak to her," she said.

"I'm afraid she would only accuse you of being influenced by me. I feel so sorry for her and want to help her if I can. But my mere existence enrages her. It wouldn't surprise me if she ordered my death when she returns from destroying Jobu, and then finds some sacrificial way of ending her own life."

"Oh dear, I do hope not."

Zandolay's childlike diagram of right and wrong was clearly no use to her in the twisted politics of revenge and hatred. The situation was beyond us both, and we sat in silence for some time until Ark and Tamon joined us. They had come directly from a conference with the Leader who had ordered that the mission would go ahead as planned tomorrow at dawn, weather conditions being favourable. Tamon and myself were to be present at take off. Any further attempt to question or prevent the mission would be regarded as treasonous. There was no more to be said.

We invited Zandolay to supper but she said she would rather return to her own apartment. After she'd left Ark said that she was very religious and she would spend the whole evening praying for God's guidance and for there to be no more war and hatred and killing and us all to be safe and happy.

"I hope God's listening for once," said Tamon.

Conscious that it might be our last time with Ark we tried to make the evening as cheerful as possible, ordered up his favourite dishes and talked about everything and anything except what was weighing heavily on our minds. We reminisced about old times and good times and absent friends and drank wine till we were too sleepy to go to bed, and Ark ordered a guard to wake us an hour before dawn.

When Tamon roused me Ark was already togged up in his leather flying suit and helmet, and had his goggles and gloves. He looked every inch the flying ace, even if there weren't that many inches to him. I dressed up warm, and Tamon suggested I bring Procter's field glasses - he had a pair of his own. Lit only by Tamon's helmet lamp it was a long journey through the dark, intricate network of tunnels to reach the launch site. The last stage was all uphill and I was out of breath as well as weak from anxiety when we entered the hangar. It was a large cavity, like a wide corridor with rails running the length of it, rising at the further end to an opening filled with the grey light of dawn. I could see the razor hawk in the shadows, and other craft being assembled, but all the lights were focussed on the great raider eagle, which positively shone with a gem-like lustre.

Four engineers surrounded it, working with intense concentration and coordination, checking, tightening and greasing the moving parts, and exchanging a few quiet words of question and confirmation. Standing as close as I could without getting in the way I examined it with astonished admiration, aware that it also might soon cease to exist and I might even become the only witness to its ever having existed. I was struck by the complexity of the controls, with all the wires and linkages routed to the joystick of the leading pilot, and connected to the controls of the second pilot, who operated the grab mechanism and wing flap when required. I guessed the city's thermal currents would be strong enough to lift the machine without much wing action. The third crew member would of course be Jobu himself. The flaps and feathers shimmered as the engineers tested them, while the fierce, staring raptor head, polished in black, white and gold, waited patiently for its prey.

Other engineers were at work cranking up the catapult and setting the release mechanism. As yet there was no sign of the Leader. We waited, nervously cheerful, clapping our hands and stamping our feet to keep warm. Feeble light from the outside world began to creep in, gleaming on the rails of the ramp, and the misty silhouette of Zinn's upper levels could just be seen, the topmost spire rising in clear air to its needle point. As the minutes passed I was trying not to hope too much that the Leader would fail to appear, and would call the whole thing off. And I was right not to. She did appear. The guards came in first and everyone stood to attention. Then she entered.

She was wearing a tight fitting leather suit and gloves like Ark's, but no helmet, her blond hair pushed back from her face which was set hard and almost white. Tragic, cold, beautiful, indomitable; an avenging angel if ever there was. Looking neither to left or right she walked straight over to the raider, exchanged a brief word with the chief engineer, then climbed inside, clipped her take-off harness, and began feeling and running her fingers over the controls. Tamon and I hugged Ark and patted him on the back and gave the thumbs up sign and he went over and climbed in too and strapped up his harness. The catapult hook was attached to the front of the raider, and while this was being done the Leader spoke to Ark. He nodded and took up his position.

The two pilots put on their goggles, and after a brief pause the leader nodded to the operative controlling the catapult. He yanked his lever, there was a sharp snap and the craft jerked forward and whanged out like a slug from an air gun. We watched it rapidly recede, and then the wings fanned open to their full glorious breadth and the great bird soared upwards out of sight.

By now I was feeling sick with apprehension, and I decided I couldn't watch to see the outcome of the mission. I looked at Tamon and knew from his expression he was feeling the same. He said, "We'll know soon enough, we might as well go back." I lent one of the guards my field glasses and asked him to bring word to us as soon as there was any news. We returned to our rooms where I stoked up the fire and put a pan of water on to make some coffee. Later Zandalay joined us. We sat waiting in silence, sipping our coffee. Time passed. Worried looks were exchanged. By now we should have heard something. Still we waited.

At length there was a knock on the door and the guard came in. He told us there was a lot of mist and smoke rising at first and visibility was poor, but now he could definitely see a body impaled on the spire. As yet, however, the raider had not returned. He said he would bring news again as soon as there was any. The same questions and fears were in all our minds. Had there been an accident? Had they been captured? Had the Leader decided to take her own life by crashing the plane? Surely she would not have sacrificed Ark as well? Tamon was the first to speak:

"If we don't hear soon we'll have to send out a search party. We'll have to find out what has happened."

We waited again, and then Tamon got up and said, "I'll have to go and organise something." But just as he got up to put on his coat there was another light tap on the door. It opened slowly and a little head appeared. It was Ark, grinning from ear to ear.

We all rushed forward and grabbed him and smothered him with hugs, and even Zandolay bestowed a demure little kiss on his cheek and said, "Oh Ark, I can't tell you how relieved we are to see you. You must tell us what happened." Ark held his hands up to ward off any further physical expressions of pleasure and congratulation on his return, and then, panting a little to regain his breath, gave his account:

"Well, before we took off the Leader had a word with me. She said there had been a slight change of plan. Instead of lifting the real Jobu we were going to lift the dummy Jobu, the sack full of dirt, and we were going to put that on the spike instead. Well, it was a piece of cake. We've lifted that hundreds of times. The Leader brought the bird up on the head wind and we hovered right above the spire and I pushed it down on the spike, no problem. "Well done Ark," she said, "now let's go for a ride shall we?" So she spiralled up, and we lofted higher and higher - we'd never been that high before, you could hardly breathe.

"We circled round and could see all the little houses and farms hidden away in the forest, and in the distance we could see the rivers and the mountains, the Tash'kaherns, and the sun glistening on the Looshin Lake. You know she loves to fly, and never stopped flying in the little hawk even when everyone else was grounded, so quick or so high no one could tell it wasn't a real bird. She says it's the only time she's happy because the world looks so beautiful from up there, and Aya's spirit is there too she says. In the end I had to shout to her 'Leader, we should go back. Everyone will wonder what's happened and be worried.' 'You're right Ark,' she yelled back, and she threw the plane into a steep dive and we plummeted down and I thought we were going to crash in to the hill and I could see the tiny hole in the side of the hill hurtling towards us.

"God knows how she did it. I just closed my eyes and prayed and then I felt the tug of the drag rope and screeching wires in the windlasses and we slammed to a halt, flung forward in our harnesses, hardly an inch from the wall. People were getting up off the floor who'd had to jump for their lives. She took her gloves and her goggles off, cool as anything. 'Thank you Colonel,' she said. 'Mission accomplished,' and the guard formed round her and she strode away."

Everyone was speaking at once, asking questions, bestowing accolades on the Leader and on Ark, but he held up his hand and said, "Friends, I'm bushed. That dive knocked the stuffing out of me. I'm going to get my head down. We'll talk about it some more later on." Zandolay immediately went into mother mode and escorted Ark to his room and helped him take his suit off and put him to bed. Then she came and fetched him a glass of hot milk and sat by him until he slept. Meanwhile Tamon and I mulled over the significance of this turn of events.

"That could be a good move," I offered.

"Hmm, yes. A bit of sideways thinking perhaps."

"That little lady is certainly some pilot."

"We need to build up the air force. Air power could play a vital role."

"What will the Zinnians make of it? That's the question."

"Did they see the raider, I wonder?"

"Perhaps not if there was a lot of mist."

"We'll find out in time no doubt. Well I'd better get to work. Those tunnels won't dig themselves, and the squad won't dig them either without me to chivvy them."

After Tamon left, Zandolay came through and gave me strict instructions not to wake Ark and not bother him with too many questions when he did get up. I promised I wouldn't. She too had to leave then, to attend to judicial matters, and I was left again with time on my hands and with questions, and worries and doubts in my mind. I was profoundly relieved at the outcome of the affair, but at the same time frustrated by my enforced idleness. I always needed to move forward, whether in space or action. To stop would be fatal. I went out and talked to the guards, but they could give me no more information, other than that the Leader had returned to her quarters and had not been seen since.

Everyone was talking about it but it was all speculation until some hard news came through from the city. Ark got up in a bit and true to my promise I didn't sound him out further. We made some toast on the fire and drank tea, and then he said he was going back to the hangar to see how the raider had stood the test, and to carry on with his other projects. He loved his planes. I managed to sleep a little myself then, to while away the time until he and Tamon returned.

When Tamon did return, news had already percolated through from the very top to the bottom of Zinn and into the caves. He was brimming with it but wouldn't tell me until Ark got back and Zandolay had been summoned. As soon as we were all together he gave his report:

"The raider came in so quickly and quietly no one saw it happen. Then it soared so high it would have been taken for a real bird if anyone had seen it. When the sack was noticed people started gathering round and debating what on earth it was, and how it got there. People stared at it nonplussed, and then at each other, shaking their heads. Jobu himself was summoned. He stared up open mouthed, and then a shift in the wind made it split open spilling some of its contents. Rabbit droppings fell in his mouth and he nearly choked to death.

Angry and spluttering he ordered the Chief Environmental Scientist and the Chief Engineer to present themselves immediately. The CES blathered on about possible freak conditions, or something that fell from a foreign aircraft, and other explanations vying with each other in improbability. Jobu ordered the CE to remove it immediately and retired to confer with Baldark and the Chiefs of Staff. Of course the CE like the CES are honorary positions held by the nobility who haven't got a clue about science or engineering and the fact is they don't have the knowhow any more even to reach the finial. Jobu's double will stay there till it rots. By mid afternoon an official explanation had been concocted - a localised tornado. Anyone heard putting forward an alternative explanation would be condemned as a 'conspiracy theorist', which as you know is now an offence subject to 'the full rigour of the law'."

After we'd finished laughing and cheering and hugging Ark

again we ordered up a feast and this time Zandolay did join us, and the rest of the evening passed very pleasantly indeed. The next morning I woke with a bit of a hangover, and the other two were also rather the worse for wear. We hadn't drunk to excess but we didn't have the body mass to absorb much alcohol. I envied them having vigorous work to go to as another idle, empty day stretched ahead of me. But at least I was comfortable, under no immediate threat, and had the company of Zinn's classical poets. I decided to occupy my time by attempting to translate some of their work into English and borrowed paper and a pen from the boys' room for that purpose.

I found the business of crafting phrases that fitted both the sense and music of the original intriguingly difficult and absorbing, so much so that I thought I might in another lifetime have been a scholar or a poet myself. One of the poems that had particularly moved me was by a poet of the early twentieth century, Hamon Persus Redire, who wrote sonnets with varying and subtle rhyme schemes, many on the subject of loss and bereavement. Curiously he seems to have known about Einstein's theory of general relativity and even more curiously to have discerned spiritual possibilities inherent in it, an escape from mechanistic science into an awareness that reality extends beyond our ability to perceive and understand it. Here is one of my efforts:

Sonnet 22

Nothing is irrevocable or absolute.
Everything returns; there is no loss.
Everything returns to what it was,
darkness returns to darkness, light to light;
all cruelty, corruption and untruth
go back into the void from which they came.
Love and loveliness are stars forever bright,
friendship is a clear unwavering flame.
Everything returns, revolves, resolves;
even time is not absolute, it bends.

The years forgive us, and are forgiven,
and the pain of loss and death dissolves
where the tyranny of the instant ends,
at last, in the stillness of fruition.

I was so wrapped up in it I didn't at first hear someone tapping on the door. It turned out to be a guard who said the Leader wanted to see me again. I had wondered if I'd be summoned to another interview, and if I were whether it would go as badly as the last, or worse. Had she come to regret denying herself the opportunity of taking revenge on the person chiefly responsible for her sister's death? If so, and if she were looking for someone to hold to account for this, I was the obvious candidate.

As before I was conducted to the door of her room, or 'cell' might be a better word. The guard announced me, ushered me in and withdrew. As before a single candle burned on the low table and she sat behind it. But the cloth case was not on it. She was holding it in her lap as if it were her baby. There were torn scraps of paper scattered around, which I took to be Zard's letter. Again she didn't look up at me, but there all comparisons ended. I saw a small unhappy child with lips softly parted, downcast eyes and tear stained face. I went over and knelt in front of her and said, "Sulibe, can I touch you now." She nodded slightly, without looking up, and I put my arms round her. She pushed her head into my chest, still clutching the bag, and I could feel her convulsions through the bag and see her blond mane shaking, and instinctively put my lips into it to make it still. After a few moments I gently eased her back and put my finger under her chin and lifted it. Her eyes slowly opened. They were steel blue, no weakness there. "You turned me," she said. "You bastard!"

"Can we be friends now?" I asked, and her reply was quite coherent though her voice was slow and thick from weeping.

"Yes, but first I have to apologise for having you beaten and starved and kept in a black hole for days on end. Can you forgive me?"

"Apology joyfully accepted. Forgiveness already bestowed."

She glanced down at the bag she was still holding, and put it down on the table. "I think perhaps it's time we buried Aya. By the pool. Just you and me and Ark. Tomorrow morning perhaps."

"Yes, I think that would be good."

Tears were welling in her eyes again. I didn't have a handkerchief so I loosened my shirt sleeve and dabbed her face with the cuff. "Ark said you felt Aya was up there with you when you were riding around in the clouds."

"Do you think that was very silly?"

"Not at all, she's free now."

"And is she really at peace?"

"She is Sulibe, and so will you be. And you will never be apart. Be patient. All will be resolved."

"Do you really believe that?" There was a note of doubt and hesitancy in her voice.

"I believe it if I believe anything. And you have to believe something."

She sighed, half nodded, half smiled, and then said in a composed voice, "Thank you Jason. We'll meet tomorrow then. I'll send a guard. I'll get them to dig the hole. You'll tell Ark won't you. Then afterwards I think you and I should have a talk about what's to be done."

So we kissed and parted, and I was able to report later that my second meeting with the Leader had been a success.

"Oh I'm so pleased," Zandolay said.

CHAPTER 23

Earth and Air

I TOLD ARK about the funeral to be held the following day. He was pleased too, and not altogether surprised as he had never known the Leader so happy as when they went for their spree in the stratosphere, and she felt that Aya was free at last. It was hardly a conventional funeral, but I asked Ark what form the ceremony might take and what would be required of us. His words were reassuring. Their funerals were simple like their weddings. The coffin was placed in the grave and the mourners stood round it in a circle. The chief mourners said a few words to the deceased and placed flowers or a memento of some kind on the coffin, and that was it. No special burial ground, no priest and no gravestone, but it was customary to plant a tree, a yew or an oak for enduring memory. Ark said his gift would be a model he made for Aya of his first plane. She liked to play with it as she was determined to fly one day despite her disability, and he had taken her for rides in a full sized craft. The model got broken of course but he'd kept the bits and was going to reassemble it for her.

I was exercised as to what I might give myself. There were no flowers now, and I had so little with me, certainly nothing in the least bit sentimental. The sapphire would have been the thing of course, but that had been reassigned to the defence budget. I decided to write out some of the poems I'd been reading and I borrowed card and thread from Ark and a piece of embroidered fabric from Zandolay to make them into a little book. We were summoned shortly after breakfast the following morning. The guard assembled but the Leader stood them down and we set off without them, carrying Aya's cushion case, an oak sapling, and our gifts. There was a brief delay at the sealed entry port while we waited for scouts to return with the all clear, and then we stepped out into the daylight.

It was my second encounter with the open air since my arrest and I couldn't but reflect on the difference in circumstances to my last, and all that had happened in between. It was bright sunshine then, and I was strangely elated at the prospect of escape from the wretchedness of my physical and moral condition. The day was darker now, and my mood sombre and confused. More snow had fallen, and by the look of the sky there was more to come. Ark said that Tamon was worried about leaving footprints and would send a party out to brush them afterwards. He'd ordered a stop to country excursions while there was snow on the ground but had to give way to the Leader on this occasion. Ark said there wasn't much risk as the soldiers were too lazy and drunk to come out when the weather was bad.

Since my reprieve and, at least partial, absolution, thoughts of Aya had become less painful, but still my desertion of her remained symptomatic, or symbolic, of a deeper failure to connect. I'd almost forgotten I was a traveller, a universal stranger. I had become not only stationary but subterranean, one of a tribe of small burrowing creatures, and there could be no more foreign seeming place to me now than the one that was once my home. But this short journey, and the memory of the occasion of its predecessor, revived my feelings of rootlessness and alienation. Somewhere in the dim recesses of my mind I heard a peevish, wizened and insidious voice chanting 'not his road, oooh no, it's not his road. He's not from here'.

We came to the pool. A disturbance in the smooth ice sheet and some frozen chunks marked the place where I was to have made my exit. A few flakes of snow were already drifting down as we gathered round the grave that had been dug on the bank. A robin perched on the recently turned heap of soil, and flitted to a nearby bough to observe the proceedings. Sulibe placed the cushion in the grave and knelt in the snow, her eyes sparkling. Ark and I knelt too and Ark spoke first:

"Dear Aya. I can't remember a time when we were not friends. You were always full of fun and I called you 'laughing water', and that made you laugh even more. And you were the bravest. You could climb any tree, and you ran the fastest. You would have become a great pilot like your sister, but one day a soldier shot you and you had to have your leg cut off. You didn't scream, or even cry, and afterwards you were just the same, as though nothing had happened. You would still have learned to fly and you used to come flying with me, and how you loved it with the wind in your hair, looking down on the world. We'll always be together now."

He placed the model buzzard on the cushion case and Sulibe spoke next:

"I know this isn't you my precious because you are inside me and all around me, and I can give this back to the earth now as we will never be apart. We are burying your suffering, and your poor little body that suffered so much is not here anymore, but your love remains and fills our hearts. You remember when mother was still alive and we used to play together and tell each other stories and were happy and carefree. My dear little sister, it will always be like that from now onwards. This is mother's ring, made of gold. She gave it to us before she died. Like our love it is precious and is a circle with no end. There is no grief or sorrow now. The only thing that lives is love, and love lives forever. Sleep now my angel, close your eyes and fold your wings."

Listening to Sulibe repeat my words it occurred to me that I sometimes said things I didn't believe, until I'd said them. God speaks in mysterious ways. Sulibe put the ring in the middle and then it was my turn and I spoke as they did, without premeditation, directly to her as if she were there. "My dear Aya, we met only briefly, but it only took a moment for me to know that what Sulibe and Ark have just said about you was true. Yours was the spirit of hope and joy, despite all the hatred and cruelty in the world. You wanted to include me in the circle of your love and I walked away, to my shame and profound regret. Please forgive me now and take me back. I love you dear child, and always will."

I placed my token beside theirs. Ark took one hand and Sulibe the other, so we formed a circle, around the circle of the grave and the circle of the ring, and remained there still and quiet for several minutes. Then we filled the grave and planted the little tree, spreading its fibrous roots in the moist soil. As we left the robin returned, hoping to find a morsel before the snow, which was falling faster now, covered the bare earth and our retreating footprints.

We returned in silence, but our hands and thoughts were linked. Outside the entrance to the mine Sulibe kissed us both. Once inside and surrounded by guards she was the Leader again. Ark left us to go to the hangar while she and I returned to the gallery. I invited her to join me for a coffee in Ark's rooms - it would be a more cheerful place to talk than her cell. She looked at me coolly and then nodded. "All right," she said.

I roused the fire and put water on to boil, while she sat comfortably and looked around bemusedly at the various tokens of homeliness and boyishness strewn about the place. And again when she sipped the coffee it was as though she was experiencing taste for the first time, or after long absence from the world of the senses. At length she brought her penetrating gaze to bear on me.

"Well Jason. I expect now you will want to return to your friends in the forest."

"No Sulibe, I will never leave you again."

"But what can you do here? You're a pacifist, and we are fighting a war."

"I can keep trying to persuade you that evasion and escape are better plans than fighting a war you cannot win."

"No we cannot win, but neither can we escape. We have no choice but to fight and die, or surrender and die."

"But you could melt into the forest. Hasn't that always been the way with you orphan refugees? The foresters are strong, kind people. They survive, and live a good life."

Sulibe shook her head and sighed. Her manner softened and became childlike again. After a pause she said, "I'd like you to stay, Jason. I need someone to talk to. There are things I can't say to the others. The news isn't good. Eldis came. You met him I believe."

"Yes, he came to see me."

"He told you about Baldark, and the Prince Shahribe."

"He did indeed."

"That was a turning point. Jobu and Baldark are now in absolute control and have suppressed all opposition. They don't have to play games any more. They've colluded with the logging company in the claim that the Looshin flood was a natural disaster and the company has been fully compensated. A new contract has been signed to clear fell the entire forest and divide it up into estates for the nobility. Naturally they won't object even if they weren't afraid to. There's a huge amount of money involved and it will be used to buy modern weaponry. All those people will be killed, or driven out, or enslaved. There's no escape."

The news stunned me. I felt weak in the pit of my stomach. After a long pause I said, "People will have to be warned. They'll have to get out of Zinn."

"There's nowhere else for them to go."

"But the outside world?"

"Doesn't want them. Won't have them. Won't even recognise their existence. I don't need to tell you that Jason. People disappear. Whole tribes, whole races. No one cares."

I was in a room without doors or windows, my trapped thoughts racing and groping round the walls but there was no exit anywhere. There was another long pause and Sulibe was the first to speak, her voice still gentle but with regained resolution.

"It would be best for you to go back and help Scottie and Elphane and your friends escape. We'll fight as long and hard as we can."

"I'll have to get word to them. Perhaps Eldis has told them already. But I won't leave you now Sulibe."

"You mean it?"

"I do. I will not leave again, whatever happens."

"Thank you Jason. You won't be much of a military asset, but I really do need someone I can talk to. I can't tell Ark or Tamon any of this. We've created a fighting unit. We have to keep up morale."

"Even pacifists defend their own. It's a mistake to think because you hate killing you lack courage, or because you are honest you lack guile. There may be some twists and turns in this affair yet."

"You see, you're making us both feel better already. It will be good to have you around."

"But I'll be bored doing nothing."

"That's just what I was thinking, and I have a specific task for you, and one which won't clash with your principles."

"I'll do whatever's in my power."

"It's in your power all right because you have those." She pointed her first two fingers towards my eyes. "There isn't much you don't see. I want you to be our recorder, our historian. I want you to write it all down in your own language. Millions die and are buried and leave no trace, and are forgotten as though they had never lived. I want us to be known and remembered. I want the world to know what it is they waste and kill. Tell them about people who live and love and breathe and hope just as they do. Tell them about heroes, about people old and young who fought for their own and faced death with courage - Procter, Scottie, Tamon, Ark . . . Sulibe. Tell them about a wonderful little girl called Aya, and how she lived, and how she died. I want those names to be remembered because they stand for the names of millions more."

"I'll do it of course, but there's one problem. I'm going to die and be forgotten here as well."

For the first time a little smile played around the corners of her mouth. "Oh no Jason. You've got nine lives, remember. By my calculation you've got at least one left."

"OK, I'll need a stack of paper and some pens."

"No problem. But there's something else you'll need as well."

"And what's that?"

"I want to show you the most special thing about us. You'll need to learn to fly."

"Really? But I'm an adult - won't I be too heavy?"

"Not now. You're not much above seven stone, I'd say. You'll be fine in the raider. I'm beginning to realise it was a good idea of mine to starve you, and I don't think you've been eating much since. But there's one thing you have to understand. We can't have bystanders. You'd be one of us - signed up - an officer. 'Captain Jason'. How about that?"

"An unexpected development, but as you wish Sulibe."

"And 'Sulibe' is OK when we're alone together. Otherwise it's 'Leader'."

"Absolutely Sulibe, and I'll make the most of 'Sulibe' while I can."

"Don't worry, Jason. There'll be lots of times I need to talk to you. I'm so glad we've forgiven each other and we are friends now."

"I am too, Sulibe."

"I shall go now and start brightening up my rooms a bit. I'm sure Zandolay will help me." She inclined her pale cheek towards me for a kiss, and then said, "You will report to Colonel Ark tomorrow morning for flight training." "I shall indeed, Leader," I replied, with a mock salute.

Ark was delighted that I had been recruited and assigned to his embryo flying corps. He said it called for a celebration and sent instructions to the chef to prepare some of his specialities, and invitations to other engineers and pilots working with him. There were twelve of us, with Tamon and Zandolay. Several of these boys and girls were survivors from the era of unrestricted flight, nostalgic about those days and longing for their return. They were very welcoming towards me and already filling my head with the thrills and spills and do's and don'ts of aerial navigation. Their enthusiasm and eagerness to impart their knowledge was such that Ark interceded to say that I'd be put off if they made it sound too complicated. "It will come naturally," he said. "We were born to fly."

Tamon was impatient with the aviators' romantic attitudes. He wanted hard facts: how many machines would be operational and when, and what armaments would they carry. He questioned the role of an air force in what would be, he believed, essentially an underground war. There was some heated debate on this question.

I did my best to appear interested and involved, while knowing that what Sulibe had told me made it all irrelevant. I also did my best to eat, but Sulibe was right about that too. I'd lost my interest in food. No one noticed or remarked on this except Zandolay. She said, "Jason you really must try to eat more. You are wasting away. You will need to build up your strength if you are going to learn to fly."

"You're quite right Zandolay," I replied. "I think it's just my enforced idleness that has made me lose my appetite, and as soon as I get to work again I shall be heartily devouring everything our excellent chef can produce." "I do hope so Jason. I was so pleased to learn that you and the Leader had overcome your differences, and there appears to be no reason now why you cannot play a full part in our endeavours." The tone was both caring and admonitory.

The one very acute reason I had for my malaise, Sulibe's chilling news, filled my thoughts completely as soon as I was alone again in my own room. Search as I could with the faculties of mind and imagination I could conjure up no exit strategy from the situation we were in. Tamon's underground war seemed the only possibility of holding out for any length of time, but if the modern weaponry the Zinnians were acquiring included enhanced blast thermobaric devices, which sucked oxygen from enclosed spaces crushing the lungs and internal organs of their occupants, the war could be over very quickly. The only course left for the children was to return to the city and their former life of poverty, slavery and abuse. They would die rather than do that.

On top of this was my concern for Scottie and Elfie, the people of the village and the Prendises, and all the forest folk. What would become of them? Mass emigration, perhaps, but where to? If Eldis would return soon I could send a message. Other than some sudden and unforeseen reversal in the flow of events I could find no hope or comfort anywhere. At any other time the prospect of flying in those miraculous contraptions, the buzzards of Zinn, would have filled me with delighted anticipation. Now the enthusiasm, the challenge, the camaraderie - everything would be a pretence. I half wished Sulibe hadn't told me what was to be. But it was a heavy burden for her slender shoulders to bear alone.

My flight training began the following day. It was demanding and intensive from the start and that was good as it helped to keep my mind from anxious thoughts. The first thing I learnt was that there was no distinct separation between the building, maintenance and flying of the craft. I had to know exactly how they were put together before I would be allowed to leave the ground in one. In any case the number, duration and range of flights was severely restricted by the need to keep the survival of the children and their birds a secret from the Zinnians as long as possible. There had to be mist or low cloud, or look-outs posted round an area for a short hedge-hopping run. This meant that most of my hands-on flying experience would be on a simulator.

So I began in the workshops. My first task was crafting 'feathers', the overlapping foils that made up the wings and tail. They had to be light, strong and flexible, and each one was slightly different in shape and profile depending on its position and function. A variety of natural and manmade materials were used, the latter derived from city waste, but the best ones were made by laminating the fibrous outer sheaf of a local bamboo plant, and paring or 'feathering' the trailing edges to the point where they were translucent. The spread out wings and tails made of these were especially life-like and were beautiful in flight with the sun shining through them. They took longest to make and were reserved for the top fliers, but local supplies had been devastated by the war. Before using the bamboo sheath I had to prove myself on scraps of plastic and metal, and each attempt was weighed and checked against templates before it was passed.

After many days of this I moved on to the fuselage, a semi-rigid frame which had evolved into the simplest structure possible to bear the stresses imposed upon it by the leverage of the wings and weight of the pilot. The joints were spliced and bound with leather thongs, and each one was rigorously tested as failure in flight destabilised the whole apparatus. Fatal crashes had occurred from a single fracture. Next came the wing and tail frames, made of seasoned hardwood. Each member had to be shaved and shaped with absolute precision, which only the master artificer's sense of touch could determine; but the greatest skill was required in fashioning the ball and socket joints, which had to move freely in some directions, less freely in others, and in others not at all. The articulation and gradation in size from the main shoulder socket to the fingers at the wingtips again called for extraordinary finesse in workmanship, and to see a wing move even in skeletal form was so birdlike it seemed alive.

Once the main framework had been thoroughly tested and approved the plumage was attached. This had to be done feather by feather in the correct order by plugging the shafts into the frame. After this, perhaps the most complex business of all, the control system was installed. Cords or sinews activating the movement of groups of feathers and individual pinions were routed through grooves, holes and eyelets to the joystick. This was primarily a lever operating through 360 degrees and controlling the opening, folding, spread and pitch of the wings, and the fanning and dipping of the tail. There was a lock position in which the wings and tail were held rigid in optimum glide configuration for high soaring. The joystick was worked from a crossbar with a series of sleeve controls which were slid from side to side as well as rotated. These operated the finer flexing of sections of the wings and tail feathers for the rapid checking and swerving necessary for manoeuvring in confined spaces, like the city streets. After this came the claw grab and landing mechanisms which had separate controls further down the joystick or were operated by the second pilot in two-crew machines.

Finally there was the head. The construction of this had more to do with art than engineering, and one elderly lad, in his late teens, was a specialist and the acknowledged master. Nevertheless I had a go and produced a weird looking raptor which would not terrify but might well perplex an enemy. Ark insisted on mounting it and putting it on his wall along with his own creations.

I gave it all my full attention and my best endeavour. Being past the age of rapid learning I had to work hard to keep up with the younger apprentices who absorbed everything without effort. Ark helped me out by giving me extra tuition in the evenings. What with the training, homework, and writing my historical record, I was fully employed. Since my return to Marchenor I had moved from sensory deprivation, through periods of lethargic convalescence and frustrated inactivity, to intense engagement with the material world. This certainly distracted me from depressing thoughts, but it also changed my perspective on life in general. War and politics became meaningless abstractions to me, and I began to understand how birds and animals simply delight in being and doing, without a thought for the future and their inevitable end. In the continuum of life, death was of no account.

Following on from construction came the maintenance course: repairing or replacing worn or damaged parts, checking cord tensions, alignment of feathers, fixed and moving joints, balance and trim, and then oiling, greasing and polishing so all was gleaming and weatherproof. I had to memorise a list of fifty-one separate checks to be carried out before every flight. Inspections were often done in pairs or teams with a ritual chanting as each point was noted and verified. For my final test in the practical engineering side I was faced with a random spread of scattered components which I had to reassemble into a complete machine. Not only did I achieve this, but my time of thirty hours was not quite the slowest out of the six of us who started together.

Then it was time to move on to flight simulators. These were complete craft suspended in a natural wind tunnel, a spacious chamber with an airflow passing through from some external source. The current varied with wind conditions and was further complicated by a system of bellows and baffles operated by the instructors, while a compost pit below replicated the effect of thermal uplift. You climbed in when the bird was on a ground frame and held on to the controls while it was hoisted up some twenty feet. To begin with there were several ropes holding it steady, but these would eventually be reduced to a single one.

Once in position the signal was given from the control booth ahead of you to open the wings and you immediately felt lift and sway, which you had to control. Invariably your reactions were too jerky and sudden, and then you over-corrected. It was scary as you were just standing on a narrow perch with very little lateral support, but it was also exhilarating, especially when you did something right and held a steady course in the gentle breeze, and then succeeded in a slight rise or deviation without losing control. In the first few days of training such moments were rare, however, and you had to wait for the guide ropes to right you and try again.

The simulator training lasted even longer than construction and maintenance, and became progressively more difficult. In the latter stages, on a single ligature in blustery conditions, I not only lost control of the craft but parted company with it, ignominiously hanging on to a spar of the upturned fuselage while it was lowered to the ground. No quarter was given: I had to get straight back in and be hauled up again. It was rather like being on a roller coaster that never stopped. And there were no passes or second class degrees. You had to be 100% efficient over and over again before your instructors would consider you a good risk to fly for real. And before that consideration could be entertained you had to more or less start all over again in the role of second pilot.

In the older machines the co-pilot had the landing, grabbing and flapping gear to operate, but in the new raider class a wider range of whole-wing actions was possible. These included strong down-sweeps to provide extra lift, drive strokes to increase propulsion, and a rapid fluttering motion for hovering. The motive power for this was provided by the second pilot, using crank handles on either side. However the lead pilot controlled and directed this operation, and as vocal instructions could be drowned by wind noise, the crank handles were wired up to receive jerks, or pulses, transmitted from the joystick. These came in a coded form which had to be interpreted precisely and immediately, and the two aviators had to become as one. It was a different discipline but equally tough, requiring total, tireless concentration. I worked in first and second positions with all my fellow trainees.

After weeks of this I realised I was becoming a bird myself. Wings, tail and claws became virtual extensions to my own body, and whenever I thought of the Zinnians I found myself staring ahead of me with the focussed wrath of hooked beak and fierce staring eyes. Perhaps I was turning into a warrior after all.

Without clocks or weather it was hard to keep track of time, but I guessed we were moving towards spring, and the first anniversary of my arrival in Zinn, when at last I was considered reliable enough to make my maiden flight. This would be as co-pilot to an experienced flier and I was pleased that Ark offered to take me up in the original raider eagle, the craft that had rescued me from the gallows and pinned Jobu's double to the highest spire of Zinn. The catapult would shoot us out into the morning mist and we'd sail up and circle round for an hour or so, and as the mist cleared descend to a hidden landing strip on the far side of the hill.

It went like a dream, in every sense the most uplifting experience of my life. A moment of sheer panic as we were flung helplessly forward into blinding white oblivion, and then the ecstasy of flight, perfect and controlled, responding instinctively to every variation of pressure and flow in the ambient atmosphere. We soared up into the blue space above the carpet of mist, Zinn's pinnacle, with bits of Jobu still hanging from it, just visibly piercing it. We spiralled up till we could see the Earth's curvature and distant outlines of the encircling mountains. Then we practised a series of manoeuvres: sharp turns, swoops, speedy escalations, headlong dives, and combinations of all of them, and hardest and most exhausting of all hovering like a kestrel, with tail fanned and pointed wings whirring in rapid circular movements. We dropped down level by level till we skirted the now visible hill slope and the landing strip passed below us. One more turn and then a steady descent, rough ground racing below us, the signal to drop the undercarriage as our shadow crossed the edge of the strip, the wings arched and all flaps flaring and the sudden drag and shudder as the talons skidded and the level earth reclaimed us.

This pioneer flight with Ark was even more memorable than my first solo attempt, a hop of about half a mile in one of the smaller craft. The programme continued with solo and two crew flights as first or second pilot, with both experienced and rookie pilots, and daily practice on the simulators when outside conditions were not suitable. I got so good I was taking risks, and had to be warned about over-confidence when one ambitious corkscrew dive nearly went wrong. I had gone down into the cavern to investigate a bevy of real buzzards and vultures that had congregated there around a small unrecognisable carcass on a ledge above the water level, squawking and flapping their wings as they competed for the tastier morsels.

Finally the day came when I stood in a line with the other apprentices to be awarded my wings, a little silver buzzard badge bestowed by the Leader with a few formal words of congratulation. It was a moment of pure pride. Not only was I the only Westerner to set eyes on the amazing buzzards of Zinn, I had now become one of them.

CHAPTER 24

Nemesis

THE DAYS AND weeks passed in an eerie stalemate that could only end in war. My time was divided between flight training and duties, and writing my account of the bird children and their fight for survival. What social life I had time for was mostly in the company of Ark, Tamon, and Zandolay. We occasionally joined in with or were joined by others but we were easiest in each other's company. Our conversations ranged over many topics and we all had stories to tell, but there was a tacit agreement between us to avoid any serious debate on the impending conflict or to talk shop in any form other than the day's budget of mild gossip and incidental anecdote. I was glad of this because my frequent meetings with Sulibe were occasions when the worsening situation we were in had to be squarely confronted. Sometimes training was interrupted by a summons, but it was usually when I returned that I was given word that the Leader required my attendance.

Her quarters were now a lot more comfortable and well lit, and Zandolay's taste in fabrics and furnishing was much in evidence. A large chamber, to which the cell was just an anteroom, had been opened up. Happy portraits of Aya and Sulibe by Ark beamed from the walls. We sat together on a settle in front of a cheerful log fire and drank tea. Sulibe usually began by asking how the course was going and adding a few tips of her own regarding any aspect I was finding difficult at the time. Then she talked about her own worries, usually some troubling piece of intelligence that had recently come in.

There had been, for example, a report that the Western High-way had been closed to normal traffic to make way for a large convoy of low loaders carrying military equipment. From the description it included tanks, armoured personnel carriers, field artillery, rocket launchers, and helicopters. She wanted to know all I could tell her about these weapons. I said I was no expert but it sounded fairly standard stuff and it would take a considerable time for ZADD to train up to using it effectively. I told her that ill-trained soldiers with powerful weaponry often killed each other, a phenomenon know by the absurd euphemism 'friendly fire'; and that there were examples of poorly equipped peasant armies, operating in terrain they knew intimately, holding out indefinitely against modernised military forces. In other words I put the best or least bad interpretation forward that I could think of, and kept my own doubts and fears to myself. Other disturbing news came to me through these meetings with the Leader. Camps were being built at various locations. Some were destinations for the weapons convoys and army training centres. Others were places where people were taken and never seen again.

At some point in the interview Sulibe's need for a shoulder to lean on became quite literal. She would just lay her head against me, and I would put my arm round her and hold her. For a couple of minutes she wanted to be a child, to be held. Then she'd open her eyes again with that wide, vague, unfathomable stare of hers and I could feel the tense determination flowing back into her body.

On another occasion I found out that the buzzards I'd seen in the cavern were feeding on the corpse of one Drev Maldock, a ten year old boy who had been exposed as a spy. The Court found the evidence against him irrefutable; he was condemned to death and Sulibe ratified the decision. She told me she had given orders that I should not be told about the affair as I would have interceded on the boy's behalf. With the knowledge he had acquired he could not have been released, and apart from the risk of his escape, indefinite imprisonment would have been costly in resources, and hardly less cruel. She said they had put a strong narcotic into his drink and he was unconscious when they threw him over the cliff. All I could offer was a shoulder of reassurance. Violence creates violence, cruelty begets cruelty. What more could be said. Like so many outcasts the world condemns for violent acts she could truly say, with Viola in *Twelfth Night*, "My manners I have learned from my entertainment here."

As well as the stress and moral aftermath of having to make such a decision there was the fear that Drev Maldock might already have passed information to the enemy. He had refused to admit or disclose anything.

The news that came through from Sammonar, via Eldis, was naturally of great interest and concern to me. The redoubtable Mordrid, Prince Shahribe's sister, had complained mightily about the treatment of her brother, treatment which she averred had led to his death. There was much covert support and sympathy for her outside the inner circle. It was believed that Baldark was prepared to start signing more arrest warrants but Jobu counter-manded this. He issued a statement of apology to the Prince's sister and widow and reinstated the latter's rank and a portion of her wealth. He said that the officers responsible for torturing the Prince had acted beyond their authority and had been disciplined. No doubt a sharp rap over the knuckles with a ruler had been administered.

Esolday had gone to live with her sister-in-law in the style to which she had been accustomed, but remained on good terms with the foresters and was allowed to visit and be visited by her children. The offer of restored status had also applied to her daughters provided they renounced all association with rebels and anarchists. Zarielle had reclaimed her title but Amarel (now a Prendis) and Elphane had declined.

Did this development indicate some flicker of humanity in the Zinnian leadership? I ventured to doubt it. It struck me as a clever move. Having shown their readiness to act with unrestrained bru-tality they yield to the entreaties of a harmless old lady and dismiss the whole thing as an administrative aberration, thus reaffirming their attachment to civilised values while leaving potential critics in no doubt that they would act the same way again in the event of any real challenge to their authority. At the same time they split the family and cover themselves against blame for any future misfortunes that may befall its dissident members.

Another item of news, which under normal circumstances would have fulfilled the happiest expectations, was now fraught with difficulty and conflicting emotions. Elfie was with child. Scottie would know by now about the impending destruction of the forest and its people. Would he allow his wife to turn down an offer of safety for herself and her unborn child even if it meant their separation? Would Elfie too be split between her love for Scottie and concern for their child's survival? I thought about these matters whenever I had time to think, but could not resolve them. Then one day Sulibe handed me a scrap of paper, creased and folded, with my name written on the front. It had reached her by pigeon post. She said the writing which covered it was in a strange script and asked me if I could understand it. I smoothed it out and read as follows:

Sairlie we miss ye, bonny lad. We baeth bide weel and hail, and a wean expectit, but we maun gang awa tae the nor whan the sodgers an' loggers come. We wull reenge awa t' thae mountains and the waste lan gin we win anither hame. We ken ye maun bide there wi the bairns. They shuilie hae muckle need o ye. The gude Lord presser and proteck y a', and grant we meet agane and be blithe and bonny as afore. Dear freen, wi a' our love and blessing, ayeways thine,
Scottie and Elfie

I translated it for Sulibe, and she gave my arm a little squeeze. She said that she'd heard the foresters planned to evacuate, lock stock and barrel, when the invasion went ahead. There was no point in losing lives in fruitless resistance. The rail line was in full operation and they'd move people and goods up to the mountains, and take up the tracks after them. There would be enough grazing on the moors and tundra for their cattle, and they'd live like nomads, but they'd also explore the mountains and find places to hide and return fire if they were attacked beyond the tree line. It was all Scottie's plan and he was their leader now, with Kombard Prendis his second in command. "Could we not follow them there?" I mused.

Sulibe shook her head. It was a harsh region. No tribe had survived there for long and no one ever returned from the Ozoora desert beyond. Wild bands descended from Genghis Khan's fearsome horsemen still roamed there, and I recognised from her description the savage scavengers I had encountered on my journey to Zinn. It would be tough for the forest folk, but hundreds of town kids as well? Not a chance.

It was a strange time and a strange way to be alive. My pre-Zinnian past was a distant memory and the future a blank. My existence oscillated between dark and secret places underground, and the wild freedom of flight. I was an adult among children and a pacifist among warriors, and though they were child warriors it was no game they were playing. I only had to think of the bones in the cavern, and my own ordeal, to remember that. I could not live with my past or my future. In all my thoughts I could find no place of peace, no avenue of hope, and I sought action, company, work and exhaustion to escape the inescapable.

It became known to us that our presence in the old slate mines was now known to the Zinnian high command, and indeed, though still unofficial, this was general knowledge in Zinn. Then even the state controlled newspapers and broadcasts had begun to talk of 'pockets of resistance' and 'remnants of anarchy', and of imminent 'flushing out' and 'mopping up' operations. Then a series of major infrastructure collapses occurred in the industrial zones. These were claimed to be the work of the resurgent anarchists. Street children were being hunted down by the authorities, and more were being rescued and brought into the mines every day, many in urgent need of food and care. Training and arming lagged behind coping with this influx and we were becoming a refugee camp as much as a standing army. The real work was getting in enough food and supplies. Tamon and his tunnellers and scouting parties were busy while the airforce kicked its heels.

In the world outside, spring had returned. Even the war-blasted area around us was bursting into life with wild flowers and saplings teeming out of the churned-up earth. But opportunities to venture beyond the sealed portals, either on foot or in the air, were becoming rarer as the weather improved and the morning mists rapidly cleared. And then the ZADD patrols returned, careering around now in their brand new personnel carriers, and a tank was seen rearing and snorting clumsily across the cratered terrain. To avoid the deadliest boredom Ark and I asked Tamon to take us on as helpers in provisioning the main camp and we had at least the satisfaction of doing something of immediate benefit to our fellow fugitives. There I was like a mother bird feeding shivering rows of sparrow chested waifs.

Tamon remained single-minded and undaunted. Problems were opportunities, setbacks were timely warnings, and he was still turning out operational fighting units equipped with a variety of serviceable firearms and lethal devices of his own design. He was now armed himself with some kind of antiquated automatic weapon, as well as Procter's old rifle, and wore a couple of ammunition bandoliers strapped across his chest. He'd probably never heard of Geronimo or Che Guevara but he could have stood in for either of them. Zandolay of course was always Zandolay, living in her own world of genteel caring perfection.

But Sulibe's mood was changing. She was still the Leader, commanding awed respect whenever she appeared outside her bunker to inspect a parade, or view progress in this or that department, her steely composure and a few terse words of encouragement visibly boosting morale. Alone with her I found her increasingly abstracted, introverted, insecure. Her eyes appealed to me for help but in a way which showed she knew I couldn't give it her. Her very strength of character was becoming a weariness to her. She longed to escape from her burden, her grief, her fate - from herself. Often we sat in silence, our thoughts unspoken, and incommunicable.

So we went on from day to day, and still we waited for the war to begin. One morning I'd been out to see if a flight was possible.

Conditions were ideal, bright sunshine and a light breeze, but a patrol had been spotted and we had to abandon the idea. A little while later I was summoned to see Sulibe. She was more withdrawn than usual. There was no news to impart, or none at least capable of a positive interpretation. I told her that I'd been out and it was good flying weather but we'd had to call it off. She was silent for a bit and then she suddenly brightened up. "Jason," she said, "you and I have never flown together. Why don't we go for a whirl in the raider?"

"That would be wonderful Sulibe. The very next time the coast is clear . . ."

"Never mind about that, we'll go now. We'll go to Zinn. You always wanted to see the place. I'll take you on a tour."

"But that's crazy. We'll be seen. We'll give the game away."

"To hell with that. They know we're here anyway." And without another word she went out and I could hear her giving instructions for the raider eagle to be prepared for flight. I protested again but she said, "That's an order Captain." I was already in my flying gear. She took hers from a wardrobe and laid it out on a table, and then she whipped her dress off right in front of me and tossed it aside and climbed into her leather suit. With tiny breast buds her body was so pale and thin I could have wept. We set out for the hangar together.

There was a buzz going round by the time we got there. Anxiously enquiring looks greeted us, but Sulibe ignored them and strode over to the raider, checking her over and firing off a few questions to the attendant engineers. Ark appeared. He raised his eyebrows towards me and I raised mine in reply. Then he took a breath and said, "May I enquire the purpose of this flight, Leader?" "Reconnaissance," she snapped. "A difficult mission, Leader. Perhaps I could be your co-pilot?" "Oh and that's another thing, Colonel," she replied. "I need to see what sort of a job you've done in training Captain Jason here."

Ark and I shook hands briefly and I climbed in after the Leader, fixing the restraint harness used during a catapult launch. Sulibe went through the control checks and I felt a positive energy coming through that even Ark's signals had never transmitted. I realised I was about to be tested to the limits, and any lingering trace of my over-confidence rapidly evaporated. The doors at the end of the ramp opened and daylight flooded in, almost blinding me but I felt the catapult linkage grip and tauten through the slender framework. And then again that surge: the trans-dimensional disembodiment of release into the radiance of the absolute.

Before I'd had a chance to recover my senses I was responding automatically to Sulibe's rapid signals and we were diving, lifting, rolling and turning almost in our own space. Her blonde mane flared and flapped in the wind. "Hey Jason," she yelled back at me, "you can really fly - we're flying together." The land below and the sky and the horizon were whirling around in a kaleidoscope with bits of Zinn at various angles edging and banking into the mix. At last it settled below us and the same sun that glittered on our outspread wings lit the towers and slender spires rising from the concentric buttresses of the city's titanic foundations. We rose higher, circled round, sloped away then turned again, and suddenly we were plummeting down in a steep dive towards the base of the lower ramparts on the dark side, hidden in deep shadow. The rush of air was roaring in my ears as I held the wings closed tight. I understood her intention now. The black wall hurtled towards us and I waited without thought, or fear, for the end. As my eyes pierced the dark, the gates of hell itself with all its stinking ordure yawned open ahead.

A split second later I realised we were flying into the city by its waste disposal outlet. I had made my entrance at last into the wonderful, terrible, mystical city of Zinn, beyond the rim of the known world, and with the foulest stench imaginable in my nostrils

Now with wings arched and tail flared we hauled in our speed, the craft veering and tipping from side to side as we air-bounced off walls and buildings; then holding steady at last we could hover and flit bird-like from place to place at will. There were shouts from below and astonished faces looked up, but we were away before their owners had time to react. The smell and darkness hardly lessened as we sailed along narrow grimy streets, our wing tips almost brushing the sides. There were heaps of trash every-where, rats scurrying and dogs rooting in it, and bodies of animals, and people too, whether alive or dead or somewhere in between it was impossible to say. Those still upright were gaunt figures in colourless, shapeless garments, hooded or shawled, moving for-ward with a kind of feverish urgency, pale faces barely lifted as our shadow passed over them. Other human forms, also darkly hooded but slim, agile and menacing, lurked in arches and door-ways. In numbers defying estimation they gathered and disappeared with equal suddenness.

But in stark contrast, substantial, visible and numerous, were the forces of law and order. There were squads of police in crisp black uniforms with blue helmets, shields and body armour, armed to the teeth and wielding canes and batons. We saw squads on the march, and one gathered around a house they'd smashed into and from which helpless, half-dressed citizens were being dragged to a waiting truck.

The military were also patrolling in their vehicles, no doubt pro-viding back-up where needed, and manning the checkpoints through which the people had to pass to get to and from their work or homes. With their sheer physical bulk and the amount of equipment they were now wearing or carrying I doubted if the soldiers could move far unaided. Scowling red faces were raised to us, heavy weapons clumsily lifted and fired, the bullets screaming off the walls; but we were gone. And everywhere the menacingly smiling, folksy portrait of Jobu II, now in one uniform, now another, now in elegant civvies - murals, statues, mosaics; no view in which part of him was not visible, a leery eye, an immaculate parting, a listening ear.

At one point where we hovered momentarily in shadow a scene flashed in front of me and imprinted itself on my brain. A heavy man, an official of some kind, encased in body armour, carrying a steel box and a large bunch of keys on a chain, was emptying coins from a meter on the side of a building. A child ran up to him, waving a small plastic knife in his fist. The official drew his baton and whacked the side of the child's skull with such force as to fling him in a lifeless heap on the pavement, and then continued his work as though he had merely brushed a fly from his eyeshield.

I saw that the houses and buildings in these streets, marred as they were by squalor and decay, were originally solid and well proportioned, with stone steps and arches and ornate iron railings and balconies, and were brightened here and there by patches of sunlight. Grass and weeds grew in corners and edges, and a blackened tree put forth a spray or two of fresh blossom. But a sudden sharp turn brought us into a region of murky twilight, pierced only by random gas flares and the lurid light from open fires and furnaces.

I struggled for breath in the foul sulphurous smoke that filled my nostrils, and I marvelled how Sulibe could find her way through the weird, fitful, labyrinthine gloom. Such faces as I glimpsed in this hellish half light were inhuman masks of pain and anger; inhuman too the hoarse, roaring shouts and visceral screams that struck my ears. The glare from factories and forges silhouetted broken facades of tenement blocks. There were fragments of streets and terrace houses, some empty and the fronts all smashed like broken teeth, others inhabited, but filthy, sordid, the original architecture defaced beyond recognition by the erosions and encrustations of poverty and overcrowding. Beyond these, lit by the same garish doomsday chiaroscuro, were areas covered with fetid ramshackle hovels and hills of raw garbage on which skeletal figures of women and children could be seen, crawling. This was the inner city, the burning core, the seething festering heart of Zinn.

Like a swift in flight we swerved, veered, banked, rose and dived, swinging the wings on to a vertical plane to thread a narrow alley, or closing them to shoot an underpass. It was a profound relief when we spiralled up through a ventilation shaft into the clear sharp air again. I now realised Sulibe really meant it when she said she would show me the city. As we climbed and circled, the class structure of Zinn passed before my eyes like the layers of a wedding cake.

We entered next another warren of narrow streets, the quarters of the lower middle classes, desperate to distinguish themselves from the hated masses below by their shabby decencies and mean conformity, their grovelling aspirations towards those just a little higher than themselves. The houses here were in better condition, though tacky additions and home 'improvements' often spoilt the clean, decorous lines of the old architects' civic vision. And here were street markets, churches and public houses with some bustle and life about them.

The agencies of law enforcement and even the portraits of Jobu receded in prominence as the house size increased from rows to semi-detached to detached, and villas and mansions standing in their own grounds. The shopping arcades and civic buildings also became more showy and aspirational, and lawns, gardens, parks and trees flourished in proportion. This was the realm of the middle class of complacent burghers, materialistic, philistine, mercenary, self-satisfied, obese; men and women of substance in every sense, with spoilt, obnoxious children.

Then the professional classes, assiduous servants of the rich and powerful and inwardly flattered by the proximity their services conferred upon them, priding themselves on the illusion of their taste, intellect and independence; creators and slaves of fashion in food, clothes, books etc., pretending to despise wealth but ready to sell themselves to the highest bidder.

Finally we ascended through the ranks of the upper middle class and aristocracy in ascending degrees of luxury and arrogance, and I could not but be amazed at the grandeur of their habitations. They were not of this world. Beyond the wonders and splendours of the architecture, aerial, dream-like fantasies floating in stone and marble, the gardens surpassed all imaginings: the subtlety and harmony of colour, the mystical intricacy of design from the vast stately cedars to the delicate ferns and mosses that fledged walls and buttresses. The fabled hanging gardens of Babylon could hardly have excelled the high palaces of Zinn, rising in the clearest, purest air to the unbelievable edifice that crowned it, the fairytale fortress of Jobu II, and his ancestors and successors to be. I could easily understand the fury of these lords of earth and sky at the ragged urchins in their rattle-trap contrivances buzzing around like flies overhead.

Robed figures now were staring and pointing in horror. We dived and scattered them and flapped, hugely and darkly at windows and galleries, piercing those gathered inside with our terrible eyes. People were running, alarm bells were sounding, ceremonial militia men were falling over each other in their attempts to deploy some ancient artillery piece. We soared above it all. I saw the tiny inner courtyard where Sulibe had intended her unprecedented feat of aerial attack, and we circled the golden spire where a few rags of her rabbit sack still lifted in the breeze. We sailed higher still into the pure, sun-filled air, only the soft flutter of our wings breaking the silence. Peace and serenity filled my entire being.

Suddenly there was a rumbling, and a roaring crescendo below us.

I looked down through the open fuselage and saw the high city of Zinn imploding, collapsing into its own space. Tower by tower it was crashing down in landslides of gargantuan masonry, cyclopean fragments tossed up like chaff, and enormous spars of corroded iron were rearing up out of the maelstrom, swinging and clashing like a battle of the giants. Sulibe was shouting "It's the girders, Jason, all the girders are bursting out," and she gave a wild buzzard cry, shrill above the thunderous din. Then followed a series of cataclysmic shocks as the outer walls cracked open with the weight of material descending on them, and the entire city disintegrated, pouring in a thunderous avalanche down the mountain.

A billowing cloud of dust rose up and enveloped us, and waves of turbulence shook our frail craft. It rocked and shuddered and I could no longer distinguish Sulibe's signals. I could see her dimly through the choking fog struggling to ride the storm, but suddenly she took her hands off the controls and turned round to face me with an expression of wild triumphant joy. "We've won," she cried. "Zinn is destroyed, forever, forever. It's all over now Jason, it's finished. We can live in peace at last!" And with this she threw her arms round me and I held her tight against my chest.

Tossed this way and that for a few moments our bird flew gallantly on, but then a wing folded and snapped, pitching us round into a spin, and we fluttered helplessly down into the boiling rubble.

A Parting

AFTER THIS everything got very confusing. I seemed to see Zinn from a great distance, as I had first seen it, but surrounded by bright yellow light. All was calm. The image slowly resolved itself into a picture, woven in the tapestry of a wall hanging - not a real place at all but a flight of fancy on the part of the artist, framed in an arabesque of foliage with exotic birds and creatures amongst the leaves. The room I was in was spacious and sparsely but richly furnished: carved and polished wood, painted screens, oriental rugs and hammered bronze. Clear sharp yellow light filled every corner from a panoramic window through which I could see distant snow capped peaks. Two buzzards soared and circled in the high summit of an intensely bright blue sky. Amongst all that was strange I saw one familiar thing. On a table nearby sat a long lost friend - my old backpack.

I was lying on a couch, perfectly still and comfortable, but when I tried to get up I found I couldn't. Only my head moved, and looking down I saw that under a light linen sheet there was very little left of the rest of me. My arms, lying inertly on the top of the sheet and seeming not to belong to me, were wasted to sticks. There were drip tubes attached to them. I lay for some time vaguely pondering how I could have survived the destruction of Zinn and what had happened to Sulibe, and how I came to be reunited with my original possessions.

Two people then entered the room, a wrinkled old man with

long lidded eyes, dressed in a saffron robe, and a boy dressed in white. While the boy's solemn expression remained unchanged the old man's face registered delight at seeing me - surprise even. He drew up a chair to my bed and said one word to the boy who left immediately. Then he picked up and held in both hands one of the hands that was lying on the bed and spoke to me, in perfect English, in a sweetly reassuring way which entirely belied the content of his speech.

He explained that I had had a serious accident. I had lost my footing on loose stones and fallen down a steep cliff. My rescuers had brought me to this monastery where I had lain in a coma for some considerable time. I hadn't been expected to regain consciousness and the doctor who attended me advised that I be allowed to die. Twice I was very close to death, but the monks had kept me alive and watched over me. Their religion required them to preserve life as long as possible, but I was paralysed from the neck down, and my organs were now so wasted that I was unlikely to live much longer. I was far too weak to be moved, so my remaining time would be spent at the monastery under his and his brothers' care.

After I had taken this in I thanked him sincerely. I said that I had assets at home which could be realised to cover the expense of my care, but he would hear nothing of it. I must banish all anxiety and rest, and all my needs would be taken care of.

The boy then reappeared with a polished silver tray. Fragrant tea was poured into delicate cups, one of which the old man gently held to my lips to sip, and he then fed me a soft fruity sweetmeat. He told me that he and his brothers would look in frequently and be at hand if I should call out, and they would attend as best they could to any need of body or spirit. Again I thanked him and them with all my heart.

As we spoke two fighter jets screamed over, Chinese wing markings. The monk's face darkened, but almost immediately he regained his composure and with more soothing reassurances he left, followed by the boy with the tray. Outside the panoramic view seemed still to be reverberating. The buzzards had disappeared.

Time passed, peacefully and pleasantly. The light changed, but nothing else. I drifted in and out of sleep, with little to distinguish one state from another, re-living or dreaming about my past life, and my past dreams. Were all my travels and adventures in the land of Zinn a dream? My hold on reality was now so tenuous and transitory it hardly mattered. Sometimes a monk would be sitting by my bedside, and at others I'd hear the acolytes whispering among themselves. Their references to 'the traveller who never moves' were sympathetic, if a touch ironic. Curiously, though they spoke in their own language, I could understand everything I heard. Usually it was the monk I had first met who sat beside me. He spoke to me again in his kindly way and we managed a bit of a conversation which seemed to be really taking place. I must have told him my name because he addressed me by it, and so I asked him his. He smiled:

"My friends call me Brother Al."

"Does that include me?"

"Certainly. I feel I've known you for a long time."

"How long have I been here?"

"We don't really consider time. We think about eternity."

"I can see you are a good man, and a true friend. Perhaps we'll travel through eternity together."

"I'd be happy to."

I didn't need to press for an answer to my question. The acolyte entered with the tray of tea and after he had put the cups and teapot on a table by the bed he lifted the tray by its rim and I glimpsed my reflection in it. I saw the face of a very old man which I only just recognised as my own. It occurred to me that Brother Al must be less old than me, and he too would have been a much younger man when I was first brought here. He would have found out my name and circumstances from the contents of my backpack. We'd been silent companions for many years, and that might explain why I felt I knew him of old. There was something familiar about his smile and the way he looked at me; and the sense of a situation repeating itself. But perhaps it always seems this way when you meet a soul mate, a kind of personality *déjà vu*.

I tried another question: "Have you always been a monk, Brother Al?"

" No. I was married once and had children. I was a farmer. We all lived together in the country, not far from here."

"What happened to your family then? - Forgive me. I've no right to be so inquisitive."

"That's quite all right my friend. My wife is dead. She was frail. We had some wonderful years together and she died as she had lived in my arms. Our two children still live and work there and have children of their own. They often visit me. But after her death I decided to retire from the world and spend the rest of my days with my own thoughts, and my happiest memories. I'm not really very religious in the conventional sense, but this was the quietest place I could find."

"Except when the jets fly over."

"Yes indeed, an unwelcome reminder of a cruel world."

"Perhaps they're just training."

"No, it's another crackdown I'm afraid."

There were moments between dream and reality when my mind became preternaturally clear. Every detail of the Zinn experience was still vivid to me, and it all seemed too connected to be devoid of any meaning. The more I thought about it the more I realised that nothing in it was invented. The subconscious mind had simply rearranged my memories and surroundings into another pattern with, it seemed to me, more explicit significance. Some of the characters had real life originals, living or dead.

Sulibe for example - I had seen her sitting on a pile of rubble that had been her home, the sole survivor of her entire family from an allied air strike. She was looking down, and all I saw first was her blond head, and then she lifted her face and held me with her strange, unseeing, traumatised stare. Aya, the victim of a land mine that had exploded years after the main killing event was over - an orphan too, but a face full of fun and excitement, full of hope too - and trust.

That was the most pitiable thing. To betray that innocence is surely the ultimate crime, and I cursed myself because I was part